Friday Night
Brides

By

Samantha Chase

FRIDAY NIGHT BRIDES

Published by Samantha Chase

Acknowledgements:

Back when I was younger, we were friends with a family who owned a bridal shop and I used to go to the shows they put on. I knew some of the models and used to wish I could be up there on the stage with them – modeling the beautiful dresses. I never hit that point, but it was always a great memory for me and something I never forgot. It was one of the main inspirations for this story.

So, Doll – and you know who you are – thank you. Not only for so many years of laughter, but for being an inspiration.

Dedication:

Writing about strong friendships is something that I love to do and I have been blessed with having some of the greatest friends in my life. Whether we've known each other since forever or only for a few years, you've all been a part of making this particular book possible.

For Linda, Lisa, Lori, Robin and Cheryl – you ladies made my childhood and teen years something that I can always look back on and smile. You've seen me at my best and at my worst and yet you're all still here laughing with me.

For Christine, Angie and Ann – you all came in to my life when I needed you most and have encouraged me and lifted me up and all I wanted to do was curl up in the fetal position and cry. There aren't enough words to thank you for that.

So this book is dedicated to all of you. Someday, I hope to have all of us in the same room together for the greatest picture ever. Love you all.

#squadgoals

Prologue

Ten years ago…

"I totally felt like a princess tonight."

"Me too!"

"Is it wrong that I didn't want to put my street clothes back on?"

Hailey James shook her head and laughed. She still couldn't understand what the big deal was. Or maybe she could. The first time in a wedding gown is always a big deal. Well…at least that's what she'd learned after going to work with her mom every weekend at her bridal boutique, Enchanted Bridal, since she was five years old. Maybe she had just become desensitized to it all.

Nah.

Sitting at a table with her three best friends at their favorite café at eleven on a Friday night was the perfect way to cap off the night. Hailey shook her head and smiled as her friends continued to gush about how exciting the night had been.

Every Friday night, Enchanted Bridal held a fashion show—sometimes they were big events at convention centers or hotels, and other times they were scaled back and small and held at the boutique itself. Tonight's was at the boutique and it was the first time in the thirteen years Hailey and her friends had been modeling in the show that her mother let them be brides. They'd started out as flower girl models when they were five so maybe she just figured it was time.

Maybe it was a big deal, she thought. After all, modeling wedding gowns rather than bridesmaid dresses made them the focus of the entire show. As much as Hailey hated to admit it, it had been kind of cool. Even though she'd been playing dress-up in some of those wedding gowns for years, it was completely different when you walked out onto a stage—with a super-hot guy pretending to be your groom—and having everyone's eyes on you.

Okay, yeah, it was exciting.

Hailey sighed. Every weekend she helped brides pick out their dresses and listened to them talk about how happy and in love they were and how wonderful their futures were going to be. It wasn't that she doubted the sentiment, but personally, she had never experienced those overwhelming feelings. And while putting on a dress that made you feel beautiful—like a princess—was great, what Hailey really wanted was to meet a guy who would make her feel like that.

And if it could possibly be one of the many hot models her mother always seemed to find each season, even better. Seriously, her mother had a knack for finding the most amazing looking men. Tonight Hailey had walked with Terrance Adams. He was twenty-three and completely hot. He'd been very nice to her but she got the impression that he looked at her like she was just a kid. So while he was nice to look at, he wasn't going to be her Prince Charming.

But she had no doubt these Friday night shows were going to be the key to finding a hot groom of her own and her ultimate happily ever after.

Resting her cheek in her hand, she laughed as Angie bragged about how great her boobs had looked in her dress tonight. Hailey would never consider talking about her boobs in public, but Angie had no filter. The four of them around this table were as different as night and day and yet…they clicked. It had been that way ever since the first day of kindergarten.

Angie was the loud one.

Becca was the shy one.

Ella was the sweet one.

And Hailey? Well, she was the sensible one. And sensible, she realized, was really just another word for boring or uptight.

Either way, it worked for them.

"You know what I think?" Becca asked them. "I think this is the start of something big for all of us. I think tonight marks our own journey toward getting to wear one of those gowns for real."

"Ugh…" Angie moaned. "We're only eighteen. Do we need to start thinking about our own weddings? Can't we just get through prom? That's causing me enough grief."

"Stop being so cynical. There's nothing wrong with thinking about or just pretending that we know what our future is going to be like," Becca admonished. "So…who's going to go first? Where do you see yourself in say…ten years?"

Even though she thought it was ridiculous, Hailey was the first to play along.

"Me," she said. "In ten years, I imagine myself being madly in love with one of those hot male models Mom always has in the show. They're perfect—and look great in a tux!"

They all laughed. "Way to be superficial," Angie teased.

Hailey shrugged. "I can't help it if I want a man who looks good."

"Me next!" Ella said excitedly. "In ten years I know I'm going to be married to Dylan. We're going to have the perfect, small and intimate wedding I've always wanted with just you guys and a handful of family with us." She sighed happily. "I can't wait!"

"Ten years?" Becca said with disbelief. "You've been dating for years already. Why wait that long?"

Ella shrugged. "Well, hopefully we'll be married by then but we really want to be financially set before we get married."

"So practical," Angie sighed. "What about you, Becs?"

"All I want is to have my own little café and be married to a man who treats me like a princess," she said dreamily. "I've heard there are guys out there who do that—treat girls like that. I just wish I could find one."

"Yikes. You're only eighteen, you know. Give it some time," Angie said. "You all are acting like you need a man to make you happy! You don't!"

"Really? So where do you see yourself in ten years?" Ella challenged.

"I'm going to grab the world by the balls and do whatever it is I want to do because I don't need a man to define me," she challenged.

Everyone went silent.

"Until some guy comes and sweeps you off your feet when you least expect it," Ella said and then giggled. "It's going to be the most fun to prove that you're no different than the rest of us."

"Bring it, bitches," Angie said with a grin.

One

"Seriously, babe. What were you thinking?"

For a minute, Becca could only stare. Was he joking? Had he been paying attention at all? "I…I thought you'd want to come and see the show. That's why we agreed to meet here," she said slowly. Unfortunately, she wasn't sure who she was trying to explain it to—Danny or herself. "You've never come to one and…I don't know…I just thought…"

He held up a hand to stop her. "Becs, look…I think you've got the wrong idea here. I'm not interested in going to some…bridal show. I mean…why would I?"

Her shoulders sagged and she gave him a patient smile as she reached for one of his hands. "Danny, this is something that's really important to me. I've been doing this since…forever! I tell you about these shows all the time and it would really mean a lot to me if you came and saw me model."

The loud bark of laughter was not was Becca was expecting.

At all.

"Um…Danny?" But when he continued to laugh, Becca pulled her hand away and began to nervously look around the parking lot. There weren't many people around at the moment—a couple of the florist trucks were parked by the curb and the delivery guys were too busy moving flower arrangements around to notice Becca and Danny—and there was some hipster-looking guy standing on the sidewalk checking something on his phone.

Clearing her throat, Becca took a step back and glared. "I don't see what's so funny about this," she said defensively, her arms crossing over her middle.

Danny McDowell had been Becca's ideal guy since the tenth grade. Of course back in high school, he never paid any attention to her. When they'd run into one another at a club six months ago and Danny asked for her phone number, Becca thought she'd died and gone to heaven. She knew part of it was because she looked a heck of a lot better at twenty-five than she had at sixteen—she had more confidence and had lost some of the weight that haunted her all through high school. Just thinking about how excited she'd felt when Danny actually approached her still made her a little giddy.

As time went on, however, she sort of found herself finding all kinds of things that really irritated her about him. Things she never really noticed back in school—he was extremely self-centered, kind of a loud-mouth, and he never wanted to do anything Becca did.

For a while she thought she could let it go, but tonight's show was important to her. Enchanted Bridal was celebrating their twentieth anniversary and it was something she had wanted to share with Danny. And she thought he'd want to share with her!

"Come on, Danny," she began, "you know why this is a big deal for me. Mrs. James is like a second mom to me and Hailey, Angie, Ella, and I have been in every show since the beginning. We're going to celebrate afterwards—cake and champagne and…it's going to be great." She reached for his hand and gave him what she hoped was a sexy smile. "I really want you there with me."

He sighed loudly and pulled his hand away before he walked around her and started to head back to his car. Becca frowned and went after him. The florist vans were pulling away and only the hipster was still around. When she caught up with Danny, she did her best to keep her voice down as she tried to figure out what was going on.

"Um…excuse me," she said. "But I'm standing here talking to you and you just walk away? What's going on, Danny?"

Stopping and spinning around, Danny raked a hand through his dark hair and stared down at her. He was easily six inches taller than Becca and normally it was something she loved, his looking down into hers. But right now, there was nothing sweet or sexy about his expression.

"Look, Becs," he began, and none too softly. "I really have no desire to stand around with a bunch of losers who are looking to give up the single life. It's a Friday night, for Christ's sake! I'm meeting the guys down at BJ's, I'm not hanging around while you parade around in a costume."

She took a step back as if he'd slapped her. "A costume? Danny, I model wedding gowns! This isn't some little game; it's a fashion show. A real fashion show!"

He snickered again. "Come on…you're kidding right?"

"What's that supposed to mean?" she demanded.

"Becs, you are no model. I mean…look at you. You're short, you're not thin and…well…" he waved his arms around to pretty much indicate her entire body. "You're just not model material." He shrugged. "The only reason you're in these shows is because you're friends with Hailey. There's no way anyone would actually choose you to be a model. Come on, blow this thing off and come to BJ's with me. I'll even let you win at darts."

Cars were starting to pull into the parking lot and for all the open space, Becca felt very closed in. "I'm not going anywhere with you," she hissed. "I'm serious, Danny. I can't believe you could say those things to me! I thought I meant something to you! I thought this was going somewhere!"

He laughed one more time. "You do mean something to me, Becs. You're fun. We've had some good times and the sex has been great but…"

But?! There was a but?! She inwardly seethed.

"But this was never going to go beyond that. I thought you realized that. I'm not looking for anything serious and…well…if I were, you just aren't my type." He shrugged and pulled his keys out of his pockets.

"Not your type? How can you even say that?" she cried. "For months we've been sleeping together and you didn't seem to mind…my type!"

He gave her another shrug and managed to look bored before his gaze landed on her chest. "What can I say? I'm a breast man." And before Becca could even respond, Danny walked around to the driver's side of the car and unlocked it. "It's been fun, Becs, but…you know. I thought you understood."

"Danny…"

"Later," he said as he climbed into the car.

Becca stood there and watched him drive away as tears welled in her eyes. When his taillights were out of sight, she let the tears fall for a minute before wiping them away. That was it? She'd invested six months with him and all that time he was only interested in her because of…because of her bra size? Becca's mind raced with all of the degrading things he'd said and she felt like she was going to be sick.

Slowly she walked over to the sidewalk and sat down on the lone wooden bench. The parking lot belonged almost solely to Enchanted, so the only traffic coming and going was from the vendors for the show tonight. Hugging her middle, she bent forward and forced herself to breathe.

All of the excitement she'd been feeling about the show and the party and the anniversary was gone. Right now all she wanted to do was get in her car, drive home and curl up in the fetal position. God, was she so hideous that the only reason a guy would sleep with her was because she had big boobs? Is that what all her other boyfriends had thought?

Every insecurity she'd ever had was now spinning around in her head, mocking her. Becca had no disillusions about herself—she wasn't classically beautiful like Hailey, or tall and glamorous like Angie. Hell, she wasn't even girl-next-door cute like Ella. But hey, it didn't make her some sort of troll either! And in her entire life, no one had ever said she wasn't pretty enough to model in the bridal shows.

The only reason you're in these shows is because you're friends with Hailey.

Oh, God. What if it was true? What if Mrs. James was losing business because Becca was an ugly bride?

Glancing around, she noticed the girls weren't there yet. If she could just get herself together, she could be out of here before they arrived and then call in sick. No one would have to know. There were no witnesses to her ever having been here! Part of her felt a little guilty because it was hard when a model didn't show up, but they'd dealt with it before and she knew Mrs. James would be able to make it work if she weren't there.

Scooping up her purse, Becca fished out her keys, stood up and wiped away the stray tears. She made it all of two steps before she tripped over her own feet and fell down on the pavement.

"Shit!" she cried. "Can I seriously not get a freaking break here?"

"Hey, are you all right?"

Oh great. The hipster.

"Yeah," she murmured. "I'm fine." Becca was surprised when he helped her to her feet and then bent over to pick up her purse and the items that had spilled out of it. When he stood back up and held her purse out to her, she was at a loss for words.

He was tall—not taller than Danny though—with the bluest eyes she had ever seen. He was wearing a knit beanie and from what she could see, his hair was a sandy shade of brown. He wore glasses and it should have made him look a little nerdy, but it didn't. With a strong jaw lightly shaded with stubble and…yes…dimples…he was almost breathtaking.

With a shaky hand she took her purse from him. "Um…thank you."

"Are you sure you're okay?"

"What? Oh…yeah. Fine. It wasn't that bad of a fall. I'm more embarrassed than anything else."

"You seemed pretty upset," he said softly. "You know…before the fall."

Great. He'd seen that too. "I guess I'm just not having a very good night."

He nodded. "Sorry about that."

Becca wasn't sure what she was supposed to say

or do, but she really did want to escape before the girls got there. "I…um…I really need to go," she said, carefully stepping off the curb and inching in the direction of her car. "Have a nice night." With a small wave, she spun around and went to walk away.

"He was wrong, you know."

Stopping in her tracks, Becca turned back around. "Excuse me?"

"That guy? The one who made you cry? I'm guessing he was your boyfriend or something, but whoever he was, he was wrong about you."

Stepping back toward him, Becca wasn't sure if she should graciously thank him or if she should be pissed at how he'd been listening.

She opted for pissed—with a hint of embarrassment.

"You were eavesdropping?" she asked incredulously.

He at least had the good sense to look embarrassed too. "It was kind of hard not to. You were standing right there."

Even though she knew he had a point, it still irked her. "Yeah, well…you shouldn't have. And you didn't need to let me know that you did."

This time he took a step toward her. "Look, maybe I shouldn't have said anything. But I stood here and watched you cry and I knew it was because of what he said and I…I just couldn't let you leave here believing anything he said."

"What difference does it make to you?" she snapped. "You don't even know me! How could you possibly say Danny was wrong?"

"Because I have eyes!" There was a hint of amusement in his tone. "I don't have to know you to see that you're a beautiful woman. And I highly doubt Mrs. James would let anyone model in her shows just because she felt an obligation!" He took a steadying breath before continuing. "Look, guys like that, they get off on putting other people down and it just ticks me off. There was no way I could just stand here and let you go home and cry some more because of that jerk. You were going to blow off the show and probably fake being sick or something and that's not fair. Not to you. And not to Mrs. James."

"How…how did you know that was what I was doing?"

He gave her a lopsided grin. "Really?"

She sighed and avoided meeting his gaze. "Okay, fine. That's what I was doing. But can you blame me? I was just dumped by my boyfriend in the middle of a parking lot after being insulted in every possible way! I think I kind of deserve a little time off to lick my wounds."

He shrugged. "Maybe. But that's just giving him the power back. It's letting him win. And believe me, guys like him do *not* deserve to win."

Now it was Becca's turn to chuckle. "You sound as wounded as I am. Did some jerk dump you today too?" He smiled. And Becca almost sighed at the sight of it.

"I'm Max, by the way," he said, holding out his hand to her.

"Becca." She put her hand in his and liked how big and firm his hand was. She smiled and gently took her hand back. "I think I'm still gonna bail. I'm not feeling very festive and I'm really not in the mood for any more witnesses to my humiliating night."

"My lips are sealed."

"Thanks." She paused. "How do you know Mrs. James?"

"I don't. I mean I do. Sort of. We just met a couple of days ago."

Becca looked at him in confusion. "But…just a minute ago you said…"

"I've heard a lot about her. And I still firmly believe she wouldn't have you in her shows, representing her business, if she didn't want you there."

"Oh." With a sigh of resignation, Becca was just about to wish him a goodnight when she heard voices behind her. A quick glance showed her it was too late to run and hide. When she looked back at Max, she saw the knowing grin on his face. "Dammit," she murmured.

"Don't look at it as a bad thing. No one's going to know what happened here unless you want to tell them."

While she knew he was right, she knew that as soon as everyone was here, they were going to talk about it—because it's what they always did. She had no secrets from her friends. Never had. And while she hated how Max had witnessed the entire scene with Danny, there wasn't anything she could do about it. The only upside was that she'd most likely never see him again.

"I should go," Becca said quietly. "The girls are all pulling up."

Max nodded. "I hope you have a good night, Becca. Go out there and have fun and don't let anything that jerk said ruin it for you."

"Thanks, Max," she said. "Have a good night, too."

This time when she turned and walked away, she did make it across the parking lot. Angie was the first to arrive and, as usual, Becca couldn't help but feel a little inferior to her friend. She was tall and curvy and confident and had a take-no-prisoners attitude toward everything.

Becca only dreamed of being so brave.

"Oh my God," Angie said as she climbed out of her sporty convertible. "I swear, the traffic gets crazier and crazier all the time. What's the point of having a convertible that lets the wind blow through your hair when you can't drive at a speed that creates a damn breeze?" She reached out and hugged Becca. "I almost did donuts in the parking lot just to get out my frustration."

"That would have been something."

They were about to walk toward the building when Angie stopped and put her hand on Becca's arm. "What's going on? What's the matter with you?"

Busted.

"What are you talking about?"

Leaning in a little closer, Angie scanned her face. "Something happened. You've been crying. Come on, out with it."

"Dammit, Ange…"

"We could wait for the girls but it might help to vent a little out here first."

It was a blessing and a curse when people knew you so well, Becca thought. With a shaky breath she went into detail about how things had gone with Danny. When she was done she looked up at Angie—expecting to see some sympathy.

"And you're surprised by this…why?"

Okay, not sympathy. Becca's eyes went wide. "What do you mean why? Not only did he refuse to come to the show but he pretty much told me that I wasn't even attractive enough to be here! I'm surprised he never asked me to put a paper bag over my face while we were having sex!"

Angie chuckled but after seeing the annoyance on Becca's face, she sobered. "Look, I get why you're upset—no girl wants to hear her boyfriend tell her she's not attractive—but Danny's always been kind of clueless. And an asshole. This isn't the first time you've mentioned it."

Unfortunately, Angie was right. "I just…" She paused. "I just thought he'd change eventually."

"You mean grow up," Angie corrected and then pulled Becca in for a hug. "That's what we all think. But there are some guys you just can't change, baby doll. Danny was a jerk from elementary school through high school. Trust me, I've known him since the second grade. You're too good for him and I told you so from the get-go."

"I know you did and I know I should have listened but…"

"But nothing. You don't need him and you totally deserve someone better." Looking around the parking lot, she sighed. "At least he didn't do it some place public. He's the type who wouldn't think twice about spewing that crap in the middle of a crowded room."

It was on the tip of Becca's tongue to tell Angie about the lone witness to the whole scene but decided to keep it to herself. "I was hoping to leave before anyone got here," she said quietly.

"What? Are you kidding me? Why?"

With a massive eye roll, Becca sighed. "Seriously? I just told you what happened and you're asking me why I want to go and be alone?"

"Don't be such a drama queen. Being alone is the last thing you need right now. You need to be here for the show and the party afterwards. You know Mrs. James always has the best parties. We'll go and play dress-up for a few hours and then kick back with some top-notch food and champagne. It will be great. Trust me."

It was true. Judith James had the Midas touch where her events and business were concerned. Tonight's event was the sort of thing Becca normally looked forward to. With a little bit of effort, she could probably get into that mindset and forget about the last thirty minutes of her life. Maybe this would be the perfect distraction. And maybe—just maybe—it would be enough of one to keep her from going after Danny and giving him another chance.

****

There were few things that Hailey James loved more than the weekend.

Wedding fashion shows were one of them.

True, it was her family's business so technically they were one in the same, but her reason for loving the show—especially lately—was because of this season's "groom."

Logan Baxter III.

Sigh.

Being the daughter of the owner and coordinator of the bridal show came with certain perks. And as soon as Hailey had gotten a glimpse of the male models for this wedding season's shows, she had pretty much called dibs on Logan. He was perfect. Beautiful, almost. With blond hair that was always impeccably cut and styled, an amazing smile and a body that should be illegal. Yup, Hailey wanted to weep with gratitude that he came into her life.

Climbing from her car she spotted Becca and Angie heading into the store. She knew she was on time and could sprint to catch up with them, but she decided to take an extra minute to fix her hair and makeup and maybe—just maybe—see if Logan arrived before she went in. She smiled. Maybe they could walk in together and have a few minutes alone before all of the chaos of the show started.

A loud banging on her window had her lipstick flying out of her hands and small scream coming from her lips. Sighing with annoyance, she reached for the door handle and almost fell out of the car when the door opened from the outside.

"What is the matter with you?" she demanded angrily as she came to her feet. "Are you trying to kill me?"

Unfortunately, she had to look up at him and knew he could probably kill her with his thumb if he wanted to. He was *that* big. Jack…something. Seriously, she had no idea what his last name was and it was perfectly fine with her. Hailey was beyond annoyed. He had a tendency to do that to her. He was one of the models—normally a groomsman—and yet he always seemed to find a way to do something to get under her skin.

He was the exact opposite of Logan. He was big and…burly wasn't quite the right word but every time she looked at him, all Hailey could think was…*big*…and imposing and just not the kind of guy you wanted to run into in a dark alley or something. He had jet black hair that was always messed up—some called it playfully tousled but Hailey often wanted to ask him if he even owned a brush. And then there were the tattoos. Lots and lots of tattoos.

Jack looked down at her and smirked. "Why are you sitting out here doing your makeup, Princess? You have an entire glamour studio inside."

Hailey rolled her eyes. "I wasn't doing my makeup," she snapped defensively. "I was simply *checking it* while I waited for my friends."

"Becca and Angie already went in."

She sighed. "I'm waiting for Ella."

"You're waiting for Logan," he corrected, crossing his arms across his massive chest.

Hailey glared up at him. "Shouldn't you be getting inside? I know my mother could use a hand moving the chairs and getting set up." She seriously hoped he would take the bait and leave. There was no way she wanted Jack to see that he was right, that she *was* waiting for Logan.

"She pays a crew to come in and do that and you know it," he said with a smile. Then he leaned in, ducking his head a little to bring himself somewhat eye-level to her five-foot-five frame. "I think you're just trying to get rid of me."

Turning away from him, Hailey reached back into her car and grabbed her purse, supply bag and keys before she faced him again. With a smug smile of her own, she slammed the car door shut and hit the remote key to lock it.

Jack chuckled and the sound only irritated her more. "Now what?" she snapped.

"You're just predictable," he said, smiling. "And cute as hell."

With a huff, Hailey turned on her heel and walked away—almost stomping across the parking lot. She hated being called cute. She wasn't cute. She was…stylish. Elegant. Classically beautiful. Everyone said so. He was the only one who would dare to call her cute—and it sounded like an insult.

It took all of five seconds before she heard him come up beside her. "Now what did I do?"

Hailey instantly stopped and she felt a small sense of satisfaction that he actually looked worried. "Look," she began with more bravado than she actually felt, "I don't know why it is you seem to keep trying to start up conversations with me or why you feel the need to be so…so…rude."

"Rude?" he interrupted incredulously. "Nothing

I've said so far has been rude, Hailey. Trust me. If I wanted to be rude to you, you'd know it."

"Oh really?" she asked sarcastically.

Jack went back to his original pose as he stared down at her. "What I was, was truthful with you, and apparently it bothers you. What's the matter, Princess? You don't appreciate when people call you out on your actions?"

In that instant she wanted to stamp her foot and scream. Why couldn't he just leave her alone and go away? But rather than give him an answer, she simply stood her ground and continued to glare at him. Silently.

It was like a standoff. Hailey had no idea how long they stood like that—she sort of got sucked into his green eyes and couldn't look away. It was the first time she'd noticed the color. They were a deep, jade green. If he wasn't such a jackass, she'd actually appreciate them.

"Why are you having a staring contest in the middle of the parking lot?" Ella asked as she came up beside them. She was all of five foot three and looked like a pixie with her blond hair and blue eyes. Staring at the two of them, she waited for an answer.

"I was trying to go inside but…" Hailey began.

"Your friend is a little annoyed that I caught her sitting out here waiting for pretty-boy Logan."

"No, I'm annoyed because you won't just go

away!"

"We're both going inside," Jack countered. "I don't see the harm in…"

Ella let out a surprisingly loud whistle and cut them both off. "I think it's time everyone went to their corners, okay?" She smiled at Hailey and turned to Jack and said, "Please."

For a moment, Hailey couldn't believe her eyes—Jack actually smiled at Ella and walked away.

"How…how did you do that?" she asked. "I've been trying to get him to go away for several minutes and it just seemed to spur him on to stay and bug me."

Looping their arms together, Ella began to lead Hailey toward the shop. "Somehow I don't think you asked as nicely as I did."

It was hard to argue with the truth. And honestly, she was done talking about Jack. Looking around, she instead asked, "Where's Dylan? Don't you guys normally come together?"

Dylan was Ella's fiancé. They'd basically been dating since the sixth grade. It still boggled Hailey's mind how someone could only date one person their entire life and then marry them. They'd often talked about some of the things Ella was missing, but she and Dylan were so in love, it bordered on nauseating.

"He's coming later for the party," Ella explained. "He had the opportunity to get some overtime hours at work and decided to take advantage of it."

"Oh. That's good."

Ella nodded. "This wedding is really starting to stress us out. The costs keep rising and our parents are doing all they can, but…they keep adding stuff. Dylan and I really only wanted something small and it just keeps growing and growing. It's taken on a life of its own."

Hailey chuckled and bumped shoulders with her friend. "They tend to do that. We've met enough brides over the years that you should know that. What made you think yours would be any different?" It was said good-naturedly but Ella still frowned. "Hey," Hailey said softly, stopping them just outside the door to the shop. "What's going on?"

Tears welled in Ella's eyes. "I just don't understand why everyone thinks they get to dictate what our wedding is supposed to be. They all had their weddings already. Why can't this be about me and Dylan? Why do our parents get to tell us how it's supposed to be?"

"Well, technically they are paying for part of it…"

"*Part*," Ella emphasized. "They wouldn't have to be if they would've let us have the wedding we originally wanted!"

"Ella, you and Dylan wanted to get married in a field of wildflowers on a beach at sunset with a harpist accompanying Justin Timberlake. That was never going to happen."

Ella chuckled as she wiped the tears from her eyes. "That was my tenth-grade wedding dream. You need to keep up."

"Fine. The last one was narrowed down to the beach at sunset with only a dozen or so people in attendance. It's a beautiful idea but you eliminated half of your friends and family. Surely there can be a compromise somewhere."

She shrugged. "I don't know. Every time we sit down with our parents to talk about it, someone throws in another couple of names of people they're adding to the guest list. It's exhausting."

"I can imagine. So what are you going to do?"

"What can I do? We'll have this big circus show of a wedding and maybe for our ten-year anniversary we'll actually get to do what we wanted."

"Well that's just sad, El," Hailey said. "I think you and Dylan need to put up a united front and confront the parents. Sure they'll be disappointed, but you have to tell them how important this is to you."

"Maybe you can do it for me?" Ella asked hopefully.

"Not a chance."

"Well…crap."

"Ella Gilmore! Did you just curse at me?" Hailey laughed.

"Technically, no. But if you give me a few minutes, I'm sure I can force myself to."

Hailey pulled her in close and hugged her. "Nah. I'll pass. You're the sweet and innocent one. I'd hate to be accused of being a bad influence on you."

"Too late," Ella teased.

Staring at the door to the shop, Hailey sighed. "Are we ready for the craziness that awaits on the other side of that door?"

Ella nodded. "You?"

Jack's image instantly came to mind, making Hailey frown. She was going to have to talk to her mother about not using him in any more of the shows. Maybe if she told her…

"Good evening, ladies."

Hailey turned and smiled. All thoughts of Jack vanished. Standing beside her was Logan Baxter III in all his perfection. Without a word, he held his arm out to Hailey and grinned. She sighed happily before turning to Ella. "I think I'm ready."

****

Judith James wiped proud tears from her eyes as she looked at the four of them. It wasn't as if this was something new—since the time the girls were five they had been featured in her bridal fashion shows and showcases. They were her models, her pride and joy.

"Is it wrong how I look at the four of you and

still see four little girls and not grown women?" she asked.

"Mom…" Hailey whined lovingly. "Every time?"

Judith sniffed. "I can't help it. You started out dressing up as flower girls and now look at you. Brides!"

"Not real ones," Angie said, fidgeting with her headpiece.

"Ella will be one before you know it," Judith said. "Which reminds me, you really need to settle down and decide on your dress, Ella. You know it will take forever to come in and then there are the alterations."

Ella nodded. "It's so hard to choose when they're all so beautiful!"

"You've worn enough of them over the years that I think you know what style is the most flattering on you and which ones are the most comfortable. All you have to do is narrow it down to your favorite," Judith said. "Why don't you come in next week and we'll have a girls' night here after hours and work on that?"

Ella looked at Becca, Hailey and Angie and smiled. "What do you say? You guys up for a mid-week girls' night?"

"Will there be wine?" Angie asked.

Judith clucked her tongue like a mother hen.

"Do you think I'd allow wine around these dresses? We'll have a bottle of champagne to celebrate Ella's choice—other than that, it's lemon water. Besides, it's better for you."

All four of them groaned.

"Way to take the fun out of it, Mom," Hailey said.

Judith gave her a disapproving frown. "Anyway…it's almost show time. You all know the drill." She clasped her hands together and looked around. "Becca, you'll go out first and you'll be escorted by Thomas. Angie you're next with Ben, Hailey you'll be with Logan and then Ella is with Jackson."

"Wait…Jackson?" Hailey asked. "Who's

Jackson?"

Ella turned to her with a chuckle. "It's Jack, Hailey. Remember? Your glaring partner?"

She blushed. "Oh." She paused for a moment. "Why is he escorting Ella? He normally does the groomsman stuff."

"We were short a groom and he's the same size as our missing one."

"But he's so…big and next to Ella he'll look ridiculous," Hailey said.

Taking a minute to consider her options, Judith nodded. "I don't think it will be a problem. Like I said, he's the same size as Gerard—who's not here tonight—and he always walks with Ella. We'll be fine."

Hailey mumbled under her breath as her mother walked away.

"What is the matter with you?" Ella asked quietly. "It's not like you have to walk with him and I don't have an issue with him."

"I just wish…I wish Mom would find someone else. He's not a good fit for this. He's rude and condescending and…"

"Jack?" Angie asked as she walked over. "You think Jack's rude and condescending? Are you crazy?"

Hailey nodded hesitantly. "He is to me."

"He's usually the first one here and helps your mom with anything she needs and he's the last one to leave. And like Ella said, it's not like you have to walk with him so…unclench. Geez."

When Angie walked away Hailey turned to Ella. "So basically everyone around here is a fan of his except me. Do I have that right?"

"It would seem so," Ella said.

She looked like she was about to say more but Judith called out for everyone to get into place and line up. It was a flurry of activity covered in formal wear. Two by two everyone lined up backstage as music began to play.

Judith took the stage first and welcomed the

crowd of two hundred to the show. When she had first opened her store, there wasn't room for a dozen people to come in at the same time. But over the years, she had gained a reputation for being the best in the bridal business in North Carolina and as her business grew, she wisely invested in the kind of showroom where she could host large events. Since that time, business had quadrupled and future brides and grooms came from several states away for one of her shows.

She beamed with pride as she shared her story with the crowd. With a nod of her head toward the group backstage she said, "And now may I present to you, my Friday Night Brides!" The curtains opened and the show began.

****

"Here's to another twenty years!"

Everyone in the room raised their glasses and toasted Judith and Enchanted Bridal—including Becca. Looking around she saw people laughing and smiling and drinking and all she wanted to do was go home, curl up in a ball and sleep for a week. Not that it was going to solve anything, but for now it just seemed like a great way to avoid thinking about what had happened earlier with Danny.

"Okay, you are being a serious buzzkill," Angie said from beside her. "This is a big night for Mrs. J and you need to snap out of your funk and be social."

"I was social all during the show," Becca said wearily. "I think I've done my share."

"For crying out loud, Becca…"

"Hey, what's going on? You okay?" Ella asked as she approached them, arm in arm with Dylan.

Becca rolled her eyes. The last thing she wanted was to share her humiliation with even more people right now—particularly the most in-love couple on the planet.

"She and Danny broke up," Angie said, firmly taking the decision out of Becca's hands.

"Oh no!" Ella cried. "When?"

With a sigh, Becca answered. "Right before the show."

"What's going on?" Hailey asked as she joined them. "What are we all huddled together about?"

"Becca and Danny broke up tonight," Ella said and Becca prayed for the floor to open up and swallow her.

"Becs…why didn't you say anything earlier?" Hailey asked.

"Can we just not talk about this right now?" Becca asked them. "Seriously, I'm not in the mood to get into it and besides, we're supposed to be celebrating." She gave Angie a pointed look.

They each looked at one another before Hailey spoke again. "Okay, it's fine. Anyway, I wanted to introduce you guys to our new photographer." Turning, she motioned for someone to come and join them.

Becca's eyes went wide right before she did her best to hide behind Ella and Dylan.

"This is Max Abrams," Hailey said with a smile. "He's going to be doing all of our event and publicity photos this season."

Becca was the last one to be introduced and she mentally sighed with relief when Max didn't acknowledge they had met earlier. "It's nice to meet you, Becca," he said with a small smile.

"You too."

Conversation flowed for a few minutes before Max excused himself to take more pictures of the party.

"I…I didn't know we were getting a new photographer," Becca said absently. "What happened to the Hendersons? They've been doing all of the pictures for years."

"They retired," Hailey said. "Mom was pretty worried about finding someone new but Max came highly recommended so…"

"Hey," Max interrupted. "Would you mind if I got a group shot of the four of you? I took individual shots of you on the runway but I'm sure Judith would love a more casual shot too."

The girls instantly lined up as Dylan stepped to the side. Becca was used to posing as a group—they'd been doing it their entire lives—but she was curious about how others saw them. Now that Danny had put it out there that she wasn't pretty enough or skinny enough to be a model, she couldn't help but wonder what Max was seeing.

She smiled even as her mind wandered. They were all different; that was a given. Angie was tall and curvy with naturally curly dark brown hair while Hailey was more of an average height with straight sandy brown hair. Ella was the shortest out of the four of them and probably had the best figure—trim and willowy and perfectly proportioned. Ella's words, not hers. And then there was Becca—auburn hair which required an entire shelf of products to tame and a short, curvy figure that tended to come off as looking stocky…and big boobs.

Damn Danny.

It wasn't as if he said anything Becca hadn't thought about herself before, but hearing it come from somebody else really hurt. Her entire life she had thought it was her own insecurity and not based on any real fact. Clearly she had been wrong.

Double damn Danny.

"Becs?" Hailey asked a minute later. "You okay? You zoned out there."

Looking around, Becca noticed that Max was gone and they were no longer posing. "What? Oh…sorry. Yeah, my mind sort of wandered there for a minute."

"He seems nice, doesn't he?" Hailey asked.

"Who?"

"Max! He seems really nice. I'm glad Mom found him. Not that I didn't love the Hendersons, but they weren't a whole lot of fun. I think Max would be cool to hang out with."

With a shrug, Becca said, "Maybe."

For the next thirty minutes, she walked around the room and socialized—all the while counting down the minutes until she could leave. After finishing the drink she had been nursing for far too long, Becca went in search of Judith to congratulate her one more time. When she turned around, however, she ran right into Max. "Oh! Sorry," she murmured, unable to bring herself to look him in the eye.

"No problem." He studied her for a moment. "You having a good time?"

Nodding, she said, "I guess."

Hands in his pockets, he smiled. "You did great out there earlier…you know…during the fashion show. I got some great pictures."

She gave him a small smile before tilting her head to study him just as he'd been studying her. "Can I ask you something?"

"Sure."

"Why didn't you say anything earlier?"

"When?"

"When Hailey was introducing you. Why didn't you mention how we had met out in the parking lot?"

"I don't know," he shrugged. "I guess…I figured it would get everyone wondering if I was there when…well…you know."

"Oh. Well…thanks. I appreciate it."

"Anyway, for what it's worth, I'm glad you stayed. It seemed like a great show—the audience loved everything that was modeled and Judith is working the room like the belle of the ball. I'm sure you would have hated to miss it."

He was right and she told him so. "I'm just ready to call it a night. I was going to go and find Mrs. J and say goodnight to her."

"So…do you do all of her shows?" he asked before Becca could walk away.

"I do. I've been doing them ever since I was five. That's how long I've been friends with Hailey, Angie and Ella."

"That's kind of cool. I'm sure she has some great pictures of all of you throughout the years." He stopped and seemed to consider his next words. "Listen, do you think you could get some of those old photos?"

"You mean of me and the girls?"

He nodded.

"Sure. I don't see why not. How come?"

"Well, it sort of just came to me how we could put together a slide show of the history of her fashion shows but have a special segment of you and your friends. I'm guessing if you've all been friends for that long that Judith is like a second mom to all of you."

Becca chuckled. "You've got that right."

"So what do you think? I know it probably would have been even more meaningful if we'd had something like that for tonight, but if you can get me some photos maybe by next week, I can put it together and present it to her after the next big show next month."

"I'm sure I can get Hailey to help out and she'll be able to do it while her mom is at work." The wheels began to turn in her head. "Do you do all of that yourself? The video and music and all that?"

He nodded again. "You tell me what you think she'll like and I'll put it on there—favorite songs or quotes. And I'll include the pictures from tonight to sort of end the whole thing."

For the first time that night, Becca actually felt excited about something. "She is going to love it! It's so sweet of you to think of doing this. But...how much is it going to cost?"

Max waved her off. "Don't worry about it. I wanted to put something together to show potential clients about all of the services I'm going to be offering and what better way than to have a bridal video? Who knows? Someday I can be the one referring clients to Judith instead of the other way around."

"She doesn't expect that," Becca assured him. "I think she just likes knowing she has a quality team working with her. She wouldn't have hired you for the season if she didn't love your work."

"Thanks."

"Well, I should go. I guess I'll see you next weekend, right?"

"It's a small showcase, right?"

Becca nodded. "Definitely smaller than this—probably only a quarter of the crowd but Mrs. J still pulls out all the stops. It will be a great way for you to network though."

"That's what I'm hoping for. I need to get my name out there a little more. I'm hoping if I can get the photography business going, I can quit my day job."

"Oh? What do you do?"

"Promise not to laugh."

That just made her chuckle. "Sorry. Okay, I promise."

"I'm an accountant."

Her eyes went wide. "Wow. Seriously? That is so completely opposite of this!"

"Yeah, I know. I caved to parental pressure and took on a career that would always pay the bills but my artistic side is begging to be let out to play."

"I can totally relate. I desperately wanted to be a chef but my parents pushed me to go to business school. I'm hoping to combine the two someday and open my own café."

"So what do you do now?"

"Right now I'm doing data systems analysis and it's sucking my will to live. I sit at a desk for eight hours and think about all the ways my soul is dying."

He chuckled. "Come on, it can't be that bad."

"It's that and worse!"

"Becca! There you are!" Judith walked over and hugged her before turning and hugging Max. "You were absolutely stunning out there tonight!" she gushed. "I had four different brides come up and ask about the second gown you modeled. They raved about how lovely you looked in it. I may have to pay you commission!"

Becca wasn't so sure it was all entirely true, but she appreciated the enthusiasm behind the words. "Thanks, Mrs. J. Just doing my job."

Judith hugged her again. "Thank you for being one of my brides." She gave Becca's cheek a gentle pat. "You looked like you were getting ready to go so I wanted to make sure I came over to thank you. And don't forget about next week with Ella's dress. I think we're going to do it on Wednesday night. Are you going to be able to make it?"

"I wouldn't miss it for the world!"

"Okay then." Turning to Max, Judith smiled. "I hope you got some great shots for me tonight. I'm looking forward to seeing them!" And before Max could reply, Judith had gone on to socialize with another group of guests.

"She's like a whirlwind," he said.

"You have no idea," Becca chuckled. "But this is a big night so she's even more revved up. She loves this sort of thing—she throws the best parties."

"So I've heard," he said with a smile.

They stood in companionable silence for another minute before Becca broke the spell. "Thanks again. For everything."

Max simply nodded.

"And I'll see you next weekend and hopefully have enough pictures and information for you to use for the slide show."

Reaching into his back pocket, Max pulled out his wallet and then one of his business cards and handed it to Becca. "If you have any questions or…anything, just give me a call. That's my cell number on the bottom."

Taking the card, Becca smiled and waved, thenturned and walked away.

Two

Ella sighed as she rested her head on Dylan's bare shoulder. He kissed the top of her head and hugged her close.

"You were beautiful up there tonight."

She smiled against his skin. "How do you know? You showed up after the show."

Dylan shook his head. "I actually got there right before the finale. The dress you were wearing…the one that looked like a silvery-blue? It was awesome."

"The train weighed a ton. I don't know how some brides do it. There was no way to move around easily in that thing."

"Well, either way, you looked great."

Placing a small kiss on his chest, she quietly said, "Thank you."

They lay there together in silence for several minutes. "You okay, El?" Dylan asked. "You're kind of quiet tonight."

She shrugged. "I don't know…so much is going on with the girls and…" She sighed. "I just can't relate to any of it."

Sitting up, Dylan looked down at her, frowning. "What do you mean?"

Ella moved away and sat up, tugging the blanket

with her. “Tonight Danny broke up with Becca right before the show. She didn’t want to talk about it, but after she left Angie told me and Hailey about it. He basically told her she wasn’t pretty enough to be modeling for Mrs. J!”

Shaking his head, Dylan continued to frown. “Not for nothing, but she should be thankful he did it.”

“What?” she cried. “How could you…?”

“Look, I think Becca’s great—pretty, too. But Danny’s always been a jackass. I never understood what the hell she saw in him. I’m glad he made such a colossally bad move. It should guarantee she won’t take him back.”

“Oh…well…I guess I didn’t think of it like that.” She paused. “I still feel bad for her, though.”

“Of course. No one wants to be dumped. And insulted. I hope she didn’t take what he said to heart.”

“She did,” Ella sighed. “She already has self-esteem issues and this just added to them. It’s going to take a while for her to get her confidence back.”

Dylan sat quietly for a minute. “And what else is going on? You said things were going on with the girls. What’s up?”

“Well…she won’t talk about it, but I think

Angie’s still upset over Sean.”

“The guy from her cousin’s wedding?”

Ella nodded.

"I thought it was just a hook-up."

She rolled her eyes. "Of course you did."

"What does that mean?"

"You know she doesn't ever gush over a guy. Hell, she doesn't gush over anything. But I think she really liked Sean. And it wasn't just a hook up at the wedding, they sort of had a…thing going."

"So what happened?"

"He travels a lot. Or at least that's what he told her. They were talking and texting all the time and then it just sort of fizzled out. From what I can guess, the fizzling wasn't on her end."

"Oh."

She shifted and faced him. "Why do guys do that? I mean…Angie's a great girl! She's beautiful and sweet and funny and…she's just awesome. Why would a guy get involved like that and then just bail?"

Dylan's eyes went wide. "You're asking me? How on earth would I know? You're the only girl I ever dated!"

Ella made a face and sighed, slouching back against her pillows. "Oh. Right."

Now it was his turn to straighten and look at her. "What's that supposed to mean?"

"Look, all I'm saying is it…bothers me how I

can't help my friends! I have no idea what to say or do when they're dealing with stuff like this. It's completely foreign to me!"

"That's not a bad thing," he grumbled.

With a patient smile, she rolled toward Dylan and put her hand on his arm. "I know and believe me, I know how lucky we are, Dylan, but…"

"But…?"

She shrugged. "Sometimes it just seems like maybe we…missed something."

His eyes went wide. "You're kidding, right?"

Ella shook her head.

Jumping up from the bed, he grabbed his jeans and pulled them on and began to pace. "So…here we are, planning our wedding after we've been together for thirteen years and you're telling me you're missing something?" When Ella went to speak, he held up a hand to stop her. "And what you're complaining about missing are the failed relationships and being able to understand what it feels like to be dumped?"

"That's not what I'm saying."

"It's exactly what you're saying!" he yelled.

"You don't have to experience getting dumped to sympathize with your friends, Ella! Plenty of my friends have had girls dump them and I feel for them—I really do—but that doesn't mean I want it to happen to me!"

She sighed loudly and looked up at him with her big blue eyes. "I don't want it to happen to me either. It's just sometimes I feel guilty. I mean…we found each other when we were so young and it's always been…" She looked at him and smiled. "Perfect. It still boggles my mind how it doesn't happen like that for everyone else."

And just like that, Dylan relaxed and sat back down beside her. Pulling her into his arms, he kissed her slowly, thoroughly. When he lifted his head he smiled. "How did we get so lucky?"

"I don't know," Ella said softly as she cupped his cheek. "I didn't mean to upset you. I get frustrated when my friends are hurting and I don't know how to make things better."

"I think both Angie and Becca are going to be just fine. Becca's going to realize real soon that Danny breaking up with her is a blessing and Angie…well…she'll just be mad for a while. Maybe you should encourage her to take up kickboxing or something. She's definitely the kind of woman who needs to get her anger out."

Ella laughed. "That she does. I'll bring it up next time I see her."

"You mean tomorrow," he said with a wink.

It was true, Ella and the girls rarely went for more than a couple of hours without talking and Saturday was usually their day to go to lunch.

"What does Hailey think of all of this?" Dylan

asked. "Thank God you have at least one friend who's not in a crisis."

"Well…"

It was his turn to roll his eyes. "Seriously? What's going on with Hailey?"

"I'm not sure. When I got to the show tonight, she was having this angry staring contest with Jackson. And for the life of me, I can't figure out why. Hailey gets along with everyone—particularly anyone who works for her mom—but for some reason, she really dislikes him."

"Wait…who's Jackson? The guy she's always walking with in the shows?"

"No," Ella said, shaking her head. "That's Logan. He's the one she's really interested in. He's sweet and handsome and she's always going on and on about how perfect he is for her, but he hasn't made a move on her or taken any of her hints."

"So who's Jackson?"

"He's who I walked with tonight. He's a really nice guy—funny, smart and he's always going out of his way to help Mrs. J—but for some reason, he just rubs Hailey the wrong way."

Dylan considered that for a moment. "I'm stumped. I've known Hailey almost as long as you have and I've never seen her argue with anyone."

"That's what I'm saying! It's weird!" She shook her head again and shifted until she was laying down again. "Why can't they have their issues separately? I think I could handle them one at a time—and with the help of the others—but all at once? I'm feeling seriously overwhelmed."

Shucking his jeans, he joined her back under the blankets, tucked her back in at his side and sighed. "All you can do is be yourself, sweetheart. No one is expecting you to solve all of their problems and besides, you've got issues of your own. Mrs. J told me you're finally going to pick out your gown this week." He kissed the top of her head. "That's great news."

"Mmm..."

She felt him stiffen beside her and decided to say what was really on her mind.

"I think I know why I can't pick a gown."

He took a steadying breath and let it out. "Why?"

"Because this wedding isn't...this isn't the

wedding we always talked about. I feel like no one is listening to us about what it is that we want."

"I know, but they're just excited. And they aren't asking for anything bad, El. It's just going to be a bit bigger than we planned."

"But..."

"Come on," he said softly, hugging her, "it's been a long day and an emotional night. I think a good night's sleep will go a long way toward making you feel better."

Honestly, she wasn't so sure. Her mind was swirling with everything that was going on. Becca. Hailey. Angie. The wedding. If Ella had her way, she'd stand up and demand that everyone listen to her. Of course she had no idea what she'd say—except about the wedding—but that was beside the point.

She wanted her friends to be happy.

And she wanted that for herself too.

The only problem was…she no longer knew what it would take.

****

"I'm ordering a burger that's as big as my head," Angie announced as she sat down.

"Make that two," Becca replied.

The waitress looked at the group of girls with a hint of confusion. "Um…today's specials are…"

Hailey held up a hand to stop her. "Just give us a few minutes. Thanks." When the waitress walked away, she turned to her friends. "I will not allow you to scare that poor girl or have a food pity-party."

"Geez *mom*….unclench," Angie muttered.

They were seated at a table at their favorite café in downtown Raleigh. It was a Saturday tradition they started their senior year of high school and other than a handful of times when one of them was sick, they never missed a date.

"The show was great last night," Ella said excitedly. "That was a huge crowd to celebrate with your mom."

Hailey nodded. "She cried at the end of the night. I stayed until the end with her and as we were walking out she started bawling at how much it all meant to her." She sighed happily. "I hope someday I have a career I feel that passionate about."

"You could just take over the business," Angie suggested. "You know that's what she's been wanting. Why are you fighting it?"

"I don't know. I guess I just want something that's mine. I know I'd never be able to live up to the hype that is my mother," Hailey explained. "And I don't want to. She's amazing."

"Still…you're a natural with it all. You should really consider it," Becca added. "I think with your marketing skills you could even take the business to a whole new level."

Hailey shrugged. "I don't know. Maybe." She took a sip of her water and looked at Ella. "Are you excited for Wednesday night?"

"Sure," Ella said a little too brightly.

"Uh-oh…" It was a collective comment.

"Okay, fine. I'm not sure if I'm excited about it. I'm not even sure I'm excited about the wedding anymore."

Becca reached out and took one of Ella's hands in hers. "Have you talked to Dylan about it?"

"I have. He seems to think it's all okay—that our families making things bigger is no big deal."

"But it is," Angie interjected. "Did you tell him that?"

Ella shook her head. "It was late and we were tired and…I don't know. He just doesn't seem to get it."

"Then maybe you should explain it to him again," Hailey suggested. "The two of you have always been in sync with each other. I can't believe he's not seeing why this is a big deal to you."

"Probably because it hasn't really affected him. No one talks to him about this stuff; they come to me—and usually after the fact. I swear, I once thought it was a blessing how our parents had become such good friends but now it's a curse. They get together and think and plot and plan and don't even bother to ask me or Dylan what we think about it!"

"Ella, sweetie, you're going to have to say something. Soon!" Hailey said. "I know this is a big deal to you because you're actually upset about it. A couple of months ago when you started planning the wedding, you glowed at just the mention of it. Now your face gets all…scrunchy. You can't keep this bottled up."

"Maybe I'm just being ungrateful," Ella said quietly. "Dylan's probably right—it's not like they're changing a whole bunch of stuff that's going to make the wedding bad." She shrugged and then waved a hand at them. "Anyway, it's not a big deal. I'm starving and a burger really does sound good."

While Ella picked up the menu and held it up in an attempt to end this particular discussion, Hailey, Angie and Becca exchanged glances. "So…yeah. Burgers," Becca said, picking up her own menu.

By the time the waitress came back, they were ready to place their orders. Once she was gone, the conversation went to neutral topics—work, the weather and food. When their meals were served, everyone took their first few bites in silence.

"Dear Lord, that's good," Angie finally said. "I swear, they have the best burgers here."

"Agreed," Becca said. "Although I should have just gotten a salad."

Without missing a beat, Angie smacked her in the arm.

"Ow! What was that for?"

"Because you let that asshole get to you! There is nothing wrong with you and as your friend, I'm offended that you're taking his words to heart!"

Slamming her burger down, she turned. "That doesn't even make sense!"

"So you're saying you aren't taking Danny's

words to heart?"

Sighing, Becca picked up her napkin and wiped her hands. "I meant about you being offended. It has nothing to do with you! This is about me!"

"Yeah, I get that," Angie snapped, "but at the same time, it's annoying as all hell how you listen to him."

"Well, sorry to annoy you," Becca said as she started to slide out of the booth.

Hailey grabbed her arm to stop her. "Okay, that's enough," she said gently and then glared at Angie. "Look, I know you're upset about Danny but that doesn't mean that anything he said was right. We have all been friends for so long and you have to know we would never lie to you."

Becca looked up at her with tears in her eyes.

"You're beautiful," Hailey said fiercely. "And you're an amazing friend and yes, it bothers us that we can sit here and tell you this for your whole life and you don't listen to it while Danny says one thing one time and you believe him." She paused while Becca wiped away a tear. "You were too good for him. We all told you from the get-go and we all sat back because you said he made you happy. Well…clearly you're not happy. And we're all sorry for it. But that doesn't mean we're going to sit here and let you beat yourself up over him."

"Sorry Becs," Angie said as she reached around and hugged her.

"I know I'm being stupid," Becca said, her voice trembling, "but it's hard when someone plays on your fears and insecurities like that. I always knew Danny wasn't the greatest guy in the world—and he certainly wasn't "the one"—but…I don't know…I just didn't expect him to be so mean."

"Look, I know it's easy for us to sit here and tell you to ignore it or get over it, but that wouldn't be fair," Ella chimed in. "Just know Danny's the only one who thinks like that."

"True that," Angie and Hailey said and then laughed.

"You guys are the best," Becca said with a small smile. "I don't know what I'd do without you."

"You'd be sad and miserable," Hailey said with a dramatic sigh.

They all laughed again and finished their meals.

"Oh, I totally forgot to ask," Ella said excitedly once their dishes were cleared away, "what were you and the sexy photographer talking about last night, Becs? Dylan and I saw the two of you talking over in a corner."

"Oh? Oh, really?" Hailey cooed. "Do tell!"

"For crying out loud," Becca muttered. "Actually, he had an idea for a gift for your mom." Beside her, Angie snickered. Becca elbowed her to shut her up. "He wants to do a slide show video for her with pictures from all of her fashion shows. Can you get those?"

Hailey's eyes lit up. "Max thought of it? That's so sweet!"

"He also wants to do a segment that is solely on the four of us and our years modeling in the shows. He's going to use the pictures he took of us last night too. I kind of told him I'd have them by next weekend. Do you think you can do it?"

Hailey nodded. "Absolutely! Last year we scanned all of the old photos into the computer and there's a file for them. I always wanted to do something like that for Mom, but I had no idea how to do it. It's so cool that Max thought of it!"

"I wonder why he talked to you about it and not Hailey," Ella said curiously.

"Oh…um…I don't know," Becca stammered and then shrugged. "Probably because we ran into each other as I was leaving. Maybe he thought Hailey was too busy doing stuff or…um…who knows really? You'd have to ask him."

While Becca fidgeted with her napkin, Ella, Angie and Hailey exchanged looks again and by silent agreement, decided to let that little bit of nervous rambling go.

For now.

****

Glass of wine in hand, Angie sat down on her favorite oversized chair and got comfortable, her cat curled up beside her. Picking up the TV remote, she began her nightly ritual of channel surfing in hopes of finding something of interest to watch.

Or at least something to take her mind off the fact that it was a Saturday night and she was sitting home alone.

In her pajamas.

Okay, the cat technically meant she wasn't alone but that wasn't something she wanted to advertise to the world either.

There was a time when she wouldn't be caught dead sitting at home in her pajamas on a weekend night, but that was before *him*. "Dammit," she cursed but continued to scan the channels.

Eight months ago she had met Sean Peterson while helping her cousin Tricia plan her wedding. The attraction had been instantaneous and what had started out as a bit of a chore wedding-planning-wise had quickly turned into something amazing. She and Sean worked together on a bunch of wedding-related activities and Angie found he was someone she really wanted to spend time with once the party was over. She had thought he felt the same way.

Clearly she was wrong.

Sure they had kept in touch and even got together for a couple of weekend getaways, but with Sean based out of Long Island and Angie in Raleigh, the strain of a long-distance relationship eventually did them in.

At least that's what she kept telling herself.

Unfortunately, it was too easy for her own self-doubt to creep up and have her wondering what it was about her that made Sean break it off. It wasn't anything new—she had been torturing herself about it for weeks and she was doing her best to keep it to herself and not bring it up with the girls. And after going off on Becca at lunch earlier, there was no way she could bring it up any time soon.

So she sat staring at the television and hoped she would eventually find something to take her mind off of men and relationships and how she didn't have either in her life right now. Trampus, her cat, stared up at her with annoyance. "Yeah, yeah, yeah," she murmured, "I know I have you." With a curse, she tossed the remote aside once she clicked over to Netflix and decided on binge-watching *The Walking Dead.*

Nothing romantic about that at all, right? She thought.

After the second episode, Angie got up, stretched and went to grab something to drink when she heard her phone—or rather the tone of an incoming text. Figuring it was one of the girls, she picked it up on her way to the kitchen.

Grabbing a bottle of water and a couple of Oreos, she walked to the living room while scrolling for the text.

And froze.

Sean: Hey. You around?

Collapsing on the couch, Angie let the water and cookies drop. "Son of a *bitch*," she hissed. "For real?" And the worst part of it all was how she was actually torn about what to do. It would be easy to just answer him but she didn't want to make things easy on him. After pretty much dumping her without a word, she wasn't sure if she should yell at him or ignore him.

Sean: Thinking about you. I know it's been a while.

And then she thought of her cousin Tricia who was married to Sean's brother, Ryan. Tricia had basically kept Angie somewhat updated on what Sean was doing—even though Angie never asked. He and his brother had an architectural construction business they had started a year ago and supposedly they were both working like mad to establish themselves. Angie understood all about hard work—she was the queen of it—but she still made time for the things and people who were important to her.

And clearly she wasn't important to Sean.

Okay, she reasoned, that wasn't really fair. Just because she was a considerate person didn't necessarily mean Sean was.

And he wasn't.

Sean: I'd really like to talk to you. Call me. Any time.

"Typical man," she muttered. Did he even realize what a complete tool he was? He'd been ignoring her for months and now all of a sudden he wants to talk and she's supposed to just drop everything and call him? She snorted with disgust. "Well…screw that." Tossing the phone aside, Angie picked up the cookies and cleaned up the mess and then took a long drink of water before settling back in for another episode of *The Walking Dead.*

The phone was technically out of sight, but her gaze kept going in its general direction. So that was it? Three little texts and the ball was in her court?

As much as she wanted to focus on the TV, her thoughts kept straying to Sean. Maybe she should call Becca or Hailey. Calling Ella wasn't really an option because as much as Angie loved her, Ella wasn't the best person to give advice on situations like this. Then again, Becca was pretty jaded right now and probably wouldn't be feeling too kindly toward any guy. That left Hailey.

"Screw it." Muting the TV, she grabbed her phone and scrolled to Hailey's number and hit send.

"H'lo."

"Hails? Are you okay?" Angie asked.

"Sorry," Hailey said around a yawn. "I was sleeping."

"It's nine-thirty on a Saturday night. Why are you already asleep?"

"Nothing else to do," Hailey said, sounding a little more awake. "What about you? You okay?"

Angie told her about Sean's texts. "Do I call? Or do I text him back and tell him to go to hell? Or maybe I just ignore him?"

"What is it that you really want to do?"

"If I knew that I wouldn't have called!" Angie said with exasperation. "I want to do all of those things but I'm not sure which one of them I *should* do."

"Okay…okay…give me a minute." Hailey paused.

"I kind of want to ignore him—at least for now—just because I'm pissed."

"But…?"

"But…part of me wants to call him and tell him directly how pissed I am."

"Okay."

"But then I think I should probably just text him so that I can't be overly bitchy." Angie sighed and then growled with frustration. "Can you understand my dilemma here?"

"I do, Ang. I totally do."

"So if you were me, what would you do?"

"Hmm…honestly?"

"Seriously?"

"Fine, no need for sarcasm," Hailey said wearily. "I'd probably text him back. Don't give in and call him—especially if you don't think you can talk to him without getting nasty and all that. Ignoring him just puts you on his level and really…you're better than that."

"Thanks."

"What are you going to say to him?"

That was the million-dollar question, Angie thought. "I'm not sure. I can't imagine why he'd contact me after all this time."

"At least you know it's not a booty call."

"How can you be so sure? Maybe it is. Oh, God…do you think it is?" Panic began to choke her. She wasn't ready for a booty call but man oh man could she use one.

"Ange, he lives like ten hours away. I would hope that if he were here in Raleigh, he would have given you a bit of a heads-up. Otherwise, it's a complete douchebag move on his part—to be so presumptuous."

"You have a point."

"I normally do," Hailey said before yawning loudly again.

"Go back to sleep. I'll talk to you tomorrow."

"What are you gonna do?"

Angie considered the question. "Honestly? I

don't know."

"Whatever you decide, good luck," Hailey said. "And call me in the morning."

"Okay. Thanks, Hails. Night."

"Night."

Turning off the TV, Angie stared at the phone in her hand while she tried to decide on what to do. Texting was the safest choice but the snarky shoulder angel kept poking at her to ignore Sean and make him sweat it out.

"I'll never sleep tonight if I don't do something," she finally admitted and made herself comfortable. Pulling up Sean's text, she took a steadying text and replied.

Angie: Just got ur message. What's up?

As if Sean was sitting there waiting for her response, her phone instantly dinged with his reply.

Sean: How are you?

"Seriously?" she muttered. "Why can't he just get to the point and forget about social chit-chat?" Rather than type the sarcastic comment like she wanted to, she went for vague.

Angie: Busy.

Sean: Oh. Is this a good time to talk? Can I call you?

Crap. The last thing she wanted was to hear his

voice right now. Sort of. If she was going to hold on to her sanity and not completely unleash all of her anger and frustration on him, this conversation needed to stay digital.

Angie: Out with the girls. Just happened to see ur text.

Liar. Liar. Liar.

Sean: Can you call me when you get home?

Her patience hit an end.

Angie: What do you want, Sean? It's been a while. I'm busy and I really don't feel like chatting.

She held her breath while she waited for his reply. On some level, Angie had hoped to keep things light, civil, but he was being a little persistent and it grated on her nerves.

Sean: I'm sorry.

"For *what?*" she cried out, rather than typing it. "Sorry for blowing me off? Sorry for bothering me? Sorry for being such a jerk when I thought things were serious?"

Meow…beside her Trampus looked up at her like he had an answer. Then he licked his paw and cleaned his face before getting up and leaving the room.

"Traitor!" she called after him. The dinging of the phone had her looking down again.

Sean: You still there?

Angie: Yeah

Sean: I really didn't want to apologize over a text but I kind of got the feeling you weren't open to talking with me

Angie: You would be correct

Sean: Wow. Okay.

Dammit. Now she actually felt bad.

Angie: Did you really think I'd want to talk to you after you pretty much blew me off?

Sean: I know. It was shitty of me.

Angie: That's not gonna cut it.

Tears welled in her eyes and she wished he would beg—maybe just a little—for her to understand. Maybe he had a good reason for blowing her off.

Sean: Five minutes. Just give me five minutes on the phone.

For a minute, all she could do was chuckle. It was like the man was living right inside her head and knew exactly what she was thinking. And quite honestly it was freaking her out.

Sean: Please

Angie: It's not going to change anything

Sean: Then use the time to yell at me. I promise not to stop you

She laughed again.

Angie: Tempting but I gotta go

And then that was it. He didn't respond and Angie felt like there wasn't anything else she could do. Yelling at him would have felt good in the moment, but ultimately it wasn't going to change anything. And until she had a clear idea of what she was going to say and knew she'd be able to say it like an adult, it was for the best that she stay quiet.

With a sigh, she put the phone down and went in search of the television remote. Settling back in her comfy chair, she started up the next episode of *The Walking Dead.*

Sort of felt like the current story of her life.

****

"What about this one?"

Wednesday night they were all gathered at Enchanted Bridal as planned and were now staring at the sixth gown Ella had tried on. Judith fussed around her—fluffing the skirt, adjusting the train.

"Are you sure you didn't try this one on already?" Angie asked. "It looks a lot like the second one you tried on.

"She hasn't tried this one on yet," Judith said with a smile as she continued her work. "That's why I gave you girls a scorecard." She rattled off the item number of the dress for them to write down. "Trust me. I have all of Ella's choices on different hooks all over the room. I just took this one out of the garment bag."

Turning to Becca, Angie murmured, "Still looks exactly the same to me."

Becca nodded. "After a while they all do. Now that she's narrowed down the style, the differences in them are going to be minute."

"Do you guys not like this style?" Ella asked nervously. "I thought we all agreed this looked the best on me. Should I try something else?"

Judith stepped in front of her and gently grasped Ella by the shoulders. "Deep breaths," she said softly. "I want you to pretend that no one else is here and you're looking at these dresses for the first time. Don't think about what other people tell you looks good on you. What style do *you* want?"

Nancy, Ella's mother, stepped forward. "We talked about this all day, Ella. You wanted a traditional gown. Lots of lace, remember?"

One look in Ella's eyes and Judith had her answer. "Why don't we take a break and have a little something to eat? I'm going to help our bride here get out of this dress while you all get the food set up in the back room. We'll be there in a jiff."

Luckily no one argued and quietly she led Ella back to the dressing room. Once the curtain was closed, she faced her.

"Okay, sweetheart, we're all alone. Why are you trying on dresses you don't want?"

Ella's eyes immediately went misty. "I…I didn't say that."

Judith smiled at Ella in a way only a mother did. "You didn't have to. Those blue eyes of yours gave you away." She cupped Ella's cheeks. "What's going on?"

Sighing, Ella turned and faced her reflection in the mirror and grimaced. "Mom and I were going through some bridal magazines today. She had a snarky comment for every gown I picked out. It didn't take long for me to realize she had something completely different in mind and I thought it would be easier if I just went along with it."

Judith stepped behind her and began unhooking the long row of buttons down the back of the gown. "From what I've been hearing, you're doing an awful lot of that lately." She paused and finished her task before asking, "You know this is supposed to be your big day, right? No one else's. Well…except for Dylan."

Ella smiled at the mention of her fiancé.

"What does Dylan have to say about all of this?"

Ella told her about the last conversation she and Dylan had about the wedding Friday night after the show. "He doesn't think any of it's bad, but he's a guy. The less decisions he has to make, the better. At least that's what it seems like." She stepped out of the gown and reached for her jeans.

"I've known you since you were five, Ella, and

we've talked a lot about weddings over the years. For as long as you've talked about marrying Dylan, your description of your perfect wedding never changed—small, intimate ceremony and you were going to wear a strapless, princess-style gown and tiara." Judith motioned to the gowns hanging around them. "And that doesn't describe even one gown you chose to try on tonight. I've worked with enough brides and their mothers. It may not be comfortable for you, but you're going to have to talk to your mom and tell her how you feel."

"But…"

"Go and eat," Judith said, an understanding smile on her face.

"Let me help you hang this back up," Ella said quietly after she finished dressing.

"I got it. I'll be out in a minute."

Ella walked out and joined everyone in the back room where there were sandwiches, salad and cookies set out for everyone to enjoy.

For the next thirty minutes, everyone talked and laughed and asked about the wedding plans. Ella did her best to look cheerful, but Judith's words kept coming back to her. She knew she was going to have to sit her mother down and remind her of whose wedding this actually was. She just wasn't looking forward to it.

"Okay," Judith called out when everyone was done eating, "are we ready for round two? I think I found the perfect dress!"

There was a round of oohs and aahs as everyone went back to the showroom and took their seats.

Ella stepped into the dressing room and stopped short. "What…?" She quickly looked around. "What happened to the dresses that were in here earlier?"

Smiling, Judith closed the curtain. "Those were all wrong for you. I did a quick run through the store and found several that I think fit the criteria."

"But…I…I didn't get a chance to talk to my mom yet," Ella stammered.

"And now you won't have to. At least…not alone." With a wink, Judith began removing the first gown from its garment bag. "I already talked to Hailey, Becca and Angie. We've all got your back."

Ella just stood there staring as if in shock.

Gently, Judith pulled her into her embrace. "If I thought for a second that any of those other gowns made you happy, I wouldn't have said a word. But like I said before, I've worked with a lot of brides and their mothers and I know when to send in the troops. And you, my dear, need your troops."

A lone tear trailed down Ella's cheek. "I…I don't know what to say," she said quietly.

Stepping back and going back to the gown, Judith grinned. "Say we may have a winner in this one. You wore it last month in the show at the Hilton.

I didn't say anything then but…" She shrugged. "As soon as I saw you in it, I just knew."

Ten minutes later, Ella got the first glimpse of herself in the gown she had marveled at when she wore it in the show Judith had mentioned. It was beyond stunning—the perfect balance between ornate beading and simplicity and the skirt was full enough to make her feel like a princess. She couldn't help but smile.

"Are you ready to knock their socks off?" Judith asked.

Ella's smile grew. "Just as long as you're ready to swoop in if I need you."

Stepping back, Judith let Ella walk out of the dressing room first and then bent down to pick up the train. "Always, my girl. Always."

****

It was the usual after-show chaos Friday night and as much as Becca wanted to chip in and help, she needed to go find Max and give him the pictures for the DVD he was putting together. She had already changed back into her street clothes and was making her way around the boutique in hopes of finding him.

After stopping a few times to talk to some brides-to-be, Becca spotted Max heading toward the back room carrying all of his photography equipment. She quickly made her way across the room and followed him out the back door. "Max!"

The wind was whipping but the torrential rains

rains that had come through earlier had finally stopped. She would have preferred to talk with him inside, but she could make do with the crappy weather—even as she cursed her long hair and did her best to keep it pulled away from her face.

He stopped and turned around, smiling when he spotted her. "Hey, Becca," he said, making his way back toward her. "Great show tonight."

She blushed. "Thanks. I um…I have those pictures for you. You know, if you still want to do the DVD." Reaching into her purse, Becca pulled out a large envelope and handed it to him. "There are a couple of picture CDs in there and a flash drive too. Hailey's been trying to organize a project like this for years so she was able to get them in some kind of order for you. I hope it's okay."

Max continued to smile. "I'm sure it'll be great. I've been thinking a lot about how I want it all to look so all I should have to do is plug in the pictures. If all goes well, I should have something for you to look at by next week. There's another show Friday, right?"

"There is. It's an off-site event at one of those massive bridal expos. Mrs. J tries to get into all of the local ones and occasionally we travel to the tri-state area to participate."

"She told me," Max replied. "I guess she wanted to make sure I'd be okay with traveling along with the show to document it all."

"I'm glad this one is only an hour away. It

makes for a late night but the driving is doable."

They both grew silent and Becca wasn't sure what else to say to him. They didn't really know each other and as much as she found him to be a nice guy, she also couldn't forget how he had pretty much seen her at her lowest moment, one that she wanted to forget.

"So I should go," she finally said. "I need to go make sure the girls don't need my help."

Max nodded. "Thanks for the pictures. I think Judith is going to like what we put together. Since the show is out of town next weekend, maybe I'll send the DVD home with you and you can show it to Hailey and the girls and give me some feedback before anything is finalized."

"Oh, that would be great. Thanks." They stood there in the darkened parking lot for another minute. "Anyway, thanks again, Max. I'll see you Friday."

"Have a good night, Becca."

As she walked back into the boutique, she couldn't help but smile. Guys like Max restored her faith a little in the male species. He seemed to be very nice and she felt comfortable talking with him. He was good looking and an interesting mix of nerdy hipster and just a little bit sexy. And she had no doubt that she wasn't his type in the least. Good looking guys like him…well…good looking guys in general never worked out for her. Look at what had happened with Danny. If Max had simply been a nerdy hipster she might have considered flirting a little – that would have made him safe in her mind - but dammit, he was too nice to look at.

With a sad sigh she made her way around the room and spotted Hailey and Logan putting chairs away. They were laughing and smiling and knowing how much Hailey was crushing on Logan, she decided to find something else to do. Turning around, she bumped into Jack. “Oh! Sorry.”

He didn’t even make eye contact with her. He was too busy staring at Logan and Hailey. “No problem,” he murmured.

Stepping around him and making her way toward the dressing rooms, she found where the girls were busy hanging up gowns and silently stepped in to help them.

Three

"So he never texted you back?" Hailey asked the next day over lunch.

Angie shook her head.

"Oh…so…how do you feel about it? I mean…are you happy? Sad? Relieved?"

"Honestly," Angie began, "I'm kind of disappointed. It's one thing to think you don't mean a whole lot to someone, but it's quite another when it's pretty much confirmed."

"Well that just sucks," Ella said as she reached across the table and helped herself to some of Becca's french fries.

"At least I can say I have closure. Sort of."

Becca held up her hand. "Maybe he was just taking you at your word and figured you really did have to go. You can't get mad at him for respecting your request."

All three of her friends stared at her like she had grown a second head.

"What? What did I say?"

"I got this," Hailey said before Angie could speak. She turned to Becca. "While I think it could be okay if he was simply being polite, the fact is that was a week ago and he hasn't tried to contact her since. If he was being sincere and genuine in wanting to talk to Angie, he would have tried to get in touch with her the following day."

"Or any of the following days," Angie added and then sighed. "Just forget it. It's not a big deal. It's not like Sean's the one or anything."

"How do you know?" Ella asked.

Angie snorted with disbelief. "Because I know."

"Yeah but…how?" Ella asked and then looked at Hailey and Becca for back up. "I knew after the first time Dylan kissed me that he was it for me."

"For crying out loud," Angie muttered. "You were in the sixth grade!"

"But I *knew*!" Ella cried and then lowered her voice. "All I'm asking is…how do you know for certain that Sean isn't the one?"

"Other than the fact that he dumped me, disappeared, blew me off and…oh yeah…hasn't tried to contact me again? Is that what you're asking?"

Ella slouched down in her seat. "Never mind."

"Okay, we're all getting a little cranky about this," Hailey said diplomatically. "Personally, I don't think it's the same for everyone." She turned to Ella. "You looked at Dylan and knew he was it for you. The majority of the population would not know at that age or even be thinking about the possibility of forever with someone, at least not realistically. You're just lucky." Then she turned to Becca. "You thought Danny was your ideal when you met him in the tenth grade. And it took you years to actually start dating him and after everything you built up about him in your mind, turned out not to be true. Correct?"

Becca nodded.

Lastly, Hailey looked at Angie. "You felt something for Sean almost from the get-go. And if we forget about the current negative situation, how did you feel about him before that? Did you think he could possibly be the one?"

"This is ridiculous," Angie said as she waved the waitress over and asked about the dessert specials.

"Avoiding the question isn't going to make it go away," Hailey sang.

Once the table was cleared and they all ordered dessert, Angie looked at her friends and glared. "Okay, fine. If we're basing this on Sean's pre-desertion days, then yes. There was a...possibility...of him being the one. But that changed! Why is it okay for everyone to see that Becca was wrong about Danny and I'm not allowed to be wrong about Sean?"

"It's not that we're saying you're not allowed to be wrong," Ella said.

"And to be fair, you all warned me Danny was a douche from the very beginning," Becca said with a grin.

"We may have only met Sean a handful of times, Ange, but he seemed like a really nice guy. Maybe you need to hear him out and see why he pulled back," Hailey said.

"Need I remind you how you and I had this conversation that night," Angie snapped at Hailey. "You know why I didn't want to get on the phone with him and the fact that he hasn't tried to contact me since that night only adds to my pissed-off mindset! How am I supposed to pick up the phone and call him now when I feel even *more* anger toward him?"

"She has a point," Becca said. "And she does have a temper. There's a good chance she'll start yelling at him and scare him off."

Ella nodded in agreement. "She scares me."

"This isn't helping!" Hailey interrupted.

"No, it is," Angie said sadly. "It really is. Obviously I need to clear the air with him otherwise I'm never going to be able to move on. And whether or not I move on with him or without him...well...that remains to be seen."

"But you'd totally rather move on with him, right?" Ella asked hopefully, a huge smile brightening her entire face.

For a minute, Angie could only stare at her. "What the hell is it like to be that happy all the damn time? Honestly, it's got to be exhausting."

Ella blushed.

"No picking on Ella," Hailey said and thanked

the waitress who was putting their desserts down on the table. "We should all be so lucky to be like her. She's the only one of us who has her shit together."

"Who? Me?" Ella asked, wide-eyed.

"You were a total rock star Wednesday night," Becca said with a chuckle. "The way you stood up to your mom? That was epic!"

After Ella had stepped out of the dressing room wearing the gown of her dreams, her mother had immediately begun to criticize. For a few minutes, she let her speak. Then Judith stepped in and—very diplomatically—explained how she's dealt with situations like this before and the importance of the bride getting to wear exactly what *she* wanted.

It took all of five minutes before Ella spoke up and unleashed her pixie-like wrath. "Enough!" she'd cried. "In case anyone has forgotten, *Mom*, this is *my* wedding! Mine and Dylan's! For years I have dreamed of my perfect day and so far you have taken over those dreams and turned them into something I no longer recognize! You see this dress?" She had fisted the satin skirt in her hands and shook it in her mother's direction. "This is my wedding dress. I'm sorry if you don't like it, but you're not wearing it. I am. And you know what? Dylan happens to love this style on me and his is the only opinion other than mine I'm worried about!"

"Is your mom talking to you yet?" Hailey asked carefully, bringing them all back to the present.

"Yeah. It took her until yesterday to pick up the phone and call. I didn't reach out to her. I needed her to see that I was serious. It was hard to confront her like that, but it had to be done."

"Does this mean she's going to ease up on the other wedding stuff?" Angie asked.

"I'm not sure yet. One thing at a time. That's all I can handle."

"What did Dylan say when you told him about it?"

Ella chuckled. "He said he was sorry he'd missed it. He likes when I get feisty." Then she blushed. "He thinks it's sexy."

"Oh…yuck. Just…no," Angie said. "We don't need to hear anything beyond that."

They ate their desserts in silence for a few minutes before Becca spoke up. "I gave Max all of the photos last night at the show. He said he'll have a video put together for us to preview by next weekend."

"Mom is going to be so surprised," Hailey grinned. "There were a lot of pictures there. Do you think he'll need more?"

Becca shook her head. "He didn't seem to think so."

"I had wanted to talk to him about it last night but everything was so chaotic. I can't remember the last time a show went like that," Hailey said.

"That's because the weather sucked and people were late," Angie added. "Hell, even we didn't get to sit and hang out like we usually do. Thank God for our Saturday date or we'd all still be in the dark about how the week went."

"Sarcasm?" Becca asked with a laugh.

"Just a little," she replied. "So Max is going to put together this video DVD thing, huh?"

Becca nodded. "He's pretty psyched about it."

"That's so nice of him," Ella said. "I can't wait to see what he comes up with."

"He's going to give us a copy to review before he finalizes it. This way we can tell him if we want to change anything."

Hailey frowned. "Did I scare him off or something?"

Becca shook her head. "I don't think so. Why?"

"I just don't understand why he won't talk to me about it."

"I don't know," Becca replied with a shrug.

"Does it really matter?" Angie asked. "He's doing something nice for your mom and it involves all of us. What's the big deal?"

"None I guess," Hailey sighed.

"So I saw you and Logan together after the show," Becca said, hoping to cheer her friend up.

"Anything new to report there?"

"No. I'm telling you, other than just blurting out that I'm in love with him, I don't know what else to do!"

"Maybe he already has a girlfriend," Becca said.

"No, no, no, "Angie said. "We've all been working together and socializing together long enough that it would have come up in conversation or we would have met the girl. Maybe he's gay."

"Not you too," Hailey mumbled.

"What? What was that?" Angie asked.

"Jack keeps saying the same thing and I think you're both crazy. I spend a lot of time with Logan. I think I would know if he's gay." She looked worriedly at her friends. "Wouldn't I?"

"I'm just saying…it's a possibility."

Hailey groaned. "I don't know which part of that bothers me more—the fact that Logan could be gay or that Jack could be right."

****

That thought stayed with Hailey all day and she knew she needed a distraction. Lunch with the girls was always great, but right now she needed to call in the big guns—her mom.

When she walked into the boutique Sunday afternoon, she was surprised to find her mom alone in her office reading a book.

"So this is what you do when no one's looking?" Hailey teased as she walked in and sat down.

Judith smiled. "Sometimes rainy days are a blessing. No one feels like going out and I get a chance to put my feet up and relax."

"I wish you'd let one of your assistants work for you on Sundays so you can do that relaxing at home. You know you don't have to be here all the time, right?"

"But I enjoy being here," Judith said simply. "Believe it or not, this isn't a job or a chore for me. I created the kind of environment here that I happen to find very tranquil."

"You could make a space like that at home. I'm sure Dad wouldn't mind."

Judith frowned but quickly put her smile back in place. "What brings you out in this miserable weather? Everything okay?"

For a minute Hailey wanted to discuss the brief change in her mother's demeanor, but decided to let it wait. "What do you think about Logan?"

"I think he's a very nice young man. Polite. Handsome. He makes a very attractive groom," she added with a sly smile. "I know you think all those things too so…why? Why are you asking my opinion?"

"I've spent a lot of time with Logan at the shows and…" She shrugged. "I think I've been kind of obvious about how I feel about him, but he hasn't said or done anything. I had hoped he would ask me out by now, but he hasn't. Does he have a girlfriend I don't know about? Am I throwing out some kind of vibe that's telling him to back off? I don't understand what's happening to make things…you know…not happen."

Standing, Judith walked over to her mini-fridge and took out a couple of bottles of water. She handed one to her daughter.

"What am I doing wrong, Mom? Do you think I'm acting too desperate?"

Judith sat back down and reached for one of

Hailey's hands and squeezed it. "I don't think you're acting desperate, sweetheart. Maybe Logan's just a little…shy."

Hailey made a face. "Mom, he's definitely not shy. He socializes with everyone before, during and after each show." She sighed. "I guess I'm just not his type."

"That's a very real possibility, but if you want to know for sure, you're going to have to come out and ask him directly. Otherwise you're just going to keep torturing yourself."

"Maybe."

"How about I pair you up with somebody different this week for the show?" Judith suggested as she sat back and opened her water.

"What good would that do?"

"I think you could observe him a little bit. See if he's flirting with any of the other girls—not our girls," she added with a wink. "Or you might see how he interacts with everyone. I think you're too close to him during the shows and maybe aren't seeing things as they really are."

Frowning, Hailey asked, "What does that even mean? How are things?"

"Hailey, you have a tendency to over-romanticize everyone and everything. All I'm saying is maybe you've built Logan up in your mind into the person you want him to be without really taking the time to get to know who he really is."

"Well I would get to know him if he'd ask me out!"

"Or you could ask him out."

"I've thought about it," Hailey admitted. "I guess I just hoped he would eventually do it." She groaned. "I'm pathetic, aren't I?"

"No, you're not pathetic. Dramatic? Yes. But not pathetic," Judith said with a chuckle. "So how about I pair you up with Jackson for Friday night?"

"Ugh…no. Anyone but him."

Judith's eyes widened slightly with surprise. "What's wrong with Jackson? Most of the other girls love getting paired with him. Some weeks there are fights about it."

"Seriously? Over him? That's crazy."

"I'm sensing there's a story there so you might as well spill it."

"I hate that you know me so well," Hailey whined.

"I'm your mom. It's my job."

"Fine," she said with a pout. "He's…obnoxious. Every time he comes near me, it's to say something rude."

"Somehow I doubt that, but go on," Judith encouraged.

"And why doesn't he ever get a haircut?" Hailey cried as she jumped to her feet and began to pace. "Would it kill him to brush his hair once in a while or maybe stop getting so many tattoos? Honestly, mom, I don't know how you let him in the shows!"

"Well, to be fair…"

"He told me I'm cute. *Cute!* In my entire life, no one has ever called me that!"

"I don't see…"

"It didn't sound like a compliment," Hailey interrupted. "I think it was a complete put-down and it was insulting."

"Okay, but…"

"A puppy is cute," she went on. "Or a teddy bear. Grown women are not cute!"

Rather than try to interrupt a fourth time, Judith just sat back and watched and listened while her daughter rambled on.

"And on top of that, he makes fun of Logan! He calls him 'pretty boy' in that same condescending tone he calls me cute in. I hate it! Of course I shouldn't be surprised, he clearly doesn't have manners. I know there are a lot more male models out there we can hire who are far better looking and with better manners than Jack!" With a loud sigh, Hailey collapsed back down in her seat and looked at her mother. "Promise me you won't use him in any more shows. Please."

Shaking her head, Judith gave her a sympathetic smile. "No can do, sweet pea. You are the only one who has an issue with Jackson and that isn't a reason for me to let him go. The other models like him, the guests and clients like him. Hell, I like him! You're just going to have to learn to deal with him."

"I could deal with him just fine if he'd leave me alone. Or maybe just not speak when I'm around. Or make himself look presentable," she murmured.

"I never knew you to be such a snob."

Hailey sat upright. "Excuse me?"

"You heard me. A snob."

For a minute, Hailey simply sputtered and tried to form a retort, but Judith cut her off before she could find one.

"For the record, he prefers to be called Jackson

and I've never seen or heard him be anything but polite and respectful to anyone. His mother and I are in the same yoga class together and we've become good friends." She gave Hailey a pointed look.

"So you're saying this is about me? That I'm the problem?"

"Well…I wouldn't say that exactly…"

"And yet you are!" Once again, Hailey jumped to her feet and looked around until she found her purse. "I can't believe you're taking his side over mine!"

"I'm not taking sides at all," Judith said wearily, placing her water on the end table and standing up. She wrapped her daughter in her arms and hugged her. "I just think you have quite a few…issues…right now that are making you a little more sensitive than usual."

"That's just another way of saying I'm being difficult," Hailey mumbled.

Pulling back, Judith looked down at Hailey's face. "I think you need to get things straight with Logan because it's starting to wear on you. Don't wait for him to make a move; you make one. Invite him to coffee after the show or maybe to dinner before it—just do something. You'll feel much better once that part of your life is a little more settled."

"I don't know…"

Judith stepped away and sat back down. "I'm sure you've already talked about this with the girls.

What do they say?"

Hailey shrugged.

"Hailey…"

"No one can figure out why he hasn't said or done anything. Becca thought maybe he already had a girlfriend, but that theory got shot down."

"And you all just left it at that?" She gave Hailey a disapproving glance.

And for some reason, in that moment, Hailey felt it was better to lie to her mother than admit what the rest of the conversation had consisted of. "We sort of got distracted by dessert and congratulating Ella on standing up to her mom. And, by the way, thank you for making that happen."

The smile on Judith's face conveyed how she knew exactly what was behind the sudden change of subject. "It needed to be done. That poor girl was miserable and I knew the exact reason why." She shook her head. "Someone just needed to give her a push."

"You're too nice. I was thinking someone needed to give her mom a hard slap in the face."

"Hailey!"

"I know, I know…"

"You really are out of sorts, sweetheart. Do yourself a favor and talk to Logan. If he's not interested then you can move on. I know you'll be heartbroken but at least you can move on."

It was pretty much the same thing Hailey had been telling herself. She didn't know why she thought her mom or her friends were going to say anything different. It would be different if Logan had even hinted about his feelings one way or the other, but he hadn't.

"Promise me you'll think about it," Judith said.

With a small smile, Hailey nodded and knew she wouldn't be able to think about anything but.

****

Friday afternoon, the girls were piled into Becca's Toyota and heading to Greensboro. "Is it wrong that we're not even there yet and I'm already wishing we had booked a hotel room for the night?" Becca asked.

"For crying out loud, we're only a little more than an hour away from home. If you're tired later, I'll drive," Angie said.

"It's not just the drive. It's just more fun when we make it like a mini-vacation. We could have relaxed after the show and got up tomorrow and ordered room service…"

"Call it what you want, but it still sounds a lot like laziness to me," Angie replied.

From the back seat, Hailey cleared her throat. "Um…so since we're doing the show tonight and have the long drive home, I was wondering if anyone would be upset if I missed lunch tomorrow."

They all turned and looked at her—except Becca who simply caught Hailey's eye in the rear-view mirror. "Why? What's going on?"

Hailey took a steadying breath. "I'm going to ask Logan to have lunch with me tomorrow."

"Finally!" Angie said as she clapped her hands with glee. "Do you know where you're going to go? What you're going to wear? Have you written down how you want to ask him?"

"Yes, yes and yes," Hailey said with a grin. "I've been waiting for what seems like forever for him to do the asking, but I'm done with all of that. I want to move this thing along and if he's too shy to make a move, then I'm going to."

"You talked to your mom, didn't you?" Ella asked.

"What makes you say that?"

"Because we've all been telling you this for months and you haven't done a thing. Just like I was with my mom. Then I spent a few minutes talking with your mom and BAM! Things are happening!"

"So you've told your mom about how she needs to reel it in with your wedding?" Becca asked. "How did she take it?"

"Well, I still haven't put it all out there. After the whole thing with the dress, I mentioned how the guest list was starting to get out of hand. I took her to lunch and explained how it was okay to *not* invite everyone we ever knew to the wedding."

"How'd she take it?"

"She got a little offended at first and then when I mentioned all the extra money it was taking to cover all of the additional guests, she finally started to see how things were snowballing."

"So then what's left?" Hailey asked. "What else is bothering you about the whole thing?"

"Where do I even begin?"

"Ella, sweetie, how long have you been keeping this to yourself? And why?" Hailey asked.

With a shrug, Ella looked down and studied her hands which were folded in her lap. "You know I don't like to complain. And I was fine with things for a while until…" she looked up. "I wasn't. It all sort of hit me at once. It was the guest list, the invitations, the menu, the dress…it just went on and on and on. And then I started freaking out because I feel like I missed out on so much because Dylan and I have been together forever and I was thinking how maybe I shouldn't be getting married at all and…"

"*What*?!" It was a collective cry from Hailey, Angie and Becca.

Ella sighed loudly. "Look, it's not a big deal. Sometimes I just can't help but wonder if getting married is the right thing. Dylan's the only guy I've ever dated. The only man I've ever slept with. What if…what if we're not really right for each other but we thought we were? What if I'm supposed to be with someone else? How do I know if we truly make each other happy if we have nothing else to compare it to?" She was nearing hysteria by the time Hailey reached over and hugged her.

"I can't believe you've been keeping this bottled up!"

Spinning in her seat, Angie faced them. "Ella, seriously, why wouldn't you talk to us about this? We talk about everything—even stuff we probably shouldn't. Like poop. None of us were going to judge you! Hell, I think we've all probably wondered those exact same things about you and Dylan for years."

"Really?" Ella asked as she pulled back from Hailey. "You're not just saying that?"

"Do I ever lie?" Angie asked.

"Nope. You're honest to a fault," Ella said with a chuckle. "I know Dylan and I love each other. But now that we're deep into planning the wedding, everything is making me freak out. I listen to all of you talk about your relationships with the guys you date and I can't even comprehend what it's like. Then I start to worry that one day Dylan's going to come home and realize there's another woman out there he wants more than me and…it's just really making me crazy!"

"I'm sure it is," Becca said. "Geez, that's a lot to be taking on yourself. What can we do to help you?"

"Actually, just being able to say it all out loud helps a lot. I know a lot of it is just the normal stuff everyone goes through, but I can't help but wonder about…you know…what I'm missing."

"You mean the joy of wondering if a guy is going to call or if he's going to dump you? The constant need to diet and always look good when you go out just in case you run into a guy or to hopefully get a guy's attention?" Becca asked.

"Or how you think you find a great guy and then have him blow you off and you are forced to sit home with your cat and wonder what it is that you did wrong and what—in general—is wrong with you that you can't seem to find a guy who wants to stick around for more than a month or two?" Angie added.

"Then there's always the fun of feeling insecure because the guy you like doesn't seem to now you exist six out of the seven days of the week and you—again—are left to wonder what is wrong with you. Yeah, Ella, you're missing a whole lot of great stuff," Hailey said with a hint of sarcasm. "You should dump Dylan and forget about how wonderful he is because there's a whole crapload of guys out there just waiting to help you sit around and second-guess yourself."

"Okay, okay, I get it. Sheesh," Ella huffed. "Try and look at it from my perspective—what if the first guy you kissed, was the only guy you ever kissed and ever would kiss? How would you feel?"

"Ugh…" Becca groaned. "Billy Thompson. Eighth grade. His braces cut my lip and it was more spit than kiss."

"Todd Reese," Angie said with a smile. "Seventh grade and he was an excellent kisser. Not that I'd still want to be kissing him—it turns out he peaked in the eighth grade in the looks department."

"Vinny Malone—also in the seventh grade. He looked like Tony Danza and was a pretty good kisser. Too much tongue," Hailey said and then made a face. "But surely Dylan wasn't a great kisser right out of the gate."

"Neither of us were but we sort of grew into it," Ella said dreamily. "Honestly, I feel like every time we kiss it just gets better."

"So then why are you thinking about kissing other guys?" Angie asked. "If you're happy with things the way they are with Dylan, why even question it?"

"Because I feel like I should! People look at us like we're freaks sometimes because we've only been with each other!"

"Being with other people isn't all it's cracked up to be. Trust me," Becca said. "If you ask me, you and Dylan are the luckiest people in the world. You know every day when you wake up that you're with the love of your life. You don't have to deal with all the crap we already mentioned and at the end of the day, you know you're going to bed in the arms of a man who loves you for all that you are."

They were all silent for a few minutes before they realized they had arrived at the hotel where the bridal expo was being held.

"Well that drive went pretty fast," Hailey said as she climbed from the car. She spotted Logan heading into the hotel and smiled. "Wish me luck, girls. I'm going after my man!"

As she walked away, Ella sighed and looked over at Becca and Angie. "I think that's what I miss the most."

"What?"

"The excitement of something new. Look at her, just going after what she wants and she has no idea how it's going to go. She's probably got butterflies in her stomach and wondering if her lipstick is okay. And then she's going to see him and smile and he'll smile back and…"

"And it can all go to hell from there," Angie said,

slamming the car door. "Don't romanticize it, El. Yes, things can go great and tomorrow Hailey and Logan could have lunch together and find out they're crazy about each other. Or, she could find out he's married and has a wife and three kids waiting at home. Not everything is like a romance novel. Not every relationship has a happy ending."

Ella frowned and turned back to watch Hailey walk through the front entrance of the hotel and smiled. "But sometimes they do."

Together, Becca and Angie walked around the car and flanked Ella and hooked their arms with hers. "Come on, Cinderella. Time to get you ready for the ball," Becca said. They laughed as they made their way into the hotel.

****

It took Hailey about ten minutes to get Logan alone. The ballroom was a flurry of activity and she took a deep breath and let it out as she made her way over to him.

"Hey, beautiful," he said when he spotted her. "How was your week?"

Everything in Hailey melted. Reaching out, she put her hand on his arm and smiled. "It was good, Logan. How was yours?"

For the next few minutes she listened to him wax poetic about his job at…

"Wait? Where do you work?" she asked.

"Starbucks."

She could only hope her jaw hadn't literally hit the floor. "Oh…that's…that's great."

Flashing his million-dollar smile at her, he nodded. "You have no idea how rewarding it is to work at a place where you help so many people."

"You mean like customer service?"

He chuckled. "No…it's more like…therapy." Then he nodded again. "I'm telling you, I am practically a therapist. People come in and they need their coffee but they also need to talk and that's where

I come in. I listen to them while I'm making their coffee. And when they leave, they're smiling."

Oh. My. God, she thought to herself. Was he being serious? "So…um…how long have you worked for Starbucks? Is it just a part-time gig until you get a job with a law firm or something like that?"

Logan laughed. "Why would I work at a law firm? Or for any firm?"

And that made her stop and think. Why had she automatically thought that?

"Offices are depressing. I think I would go crazy being cooped up in an office or—God forbid—a cubicle all day. I would seriously lose my mind."

She made a non-committal sound and tried to come up with an excuse to walk away.

"You should come in some time," he said. "I work at the one about two blocks over from the bridal shop."

Remembering her mom's words about being a snob, she decided that maybe there was something to it. Here she was judging Logan because he worked part time at a coffee house rather than having a serious office job. "Funny you should mention that," she finally said. "I was going to see if you wanted to have lunch with me tomorrow."

His eyes twinkled at her. "Really? That sounds great. I have to be at work at two but if you don't mind an early lunch we'll call it a date."

There they were—those little words she had been dying to hear for months and all she felt was…nothing.

Seriously nothing.

Rather than examining that too closely, she rattled off the name of a café she knew of near the Starbucks and was relieved that he knew where it was. "I need to go and get ready. I guess I'll see you backstage in a bit."

Logan turned and waved before walking away and Hailey stood rooted to the spot. She racked her brain for any previous conversations with Logan that had been…bizarre. None came to her. This was something she definitely needed to talk to the girls about. Turning around, she took all of one step before she ran into someone.

Jack.

Correction…Jackson.

"Hey, Princess," he said smoothly.

Once again her mother's words came back to her so she bit back her instinct to say something snarky and opted to try and be pleasant. "Hey, Jackson. How are you this evening?"

His green eyes widened with shock for the briefest of moments before a slow, lazy grin covered his face. "I'm doing well, thank you. And yourself?"

She smiled. Or at least she hoped she was smiling. "Fine, thank you." Pausing for a moment,

Hailey figured she had been the bigger person and now needed to go and find her posse and tell them all about…

“So…pretty boy works at Starbucks, huh?” he chuckled. “I hear there’s a tremendous future in that.”

“Were you…?”

“Oh but wait…he doesn’t only serve coffee; he’s like a therapist too.” Jackson’s entire face lit up with mirth and Hailey wanted to smack him.

Doing her best to rein in her temper, she crossed her arms across her chest while tapping her foot. “Well I guess I have my answer.”

Jackson instantly sobered. “Answer to what?”

“The question of whether or not you have any manners whatsoever. Obviously you don’t.”

“Oh really? And you came to this conclusion…how?”

“You purposely stood there and eavesdropped on my conversation with Logan! It was clear we were having a private conversation and anyone with an ounce of common sense would have noticed that and moved on. But not you!”

“Fine,” he said solemnly. “I’m sorry I listened in on your conversation.”

Hailey waited for the punchline, but there wasn’t one. “Thank you.” Unwilling to accept that he wasn’t waiting to make another joke at her expense, she waited another minute. “Well then…I need to go and start to get ready. Have a good night.”

“You too, Princess,” he said with a grin. It wasn’t more than ten seconds later when she heard him say, “Enjoy your *date* tomorrow.”

She should have followed her gut instinct and slapped him when she had the chance.

****

It was after midnight when they were finally walking back to Becca’s car. As she originally thought, she was tired and really wished they’d booked a room for the night.

“Becca!”

Turning around, she saw Max jogging toward her. In all of the normal chaos with getting ready for the show, she had completely forgotten to seek him out and see if he had the DVD ready for her.

“Hey, Max,” she said with a smile.

“I was afraid I’d missed you,” he said. The parking lot was starting to empty around them as models, vendors and guests were finally starting to leave. “I have the DVD for you and the girls to look at.” He reached into his satchel, pulled it out and handed it to her.

“Thanks! We’re all looking forward to checking it out. It probably won’t be until some time tomorrow or Sunday. Saturdays are normally our day to get together for lunch, but Hailey’s got a date and we won't want to watch it without her." For a minute she felt like she was rambling, but with Max it didn't really seem to matter. He was looking at her and smiling and she was finding that she really liked his smile. "So…"

"Take your time," he replied and then looked around the parking lot. "Did you drive here alone?"

She shook her head. "I drove but the girls all came with me. Honestly, I wish we had just splurged and booked a room so that I didn't have to drive at this hour."

His expression turned serious. "You shouldn't drive if you're tired. Maybe one of your friends can drive instead."

Was it wrong that her heart skipped a beat at his concern? "I'm sure Angie would drive in a heartbeat and really, I should be fine. But I know I'm going to sleep well tonight and definitely wake up late tomorrow."

Max nodded. "Where are you parked?"

"Just back over there," she said, pointing to the far left corner of the lot.

"Come on, I'll walk you over." Together they turned and walked in that direction. "So I know I said to take your time with the DVD and all, but do you think you could maybe…call me and let me know what you think after you watch it?" he asked.

"Sure. That shouldn't be a problem."

“I’m not trying to rush you or anything,” he quickly added, “but I’d really like your opinion.”

Becca looked up at him and smiled. “I’m sure it’s going to be great, Max. Hailey may have a few suggestions—that’s sort of her thing—but I promise she’ll be cool about it when you talk to her.”

His expression—and his steps—faltered for a second.

She stopped and looked at him questioningly. “What? What’s wrong?”

He shook his head as if to clear it. “Nothing. It’s…never mind.”

When Max started to walk again, Becca put a hand on his arm to stop him. “No, come one. What did I say? I didn’t mean to imply that Hailey or any of us is going to find fault with the video, Max. I’m sorry if it came out that way.”

He shook his head again. “It’s not that, Becca.”

“Then what?”

With a small sigh, Max shifted his arm until Becca’s hand fell and then he took her hand in his. “I thought I was being cool about this and getting you to call me without being obvious,” he began. “And then you mentioned having Hailey call and…well…” His gaze met hers. “I’d really like to get to know you. Talk with you for more than five minutes every Friday.” He chuckled. “Not that it hasn’t been nice, but…I don’t know…I think you’re great and I’d just like the chance to spend some time with you.”

Becca felt as if time was standing still. Or maybe it was just her.

"Becca?"

Max wanted to get to know her? Really?

He nervously shifted on his feet and looked in the direction of her car. "Um…it looks like Angie and Ella are waiting by the car. We should…uh…we should probably go." Without looking at her, he turned to walk away.

"Wait…Max?"

He turned around and took a few steps toward her.

"I…wow…I don't know what to say. I mean…I really like talking with you and I just never thought…you know…that you might want to hang out with me other than when we're here at the shows."

His grin was slow and sweet. "Why wouldn't I?"

The last thing she wanted was to remind him of how they first met but it must have shown on her face.

"I know exactly what you're thinking," he said. "And I hate how you're letting that jackass have that effect on you. I look at you and I see an amazing woman. You're sweet and funny and beautiful!" Taking a step back, Max cleared his throat. "We may not know each other very well, but I'd like to change that."

This had to be a dream because things like this never really happened to her. Nice, good-looking guys never asked her out. At least not like this. It wasn't that Becca didn't date a lot—she did—but the guys she dated weren't nearly as…together as Max was.

"I'd like that," she said shyly.

And his grin turned into a full-blown smile. Holding out a hand to her, he clasped her hand in his and together they walked back toward Becca's car.

"Can I take you to lunch on Sunday?" he asked before they got close enough for Angie and Ella to hear.

She didn't trust herself to talk, so she nodded.

He stopped them just a few feet shy of the car and faced her. "Call me tomorrow and we'll pick a place to go, okay?"

"Okay." Becca was afraid to meet his gaze because she knew he'd be able to read her thoughts too clearly. She wanted to kiss him—but not with an audience.

Squeezing her hand, he leaned in and placed a rather chaste kiss on her cheek. "I'll talk to you tomorrow."

She stood and watched him walk away before turning and meeting the knowing smirks of her best friends.

It was going to be an interesting drive home.

****

It was quiet.

Too quiet.

Hailey looked around the car and wondered why no one was talking. They had been on the road for fifteen minutes already and it wasn't like them to not talk—especially after a show. Unable to stand it any longer, she blurted out, "I asked out Logan tonight!"

"Shut your ass!" Angie cried as she spun in her seat to face Hailey. "What did you say? What did he say? Oh my god, this is so exciting!"

Everyone started talking at once and Hailey suddenly questioned why she didn't appreciate the silence. "Okay, okay…it's not a big deal."

"Are you going to dinner tomorrow night?" Ella asked anxiously. "Someplace romantic?"

"Wait…when did this happen?" Angie asked. "After the show?"

Hailey shook her head. "No, it was before the show. I tried to tell you guys, but you and Ella were getting your hair done. I told Becca and…"

"And you didn't say anything?" Angie cried as she spun and looked at Becca. "And while we're at it, what's with Max kissing you and then you not saying anything? What is going on all of a sudden?" Her voice got louder and louder as she spoke.

"Max kissed you?" Hailey asked excitedly.

"Oh, yeah! Becca and the sexy photographer! That's awesome!" Ella chimed in.

"Weren't we talking about Hailey and Logan," Becca said, keeping her eyes on the road.

Immediately, everyone's attention went back to Hailey. "So…um…yeah. We're having lunch tomorrow."

"But lunch is our thing," Ella reminded her.

"I know but…he had to work so…"

"On a Saturday?" Angie asked. "What kind of office is open on a Saturday?"

"Thank you!" Hailey cried and then slouched down in the back seat.

"What? What did I say?"

"I automatically assumed Logan worked in an office. He's always so put together and well-dressed that it never occurred to me that he did anything else."

"And he doesn't?" Ella asked.

With a loud sigh, Hailey ran a hand over her face. "He works at Starbucks."

There was a collective groan in the car.

"Not that there's anything wrong with that," she quickly amended. "I just…well…I was surprised."

"Does he manage the Starbucks?" Angie asked.

Hailey shook her head. "He works there. Part-time."

More groans.

"Did he mention if he was living in his parents' basement?" Angie asked and then laughed. "Because that would just be the icing on that train wreck of a cake."

"We didn't get into it but I have a feeling I'll find out tomorrow." She sighed again. "Am I really such a snob?"

"What are you talking about?" Ella asked.

Hailey told them about her conversation with her mother. "I mean…it shouldn't matter if Logan works at a Starbucks or is the CEO of some company. He's still the same person."

"Who smells of coffee," Angie mumbled.

"Ugh…this is bad, isn't it?" Hailey asked nervously.

"No," Becca replied. "Like you said, it shouldn't matter what he does for a living. Not everyone is working their dream job. None of us are. Maybe he's looking for something bigger and better and needed to work there to pay the bills. You have to applaud his work ethic then, right?"

"I guess," Hailey sighed. "But what if…"

"…he's working there because he doesn't want to have another job?" Angie finished for her. "Yeah, that would bother me. I think it's great he's working and has a job but at his age, he should be training for a managerial position or looking to buy a damn franchise."

"He mentioned how he would hate to work in an office. That's a bad sign, isn't it?" she asked, her voice verging on hysteria.

"Okay, deep breaths," Ella said softly, putting her hand on Hailey's. "You're getting upset over nothing. You need to go and have lunch with him tomorrow and get to know him. I know it's going to be hard for you, but you have to go in with an open mind and put your expectations aside. Don't judge."

"I know you're right," Hailey said, "but how do I do that?"

"I don't think it's possible," Angie said matter-of-factly. "You can go in there tomorrow and paste a smile on your face but you know the entire time you're going to be silently waiting for him to say something to confirm all of your worst fears."

"Angie!" Becca cried. "For crying out loud! When did you get so damn cynical?"

"Seriously? Are we just meeting?"

"No…it's okay," Hailey said, "she's right. That's exactly how I'm going to be. No matter how much I think I can go in there with an open mind, I probably won't. I'm going to be asking him questions to try to prove me wrong while knowing I'm going to be disappointed."

"Well I'm disappointed in you," Ella said sadly.

"You are being a snob. Logan's a perfectly nice guy and you're judging him for all the wrong reasons. So he isn't working in an office. So what? It doesn't make him a bad guy! Dylan works in construction. He does manual labor. Every day he comes home and he's dirty and smelly and sweaty. He's never going to wear a suit to work but he's the greatest guy I know! Do you think Dylan's a slacker because he wears jeans to work?"

Hailey's eyes went wide. "What? No!" Then she growled with frustration. "It's not the same thing, Ella."

"Yes it is," Ella replied defiantly. "You're sitting here blatantly putting Logan down—and judging him—because he doesn't have the kind of job you think he should. Well, neither does Dylan." She crossed her arms across her chest and turned to look out the window.

"Okay, I think everyone needs to calm down," Becca said soothingly. "Everyone is entitled to their own opinion. We all know and love Dylan and have for years. He's one of the most hard-working guys I've ever met and personally, I think it's cool that he's in construction. Plus, he can fix anything and everything. You are very lucky, El, because he's the kind of man who will be able to do everything you need on your house and cars."

"Plus he looks damn fine in a pair of jeans," Angie teased.

"Oh, shut up!" Ella said right before she broke out in a fit of giggles. "But he totally does!"

They all laughed for a minute and then the car grew silent again. Hailey sat and watched the scenery go by. She was beyond ashamed of her behavior, her words and her attitude. It wasn't Logan's job that had first attracted her to him. It was his smile and his kindness. He had a great sense of humor and he was just beyond good-looking.

So maybe he didn't have a great job. So what? After fawning over him for so long, didn't she owe it to herself to stop being superficial and genuinely get to know him? That's not to say she could change who she was and how she thought in the next twelve hours, but she could certainly try. Logan deserved that much.

"So what happened with Max?" she said to break the long silence.

Becca told them about her conversation with Max. "Honestly, I was speechless. I had no idea he was even remotely interested in me. I'm usually just a step above a bumbling idiot when I'm around him. Danny really did a number on my self-esteem."

"Max seems like a great guy," Hailey said. "I think it's great you're going to go out with him."

"He gave the DVD for us to look at. I knew you weren't going to be coming to lunch tomorrow but maybe afterwards you can meet up with us and we'll all watch it together."

"I have to admit, I'm really excited to see what he created," Hailey said. "It was something I always wanted to do for Mom but I'm not creative that way. And you just know she's going to love it."

"I think so too," Becca replied. "He asked me to call him after we watch it and then we can talk about where we want to go for lunch on Sunday."

"Ooh…nice," Angie said. "Dinner as a first date could be intimidating. I think it's very cool how he made it a lunch date first. He's very considerate."

Becca blushed. "I'm not sure I'm ready for this."

"What? Going out with a nice guy?" Angie asked.

"No…just going out with any guy. It's only been a couple of weeks since the whole Danny disaster and it just feels weird."

"Well it shouldn't," Ella said. "Max is nothing like Danny and you need to start believing in yourself. The fact that he seemed just as nervous as you are tells me that Max is a good guy. Go and have lunch with him and get to know him. Tell him you need to take things slow if it makes you feel better but don't cut yourself off from the possibility of a great relationship because some jerk made you doubt yourself!"

"I agree," Angie said. "He seems like a nice guy and if Mrs. J hired him, it's sort of like getting a seal of approval."

Hailey leaned forward and popped her head toward the front seat. "Agreed."

"So just to be clear," Becca said, "Hailey, you're going to lunch with Logan tomorrow, right?"

"Right."

"Well…since we're obviously going to be getting home late tonight, I know that I, personally, am going to sleep in," Becca said. "Why don't we skip lunch and maybe you can all come to my place for dinner? We'll get some Chinese takeout and watch the DVD and just relax. What do you think?"

"Perfect!"

"Count me in!"

"I'll bring the wine!"

With a chuckle, Becca shook her head. "I love how we are all on the same page."

"But you have to promise not to watch it without us," Hailey said. "I want it to be a surprise for all of us."

"Deal. Trust me, my plan is to sleep late, do laundry, and wait for one of you to bring me Chinese food."

"You'll have to eat something before then," Ella said.

"Fine. I'll have a peanut butter and jelly sandwich," Becca sighed dramatically. "But other than that, I'll wait to binge on dumplings."

"Someone is bringing dessert too, I hope," Angie said. "I'm bringing the wine." She turned in her seat.

"Hailey, you pick up the food—you're closest to the takeout place—and Ella, why don't you bring your famous brownies?"

"It's going to be like a food orgy," Becca sighed. "I'm not sure I should do that the night before a date."

There was a collective groan of frustration in the car at her statement.

"Okay, okay…forget I said anything!" Becca huffed. "Sheesh."

After that they all quieted down and began to unwind. Thirty minutes later they were back at Enchanted Bridal where they had met that afternoon. Becca pulled into the parking lot and parked next to Angie's car. "I am going to crash hard in my bed."

Everyone began to climb out. Dylan was parked two spots over and in no time he was beside them sweeping Ella up in his arms and kissing her.

"I really want to be annoyed by their constant PDAs," Angie murmured, "but they're too damn cute."

"I know," Becca sighed. "Too bad it's not like that for everyone."

"I have a feeling you and Max are going to be like that."

I wish. She had to bite her tongue to keep from saying it out loud. "We'll see," she said instead. "Be careful driving home and I'll see you tomorrow. Did we decide on a time?"

“How about six?” Hailey suggested.

“Works for me,” Angie and Becca agreed. They called out the time to Ella who gave them a thumbs up as she climbed into Dylan’s car.

“Okay, girls,” Hailey said as she straightened and pulled her keys out of her purse. “Wish me luck tomorrow!”

“It’s going to be good,” Becca said. “You’re going to have a great time and finally get to know Logan.”

“Open mind,” Angie said. “Just remember to go in with an open mind. Pretend you’re just meeting him on a blind date or something.”

“Ooh…good idea!” Becca smiled. “Do that!”

Hailey rolled her eyes. “I’d like to see how easily either of you could do that. It sounds good in theory, but the reality is…”

“Stop!” Angie cried as she slammed the car door shut. “Just stop! Either you’re going to try or you’re not. End of story! You’ve been panting after this guy for a year and you’re going to let something stupid like his job change all that? He works in a coffee house, Hails, he’s not a serial killer. Just relax and…you know…not be you for a little while.”

They stood on opposite sides of the car staring at each other for a long minute before Becca spoke up. “I think we’re all a little tired and cranky and it’s time to call it a night.” She looked at Hailey. “Have fun tomorrow and I can't wait to hear all about your lunch." Then she turned to Angie. "Be careful driving home and maybe bring an extra bottle—or two—of wine. If we have to, everyone can crash by me tomorrow night."

They had a group hug—minus Ella—and each got in their cars and headed for home. Becca couldn't wait to crawl into bed. She had a feeling she was going to need to rest up for their get-together tomorrow night.

Four

With no plans for lunch, Angie took advantage of the time at home to do all of the chores and cleaning she had been procrastinating over—laundry, dusting and vacuuming. The only real perk she was finding was that she could stay in her yoga pants for the majority of the day.

Sometimes it was the little victories.

With her second load of clothes in the wash and the floors cleaned, she decided it would be a good time to stop and make something light for lunch. She chuckled when she looked at the clock and saw it was the normal time she and the girls would be ordering theirs.

"I think I'm in a rut," she said as she walked into the kitchen. Trampus was sitting by the back door staring at her. "Yeah, I know…but I was busy." Opening the back door, she stared down as the cat gave her a quick glance over his shoulder before walking out. "Now lunch," she murmured as she closed the door.

The contents of her refrigerator did not look promising. Everything in her crisper drawer looked like it had died a slow and painful death. "Great. Now I've got to add 'clean the refrigerator' to my list." With a curse, she shut the refrigerator and walked over to the pantry. It wasn't much better. When her doorbell rang, she said a silent prayer that it was a lost pizza delivery guy.

Opening the door, she put a smile on her face and then froze.

"Sean?" *Holy crap!* "What are you doing here?" A million things raced through her mind, but first and foremost was how she had answered the door while wearing her yoga pants, an oversized t-shirt, no bra and with her hair up in a ponytail.

It was the quadfecta of horror.

Sean's smile was slow and easy and if anything, he seemed just as happy to see her as he always was. That made Angie frown. She knew she looked hideous right now compared to every other time she and Sean had been together. Either he had some serious vision issues or he was a good bullshit artist.

"Hey," he finally said as he stuck his hands in the front pockets of his jeans. "How are you?"

That was it? That's what he had to say? Although…to be fair…Angie wasn't exactly sure what the proper protocol was for people showing up unexpectedly on someone's doorstep. "Um…good."

He nodded. "Can I come in?"

The only silver lining in sight was the fact that the house was somewhat clean. Stepping back, she motioned for him to come inside. Sean had only been to her place once. Over the course of their relationship, they tended to meet up at other places—hotels, resorts and other neutral places that were out of town for both of them. It worked out better that way and she had enjoyed it.

Closing the front door, Angie leaned against it and watched as Sean walked around her living room. Her home was a small craftsman bungalow. It was a rental but she had totally put her stamp on the place with paint colors and furnishings. She may not own it, but everything about it screamed Angie.

"This is a great room," Sean said as he turned and faced her. Then he simply looked at her and smiled.

"I like it," she said casually with a small shrug.

"I wasn't sure if you'd be home. I know you go to lunch with the girls sometimes, but I decided to take a chance."

"Why?"

He sighed and for the first time since she'd opened the door, he looked a little less confident. "You didn't text or call me."

"Did you really…?"

"I know why you didn't," he quickly interrupted. "It was wrong of me to go about things like that. It was cowardly. You deserve better than an apology by text. That was crappy." He paused as his expression grew serious. "I'm sorry."

It was on the tip of her tongue to argue how she preferred the whole texting thing because this seemed incredibly awkward, but she didn't. "What exactly are you apologizing for, Sean?" she asked, stepping away from the door. "For the crappy apology? For not calling me any sooner? For ending the relationship without an explanation? I guess you can take your pick because they were all crappy things to do."

Sean took a couple of steps toward her and stopped. "I'm apologizing for all of it."

Angie took a steadying breath and let it out slowly. "O-kay."

"You know how I used to do a lot of international construction stuff before Tricia and Ryan got married, right?"

She nodded.

"Well, after I had the accident, Ryan and I decided to go into business together."

"This isn't news, Sean."

He held up a hand to stop her. "Just…give me a minute to explain." He paused. "Ryan and I always got along fine. At least we did until we started working together." He shrugged. "We were both so used to being in control that it was hard to share responsibilities and actually talk to each other about the things we wanted to do. It didn't take long for me to realize we had made a mistake. Things weren't working out and we were fighting all the time and then Tricia would get involved because she's my best friend and Ryan's her husband and she tried to play peacemaker, but all it did was leave all of us pissed off."

"She never mentioned any of this to me," Angie said quietly.

"She wouldn't," Sean said. "I think she always figured Ryan and I would work things out. She knows us both so well and she knew if given a little bit of time, we'd get through it."

"And did you?"

He shook his head. "I took off and took a job down in Brazil. It was a six-week gig and I just needed the time away to figure out what I wanted to do with my life."

"And you didn't think to call and let me know any of this?" she asked sarcastically and then she cursed under her breath. "So I was good enough to slip away for dirty weekends with, but you didn't think enough of me to tell me you were leaving the country?"

"It wasn't like that…"

"It was exactly like that!" she cried. "From the first moment we met, you pursued me and I didn't put up much of a fight! You talked big about how much you wanted me and all that crap but in the end that's all it was—it was only about the sex to you!"

Closing the distance between them, Sean gently grasped her shoulders. "No! It wasn't! I…*shit*! Angie, the first time we met, you pretty much knocked me on my ass! You were like my every living fantasy come to life. And the fact that you wanted me too was pretty freaking incredible."

"And yet you were able to leave the country…"

"It wasn't about you!" he yelled and stepped away. He raked a hand through his hair before looking at her again. "I was pissed off at Ryan and even at Tricia. She was my friend first and as childish as it sounds, I still felt like her loyalty should have been to me. So I took off. Hell, I didn't even tell my mother where I was going. For two weeks, no one knew where I was."

"But I bet you eventually called them and let them know."

"You may not believe me but the only reason I did was because they were relentlessly calling the company I had sub-contracted with and harassing them. It was the only way to make them stop."

"All you're doing is proving that you're a completely selfish jackass. You know that, right?"

Sean nodded. "I can't change what I did. I wish I could. Honestly, I don't care if I upset my family, but I do care that I hurt you. It was never my intention. At the time I was angry and frustrated with pretty much every aspect of my life. I didn't want to burden you with all of my bullshit. All I can say in my own defense is that I wasn't thinking rationally."

Angie sighed. "Yeah, well…it is what it is. I appreciate you explaining all of this to me, but unfortunately it doesn't change anything."

"But…"

Walking around him, she went to her comfy chair and sat down. "Look, you and I clearly didn't know each other as well as we thought we did. I thought we were moving forward and were serious, but when you were struggling with something big, I wasn't even a consideration. I'm probably not going to get over that any time soon."

Sean sat down on the sofa and faced her. "I know. But…do you think in time…?"

It would have been so easy to say yes, to tell him she just needed some time to process it all. Hell, she could probably be over it by tomorrow if she sat down with the girls tonight and talked about it, but there was more to it than that. "Sean, who's to say that in another couple of months, something else isn't going to come up that pisses you off? Can you honestly sit here and tell me you aren't ever going to take off like that again?"

"I can," he said earnestly and reached for one of her hands. "I used to get a thrill out of taking the jobs no one else wanted. I enjoyed the freedom of being myself without anyone really looking over my shoulder, and no family around to question me. It was a completely selfish way of life. I realize that now. I probably should have realized it years ago. But now that I've watched everyone around me starting to have a life, I see that I want that too."

"Wait…what?" she asked incredulously. Maybe she was reading him wrong, but all of a sudden this seemed way more serious than she was prepared for.

"Tricia and Ryan are married and planning on having kids soon. Hell, I wouldn't be surprised if I got the call that they were pregnant already. She's so damn happy and my brother —who I have since reconciled with—is like a different man. He smiles all the time and when he talks about Tricia, he's like someone else. And then my mom married Paul and after being a widow for so long and the fact that she was always such a free spirit…well, it's nice to see." He sighed. "They're all settling down and I've been living like some sort of nomad."

"There's nothing wrong with…"

"I don't want to live like a nomad, Ange," he said softly. "When I think about my life and where I want to be, I think of you."

Oh. Shit. "Um…"

"I screwed everything up. I know that. But I want a chance to make it up to you. I want us to start over and not look at this as some casual relationship. I think you're amazing," he said with a smile. "And…I think if you can find it in your heart to forgive me, you might even admit you think I'm a little amazing too."

Angie couldn't help but chuckle at that. It was typical Sean. He was more cocky and confident than he should be, but he was goofy enough about it that he didn't come off as being offensive. And dammit, she didn't want to be feeling all soft and sentimental about him, but she was.

He gently tugged on her hand. "I know it's not going to happen overnight, but I really want us to give it a try—to be even better than we were before."

"Sean…"

With her hand still in his, Sean stood and pulled her gently to her feet. It didn't take much to have her pressed up against him. His hand came up and caressed her cheek. "Promise me you'll think about it," he said as he leaned forward and kissed her cheek.

She closed her eyes and willed herself not to melt against him.

Raising his head, Sean looked into her eyes and gave her a slow, sexy grin. "I'm not going to push you for an answer right now. I know better than to do that. But I want you to know that I'm not giving up. I know you're pissed off at me and rightfully so, but I also believe that given a little bit of time, you'll see how we fit." His finger stroked down her cheek. "And we have since the minute we met."

Dammit, he was right. Angie prided herself on being strong and independent. She didn't rely on anyone for anything, but standing like this with Sean had her wishing that she could just be a little softer—the kind of woman who could listen to what he was saying and simply accept it without argument.

Pulling back a bit, she looked him in the eye. "I will think about it," she admitted softly. "But you have to know that you seriously broke my trust in you. It's not something I take lightly. If I'm going to be all-in with you, or with anyone, trust is key. And to be honest with you, I'm not big on second chances."

Sean nodded. "Duly noted."

Unable to help herself, she rolled her eyes as she chuckled. He was always way more laid back than she was. He always saw the brighter side of things. They complemented each other almost perfectly. "I'm serious, Sean. It's going to take more than a grin and a kiss for me to believe in you again."

"Sweetheart, I am willing to do whatever it takes for you to realize I'm serious here. You tell me what it is you want from me, and I'll do it. Do you want me to leave right now and wait for you to call me? I'll do it." He paused and pulled her in close again and rested his forehead against hers. "Or do you want me to stay?" he asked, his voice like silk. "I'll spend the entire day doing whatever it is you want."

Angie couldn't help the small gasp that came out or how her eyes went just a little wide.

Sean switched the angle of his head just slightly until their lips were almost touching. "Whatever. You. Want."

And then he kissed her.

****

"Oh my God!" Ella cried. "What did you do? Did he stay? Did you do it? Was it good?" She fanned herself wildly and then looked at Becca, Hailey and then back at Angie. "Was it wild and intense? Oh…I bet it was wild and intense!"

Angie looked at her for a minute before turning to Becca and Hailey. "I think we may need to turn the hose on her."

"Definitely," Hailey agreed. "But you still haven't answered the question."

Looking at her three friends with a sassy grin, Angie stood and went to grab another bottle of wine. It wasn't until she sat back down and poured herself a glass that she finally said, "He stayed."

"I knew it!" Ella shouted.

"And…?" Becca asked anxiously.

"He cleaned my house," Angie said with a hint of satisfaction.

"Wait…what?" Ella asked.

"Sean stayed all day and cleaned my house—even Trampus' litter box. It was awesome."

Hailey frowned. "Let me get this straight—the guy you're crazy about comes and pretty much begs you to take him back and then promises you a day of…pleasure, and you decide to take that and turn it into making him clean? Why?"

Angie's laugh was a little maniacal. "Don't you see? It would have been easy and predictable to jump back into bed with him. And believe me, I wanted to. The things that man can do…" She mimicked Ella's earlier fanning of herself. "But that wasn't going to prove anything. I already know we're physically compatible. That wasn't the problem. I need to see if Sean's going to stick around for the day-to-day stuff and when I'm just being a bitch."

"Why would you *want* to be a bitch?" Becca

asked.

"Sweetie, we're all bitches," Angie said. "And sometimes we need to not suppress the urge and sit back and see what happens." She took another sip of her wine and looked over at Hailey. "Which brings us to you."

The frown was still in place. "What about me?"

"You've been awful quiet since you got here. You managed to talk about the weather, the traffic and the funny conversation you had with the cashier over at Panda Palace, and yet we haven't heard a word about your big lunch date with Logan."

Grabbing the bottle of wine, Hailey poured herself another glass.

"That can't be a good sign," Becca murmured.

"Uh-oh…did you let your inner bitch out?" Angie asked with a smile.

Without answering, Hailey took a drink.

"Okay, if she's not ready to talk about it, then we shouldn't push her," Ella said softly as she reached for the plate of dumplings. "There's two left, who wants the other one?"

Angie snagged the other one and put it on her plate and for several minutes, they all seemed focused on divvying up the last of the takeout. "Oh for crying out loud, Hails, just tell us! It can't possibly be that bad!"

"Ange…" Ella started but noticed Hailey holding up her hand to stop her.

Looking at each of the girls, Hailey took hold of her wine glass and smiled weakly. "It was awful."

"No!" The girls collectively cried out.

She nodded. "I cannot believe he's just so…not what I thought he was!"

"What do you mean?" Ella asked.

"He was polite and personable like he always is but…that's it. There's nothing else there."

"That doesn't even make sense," Angie argued.

"Trust me on this one. Logan is great and sweet and funny, but there's no substance to him. No depth. He lives in the moment with no thought for tomorrow or next week or next month! He's like a frat boy!"

"Please tell me he doesn't still live at home," Angie said, doing her best to hide her mirth.

Hailey glared at her. "I wish I could. In the room over the garage."

The laughter that followed by all of them was brief. "So what are you going to do?" Becca asked. "I mean…is this it? Are you over him now?"

"I…I honestly don't know," Hailey admitted. "I look at him and I just think…what if?"

"But you've seen who he is," Ella chimed in.

"You can't change him into someone or something else, Hails. That's not right."

"Or…" Angie said, placing her glass firmly down on the table.

"Or…?" Hailey responded.

"Or you can just accept that he is who he is…that it's not going to go anywhere…and maybe have a fling with him."

"I can't just have a fling," Hailey said primly.

"Why the hell not?" Angie snapped. "Everyone can have a fling and there's nothing wrong with it. If anything, you more than anyone else I've ever known needs to have a fling!"

"What?" Hailey cried. "I do not!"

"Yeah, you do! You're so uptight all the damn time that I think it would do you good to just go out and get laid just for the sake of doing it! And who better than the guy you've been lusting after but see no future with? It's freaking perfect! It's like having your cake and eating it too!"

They were all silent for a moment.

"I hate to say it," Becca said, "but she kind of has a point. You can get Logan out of your system and then go back to looking for the perfect man."

"But I thought Logan was the perfect man!" Hailey whined. "How the hell am I supposed to know what that even looks like anymore?"

"You don't," Angie said. "This is all sounding like what we talked to Ella about the other night. The dating world? It sucks. It's a lot of work and it's exhausting and sometimes it's going to just let you down. You looked at Logan and only saw what you wanted to see. Next time you'll know not to judge a book by its cover."

Hailey put her hands over her face and sighed. "Oh God…my mom was right! I am such a snob!"

"Uh…yeah," Angie said. "You are. We all know it and yet we still love you."

She dropped her hands. "Seriously? You all think I'm a snob?"

Becca looked away as Ella jumped up and began clearing away the takeout containers and Angie took a slow sip of her wine.

"Great. *Great*! So…my mother was right. I'm a snob and everyone knows it," she huffed. "Now what?"

Putting her glass down, Angie leveled her with a stare. "You have a fling and move on."

"But…I don't…how…?" Hailey sputtered helplessly.

"Use your words," Angie teased.

Ella sat back down and smiled patiently. "I hate to say it, but you totally need to leave your comfort zone, Hails. Normally I don't believe in the fling thing, but in this particular situation, I think it's what you need to do."

"If you don't," Becca began as she took her seat again, "you're always going to wonder about it. For all you know, the sex could be really bad and then it will totally cure you of your feelings for him."

"But what if the sex is good?" Hailey asked earnestly. "Like mind-blowingly good? Then what?"

"Then you keep flinging until you're done," Angie said matter-of-factly then shrugged. "Why are you overthinking this? You like this guy. You think he's hot. And in this instance, you get to have sex with him without worrying about whether or not he's going to be able to support you financially in the future. No strings. No hassles. No worries."

"Isn't that how you went into things with Sean?" Hailey asked with a hint of snarkiness.

"As a matter of fact it wasn't," Angie countered. "It was lust at first sight for the both of us. We were always on the same page from the get-go."

"But it was all about no strings and worries and all that happy horseshit," Hailey replied. "And now look where you are."

"I don't think we need to get pissy," Becca interjected.

"Don't worry," Angie said, her eyes never leaving Hailey's. "I don't see it that way. Hailey actually has a point. So…yes. In the beginning Sean and I were just having fun and then my feelings changed. Apparently, so did his. We didn't talk about it before. From this point forward, however, we will. I knew I liked Sean and I knew what he did for a living and I've met his family. Hailey—on the other hand—based all of her feelings simply on Logan's looks. That's the difference."

"God," Hailey huffed, "you really can be a bitch." She stood and walked out of the kitchen.

With a sigh, Becca got up and went after her. She found Hailey by the front door putting her shoes on. "Don't go," she said. "You threw down the gauntlet. You can't honestly say you're surprised she came back at you."

"Yeah, but…"

"And nothing either of you said was a lie. You did base your opinion of Logan on his looks without getting to know him and Angie went into her relationship with Sean as a fling. I think things got a little out of hand, but since when do we tiptoe around each other?"

Hailey's shoulders dropped and she leaned against the front door. "You know what kills me more than anything?"

"What?"

"I'm really this shallow."

"Hails, you're not shallow. You're disappointed Logan isn't exactly who you built him up to be. It doesn't make him any less of a good guy. But…we're also at the age where we're looking for a man who is going to take care of us. Or in the very least be a partner with us. It may not be politically correct to admit it, but there it is." She shrugged and took one of Hailey's hands in hers and squeezed. "Don't go. We still have the DVD to watch and we have to watch it together."

Hailey seemed to consider her options for a minute. "Will we get to be here when you call Max and let him know how we liked it?"

Becca blushed. "I don't know. I'm really nervous about calling him."

"Why?"

"Because it's not really about the DVD. You and I both know that. He was giving me a reason to call him so he could ask me out."

Hailey smiled. "It's kind of cute if you ask me."

Becca agreed. "Am I crazy for going out with him so soon after my breakup with Danny?"

"Hell no! I think going out with Max is going to be a great thing. He's super sweet, considerate and it's kind of obvious that he's really into you."

"Yeah…well…if I'm being honest…I'm really kind of into him too."

Hailey's grin widened. "Aww…aren't you adorable!" She pulled Becca in for a hug. "Fine, we won't hover when you make the call, but you have to promise to call us all when you get back from your date."

Becca pulled back and smiled. "Deal." Moving away, she walked over to the TV and turned it on. "I already have the DVD in."

"Why didn't he just upload it and send it to you? I didn't think anyone even used DVDs anymore."

"I guess it's like having a hard copy for copyright purposes," Becca said. "When it's all done and edited, I'm sure we can ask him to send us each a copy of the file. Hopefully he won't mind."

"Maybe."

"Come on, you two," Becca called into the kitchen. "We're going to watch the DVD now!"

Angie came into the living room first and eyed Hailey warily. "Are we cool?"

Hailey nodded. "Yeah. I'm sorry. I overreacted."

They hugged it out just as Ella walked in. "Oh, thank God. That was awkward."

Together, they sat down around Becca's living room as she hit play on the remote. For the next thirty minutes, no one spoke. Max had taken all of the pictures and set them to a beautiful orchestral soundtrack. Every once in a while he cut away to some audio of Judith talking during a bridal show but the story was generally told with the musical soundtrack.

At the end of the DVD, the words "Friday Night Brides" came across the screen. They each looked at one another and then gasped at the picture that came up first. It was the four of them dressed up as flower girls in their very first show. And from there, it flowed easily as the pictures showed how they had grown and transformed from young girls, to teenagers, to the women they were now. All of the dresses—flower girl, bridesmaid and bridal—were there. Some of the photos showed them posing as a group, while some were individual shots.

The final picture was from the anniversary show when Judith had come up on stage at the very end and stood in the middle of their quartet. Each of them were smiling—beaming really—and the shot perfectly captured every emotion they were feeling.

When the screen faded to black, the room was silent.

Becca looked around and saw that, like herself, everyone was a little teary. "Wow," she quietly. "That was…"

"Amazing," Hailey finished for her. "I know I saw all of those pictures dozens of times in my life, but never like that. What Max did was…"

"Beautiful," Ella said, her voice filled with wonder. "I can't believe he was able to put something like that together in a week! The pictures he chose were perfect and the music just added to the emotion and it was all just so…"

"Un-freaking-believably awesome!" Angie finished.

"You always take it a step further," Becca laughed.

"Go big or go home," Angie chuckled and raised her wine glass in a mock salute. "That was incredible. Hails, your mom is going to love it. I don't think I'd change a thing."

"Me either," Ella said. "And I'm telling you now, Dylan and I are going to book Max as our wedding photographer. If he can do something as amazing as that, then I definitely want to book him before the word gets out about how great he is."

"He's going to love that," Becca said. "Can I mention it when I talk to him later?"

Ella nodded. "Absolutely! Dylan and I haven't really talked about a photographer yet, but once I tell him about Max's work, he'll be on board. And I'm already thinking about the kind of wedding video I want!"

"With all of the years the two of you have been together, Max will have plenty of photos to use for the montage," Hailey said with a smile.

They all stood and went back to the kitchen. "Anyone want coffee or tea with their brownies?" Becca asked.

"Any chance you have some ice cream?" Hailey asked. "That video left me with an overwhelming need to overload on chocolate."

"It was pretty emotional," Becca agreed as she pulled a carton of ice cream from the freezer. "Have at it."

For the next hour they talked about the video and food and Ella's wedding and Becca's upcoming date with Max. By the time everyone left, Becca was only mildly nervous about making the call.

Walking into her bedroom, she changed into an oversized t-shirt and went through her nightly routine—washed her face, brushed her teeth, and procrastinated for as long as she could. Max's business card was sitting on her nightstand along with her phone. It was almost eleven o'clock and now she wondered if she was being completely rude.

Only one way to find out…

"Hello?"

Just the sound of his voice made Becca smile. "Hey," she said softly, "it's Becca. Sorry I'm calling so late."

"I was afraid you weren't going to call at all," he admitted with a nervous chuckle. "How are you doing?"

"I'm good." She told him about her night with the girls and how things almost fell apart. "It doesn't happen very often, but every once in a while, we get a little…snippy."

"That's not a bad thing," Max said. "It's not possible for everyone to get along and be happy all the time. You're four very unique women. But it's great how you were able to put it all aside so quickly."

"Well, watching your video really helped."

He was silent for a moment. "So…? What did you think?"

She couldn't help but smile at the uncertainty in his voice. "Max?"

"Yeah?"

"It was amazing," she said. "Absolutely amazing. By the time it was over, we were all crying."

"Really? You're not just saying that?"

"Trust me. I wouldn't say it if I didn't mean it," she said honestly. "We were all blown away with how you were able to put something together so amazing and beautiful on such short notice. Ella is going to be calling you to book you for her wedding."

"Seriously? That's great! The only weddings I've done so far have been for friends and family, but…uh-oh."

"What? What's the matter?"

"I probably shouldn't have admitted that to you. Ella is going to want someone with a little more experience than me."

She laughed out loud. "Max, do you even hear yourself? You do incredible work! You are a very talented artist and it doesn't matter how long you've been doing this for! We've worked with photographers who were in the business for years whose work wasn't even half as good as yours!"

“I’m seriously not fishing for compliments, but I have to admit, you’re good for my ego.”

His admission had her smiling again. “Well it’s the truth.”

He paused for a minute. “Would you still like to have lunch with me tomorrow?”

Becca knew she wanted to go out with Max. More than she thought she would. But first dates were always so awkward—sitting across from each other and sort of having an informal Q&A while you ate. It wasn’t her favorite thing to do. Although if she had to choose between going to lunch or dinner on a first date, she’d definitely choose lunch.

“Becca? You still there?” He chuckled. “If you’d rather not go, you can just tell me. I’ll understand.”

Even though Max couldn’t see her, Becca blushed as she smiled. “I would,” she said shyly. “I really would like to have lunch with you.”

“The weather’s supposed to be great tomorrow,” Max began and Becca could hear the relief in his tone. “I was thinking of maybe grabbing some sandwiches and hitting a park or something. You know, something casual. What do you think?”

In that minute, Becca thought Max just might be too good to be true.

****

"And then…there was this beautiful montage of me and the girls from just about every show we ever did with Mrs. J," Ella said excitedly. "I'm telling you, Dylan, it was so beautiful I cried!"

"And that's a good thing?" he asked with a smirk.

Ella had just gotten home from her dinner with the girls and had not stopped talking since she walked in the door. The townhouse she and Dylan rented was only a couple of blocks away from Becca's house and even on the three-minute drive, she had been overcome with excitement to tell Dylan all about what Max had created.

"I want us to sit down with him and talk to him about the wedding," she said. "And I definitely want him to do the kind of video he put together for Mrs. J." She sighed happily. "It will be something we're going to show our kids and our grandkids and it's going to be wonderful." She was sitting on the couch by now and kicking off her shoes and smiling at Dylan.

"Why don't you give him a call tomorrow and set up a time for us to talk to him? Or maybe we can just arrange to talk to him after the show on Friday. What do you think?"

"Oh!" she gasped. "I completely forgot to tell you, Becca's going out with him tomorrow! On a date!"

Dylan's eyes went wide. "Really? How did that happen?"

Ella told him about how Becca and Max had sort of hit it off after his first show and how Max clearly had a crush on her. "I'm so proud of her," she continued. "I was afraid she was going to stay in a funk over Danny, but it seems like Max is helping her get over it. Fast."

"I've said it before and I'll say it again," Dylan said, "Becca was too good for Danny."

She relaxed on the sofa and let out another happy sigh. "I missed you tonight."

Dylan rose from his spot on the recliner and walked over to her, holding out a hand to bring her to her feet. When she was pressed up against him, he kissed her thoroughly. "How much did you miss me?"

Ella couldn't help but grin at his words. "A whole lot," she said breathlessly as she raked her hands up into his sandy brown hair and pulled him back down for another kiss. If there was one thing she loved, it was the way Dylan kissed. He started out slow and sweet and then let it build. "Let's go upstairs."

Without a word, Dylan took her by the hand and led her up to their bedroom. They'd been living together for two years and Ella still loved the fact that the place was theirs. For so many years they'd had to sneak around or get a hotel room and having the freedom to go up to their own room and make love in their own bed was as close to perfect as anything could be.

As soon as they crossed the threshold, Dylan gently pulled her back into his arms and immediately went back to kissing her. The fact that he wanted her just as much as she wanted him had her more than ready.

They moved around the room in each other's arms as if their steps were choreographed. His hands began a slow journey from her hips and slipped under her shirt, moving the fabric up and over her head. Once it hit the floor, those work-roughened hands gently cupped her breasts and Ella sighed at the contact. It never ceased to amaze her how, after all this time, it was always so good.

They knew exactly how to touch each other, how to kiss, how to move. To some people, they'd say it was boring, but Ella didn't mind. And from the feel of Dylan's arousal pressing against her belly, she knew he didn't mind either. There was something to be said for knowing your partner, your lover, so well that being intimate wasn't simply about acrobatics or sex marathons.

"You're thinking too hard," Dylan murmured, his breath hot against her throat. "Clear your mind, Ella, and let me make you feel good."

His hands moved to her hips and immediately began sliding her yoga pants down, along with her panties. That was the beauty of girls' night—dressing comfortably. And now she was even more thankful for it. Slowly, she shimmied and kicked the garments aside and shamelessly rubbed herself against Dylan.

"One of us is majorly overdressed," she said just

as his head dipped to kiss the swell of her breast.

Lightning quick, he straightened and pulled his t-shirt up and over his head and then went to work on shucking his jeans. In nothing but his boxer briefs, he gently pulled her toward the bed and then down on top of him. His kiss became more urgent as he rolled her beneath him.

"Dylan," she purred, loving the feel of him. Her hands raked up and down his back and then back up into his hair. He murmured how much he loved her as he began to kiss her from her lips, to her jaw, her throat and breasts.

She particularly liked it when he kissed her there.

This was how it was meant to be—slow and sweet and sexy. Those were the words that always came to her mind when she thought about Dylan. Everything he did and how he did it, was his way of showing her how much he loved her.

His mouth worshipped her.

His hands worshipped her.

Soon she was panting beneath his touch. "Dylan…I…I need you. Please."

Dylan lifted his head and smiled at her. "I need you too, sweetheart. Every minute of every day." For a minute he moved off of her so he could slide his boxers off and then he was back, positioned between her thighs and kissing her softly. "You know what I wish?"

She shook her head as her legs wrapped around his waist.

"I wish we were already married and working on having a baby," he said, his voice low, his expression serious.

"You do?" she asked in wonder. Ella already knew they both wanted kids, but they hadn't really talked about the timing.

Dylan nodded. "Ella Gilmore, the thought of you being my wife and us making a family? It's all I think about lately. We've been planning this wedding for so long and it just seems like it's never going to get here."

Suddenly sex was the last thing on her mind. She shifted slightly beneath him. "Why haven't you said anything before? I thought…when we set the date, you were okay with it. We talked about taking the extra time to save up some money and…how long have you felt like this?"

He shrugged and rolled off of her and onto his side. "I don't know. We always talked about getting married and the kind of wedding we wanted and it wasn't until you mentioned it last week about how frustrated you were getting that I realized that it was getting to me too. Just not for the same reasons."

"Dylan…"

He placed a finger over her lips to stop her. "I'm not saying I want to cancel the wedding or anything, but I just wanted you to know how I feel. Maybe this wasn't the right time to bring it up." He shrugged again. "Honestly, if it were up to me, we'd be married next weekend by a justice of the peace and invite everyone over for a barbecue or something," he said nervously and then met her wide-eyed gaze. "But I would never ask you to give up your big day, Ella. Never. I love you and I guess I needed to say these things out loud." He rolled onto his back and seemed to sag with relief. "Actually, it feels really good to finally say it out loud. I tried to talk to my dad about it, but I chickened out. And then I was talking to Tommy at work and…I don't know…I couldn't make myself do it. I didn't want anyone to think I was acting like a chick or anything."

She reached up and cupped his cheek. "Baby, you don't ever have to keep these things to yourself. Gosh! Do you have any idea how relieved I am to know you feel this way too?"

Now it was his turn to go wide-eyed. "So what are you saying?"

She nibbled her bottom lip. "I don't know. I just…I don't know if I want to go to a justice of the peace but maybe…maybe we scale back and move the wedding date up. What do you think?"

Dylan studied her for a moment. "You know our parents are going to freak out."

Ella nodded. "I know. But it's not their day. It's ours. They had their own weddings and had them the way they wanted. It's our turn." She smiled shyly. "I think we all lost sight of that fact for a little while. But now that you and I are both on the same page, we can make a united front and tell them we're taking our wedding back." She giggled. "I'm almost tempted to call my mom right now and tell her!"

A slow smile tugged at his lips. "How soon are we talking?"

"Hmm…I just ordered my gown and…I hate to say it but…I really want it. I want to wear it even if we do scale everything else down. It's so beautiful and I know it's crazy because I get to wear beautiful wedding gowns all the time, but this will be the first and only time that it's mine. Is that wrong?"

"Ella, you know how much I love seeing you in those gowns. Every time I come to one of Mrs. J's shows, seeing you modeling those gowns makes me feel like the luckiest man alive. You're beautiful."

She sighed. "Mrs. J put a rush on it for me and it will be here in a month."

"Why'd she rush it?"

Ella rolled her eyes. "Alterations can be a nightmare and she wanted to make sure I had plenty of time to get them done and not freak out over it. She said the sooner we got it done and out of the way, the sooner it would be one less thing on our plate."

"God, I love that woman. She's a genius."

"I know. I almost wish she were my mom. It would be so much easier making her understand why we want to change things up."

"So what are you thinking? What kind of

timeframe are we thinking about?" he asked.

"Our wedding is still eight months out. Do you…" She paused. "Do you think we can move things up? Like…to maybe three months? Is that possible?"

"We can do whatever we want, sweetheart. I'm sure there are going to be some repercussions for changing the date and we may lose a little money in the process but if we scale back in other ways, we should be all right." His smile broadened. "So…are we good? Are we really going to do this?"

She nodded eagerly. "I think we are!"

"I take it this makes you happy?" he teased.

"Oh, Dylan!" she wrapped her arms around him and hugged him tight. "I was beginning to feel like we were going to get stuck with some sort of circus of a wedding and that you were all right with it!" She kissed him soundly on the lips. "I'm so glad you said something! So relieved!"

"I didn't want to be the jerk who made you give up your big wedding. From what I've seen and learned from all those bridal expos you model in, weddings are a big deal to the bride."

Ella shook her head. "It was never about the party, Dylan. All I've ever wanted was to be your wife."

"That's good," he said softly, rolling her beneath him again, "because all I've ever wanted was for you to be my wife."

"It's going to be so good, isn't it?" she asked, her eyes scanning his face. "All that unnecessary pressure…gone." She sighed. "So…so…good."

"Better than good," he promised. "We're going to do this wedding our way like we should have from the get-go and then we're gonna have babies and buy a house and be happy forever."

Tears began to well in her eyes, but when she tried to turn away, Dylan gently cupped her cheek and then wiped away the few that fell with the pads of his thumbs. "Don't cry," he said and kissed one cheek and then the other.

"They're not sad tears," she said. "They're happy ones. I love how we're in sync with each other on this."

He kissed her lips again. "Always." He paused. "Do you trust me, Ella?"

"Always."

Dylan let one hand skim down her cheek and down her body to her thigh. He lifted it and guided her to wrap it around him and then did the same with the other. "Let me love you," he murmured against her lips. "Let's forget about everything else and just focus on this. Us."

He slid into her and Ella gasped and then sighed his name. She was ready for him and locked her legs even tighter around him. Ella was finding it hard to focus on anything but the feeling of Dylan moving inside of her. Arching her back, she moaned with pleasure. There was no way sex could be this perfect for anyone else.

"You're so beautiful," he said as he rocked into her again and again. "And you feel so damn good, Ella. You're so sweet. And you're all mine."

That made her smile. Because more than anything in the world, it was exactly what she wanted to be.

All his.

Five

"I'll see you after the show," Max said with a smile as he kissed Becca gently on the cheek. She watched him walk away and stood there frowning.

"Uh-oh," Angie sang as she walked up. "Somebody looks cranky."

It had been two weeks since their first date and Becca was growing increasingly frustrated. "Shut up," she mumbled and turned to walk toward the dressing rooms. Tonight's show was local but at the convention center. It was a huge bridal expo—the kind she normally looked forward to—but she was beyond distracted.

"What's going on?" Angie asked, grabbing Becca's arm to keep her from walking away.

"It's nothing."

Angie rolled her eyes. "Right. Don't bullshit me. You're clearly annoyed about something. Your face is all scrunchy and you're in a mood. So you can either tell me now and get it off your chest so you're not scowling on the runway or you can stew in it until Mrs. J has to step in. Your choice."

With a huff, Becca grabbed Angie by the hand and led her to a quiet bench outside the ladies' room. "It's Max."

"Really? I thought you guys were getting along great? You were practically doodling your names in hearts at lunch the other day."

"Yeah…well…it's just…" She paused and sighed. "He hasn't kissed me yet."

Angie's eyes went wide. "For real?"

"Totally for real."

Sagging against the wall behind her, Angie sighed. "Wow."

"That's what I'm saying," Becca murmured. "We've seen each other almost every day since our first date and every time he goes to leave, he kisses me on the cheek. He doesn't even try to do anything more!"

"Have you thought about just kissing him? Like grabbing his face and laying one on him?"

"Of course I have! Every time he leans in I think about it!"

"So why haven't you done it?"

Becca shrugged. "I chicken out. What if I'm misreading all of this? What if I'm looking at this like he's really into me and he's looking at this like we're buddies? Or pals?" She groaned. "Ugh…what could possibly be worse than being relegated to the friend zone?"

"What are you going to do?"

"I don't know, Ang. I really love hanging out with him—he's sweet and funny and we have so much in common—but if he's only looking at this as a friend-thing, I don't know if I can keep that up."

"Then you're going to have to talk to him," Angie stated firmly. "This is no different than what we talked about with Hailey and her situation with Logan."

"It's not the same!" Becca interrupted.

"It's exactly the same! You have got to stop sitting back and making assumptions. You are going to have to leave your comfort zone and just flat-out ask him what's going on."

"Dammit. I was hoping to avoid all of that."

"Tough luck, buttercup." Angie stood and pulled Becca to her feet. "Come on. Let's go get ready."

"I'm so not in the mood…"

"You will be once things get going. And tomorrow at lunch, we'll pow-wow on how you can bring this up with Max. Plus, we have to get Hailey to make a commitment to seducing Logan and getting that whole thing going." She sighed dramatically. "Seriously, you guys are exhausting."

"Yeah, yeah, yeah…big talk from the girl who has been rather quiet about her own love life."

"I promise to share all tomorrow."

"We'll see," Becca replied, but she wasn't holding out much hope. If everything went the way she was imagining it, they'd spend a lot of time getting on Hailey about her plans with Logan and then turning all of their attention to her and Max. By the time they covered those two topics, lunch would be over.

For the next hour, it was the usual pre-show chaos—hair, makeup and last minute alterations. Becca did her best to push thoughts of her and Max out of her head. She was dressed and lining up back stage. Tonight she was paired up with Jackson. For the life of her she still couldn't understand why Hailey hated him so much—he was good-looking and polite and he must have sensed that she was in a funk because he kept cracking lame jokes to make her smile.

Mrs. J came out to give them all the usual pep talk. "We've got a full house out there tonight. I heard attendance was near five hundred. After the finale, I would appreciate it if you could all mingle with the crowd in your gowns and tuxedos and give them any information you can about the shop, what you're wearing, our contact info…all that good stuff." She beamed at them all. "I'd like you to walk around in pairs—mainly because I know you ladies are going to need a little assistance with your gowns, so gentlemen, do what you can to make sure no one gets stepped on."

Off in the distance, music began playing and the emcee announced that the show was about to begin.

"Have fun everyone and just plan on meeting and greeting for about thirty minutes after the show, okay?" Clapping her hands together, she smiled brightly. "Good luck out there and have fun!"

Becca and Jack were third in line and for a little over an hour, she pasted a smile on her face as she modeled four different gowns. At the end of the show, all of the models lined the stage and listened as Mrs. J told the guests they were free to speak to them for the next half hour. It was on the tip of her tongue to fake a headache and head backstage, but Jack squeezed her hand and smiled. "Come on. It won't be so bad. Quick and painless. I promise."

She wished she could believe him. But mingling with the crowd meant she would probably spend a lot of that time scanning the crowd for Max and then overanalyzing his every look and word. Maybe lunch with the girls tomorrow and their potential pow-wow was a good thing.

As directed, she and Jack stepped down from the stage and began walking through the crowd.

They hadn't gone more than a few feet when he leaned down close and whispered in her ear, "Tell you what…let's do our best to keep a smile on our faces as we make a beeline for the farthest corner of the room and maybe out one of the doors?"

Becca looked up at him with surprise. "Are you serious?"

He nodded. "Look, obviously you're uncomfortable and there are fourteen other couples walking around to keep people busy. If we just act casually, we can slip out the door and hide out until it's time to go."

She almost wept with relief. "If you can make

that happen, you'll be my new hero."

"Come on," he said, straightening. "Let's do this."

For the first time that entire evening, Becca felt hopeful. With her arm linked through Jack's, they began to walk through the crowd. They smiled and waved at a few people, but luckily no one stopped them.

"Almost there," he said quietly and then nearly stumbled as Becca came to a complete stop. Turning to look at her, Jack's immediate reaction was concern. "Are you okay?"

Becca knew she must have gone pale. Everything in her seemed to stop.

Standing not two feet in front of her was Danny—with his arm around a tall, willowy blonde.

"Becca?" Jack asked.

"I…sorry…" she mumbled. "Can we just keep…?"

"Oh my God!" the tall, willowy blonde beamed when she spotted Becca. "I was so hoping you'd come our way! I love this gown! Danny," she said over her shoulder, "this is it! This is the one!"

To his credit, Danny looked just as uncomfortable as Becca felt.

For all of three seconds.

"I knew I would find the perfect gown here

tonight," the blonde was saying and then she turned and hugged Danny. "Thank you for coming with me." She paused and then gasped. "Oh! Is it bad luck if you see the dress?"

"I doubt it, baby," Danny cooed and kissed her. Thoroughly. Then he raised his head and looked at Becca with a smirk before returning his attention to the blonde. "I think this dress would look good on you. Real good."

Jackson—bless him—cleared his throat before anyone could say anything else. "If you're interested in the dress, you can go up to the podium and talk to Mrs. J. She's taking appointments and can give you all the information on it."

"Ooh, Danny, come on! I don't want to miss her!" The blonde took Danny's hand in hers with a giddy squeal. "This is so exciting!" She turned to Becca and Jack. "Thank you so much!"

They started to walk away when out of the corner of her eye, she saw Danny trip and fall. The skinny blonde cried out as she tried to help him up. Becca wondered what happened when she noticed Jack's grin. He winked down at her. "Come on. Let's go."

It took a minute for her heart to stop racing. Jack got her out into the hallway and immediately found a refreshment table and grabbed her a glass of water. He put it in her hands but didn't let go. "Drink."

She forced herself to drink and then looked up at him sadly. "Thank you."

"That was your ex, right?"

Becca nodded. "How did you know?" Danny had never come to any of the shows or any of the parties Mrs. J threw, so she was mildly curious.

"The look on your face said it all. And his, too—at first." He cursed under his breath. "I'm sorry. I know that sucked."

She nodded again. "I had no idea he was dating anyone else—let alone engaged."

"How long since you broke up?"

The reality of it all had her stomach clenching. "A month."

Jack frowned. "I hate to say it…"

"I know. Clearly he was dating us both at the same time," she finished quietly. "God, I'm such an idiot! Everyone warned me, but I didn't listen."

"Hey," he said softly, cupping her cheek. "You are not to blame here. He is. Guys like him…" He paused. "Guys like him are skilled liars. I'm sure his fiancée has no idea he's been screwing around." Then he grinned. "But I can inform her if you'd like."

Becca couldn't help but chuckle at the hopeful look on Jack's face. "Thanks, but…" She shook her head. "That wouldn't be very nice."

"Actually, it would be," he corrected. "Looking back, don't you wish someone had told you he was seeing someone else rather than finding out like this? And, before you answer, you know there's a very real chance he's going to keep doing it. Hell, he probably has someone else on the side already."

"So she should benefit from me being stupid?" Becca asked incredulously and then shook her head again. "No. I'm not going in there and making a scene. I say let her find out just like I had to."

Jack studied her for a minute. "Your call," he said and then sighed. "Come on. We'll make our way toward the dressing rooms. If Mrs. J says anything, I'll let her know what happened, okay?" Holding his arm out just like he did backstage, he smiled and waited for her.

Nodding, Becca took his arm and quietly they walked toward the entrance to the dressing area. At the door, he stopped and stepped in front of her. "Are you going to be all right?"

"Eventually," she said sadly. "Just not tonight." Then she groaned. "Honestly, this entire night has sucked."

"Hey!" he said, feigning offense.

That made Becca chuckle. "You were the highlight, but trust me. The rest of it really sucked."

"Want to talk about it?"

She shook her head. "I think I'm going to go and get changed and head out before the girls even get back here. But thank you." Standing on her tiptoes, she placed her hands on his shoulders and kissed him on the cheek. "I knew you were one of the good ones."

Jack waited until Becca was in the dressing room before walking away.

****

"Change of plans," Hailey said later that night. After she had gotten back to the dressing room she had caught Becca sneaking out and stopped her. With a little bit of persuasion, she convinced her to stay for a little while. Now Angie and Ella were with them and they were having a drink at the hotel across from the convention center.

"What plans? When?" Ella asked, looking at each of them. "I'm confused."

"Instead of our usual lunch tomorrow, we're going to have lunch at my mom's. I want to show her the DVD Max made and I figured we'd make an afternoon of it—lunch by the pool and margaritas. What do you think?"

"Ooh…that sounds good," Ella said. "Any chance there will be someone there to serve us margaritas by the pool?"

"Keep dreaming," Hailey said with a grin. "Is everybody in?"

"I'm in!" Ella said excitedly. "Dylan's helping his dad with some painting tomorrow so I have all day."

"I'm in too," Angie said. "And I don't have to

answer to anyone so I can come and go as I please."

"Sean's not visiting this weekend?" Hailey asked. Ever since his arrival on Angie's doorstep, Sean had been true to his word—doing his best to win Angie over. Hailey assumed since it was the weekend he would put in an appearance.

Angie shrugged. "He asked if he could come and visit, but I put him off."

"Why?" Ella asked. "If you're serious about giving him another chance, then you are actually going to have to see him and spend time with him. You can't have a relationship via text, Ang."

"It's not just texting," Angie said defensively. "We've talked on the phone a couple of times."

"But…?" Hailey prodded.

"But…I don't know. He's busy with work, I'm busy with work and I just wanted him not to be here this weekend."

"Yeah but next weekend we'll be in Charlotte at another expo," Becca reminded her. "Or are you inviting him there since we're getting hotel rooms?"

Angie blushed.

"Nice," Hailey said approvingly. "That's a good plan."

"Plus, it puts us back—sort of—the way we were before. We used to meet up on the weekends on neutral territory."

“Maybe that was part of the problem,” Ella said. “If this relationship is going to go anywhere, you’re going to have to let him into your world a little bit.”

“I know. I’m working on it.” She paused and took a sip of her wine. “Which reminds me…what about you, Hailey? Are you going to take advantage of our lodgings next weekend and make your move on Logan?”

Hailey choked on her drink. “What?”

Angie chuckled. “You heard me. We’ve all given you a little time and space with this, but it’s time for you to make a decision. Are you going to make your move or not?”

“I…I’m still not sure.”

“Oh for crying out loud!” Angie cried. “Why not?”

“I’ve never had to do that before!”

“Seriously? You never made the first move?” Becca asked.

Hailey shrugged. “Honestly? No.”

“Wow,” Becca murmured and picked up her own drink.

“It did cross my mind to take advantage of our time away next weekend, but I’m not sure how to go about doing it.”

“Well don’t look at me,” Ella said quickly. “The last time I made a move it was to slip a note in

Dylan's locker telling him I liked him."

"Yikes," Angie muttered.

"Hey! There's nothing wrong with that," Ella said defensively.

"I know, I know," Angie replied. "But that just seems like a lifetime ago."

"Hello?" Hailey interrupted. "I'm seriously looking for some guidance here!"

"Okay," Angie said, resting her elbows on the table. "After the show Friday night, you know we'll all be staying overnight. No one is going to want to make the three-hour drive home so you know that's going to include Logan."

"Okay," Hailey said.

"More than likely, we'll all end up hanging out at the hotel bar—just like this. You come in, chat with him a little, maybe buy him a drink and then…ask him to join you in your room."

"Just like that?"

Angie nodded. "Just like that. It's not that hard to do. You should probably have a glass of wine just because…well…it's you and you're going to need to relax a little. And then you pick a room and enjoy the night."

"I have a feeling it's a little more complex than that," Hailey said.

"Only if you make it that way," Angie said and then looked over at Becca. "And now you. You look even more miserable than you did before the show. What happened?"

Without making eye contact with any of them, Becca told them about her run-in with Danny and his fiancée.

"No!" they all gasped.

She nodded. "I completely froze. Thank God Jack was there because I swear I thought I was going to be sick."

Ella reached over and squeezed Becca's hand.

"Did he say anything to you?" Hailey asked.

"No. He just gave me that stupid smirk. And then he kissed her right there in front of me." She snorted with disgust. Then she chuckled and told them how Jack had done something to make Danny trip. "It was a little bit awesome how he did that—kind of like a ninja. I never even saw him move."

"So…Jack like…defended you?"

Becca nodded. "He was really sweet. He knew I was already having a crappy night and seeing Danny was the last thing I needed."

"Why? What else happened?" Ella asked.

Becca told them about Max. "So basically in the last several hours, I've had to deal with my ex-boyfriend and his fiancée—who he was probably dating while we were dating—and the fact that my current boyfriend—who may not even be my boyfriend—doesn't find me attractive either and may very well only think of me as a friend. I'm too hideous to attract anyone!" She was breathless by the time she was done.

The girls all looked at one another silently before Hailey spoke up. "Okay, I know it all looks bad right now, but I think if you go and talk to Max, you may find he's just shy. Or being considerate."

"There is considerate and then there's not interested. He kisses me on the cheek like I'm his sister or his buddy. I'm telling you, I completely read all the signals wrong and now I'm stuck in the friend zone."

"I hate the friend zone," Angie agreed and picked up her wine.

"But you're going to talk to him about it, right?" Ella asked.

"I don't know," Becca sighed.

"Oh no…" Hailey said quickly. "You all pushed me into going out with Logan and now possibly seducing Logan…"

"Not possibly," Angie corrected, "you're doing it."

"An-y-way," Hailey said tightly, "you have to talk to him. There really is a good chance he's just treading slowly with you. That doesn't make him a bad guy."

"Maybe," Becca said. "But what if I'm right? What if he only sees me as a friend?"

"Then…you'll be hurt for a little while and

you'll move on," Ella said. "I'd rather find out now than go on and invest any more time in a relationship."

"She has a point," Angie said. "Rip off the bandage now and get it over with."

"But not tomorrow," Hailey said. "Tomorrow we're going to sun ourselves by the pool and relax and show my mom her gift." She looked over at Becca with a sympathetic smile. "And I'd rather we all still like Max while we're doing it rather than cursing him. He really did a great job on the DVD and Mom is going to gush."

"Fine. I think I'm supposed to see him on Sunday. I'll wait and talk to him then."

"Good girl," Angie said and then yawned. "Let's get going."

"You okay to drive?" Hailey asked as they stood, motioning to Angie's glass.

"I only had half a glass."

Together they walked out to the parking lot and waved as they went their separate ways.

****

Later that night, Hailey lay in bed thinking about her conversation with the girls.

Seduce Logan.

Two little words and yet they seemed to carry a lot of weight. Ever since their lunch date, they had talked a couple of times on the phone and he had texted her twice, but all of their interactions had been fairly…generic. Logan never hinted at wanting to go out again and most of his conversations seemed to center around upcoming shows and maybe doing some other modeling gigs.

She supposed that was something. He was good-looking and if he really put an effort into it, Hailey didn't doubt Logan could get some print work in magazines or catalogs, maybe even a commercial or two if he was lucky. He asked for her advice and her opinion and while it was nice it was still…generic.

Sighing, she rolled to her side and turned out the light. It wasn't supposed to be this hard, was it? All of her life, relationships had come easily to her. Not that she liked to brag, but she was the first out of her friends to have a boyfriend—Kenny Miller, seventh grade—and since then, she'd never gone for long without one.

Until she met Logan.

"Well damn," she murmured. Hailey knew it wasn't a coincidence. Logan had started modeling for Enchanted not long after Hailey and her boyfriend of two years had broken up. The timing had been perfect.

Or so she thought.

Had she known that almost a year later she'd still be waiting for Logan to make his move, she might have re-thought things.

She shook her head. No. That wasn't true. She would most likely still pine for him silently. This was all new territory for her. And unfortunately, she no longer felt like her normal, confident self. Ugh…now she could understand how Becca had been feeling. And she sure as hell didn't like it.

"Note to self, apologize to Becca tomorrow."

Not that Becca would hold it against her.

For the most part, Hailey's previous boyfriends had all been the ones to ask her out and they tended to end on good terms. That was a good thing, right?

Or…

Or maybe she just hadn't cared enough to be upset when the relationship ended. *Crap.* Where the hell had that thought come from? Hailey knew she was a very caring and empathetic person. Racking her brain, she tried to think of an ex-boyfriend who she was really upset over breaking up with.

None came to mind.

"Yikes," she groaned. "Second note to self, ask the girls about that one." Surely she had to have been upset about a breakup at some point. Was she just blocking it out? After another minute or two she had her answer. No. Not once could she remember crying over a breakup or even being the one to get dumped. Normally she was the one to end the relationship. "Oh God…I'm *that* person."

How was she supposed to feel confident about going after Logan now? What if he rejected her? What if he told her he simply wasn't interested? Now everyone was going to know about it because she'd been so damn vocal about her feelings for him.

"Okay, calm down," she told herself as she rose from the bed. All this negative thinking had given her a headache and she needed to take some Advil or something.

Padding to her bathroom, her mind raced. Why did thoughts and ideas like this have to hit when all she wanted to do was go to sleep?

Five minutes later, she was back in bed but her mind was still swirling. There was nothing she could do about her previous relationships. They were done and over with. And if she was honest, there wasn't anything wrong with going after what she wanted. And that was Logan. For weeks she had been encouraging everyone else to be brave—Ella with her mom over the wedding, Becca with her breakup with Danny, and Angie with her relationship with Sean. Shouldn't she be practicing what she was preaching?

Pulling up her blankets, Hailey shifted around until she was comfortable and then let out a very loud sigh. It was going to take effort to get to sleep now, too.

"It's okay," she said quietly. "I have direction now and starting tomorrow, I am going to start putting it all into action. This time next weekend, I won't be alone in bed."

The thought put a smile on her face. Closing her eyes, she let herself dream of how wonderful it was all going to be.

****

"This is the dream. I think we need to do this every weekend. Forever," Angie said.

"This is North Carolina, not Key West. We would have to contend with winter weather," Ella replied.

"So we'll move," Becca added.

"Then I vote for Hawaii," Hailey lazily chimed in.

Judith James came out of the French doors that led to her yard and smiled. All four of her girls were sunning themselves on the chaise lounges beside the pool. It was the perfect day for it—sunny but not too hot—and they all look completely relaxed. Carrying a tray of margaritas, she walked over to them. "Here are your drinks, ladies."

Hailey sat up and shielded her eyes from the sun. "Thanks, Mom. You totally didn't have to do this. We would have come inside eventually and made them."

"Yes, well…you said that an hour ago and I wanted one too," Judith said with a sassy grin. She sat down on one of the empty chaises and got comfortable. "It's times like this I really wish we had a pool boy. Or at least someone to just make the drinks and serve us."

"We should totally do that one weekend, Mrs. J. I think we'd all chip in for it," Angie said.

"Maybe we'll have to do something at the end of the summer. A big party here at the house so everyone can swim and we'll have it catered," Judith said, thinking out loud. "I'll invite all of the models and everyone who helps with the bridal shows. Oh, it would be so much fun!"

Then, just as quickly as she had sat down, she was back up and walking toward the house with her drink and murmuring about caterers and party rentals.

"Does she ever sit still?" Becca asked from her chaise.

"Never," Hailey replied.

"She has no idea what she's missing," Angie said with a sigh. "Because this is glorious."

"I think I'm going to go in the water. Anyone want to join me?" Ella asked. Two minutes later, she and Angie dove into the pool.

"Can I ask you something?" Hailey said quietly, turning to look at Becca.

"Sure."

"Do I seem…cold or unfeeling to you?"

Becca lifted her sunglasses and looked at Hailey as if she were crazy. “What are you talking about?”

Turning slightly in her seat, she faced Becca a little more head-on. “I was lying in bed last night and it came to me how I’ve never been upset over a breakup.”

“That’s not true,” Becca said. “Is it?”

Hailey nodded. “I was up half the night trying to think of a guy I truly was broken-hearted over and I couldn’t think of one.”

“And that makes you think you’re cold and unfeeling? Maybe those guys were just jerks.”

“No…that was the other thing, all of the guys I dated were good guys. They never cheated and they weren’t bad in any way, shape or form. I was the one who ended all of them and it was normally over silly stuff.”

Becca studied her for a minute. “Maybe now your reasons seem silly, but at the time, I’m sure it didn’t feel like that.”

“Maybe,” Hailey sighed and sat back on the chaise.

“Hails, you are a great person. What’s this all about?”

“It’s bothering me that I am having to work so hard and think so much about this whole Logan situation. I’ve never had to do that before. Then that got me thinking about why I’ve never had to do it before and…you know…it just snowballed." She sighed. "Why is this so damn hard?"

"It normally is. You've just been fortunate. The rest of us have to work at it. Look at how long I worked at getting Danny to notice me." Then she stopped. "Scratch that. Bad example."

"No," Hailey said, sitting back up. "You're right. What if…what if Logan is like Danny? What if I finally get this guy who I've built up in my mind to be so fantastic and it turns out he's a real jerk?"

Becca sat up and shook her head. "Not gonna happen."

"How do you know?"

"Because everyone warned me about Danny. Everyone saw he was a jerk and wasn't good for me and I ignored them. Everyone who meets Logan can see he's a great guy. Your mom is a great judge of character. She wouldn't have hired him if he wasn't a quality guy."

"She hired Jackson too," Hailey mumbled.

"Hey," Becca said firmly, pointing a finger at her. "Need I remind you how Jackson came to my rescue last night? In my book that makes him a quality guy too. You're not allowed to pick on him. Ever."

Hailey rolled her eyes. "You can't say that. Just because he did one nice thing…"

"He does plenty of nice things. You just choose

to focus on the things you—and only you—seem to think aren't nice. And to be honest, I think you overreact to most of them."

"I don't see it that way, but for the sake of an argument, we'll just have to agree to disagree." Hailey reached for her drink and took a sip. "Oh, that's good. Someday Mom is going to teach me how to make a margarita this delicious."

Becca chuckled. "She does have a gift with them." She stood and stretched. It felt good to be out in the sun in the privacy of the James' backyard. It was the only place she would allow herself to wear a bikini. Adjusting the bottoms, she did a little shimmy and turned toward the pool. "I think I'm gonna…"

"Girls! Look who's here! Max!" Judith called as she came back out to the yard arm in arm with Max.

"Oh shit!" Becca cried as she spun and reached for her cover-up and quickly slipped it on. When she straightened, she couldn't make herself look directly at Max.

Hailey—thankfully—jumped in. "Max! So glad you could make it!"

Becca's head snapped to the side. "Make it?"

Nodding, Hailey smiled. "I called him this morning and invited him to join us. He's the reason we're here today and I thought it would be great if he could be here."

Judith looked puzzled. "What are you talking about?"

Angie and Ella climbed out of the pool and grabbed their towels after greeting Max.

"Well," Hailey began, "Max put together a little surprise for you and the girls and I got a preview of it last weekend and that's why we're here today, Mom. To share it with you!"

With a gasp, Judith looked from Hailey to Max. "What in the world?" she asked, tearing up. "I don't even know what it is but I know I'm going to love it!"

"I have it inside," Hailey said. "So if you're okay with it, we can all go inside and see it."

Judith held up a hand to stop her. "Actually, I need about fifteen minutes. I'm about to go in on a conference call with the Nashville people. They're wanting to do an entire weekend event and we're trying to coordinate schedules."

"Don't they have bridal shops in Nashville?" Angie asked.

Judith smiled and winked. "Not as good as ours." Then she turned and walked away.

Becca wished she could do the same thing. When she got Hailey alone later, she was going to strangle her. It was bad enough she was feeling ten kinds of inferior thanks to last night's run-in with Danny. Did she really need to have Max see her and her chubby body in a bikini?

"Excuse me," she mumbled as she turned and walked quickly toward the small pool house at the far end of the yard.

Hailey inwardly groaned as she watched Becca's retreat. She turned to Max and pasted an overly bright smile on her face. "So…yeah. So glad you could come over for this. I think my mom is going to freak out—in a good way—when she sees the video."

Max wasn't really paying attention. He was staring hard at the pool house.

"Um…yeah…," Ella added awkwardly. "And Dylan and I can't wait for you to help us with our wedding video. I know we're downsizing everything, but we decided we still want a video."

When Max still didn't say anything, Hailey looked at Angie and silently begged her to do something.

"So…Max," Angie said, picking her margarita back up, "do you find Becca even remotely attractive?"

"*Angie*!" Hailey and Ella cried in unison.

"What?" Max asked incredulously, finally tearing his gaze from the pool house.

With a shrug and a small glare at the girls, she faced Max. "Look, Becca…well…she kind of thinks you're not interested in her."

Ella groaned and slowly sat down on her chaise and put her face in her hands.

"Why would she think that?" he asked. "We've been spending a lot of time together, we talk on the phone all the time…I…I don't understand why she would think I wasn't into her."

Reaching out, Hailey put a hand on his arm. "Okay, I know it's not our place to say anything but being that *somebody…*" she paused, glancing angrily at Angie, "put it out there, it's only fair that we explain."

Max sighed heavily. "O-kay…"

"Look, she's been hurt," Angie said. "Her ex did a real number on her and she's always had a self-esteem problem so really, you were going to have an uphill battle no matter what."

"I know all about her ex and what he did."

"She told you?" Hailey asked.

"No," he said quietly, swiping a weary hand over his face. "I was there that night when it happened. He pretty much broke up with her right in front of me. She was devastated."

"Oh…no…" Hailey groaned. "She didn't tell us."

"Yeah…well…" he began, "I didn't say anything to anyone either. It wasn't my place." He paused. "I talked to her after he left and told her he was crazy, that she was beautiful. But I guess she didn't believe me."

"Wow," Angie said. "You said that to her and you didn't even know her?"

He nodded.

“Quality guy,” Hailey whispered.

“I’m still confused,” he said. “I don’t get why she just took off like that.”

Ella stood up and said, “For starters, she was feeling insecure because…you know…you haven’t tried to kiss her or anything.”

“Yeah but…”

“And, knowing her like we do, she was embarrassed that you saw her in a bikini,” Ella finished.

Max’s eyes went wide. “Seriously? Why would she be embarrassed? She’s got an amazing body! Why would she think otherwise?”

Angie started to talk but Hailey stopped her. “I think we’ve said enough. You should probably go to the pool house and talk to her.”

“I’m not sure she wants to talk to me,” he said. “I mean she essentially ran away as soon as I got here. I don’t want to upset her any more than I obviously already have.”

“Yeah well, if you don’t go and talk to her, she’s probably going to still be upset,” Angie said. “You should just go and at least try to talk to her.”

Max looked longingly at the pool house. “I don’t know…”

Hailey gave him a gentle nudge in that direction. “Go. And take your time. We’ll wait to watch the video until you’re both there.”

"But what about…"

"Trust me. This is more important," Ella said.

With a fortifying breath, Max stepped around the three of them and walked toward the pool house.

"Do you think she's going to listen to him?" Ella asked quietly when Max was out of earshot.

"I don't know. She can be stubborn," Angie said.

"Yeah but this is going to be a good test of what kind of man Max is." She smiled. "I think this is going to be a game changer."

****

Becca paced back and forth and cursed herself for the hundredth time.

Running away like that? Yeah, not her finest hour.

At the time, it had been imperative for her to get away. The backyard was like a safe haven—no one else came in and she was free to just be herself—and that included wearing a skimpy bikini she had no business wearing.

And now she was going to have to deal with the fact that not only did Max already find her unattractive, but seeing her in a bikini had probably been the final nail in that coffin. Once he got a look at her practically naked, she was fairly certain he was high-fiving himself for not getting involved with her. She glanced out the back window and wondered if she could climb out and go through the bushes and escape.

Then she remembered she didn't have her purse or her car keys so essentially she was stuck.

"Dammit." Turning around, she walked over to the full-length mirror that hung on the wall outside the large changing room. The pool house was a great space—a living area with a small kitchenette, a full bathroom and a changing room. Growing up, she and the girls would come in here and pretend it was their house where they all lived together. The memory made her smile.

Then she checked out her reflection.

Her breasts were bigger than she wanted, as were her hips. The only thing saving her from being completely horrified by her body was the fact that she had a fairly small waist—she pulled off the hourglass figure all right. Unfortunately, she longed to be thin and willowy like Ella and Hailey. Angie was curvy like her, but Angie also was about five inches taller so she looked way more proportioned.

Pulling her cover-up tightly around her, Becca groaned. Was Max still out there? Had they all gone back into the house to watch the video? She could only hope so.

Walking over to the refrigerator, she pulled out a bottle of water. Behind her, she heard the sliding glass door open and figured it was probably one of the girls coming to check on her or tell her that she acted like an idiot. So fine. She did and eventually she'd get over it. With a sigh of resignation, she said, "Look, I know I…" But when she turned around, she gasped at the sight of Max standing in the doorway. "Max! What…what are you…?"

He slowly walked toward her and didn't stop until they were toe-to-toe. Reaching up, he cupped her face in his hands, lowered his head and claimed her lips with his. It wasn't a sweet, getting-to-know-you kind of kiss, it was deep and wet and all-consuming.

Becca clutched the front of his shirt and immediately melted into him. His tongue traced her lower lip until she opened for him. It was so unexpected, so wild that her head began to spin. *This was Max*? This was polite, mild-mannered, only-kissed-on-the-cheek Max? His hands caressed her cheeks and then raked into her hair where he gently tugged it free of the ponytail she had it in.

Oh. My.

Just as quickly as it had started, it ended. Max lifted his head and gently gripped Becca's shoulders and spun her around so she was facing the mirror. They were both breathless and Becca's eyes were slightly glazed. She reached up with a trembling hand to touch her lips as she met his intense gaze in their reflection.

Without a word, Max's hands came up from behind and he gently stroked her cheeks. Becca sighed and leaned back so they were touching.

"You are so damn beautiful to me," he said gruffly. "From the first time I saw you, I thought that."

She went to shake her head no, but his words stopped her.

"Yes. I saw you standing in the parking lot and thought to myself that you were the most beautiful woman I had ever seen. It killed me to hear what that jackass was saying to you, but at the same time I was thankful because it meant you were no longer involved with him."

"Max…"

Slowly, his hands skimmed down from her face to her throat and shoulders. With his eyes firmly on hers in their reflection, he began to move her cover-up aside, opening it so he could see what she was wearing underneath. His hiss of breath at the sight of her in the midnight blue bikini had Becca's mind reeling. What was he really seeing? Was his reaction one of arousal or disappointment?

Boldly, one hand came up and cupped her breast. "I was trying so hard to be a gentleman with you. I knew you had been hurt and I didn't want to rush you. Every time we've been together, I've had to fight the urge to touch you."

Becca wanted to tell him how much she wanted him to touch her, but his fingers were slowly teasing her nipple and she couldn't make herself form a word.

"I've lain in bed at night and thought about you,"

he murmured, turning his head so his hot breath was on her throat. His tongue gently licked where her pulse was beating madly. Then he let his other hand drift down to her waist, then her hip and then over until he was cupping her mound.

She sighed his name at the contact, could feel his arousal pressing up against her back.

His fingers began to move slowly—one caressing her nipple while the other traced lazy circles over the fabric covering her sex. A low moan came out and it seemed to encourage Max to be a little bolder.

His touch became a little more certain, confident. His lips never left her skin as his hands had her squirming and writhing against him. "You're so beautiful," he whispered again. "So sexy."

No one had ever called her beautiful before and as much as she loved hearing those words from him, she couldn't stay focused on them, not when his skillful hands had her climbing toward a release. His name came out on a gasp as he placed a little more pressure between her legs at the same time he gently bit the sensitive spot where her neck and shoulder met.

And that was all it took for her to soar.

Max held her against him as she rode the wave of her release, gently kissing her the entire time.

Slowly, Max shifted and moved his hands so they rested on her waist as he turned her toward him. He swallowed hard as he looked down at her. "Becca, this isn't what I came in here for. But one look at you and…" He gave her a lopsided grin. "This isn't the time or the place for this and as much as I want you, I can wait. But I needed you to know how I feel."

Becca rested one hand on his chest. "Tell me again," she said, so softly, so quietly she wasn't sure he could even hear her.

He tucked a finger under her chin. "I think you're beautiful and I want you very much."

"I want you too."

A slow smile crossed his face. "Let's go inside and watch the video." He paused. "And then…come home with me."

It was exciting and terrifying for her all at the same time. This was what she wanted—what she had been waiting for—and now that it was here, old doubts began to creep back in.

"You're thinking too hard about this," he said quietly, interrupting her thoughts. "I won't rush you, Becca. Ever. We can go into the house and later on, I can go home and you can go back to your place and we'll go out tomorrow like we had planned. It's completely up to you." He took a step back and took one of her hands in his. "You ready to go and join the others?"

Actually, what she was ready for was locking the door and letting Max finish having his way with her. No doubt the girls had encouraged him to come after her and if they stayed in here long enough, they'd figure out what was going on. But so would Mrs. J and that was definitely not a conversation she wanted to have.

Nodding silently, she smiled when Max squeezed her hand.

As they walked across the yard, Becca mentally crossed her fingers and hoped they'd be able to leave as soon as the video was over.

Six

"I don't understand why you didn't just drive here with Max," Angie said. "You guys are sharing a room, Bec[illegible] it wouldn't [illegible]ve been a big deal if we all didn't ride [illegible]

Becca [illegible]re about logistics. His office is [illegible] and he knew he had to stay at wo[illegible]ew how we normally make a da[illegible] from work and get on the road at [illegible]e. He'll be there in time for us to grab a [illegible]dinner, and then we'll go and get ready for the ex[illegible]"

Angie laughed. "Nice! That was smooth. A quick…*dinner*. Right."

"Oh, stop," Ella said. "Leave her alone. We all remember what it feels like in the beginning of a relationship."

"I'm surprised you do," Angie teased. "You and Dylan were…what…twelve?"

Rather than answer, Ella just waved her off. "And what about you, Hails? You ready to make your move tonight?"

Hailey was sitting in the back seat beside Ella. "I think so," she said nervously. "I have to admit, every time I think about it, I feel like I'm going to throw up." She looked at her friends. "That's normal, right?"

"Uh…"

"Well…"

"Hmmm…"

"Oh come on, you guys!" Hailey cried. "You know I've never done this before!"

"Maybe after the show you'll feel better," Becca suggested, smiling in the rearview mirror.

"And after a couple of shots," Angie added.

"We are not sending her to make her move on Logan while she's drunk," Ella said defensively. "Although, you probably should have a glass of wine." She shrugged. "Just saying."

"Why does everyone keep saying that?" Hailey asked.

Becca and Angie looked at one another. Becca spoke up before Angie could. "You're just a little…wound up sometimes."

"Wound up?"

"Yeah, you know…you always like to be in control and have things done a certain way," Becca said, trying to sound diplomatic—like what she was saying was helpful and not hurtful. "It's not a bad thing, Hails. But in this particular scenario, you are going to need to relax a little bit. You can't go and approach Logan in your usual way. And considering how uptight you've been about the whole thing, we're all just saying that a small drink may help you loosen up a bit."

"But not drunk," Ella added. "You don't want to go in there drunk."

"There's something to be said for drunken sex," Angie said with a devilish grin.

"Why would anyone even *want* to have drunken sex?" Hailey asked, completely perplexed. "That would just be…sloppy and…and…a waste of time!"

Angie laughed. "And that's why you can't go in there drunk. Because that's what you think is going to happen."

"Well…isn't it?"

Angie shook her head. "Sometimes it helps you loosen your inhibitions and makes the experience really good. You're relaxed and…sometimes…it even heightens the experience."

Hailey frowned. "I don't believe that for a second."

Rolling her eyes, Angie said, "Fine. Don't believe me. Your loss."

"Becca," Hailey said earnestly, leaning forward between the two front seat, "have you ever had drunken sex? Is she lying to me?"

"Um…I'm right here," Angie said flatly.

"Shh!" Hailey hissed. "Becca?"

"I'm not gonna lie to you…I'm not saying you have to get completely shit-faced, but I've had some really good sex after a couple of drinks."

Hailey huffed and leaned back in her seat. "Damn."

"Told you," Angie said with a grin.

"Last New Year's, Dylan and I shared a bottle of champagne after we got home from the party," Ella began. "That was a great night." She giggled. "Seriously, the sex that night was amazing."

Hailey glared at her. "Seriously? You too?"

Ella continued to giggle. "What can I say?"

"Okay, so one glass of wine," Hailey sighed. "I still can't believe I'm doing this."

"It's about time," Angie said. "If it were me, I would have pounced months ago."

"Yeah well…I've never had to…pounce. I kept hoping Logan would."

"Clearly you were wrong," Angie countered. "So what are you going to wear? What are you going to say?"

Hailey squeezed her eyes shut for a moment and then let out a weary sigh. "I brought my pink sundress. You know, the one I wore when we went to see *Wicked*."

"Good choice," Ella said, reaching out and squeezing Hailey's hand.

"And what about underwear? What did you go

with?" Angie asked. "Lace? Thong? Commando?"

"Ugh…really?" Hailey whined, but when Angie continued to stare and she notice Ella and Becca doing the same, she shook her head. "White lace."

"Ah…virginal," Becca said. "That could work."

Hailey looked worriedly at them. "What? Do you think I should have gone for more casual?"

"No, no, no. That's not what I'm saying," Becca quickly amended. "You should wear something you're comfortable with. And that definitely sounds like an outfit you're good with."

"But it's lame," Hailey said. "Right? It's totally lame."

"Nobody said that," Ella said. "I think it sounds perfect for you and Logan."

"What does that even mean?" Angie asked, turning in her seat.

"Logan looks like he just walked off the pages of a J. Crew catalog," Ella said. "He is always dressed impeccably. So the dress Hailey chose will work perfectly. They'll be very balanced."

Angie groaned. "They're having sex, not posing for a yuppie photoshoot."

"What would you suggest she wear?" Ella snapped, losing some of her composure. "A leather skirt, crotchless panties and hooker heels? Sheesh!"

"A thong could work," Angie said calmly. "That

would be…"

"Enough!" Hailey yelled. "I am already freaking out about tonight and I don't need all of this yammering about my choice of panties!"

Everyone grew quiet. When they pulled off the interstate at the exit for their hotel, Becca spoke up. "Okay, we're almost there so everyone needs to play nice and get along."

No one answered.

By the time she parked the car and they all got out, it was as if nothing had happened earlier—they were all chatting about the show, the hotel and what they were having for dinner. The absurdity of it all made Becca chuckle.

****

"This is going to be so much fun!" Ella said, bouncing on the bed. "You and I never have a room to ourselves!"

Angie rolled her eyes. "Easy there, Tinker Bell. Don't go getting all excited. We're simply sleeping in here tonight. No pillow fights, no telling ghost stories."

Ella frowned. "Do you have to put me down all the time? Geez. Can't you—just for once—be pleasant about something?"

Now it was Angie's turn to frown. "Okay, fine," she sighed, sitting down on her own bed. "Look, I don't mean to say things like that all the time, but it just comes out naturally."

"Yeah well, you should work on that."

"Sean says the same thing."

Ella instantly perked up. "Really? Like recently? What did he say? Are you going to see him soon?"

"This is the kind of thing I'm talking about!" Angie cried, pointing a finger at her. "Do you have to be so…perky? Can't we just have a normal, non-excitable conversation?"

Crossing her arms, Ella muttered, "Fine."

Angie sighed. "Okay, so we talk every day. And that's not an exaggeration. He calls me every night when he knows I'm just sitting alone, just me and Trampus, and doing nothing. It's…" She stopped and shrugged. "It's kind of nice. We didn't do that before."

"So it seems like he's really trying. I'm sorry he couldn't make it this weekend."

"Me too," she replied, sighing again. "And he is—he's really trying. And…I don't know…he's doing all the right things and saying all the right things and yet…"

"You still don't trust him."

"Exactly."

"There's going to come a time when you're

going to have to get over your fear and decide if you really want to move forward with him or not. He's not going to wait forever."

Angie's eyes went wide. "Ella Gilmore, did you just give me a reality check? Like a for real reality check?"

Ella grinned. "I am capable of that every once in a while."

"Yeah but you're usually more of the rainbows-and-unicorns type where everyone is always happy and everything works out."

She shrugged. "Sometimes they don't. And sometimes you have to have the guts to make that decision."

Angie got more comfortable on her bed and smiled. "Oh there's a story there," she said. "Come on. Out with it."

Ella didn't even pretend not to understand. "Dylan and I moved up the wedding date."

"No!"

Ella nodded. "And we broke the news to our parents last night."

"How did it go?"

"How do you think? My mother cried. Dylan's mom told us how disappointed she was…it was like a giant soap opera. You would have thought we said that we'd broken up. It was crazy. But we stood our ground and took control of our wedding back."

“And how do you feel now that you’ve done it?”

“Honestly?”

Angie nodded.

“It…it didn’t offer the relief I thought it would.”

“Uh-oh…”

Ella nodded. “I know.”

“So there’s something else bothering you.”

Ella nodded again.

“Well…? What is it?”

Tears began to well in her eyes. “I thought it was the pressure of the wedding that was making me stressed. Then Dylan and I talked and agreed that we would downsize and change the date.”

“But…?”

“But now he’s talking about us starting a family right away.”

Angie’s eyes widened. “Like…right away, right away? As in…now?”

Ella nodded.

“Shit. That’s a little out of the blue.”

“I know. And part of me is completely on board and then I look at you and Becca and Hailey and…I feel very alone.”

“Seriously? We’re together all the time.”

"Not alone like that," Ella huffed. "It's more like I'm alone in all of this—just me and Dylan. We're getting married and having kids and all of my friends aren't."

"I hate to break it to you, El, but we're all not ready to run out and get married. And that's not a bad thing."

"I don't know…I always pictured this happening for all of us at the same time. Then our kids would all be friends and we'd all be going through the craziness of figuring out how to be grown-ups together."

"We are. But we're all growing into different adults. And again, it's not a bad thing."

Ella's shoulders slumped. "I know. Sometimes I just feel like maybe I'm missing too much."

"We've been over this before," Angie reminded her. "The stuff you're missing? It's not that great. I wish I were in a relationship that was stable and secure with someone I knew I could trust. Do you have any idea how lucky you are that you get to go home to Dylan every night and know he loves you?"

"I do. I know I'm sounding ungrateful…"

Angie shook her head. "It's not ungrateful. You're getting ready to take a huge step, El. It's okay to be scared."

"You're the only one who thinks so. Everyone teases us about how nothing is going to change because we've been together for so long. And maybe they're right. Maybe I'm freaking out over nothing."

"Don't ever let anyone belittle your feelings. I know I do that sometimes—and most of the time I'm joking—but…you have a right to feel the way you do. And yeah, maybe a lot of things won't change for you and Dylan once you're married. But there are going to be changes. You're going to have kids and you're going to buy a house and neither of those are small things. But know this, El, it doesn't matter how long the two of you have been together. Your journey is really just beginning."

Tears freely flowed down Ella's cheeks. "Dammit, Ange," she said, standing and walking to grab some tissues from the bathroom. "That was…that was exactly what I needed to hear." She came out of the bathroom and walked over and hugged Angie. "Thank you."

"Yeah well…don't tell anyone about it. I kind of enjoy being the hardass of the group. If you let it out that I have a sensitive side, I'll have to kick your tiny, pixie ass."

Ella pulled back and chuckled. "Duly noted."

"Okay, let's go downstairs and grab an early dinner. Then we can come up here and do our hair and makeup in the room rather than downstairs in all of the chaos. What do you think?"

"Sounds like a plan. Let me just go and fix my makeup." She turned to walk back into the bathroom. "Should we call the girls to join us?"

Angie shook her head. "Becca's meeting up with Max and I'm thinking Hailey needs the time alone to get her head in the game for tonight."

"Do you think she's really going to go through with it?"

"I don't know. I think she *wants* to go through with it, but I have a feeling it wouldn't take much for her to chicken out."

"Oh, don't say that. I want to believe she's going to do this and that she and Logan will work out."

Angie was checking her own reflection in the mirror. "You don't think there's a chance that Logan's not going to be interested?" she asked casually.

Ella froze and met Angie's gaze in their reflection. "Why wouldn't he be? Hailey's beautiful and they seem to get along great. Why would you even think that?"

"Honestly, I don't think he's the one for her."

"Oh really? Why?"

She shrugged and then turned and leaned against the vanity. "First of all, he's not a motivated guy like we know Hailey wants. Logan's a nice guy and all, but if he's a slacker now at his age, it isn't going to change when he's older."

"True."

"Then there's the fact that he's pretty."

Ella chuckled. "And what's wrong with that?"

“He’s the kind of pretty that requires maintenance. That will eventually grate on Hailey’s nerves.”

“I don’t think so. She’s known him long enough to figure that out and it hasn’t stopped her yet.” She applied some lip gloss and turned to Angie. “What else have you got?”

“You know what…it’s nothing. Don’t mind me. I’m sure it’s going to go great,” Angie said swiftly and walked out of the bathroom to grab her purse.

“Come on,” Ella said, hot on her heels. “There’s more! And you badgered me to tell you all my stuff so…out with it!”

“First of all, I didn’t badger you.”

“Whatever. Now tell me!”

Angie sighed. “Don’t you think it’s odd that he’s never brought a date to any of the events Mrs. J has? Or any of the shows? We’ve all done it at one point or another. But Logan’s always alone. And he flirts with everyone.”

“So…?”

“So maybe it is a red flag that he’s not looking for a relationship. Hailey is! Hailey is the poster child for wanting a relationship. She may think she can do this fling thing but I think if Logan were to tell her it’s all he wants—right to her face—she’ll bail.”

“And forever wonder…”

Angie nodded. “Exactly.”

"Well that sucks."

"You should have just let me drop it."

"Yeah well…curiosity and all that."

"You know me, I tend to think of the worst-case scenario in everything. She's going to be fine. But I think it would be helpful if I don't talk too much around her tonight. I don't want to scare her off."

"Good point." Ella grabbed her purse and room key. "So let's go and eat and when we see her later on downstairs for the show, let's keep the conversation neutral or show-related."

"I hope I can keep my mouth shut."

They walked out of the room, the door closing behind them. "Then pick on Becca. We know she's having a sexy dinner with Max right now. And really, I'm doubting food will be involved at all. If you feel the need to talk about anyone's sex life, go to hers. She'll turn twenty shades of red and that should help you get your mean-girl fix."

Angie laughed. "You know what, Ella?"

"What?"

"I think I may have underestimated you all these years. Behind your tiny Tinker Bell exterior, you're a little bit of an evil genius."

Ella beamed. "Coming from you, that is definitely a compliment."

****

The fashion show was its usual success.

Everyone was happy and excited and planning to meet up for drinks down in the hotel bar.

Hailey felt like she was going to throw up.

Up in her room she checked her reflection for the tenth time. Everything was perfect. She looked—if she did say so herself—stunning. Her hair was perfect. Her makeup was perfect. And her dress, paired with a pearl necklace, was the perfect balance of sweet and sexy.

Perfect.

Yeah, she needed to work on her vocabulary because right now the word *perfect* also felt boring.

A quick glance at the bedside clock showed it was almost eleven. The show had ended a little over an hour ago and she knew everyone would have had time to go back to their rooms and do what they needed to do and be down in the bar by now. She had purposely waited to go—she wanted to make a bit of an entrance. Smiling one last time at her reflection, she took a steadying breath and let it out slowly before grabbing her purse, which contained condoms and her room key.

After the show, the girls had asked her if she wanted them with her, but she had said no. They were all a little surprised by the admission. Something like this was huge and normally they would all be around for emotional support. But Hailey had looked at Becca—who was wrapped in

Max's arms—and knew the two of them had better things to do than come and watch her hit on Logan. Ella was yawning and Angie had briefly mentioned in passing how Sean was supposed to call her tonight. So yeah, it was the right thing for Hailey to be going solo.

Her heart was beating frantically on the way to the elevator and she was seriously glad she had ten floors to ride down to calm it. Looking down at her white shoes, she frowned. *Maybe I should have gone with something a little less bold,* she thought. *Something a little less stiletto and more kitten.* The doors rang as they opened and when she looked up, she gasped.

Jack.

"Well, look at you, Princess," he said with a smile. "Hot date?"

Stepping inside, she mentally groaned. Ignoring him for a moment, she hit the lobby button. "Just going down for a drink."

Beside her, Jack smiled and nodded as he moved a little closer, his hands clasped in front of him. He inhaled deeply. "Where are the girls? They meeting you down there?"

Why wouldn't he just shut up? "No, actually. They all had plans. I just thought I'd go and meet up with everyone from the show and have a glass of wine." She glared at him. "That's allowed, you know."

He held up his hands in mock surrender. "I never said otherwise." Then he studied her. "You sure put in a lot of effort for the hotel bar. You sure you don't have a date waiting for you?" he teased.

Hailey couldn't help it. She rolled her eyes. "Why are you so interested? And what are you doing roaming around the hotel? Don't you have some place to be?"

Jack nodded. "Same as you, Princess. Hitting the bar for a night cap."

Well damn, she thought. There wasn't time for a snappy comeback; the doors to the lobby opened. Jack motioned for Hailey to go first and she could feel him staring at her back. Unfortunately, there was no way to get rid of him now and that meant he was going to be watching her hitting on—and hopefully leaving with—Logan.

They walked in the direction of the music playing and at the door to the lounge, Hailey stopped and looked around, clutching her purse in her hands. It didn't take long for her to find Logan. He was standing near the bar talking to a couple of guys—one was another model from the show, but she didn't recognize the other one.

Jack had stopped beside her and seemed to know who she was looking at. He let out a low chuckle.

"What? What's so funny?"

"You're down here for Logan?" he asked incredulously, unable to hide his grin. "That's what this is all about? The dress, the heels…" He motioned to her entire body. "Whatcha wearing under your dress, Princess? Silk or lace?"

Her eyes narrowed at him. "You know what? You're incredibly crude," she snorted. "And you know what else? It's none of your business. Logan and I talked earlier and he mentioned he'd be down here. And if you look around, so are a lot of people from the show."

"And if you'll notice, most of them are dressed casually. You're the only one who looks like she's going to a cotillion and not a bar."

"I'm not…" She snapped her mouth closed. He had her there. Maybe it would have been smarter to go casual, but it was too late now.

Jack leaned down and whispered in her ear, "You are and trust me, you're wasting your time."

The feel of his breath on her skin had her tingling unexpectedly. Hailey pulled back and stared at him.

Jack nodded. "Look, you've got no reason to believe me, but…believe me. If you're thinking of going in there and hitting on Logan, you're going to be disappointed."

Every fiber of her being told her to believe him,

but he had said it with just a hint of condescension that had her spine stiffening. With a forced smile, she simply walked away and made her way to the bar.

"Logan!" she said as she got closer.

"Hailey!" he replied, beaming at her. "Look at you! Beautiful as always." He wrapped her in his embrace and for a minute, Hailey felt like all was going to be right with the world. When he pulled back, he kept one arm loosely wrapped around her waist. "Let me buy you a drink."

She smiled back at him. "Thanks, I'd love a glass of white zinfandel with a twist of lime. Please."

Logan ordered for her and then turned to his friends. "Hailey, you already know Jimmy," he said, motioning to Jim Miles, who had been modeling for Enchanted for two years now. "And this is George."

Hailey reached out and shook his hand with her smile still in place. "It's nice to meet you, George."

"You too, Hailey. Logan talks about you all the time," George said.

"Really?" she asked sweetly. "All good stuff, I hope."

"Of course," Logan said, hugging her close again. Then he looked a little beyond her. "Jackson! Good to see you! I thought you were heading back upstairs?"

Jack shrugged and gave Hailey a smirk. "I was thinking about it, but then I spotted Hailey and decided to have one last drink."

She glared at him briefly before turning back to George. "So George, do you live here in Charlotte?"

He reached out and snagged Hailey's drink from

the bartender and handed it to her. "No, no, no…I'm back in Raleigh. But I've never been to one of the shows and Logan's always telling me how great they are, so I decided to tag along with him."

"Oh," she said, keeping her smile in place. "That's nice of you."

Her mind was rioting. Something seemed…off. She couldn't quite comprehend why one of Logan's buddies would give up a Friday night to come to a bridal show—especially one that was three hours from home. Friends didn't normally do that sort of thing. The only time she knew of people doing that was when they were…

Oh.

Slowly, she looked over at Jack and saw what almost looked like an apologetic smile on his face—as if he realized that it was finally hitting her.

Oh.

Taking a larger drink of her wine than she should have, Hailey carefully put the glass back on the bar. Without being too obvious, she put some distance between her and Logan—and backed right into Jack. His large hand rested low on her hip and combined with his entire body behind her, Hailey felt the need to sag against him for support.

And later she'd have to examine the fact that she was really enjoying the feel of him, the heat of him, the…everything of him.

"George and I have been living together for

about a year," Logan said as Hailey realized she hadn't been paying attention. "He normally works on the weekends but I convinced him to come with me this time." The two smiled at each other before facing Hailey again.

"That…that's great!" she said cheerily and when she saw Logan's arm go around George's waist she felt…relieved.

Wait…*what*??

It hit her that she honestly felt relief. For so long she had been pining after the Logan that she had created in her mind and when she started to see him for who he really was, Hailey felt that maybe she was hanging on for the wrong reasons.

Like she didn't want to admit she'd been wrong.

That was something she was going to think about later too. For now, she kept a smile on her face and listened to George talk about his work as…go figure…a lawyer. Great. It was completely unfair that Logan was the one who got to date a lawyer.

"I think the day is finally catching up with me," she said a few minutes later. "I think I'm going to head up to my room." Leaning in, she hugged George, Jim and Logan goodbye and did her best to keep her back to Jack. There was no way she could look him in the eye right now. "Thanks for the drink! I'll see you next Friday!" she said with a wave as she maneuvered around Jack and quickly walked out of the bar.

Fearful she was going to trip if she ran in her stilettos, Hailey quickly pulled them off and ran for the elevator, hoping to jump in one before anyone saw her.

With a sigh of relief, the doors opened just as she was approaching and she stepped in, hit the ten button and sagged against the side of the elevator. The doors were just starting to close when all of a sudden Jack stepped in.

She wanted to cry.

To his credit, Jack didn't say a word. When the elevator doors slid closed, he kept his gaze focused straight ahead, as if Hailey wasn't standing two feet away. She noticed how he didn't hit a button, but to question it would require her to speak to him, and right now, she just wasn't sure she could do that.

Finding out Logan was gay wasn't an issue. It didn't change the fact that she thought he was a great guy; it just meant she could now focus on how he was a great friend. Her real issue was that Jack had called it weeks ago and then he had stood there and witnessed her finding it out for herself.

He did warn her.

More than once.

It was her own fault she chose to ignore the warnings.

Quietly, she took her key from her purse and kept her gaze trained on the floor until the doors opened. When they did, she stepped around Jack and finally released the breath she didn't realize she'd been holding.

Hailey made it only a few steps when Jack came up beside her, took her hand in his and began to walk.

"Hey! What are you…?" They stopped at the room across from hers and she realized Jack was opening the door. "Jack? What in the world…?"

As soon as they were in the room, Jack spun her around until her back was against the closed door. There was a fierce look in his eyes that made Hailey's go wide..

No one had ever looked at Hailey this way. His eyes were such a deep green that she couldn't make herself look away. She kept waiting—waiting for him to say something, to do something—but he didn't. He stood close enough that they were almost touching—she could feel the heat of him again—but he made no move to really touch her.

It was maddening.

Her breathing was slightly ragged and for the life of her, she couldn't say why. Hailey wasn't afraid of Jack. Not really. He was the first man who didn't treat her like she was fragile and this little detour into his room had her feeling a little manhandled.

And she actually liked it.

Taking a steadying breath, she let it out and slowly licked her lips. Jack's gaze narrowed in on that movement, but still he said nothing.

Frustration and…arousal…were battling within Hailey. This was getting ridiculous! Why had he even brought her here if he wasn't going to do anything? The least he could do was tell her why! He owed her that much! Then she stopped that train of thought because really, she didn't want to talk.

She wanted Jack to kiss her.

And if she was reading the situation correctly, it would seem as if he wanted that too. Maybe she should just tell him it was okay, that he could kiss her, that she wanted him to.

Damn.

Hailey knew immediately what she wanted to do. Hell, she had been preparing herself all day to make a move on Logan. She figured she'd flirt, have a drink with him and they'd go back to her room where they'd make love. It was going to be sweet and perfect and…boring. It wouldn't be that way with Jack. She had a feeling it would be wild and frantic and anything but sweet and boring.

With her mind made up, she dropped her shoes and purse, closed the distance between them, cupped her hand around his neck and brought his head down as she went up on her toes and kissed him. And then…

Holy. Hell.

If Hailey thought she was in control, she was sadly mistaken. Jack's arms banded around her as he lifted her. Hailey's legs wrapped around his middle.

And it was everything she thought it would be—wild and frantic. It was all teeth and tongues and…good Lord, the man was hard everywhere.

Jack lifted his head abruptly and looked at her and Hailey was certain she looked dazed. "Do you have any idea how long I've wanted to do that?"

Her eyes went wide.

"Yeah," he said gruffly. "I've had to stand back and watch you chase after Logan and it just about killed me."

She swallowed hard. "Why…why didn't you say anything?"

"Seriously? You barely tolerated me when I tried talking to you about anything." He rubbed up against her and Hailey couldn't help but moan. "God you feel so good in my arms." And then he was kissing her again. Slowly he walked them over the bed and gently placed her down on the mattress before straightening and looking at her.

Hailey wanted to squirm under his appraisal. Her dress was bunched up practically to her waist, she knew her hair was a complete mess and yet he was looking at her like she was the sexiest thing in the world.

"Damn, Hailey," he hissed, reaching out and stroking a hand up her leg. "You certainly dress to impress."

Remembering how she had agonized over what to wear tonight – for Logan – she blushed and tried to fix her skirt. Jack's hand stopped her.

"Don't," he said firmly, his voice like a growl.

"I…I just feel a little foolish…"

"Yeah…I'm not gonna lie. I hate knowing you dressed like this for somebody else. But you're here with me now." He paused, his expression serious and a little vulnerable. "Do you want to be here with me, Hailey?" Slowly his hand began to slide over her leg—skimming her calf, her knee and finally her thigh.

She couldn't speak even if she wanted to. Slowly, she nodded.

A slow smile crossed Jack's face. "I need to hear you say the word." His hand was now tracing a lazy pattern on her thigh. "I need for you to tell me you want to be here with me."

Swallowing hard, Hailey licked her lips and met his gaze. "Yes."

"Thank God," he sighed right before he crawled over her and began kissing her again.

She was on sensory overload—that was the only way to describe it. Jack simply overwhelmed her—his size, his strength and his obvious desire for her. And as much as she was enjoying the way his hands were sensuously moving all over her, her own hands began to twitch with the need to touch him.

Normally, Hailey was very reserved in bed. Sex was always…nice. But when Jack's tongue began to trail down between her breasts, she almost bucked off of the bed. Reaching out, she tugged at the dark polo shirt he was wearing—pulling it up until Jack sat up and quickly pulled it off. Her eyes went wide at the sight of him.

Muscles.

And more muscles.

And then the tattoos.

Hailey swallowed hard because in all of her life she had never seen anything sexier than Jackson. Slowly, she raised her hand and touched him. Her palm rested lightly on his abs and when she looked up and met his gaze, she simply couldn't breathe. There was so much heat and need in those jade green depths that it almost scared her.

As much as she didn't want to look away, Hailey couldn't help but let her eyes wander all over his body. She had never understood the fascination that people had with six-pack abs or tattoos. But right now, she totally did. Tearing her gaze from his, Hailey looked at his body art.

There was some sort of tribal design on his right shoulder that trailed down onto his bicep. On his chest was a dark phoenix rising from the ashes and beside it was an ornate cross with the phrase "time waits for no man." The designs flowed together and across his chest to his other shoulder with a slightly less intense tribal design. Her fingers traced it all before looking up at Jackson's face.

“They’re beautiful,” she whispered.

A small smile played at his lips. “I didn’t think you were into them.”

“I had no idea they’d be so…sexy.”

A husky chuckle came out as Jack’s hands began

to lift her dress up over her hips. “I like you in white lace, Hailey.” One finger played with the pink bow at her hip bone. “It’s both sweet and sexy as hell.” He toyed with the bow before hooking his finger around it and pulling her panties off. When Hailey went to take her dress off completely, he stopped her. “Let me.”

He lifted the fabric slowly as if savoring every inch of her that was being revealed. And as much as Hailey was enjoying all of Jack’s attention, her body was craving more. Gently pushing his hands aside, she whipped the dress up and over her head and quickly removed the white lace bra too. Scooting up onto her knees so they were chest to chest, she gave him a sexy grin.

Jack’s breath was a little ragged as he looked his fill. “I was trying to go slow here, Hailey, and be gentle.”

“Somehow I get the feeling that’s not how you really are.” She leaned forward and kissed his chest. “And I don’t want slow and gentle.” She looked up at him.

“What do you want?” he asked, his voice a near growl.

"Everything."

In the blink of an eye she was on her back with Jackson sprawled over her as he kissed her. Her hands found their way up into his hair and she marveled at how thick it was and wondered why she thought he should cut it. It was a little thrilling to sink her fingers in and hold on.

When she said she wanted everything, Jack was clearly ready to deliver. He quickly stripped and was back to letting his lips and tongue kiss and discover every inch of her until she was crying out his name in pleasure.

And then he stopped.

"What?" she asked breathlessly. "What's the matter?"

"Condom," he said and then cursed. "I…shit!" Climbing off the bed, he spun around and stalked over to his overnight bag and began rummaging through it frantically.

"Jack?"

"Gimme a minute," he snapped.

"Ja-ack," she sang.

"I know I should have one in here." He cursed again

"Jackson," she sang out sweetly and when he turned around in frustration, she waved playfully at him, holding one of the condoms she had put in her purse.

His grin was slow and slightly predatory as he walked back over to the bed. Snatching the condom from her hand, he slowly crawled back up her body and took her hands and braced them on the pillow behind her head. “Brace yourself, Princess,” he growled.

There was something incredibly exciting about his warning, Hailey thought, and rather than scare her, it made her want to be bold. Wrapping her legs around his waist she whispered, “Bring it.”

And that unleashed everything. Foreplay was over, Jack shifted and slid right into her as Hailey gasped his name. Jack looked down into her face as he filled her over and over and she loved the play of emotion she saw there. But for as much as she did, she needed more—more of a connection to him as she felt herself climbing toward another release. Her hands were being held down by one of his so she couldn’t simply pull him down toward her.

Panting his name, begging him for more, she finally said, “Kiss me, damn you!” and he did. And then he kept on kissing her until they both found their release.

When Jack rolled beside her and tucked her in at his side, Hailey knew her world was never going to be the same.

And for the first time since she walked into Jack’s room, she was afraid.

****

Ella was sound asleep in the next bed and Angie was wide awake in hers. She and Sean had been texting back and forth for an hour—mainly because she didn't want to keep Ella awake by talking on the phone.

So far they'd covered all of the usual topics and Angie was fine with that. It was safe—the weather, food, sports—she would be fine just as long as they didn't get into anything personal. She told him about her rough week at work and how she was growing tired of working for someone else.

And yes, in her mind, work was still [illegible] and neutral topic.

Sean hadn't responded in a few minutes and she took the time to get up and grab a bottle of water before crawling back into bed. Her phone beeped a minute later with his reply.

Sean: I'm coming over tomorrow and taking you to dinner

Angie: What?

Sean: I was going to surprise you, but I didn't want to risk missing you

Angie: How did we go from talking about work to this?

Sean: I thought you could tell me more about it in person

Angie: What if I already have plans?

Sean: Change them

If it weren't for the fact that she would certainly wake up Ella, she would have called him and given him a piece of her mind. She didn't like being told what to do and she certainly didn't like being manipulated. Glancing across the room, she almost considered risking it, but quickly changed her mind.

Sean: You still there?

Angie: Unfair

Sean: Why? Were you hiding? Lol

Angie: I feel like you're taking advantage of the fact that I can't freak out over text

Sean: Sure you can. There are plenty of angry emojis you can use

Angie: Smart ass

Sean: Ok...you're kind of right

Angie: At least you're being honest

Sean: Told you. I'm not messing around any more

Angie: I don't know what to say to that

Sean: Say yes

Angie: I don't know...

Sean: We'll go for some big-ass steaks. I know they're your favorite

Angie: Lol

Angie: It doesn't make me sound very girly

Sean: You're perfect exactly the way you are

Well that was a new one. No one had ever called her perfect. Angie knew her faults—and normally, so did everyone else. The fact that she was really being difficult with Sean and he was still working hard to win her over made her feel…hell…she wasn't exactly sure. For the first time in her life, she felt special.

Like she was good enough.

As much as she and the girls tended to cheer one another on no matter what the situation, there were still times when it didn't really make things better. After all, they were friends. Best friends. But as such, they were supposed to love each other—even when one of them was being unlovable. The simple fact that Sean not only accepted her bitchy attitude but still wanted to be around her told her that maybe he was telling the truth. Maybe he was done messing around.

And maybe—just maybe—she really was good enough.

Sean: Ang? You still there?

Angie: Yeah. I'm still here

Sean: If you don't want me to come, I won't

Angie: I want you to come over. I want to go to dinner with you

Sean: Are you sure?

Angie: Yes

Sean: Is it me or just the steak?

Angie: Would it be wrong if I said both?

Sean: Lol

Sean: No it wouldn't be wrong.

Angie: Whew!

This was one of the things she had always enjoyed about her relationship with Sean—the bantering. Whether they were talking on the phone or in person, they had a similar sense of humor which meant no one got offended.

It also meant they never had any real in-depth conversations.

Over the last couple of weeks, Sean had been trying and occasionally, Angie had let her guard down and shared some aspects of her life she normally reserved for her talks with the girls. And the great thing was…Sean actually listened to her. He didn't try to fix anything and he didn't offer her any advice. He simply listened because he knew she needed to vent.

If she had to take a guess, she'd say their time for keeping everything light and breezy was slowly coming to an end. Not completely, but she was going to have to do more than go for laughs when they talked.

Dammit.

Sean: What time should I be there?

Angie: We should be back in town around three

Sean: Don't worry, I won't be sitting and waiting on your porch

Angie: You could if you wanted to

Sean: Don't tempt me

Angie: How about we say 5?

Sean: I can do that

Angie: K

Sean: It's late. I'm sure you're tired so I'm going to say goodnight

Angie: Yeah. It's been a long day

Even though she was tired, Angie knew she could have kept talking to him all night. It seemed crazy how all of a sudden—over just a few short sentences—she actually wanted to talk more. She sighed. Tomorrow night would be here soon enough and if she really put her mind to it, she could possibly surprise him by being the first one to stray from safe topics of conversation.

Maybe.

Sean: I'll see you tomorrow

Angie: Yes you will

Sean: Goodnight <3

Angie: Goodnight <3

Seven

"Okay, is somebody going to explain to me why I had to give up my waffles in bed so we could be in the car this early?" Angie asked.

It was nine in the morning on Saturday and they were all back in Becca's car. "That's what I'd like to know," Becca said sleepily. "I was perfectly content to sleep in this morning and had planned on one of you driving my car home so I could ride with Max."

"Yeah well…sorry," Hailey said quietly from the back seat. "I just…I needed…I couldn't stay at the hotel a minute longer. I had to leave."

"Oh no," Ella cried. "Was it because of Logan? Did last night not go well?"

Angie turned in her seat and faced them. "Was the sex bad? Like awkward bad?" Then she gasped. "Are you totally traumatized by the whole thing?"

Becca pulled out of the parking lot and onto the highway. "In case anyone was wondering, I had great sex last night and was hoping for more of it this morning!"

"Oh shut up," Angie sighed. "We spotted your good-sex glow from across the lobby. You can brag later. Clearly we have an emergency here."

"Right. Sorry, Hails," she said while looking in the rearview mirror.

"No problem."

"So?" Ella asked. "What happened?"

"Logan's gay."

"What?" they all cried.

Hailey nodded. "It's true."

"And he waited until you got him alone in your room to tell you?" Becca asked. "That's just wrong."

"No, no, no," Hailey said and then she told them about her interactions with Logan—and George—at the hotel bar. "And you know what the strange part is? I was kind of relieved."

"Okay…so…that's a good thing, right?" Ella asked uncertainly.

Hailey nodded. "It was like I didn't have to feel bad about being disappointed about Logan not having the kind of career I wanted him to have or of him falling short of my crazy expectations. And…FYI…George is a lawyer."

"Go figure," Angie said.

"I know," Hailey agreed.

"Wait…so now I'm confused. If you didn't sleep with Logan and things went well with him—and George—last night, why did you want to leave so early?" Ella asked.

Hailey groaned.

"Oh my God! You totally slept with someone

else!" Angie cried, clapping her hands excitedly. "Am I right? Am I right? Who was it? Was he hot?"

Hailey groaned again.

"Well that's not a good sign," Becca said.

Ella reached over and squeezed Hailey's hand. "It can't be that bad."

"Trust me…it is."

Ella looked worriedly at each of her friends before focusing on Hailey again. "Are you okay? I mean…are you…are you hurt?"

Hailey shook her head.

"Okay, you're starting to freak us all out, Hails," Angie said. "What happened? Use your words!"

"It was Jack," Hailey mumbled.

"Who?" Becca asked. "I can't hear her."

Hailey mumbled his name again.

Angie turned the radio off and spun back around. "Who?"

"It was Jack!" Hailey cried out. "I slept with Jack! Jackson! There! Did you hear it that time?"

There was a collective gasp.

"I know," she said, placing her hands over her face. "I can't believe it either."

"There is no way you are going to tell me the sex was bad," Angie said. "That man is like sex on a stick."

Hailey shook her head, refusing to look up.

"So wait…was the sex bad or not?" Ella asked. "I'm not sure what exactly you're shaking your head about."

That made Hailey look up. "The sex was incredible. Off-the-charts fantastic."

"But…" Becca prompted.

"But…it was…it was a mistake," Hailey replied with a shaky breath.

Angie's gaze narrowed at her. "Uh-uh. No way. I'm not buying it. No one says incredible sex is a mistake. It just doesn't happen."

"Why would you think it's a mistake, Hails?" Becca asked.

Ugh. Where did she even begin?

"We've got a three-hour drive," Angie reminded her, "and nothing to do but wait you out. Your choice."

"Fine. Okay. The sex was…amazing. It was wild and intense and…and I've never felt so completely out of control in my entire life!"

"O-kay," Ella said cautiously. "That's still not a bad thing."

"No, I know that," Hailey replied, "but it just never should have happened. I got all dressed up for

Logan. I was prepared for a night with *Logan*."

"Yeah, but it was never going to happen," Becca said. "So you moved on. Not a big deal."

"But it is!" Hailey cried. "I don't even like Jack! He's rough and crude and…"

"Sexy as hell!" Angie yelled back. "And what exactly is your gripe with him? He's a nice guy—always friendly and helps out with all the shows. He's friends with everyone."

And that was really the million-dollar question. What *was* her gripe with him? Sure he was rough around the edges and had tattoos but…she groaned out loud as she remembered licking each and every one of those tattoos.

"Someone's having her aha moment," Ella sang and then giggled. "Sorry."

"No. You're right. I am having an aha moment," Hailey said. "I'm being a snob again!"

"Oh no," Angie grumbled. "Not this shit again."

"Hailey…" Becca began.

"It's true! I look at Jack and I'm like…tattoos, get a haircut and I'm totally judging him because of how he looks!"

"Then you're judging him completely wrong," Angie said with a grin. "Because the man is seriously hot. He's got the whole bad boy thing going on. It's very attractive. Ask any of the other models. Hell, I'm sure even Logan thinks he's hot!"

“Please…I can’t even think of that.” She paused. “And he may be nice to everyone but he’s normally teasing me about something.”

“Okay but it’s just that—teasing. He’s not mean, Hails,” Ella said. “He tried to warn you not to go and hit on Logan and then he was there when you did. Did he tease you or mock you for it afterwards?”

Hailey shook her head.

“If he was going to tease you and be mean about it, there was his perfect opportunity,” Angie said. “So really, you gotta give him points for that one because he could have totally rubbed your face in it.”

“You’re right. All of you. I know it, but…” Hailey sighed, “but it doesn’t change everything. I can’t take back sleeping with Jack, but it’s all that’s going to happen. It certainly can’t happen again.”

“Why not?” Becca asked. “If you said the sex was great and you can admit that you misjudged him, why not let it happen again?”

“Well…”

“Oh my God…you snuck out on him!” Ella cried out, gasping. “You totally ditched him this morning and did the walk of shame to your room and that’s why we had to leave!”

Hailey felt the blush heating her body from head to toe.

“You didn’t wake him up before you left?” Angie asked, her eyes a little wide.

"No," Hailey said quietly. "I…I pretty much put my dress on, grabbed my shoes and purse and left."

"So there's no trace of you in the room?" Ella asked. "Not even a note?"

Hailey shook her head. "I…my panties are still there. I couldn't find them so I just…left."

Silence.

And more silence.

And still more silence.

"Oh come on!" Hailey finally said. "Now you all decide to clam up? You've had a hell of a lot to say about just about everything over the years and this is the thing that makes everyone go quiet? Seriously?"

Becca cleared her throat. "Okay. I'll go first." She paused. "Personally, I think you're scared. I think that on some level you *do* have feelings for Jack—that aren't hate—and last night meant more to you than you're willing to admit."

"I'm not so sure about that," Angie interrupted. "I'm going to need more info for clarification purposes."

"Oh God…" Hailey groaned.

"Who initiated the sex?" Angie asked.

"He took me to his room," Hailey said defensively.

"Yeah, yeah, yeah…he took you to his room.

Maybe he took you there to make sure you were okay after finding out that the guy you've been chasing after has a boyfriend. Did you ever think of that?"

"No."

"Okay, so the question still stands—who initiated the sex? Who kissed who?"

"I did," Hailey said quietly, staring down at her hands.

"What? You did?" Becca asked from the front seat giddily. "I can't believe you made the first move! I'm so proud of you!"

"I practically climbed him like a tree," Hailey said and covered her face again.

"Okay, no more of that," Ella said, pulling Hailey's hands down. "You're a big girl who obviously went after what she wants, so what's the problem?"

"Kissing isn't sex," Angie commented blandly. "So you kissed him. You've kissed other guys without it leading to sex. We all have."

"Not me," Ella murmured.

"Not the time, El," Becca replied.

"We kissed and then Jack carried me over to the bed. He asked if I wanted to stay and I said yes." Hailey looked at her friends. "So it was really a mutual thing. My throwing myself at him pretty much put the whole thing in motion."

"And you're going to sit there and honestly say you're fine with it never happening again?" Angie asked with disbelief. "For real?"

"Why was it okay for me to have a fling with Logan and not Jack?" Hailey asked accusingly. "Why was everyone on board with me having *one* wild night with Logan and walking away but now that I went and did that with Jack, I'm wrong?" Her voice was nearing hysteria and she sat back with a huff and turned her gaze out the window.

The next ten miles were spent in silence. Becca pulled off the highway and into the parking lot of an IHOP. Without a word, she turned the car off and climbed out. By the time she was opening the door to the restaurant, Hailey, Ella and Angie were right behind her. Once they were seated, she looked at her friends and smiled.

"It seemed like a good time for a waffle break," she said.

As soon as their orders were placed, Hailey apologized. "I shouldn't have freaked out like that," she began and then turned to Becca. "I'm sorry you had to leave Max this morning." Then she turned to Angie. "I'm sorry I got pissy with you." When she looked at Ella, she chuckled. "And I'm sorry you think all of this crazy bullshit that we all go through with relationships is even remotely appealing to you. Cherish what you have with Dylan because seriously, this stuff is painful."

They all laughed.

"Since we're all feeling a little calmer," Ella began, "I think maybe we should put all serious conversations to the side—at least during breakfast."

"Agreed," Hailey said, reaching for the coffee they'd just been served.

"I heard your mom finalizing the plans for next weekend's barbecue," Becca said to Hailey. "I think it's a great idea. I'm glad she's doing it."

"Me too. I thought she was going to wait until the end of the summer to do it, but she was so excited that she couldn't wait. She's always wanted to do it but my dad's been a bit of a stickler about it," Hailey replied.

"Why?"

"He feels like she already spends too much time on the business and when she's home with him, he wants to spend time with her—without anything related to weddings. So I'm surprised she got him to go for it."

"I would imagine it's hard for him," Ella said. "She does give all of herself to the brides and the business and then every weekend with the shows…but then again, your dad always seemed to have the patience of a saint."

"I think so too," Hailey said. "But lately it feels like they're just co-existing with each other."

"Do you think your mom will ever retire?" Angie asked.

Hailey shook her head. "I can't see her doing it. She keeps talking about me taking over the business, but I've told her a thousand times, I couldn't compete with her. And seeing how much of herself she gives to it, I don't know if I'm willing to do that."

"To be fair, it wasn't always like that," Becca commented. "The business has grown so much and if you took it over, she'd be there to help you in the beginning and then you could get an assistant and delegate."

"I suppose. I still don't know. I do love working with the brides and our shows but…I don't know if I'd love it if I had to do it for the rest of my life."

"Your mom is lucky," Angie began. "She found something she loves to do and made a career out of it. I envy that." She took a sip of her own coffee. "I don't think any of us can say the same."

"I know I can't," Becca said. "Although, someday I'd like to think that I'll be brave enough to leave the security of my cubicle and take the risk…do my own thing."

"I think you'd make an awesome café owner," Hailey said.

"Thanks."

"At least you guys have some idea about what you want to do," Ella said. "I hate to admit it but…I don't have any dream job. I really want to be a mom. I always have. And not a working mom, but a stay-at-home mom, full-time." She sighed. "Don't get me wrong, I love working at the daycare center and I get to snuggle babies all day long, but I'd like to stay home and someday just snuggle my own babies." She looked up at them sheepishly. "I know you all probably think it's lame…"

"Why would you even say that, El?" Becca asked. "When have we ever put you down about anything?"

Ella shrugged. "Well…you all make fun of me because of how I feel about missing out on stuff because I've only ever dated Dylan."

"Oh geez," Angie mumbled. "Again? Didn't we talk about this last night?"

"Fine. Yes we did. But I can't help how I feel. My life is…barreling forward like crazy and I feel very alone in the whole thing." She held up a hand to stop Angie before she could interrupt. "I know what you said last night and I get it. I do. But that doesn't just make these feelings go away."

"Seriously, I thought we were going to eat waffles and talk about the weather," Angie said with a hint of exasperation. "Why is everyone in crisis mode right now?"

Hailey turned to Angie. "You're in a crisis? What crisis? I thought things were going well with Sean?"

"And I thought we weren't going to talk about this stuff over breakfast," Angie snapped. "All I want is a Belgian waffle and some breezy conversation. Is that too much to ask?"

"And we're back to snippy again," Becca murmured. "Awesome."

They all grew silent, sipping their coffees and checking their phones until the waitress brought out their meals. After a few bites, Becca put her fork down and sighed.

"So sex with Max is like the best sex. Ever!" she said with a huge grin and then burst out laughing. "I'm not kidding you, the man is like some sort of sex god. I've had more orgasms in the last week than I have since I lost my virginity!"

And just like that, things went back to normal.

****

Angie angrily stared at the pile of clothes on her closet floor. "This should not be this difficult," she muttered as she went back to searching for something to wear. Sean was due to arrive in a little less than an hour and she wasn't pleased with any item of clothing she owned.

Stomping from the closet in her bra and panties, she tripped over Trampus on her way to grab her phone. Scrolling quickly, she pulled up Hailey's number.

"Hey, Ang!"

"Okay, I am officially freaking out."

"Uh-oh..."

"Yeah. Uh-oh. I'm totally screwed here."

"What's going on? Is Sean still coming?"

"He is but I can't find anything to wear! Everything is either too dressy or too casual or too squeezy…"

"Squeezy?"

"You know, too tight to go out to eat in. And I really don't want to break out the Spanx. I'm not prepared for that kind of workout."

"Plus it would suck later when you're trying to undress each other," Hailey said and then snickered.

"Seriously not helping right now! What do I do?"

"Okay," Hailey began, sounding serious, "where are you going for dinner?"

"I don't know."

"Then how do you know what you've picked out is too dressy or too casual?"

Angie sighed with annoyance. "Okay, let's just assume we're going fairly casual. At least I hope we are. I'm not going to put on jeans and a t-shirt!"

"Of course you're not," Hailey said patiently. "You can do a step up from that and still look nice—without looking like you're trying to impress." She paused. "Or are you trying to impress?"

"I don't know what the hell I'm doing. Honestly,

I wish he would have just said he was bringing over a pizza or tacos. I would be totally cool with that."

"You are going to have to come to grips with this new phase of your relationship. It's obvious Sean is looking for more than dirty weekends and booty calls."

"Booty call? Did you seriously just use that phrase?"

"What? It's still a thing," Hailey said defensively. "And I thought you wanted my help."

"You're right, you're right. Sorry."

"Okay then…the weather is great tonight so I think you should go with a pair of capris—preferably your black ones—and the turquoise halter with the little bit of beading on it that you wore last month when we went out to celebrate Becca's birthday."

Angie stepped back into her closet and found the outfit and examined it. "You don't think the halter is too much?"

"Too much what?"

"Is the beading too fancy?"

"You wore it to the Cheesecake Factory. I think you're safe."

"I really could do with a little less sarcasm right now, Hails. I'm already on edge!"

"I don't understand why you're freaking out so much. It's a date. A date with a guy who you've already been in a relationship with. I could see if this was a first date or even a blind date, but you and Sean were pretty exclusive before he…"

"Took off without telling me and blew me off?"

"You know, when you say it, it sounds really bad," Hailey said. "And he's already explained it to you and apologized for it so you have to decide if you're going to let it go or if you're going to keep harping on it."

Collapsing on her bed and lying down, Angie let out another sigh. "For the most part I'm over it. Just every once in a while it comes back and bites me in the ass and makes me crazy."

"So what are you going to do about it? Because you know you'll never be able to have a decent relationship with Sean if you're going to let this thing keep creeping in."

"I just don't know how to *not* let it keep creeping in," she replied honestly. "And on top of that, I don't know how to handle this change in the relationship."

"Why?"

"It was casual before, you know? We would meet up for a weekend, have crazy-monkey sex and then go our separate ways. There were flirty texts and calls but it was all about what we were going to do the next time we got together. Now…now it's like a real relationship. Sean wants to talk to me—like really talk to me—and he wants me to talk to him."

"And not your usual snarky stuff."

"Exactly."

"Okay, *now* I see why you're freaking out."

"What do I do? How do I not act like a complete babbling idiot because I'm feeling self-conscious?"

"How about telling him that?"

"Seriously?"

"Uh-huh. When Sean gets there tonight, sit him down and tell him how you're feeling a little out of your comfort zone."

"He'll think I'm being an idiot."

"No," Hailey countered, "he'll appreciate that you're really talking to him—that you're trusting him with your feelings and it will open the door for some good dialogue between the two of you."

"Sounds like a damn episode of Dr. Phil."

"Get all that snarkiness out now, my friend, because you're going to need to reel it in later."

"Dammit." Looking at her bedside clock, she cursed. "I've got to go and get dressed. He'll be here in about fifteen minutes."

"Call me tomorrow and let me know how it goes."

"I will," Angie said. "And Hails?"

"Yeah?"

"Thanks."

Once she hung up the phone, Angie sprang into action. She pulled on the capris and then the halter and after looking in the mirror, she frowned. There was no way to wear the halter with a bra. Technically she already knew that but didn't want to seem like she was being slutty for not wearing one. Pulling it off, she readjusted everything and then checked her reflection. "Hails may be a little bat-shit crazy, but she's an excellent fashion consultant," she murmured as she walked back to her closet.

It looked like a bomb had gone off in there and not wanting to deal with it, she simply kicked everything into a corner, turned off the light and shut the door. Her bedroom was spotless because…well…because she had a feeling she knew how the night was going to end. So she had spent a little extra time tidying up and changing the sheets and making sure everything was in order.

Truth be known, she missed that part of her relationship with Sean. Not that sex was the only thing she missed, but they had physically clicked from the get-go and Angie knew from experience that that sort of connection wasn't easy to come by. They may both go into this date thinking it's a getting-to-know-you-again thing, but she knew if she had her way, this was where they'd end up.

Fingers crossed.

Walking out to the living room, she smiled when she heard the knock on the door at exactly five. Her smile grew when she opened the door and saw Sean standing there. He was dressed somewhat casually in a dark pair of jeans and a dress shirt that was untucked. “Hey,” she said as she moved aside to let him in.

“Hey yourself,” he said softly, kissing her on the cheek. “How are you doing?”

Did she just throw it out there now about how she was unnerved or did she wait?

“Good,” she said, opting to wait. “I’m good.” She shut the door and turned to see him taking a seat on the couch. “Can I get you something to drink?”

Sean shook his head. “I’m good. Thanks.” He seemed very relaxed as he made himself comfortable. “I’m sorry that I missed meeting you in Charlotte yesterday and seeing the show. What time did you get home?”

“Just a little after noon.”

His eyes went a little wide. “Wow…that’s earlier than you thought. Everything okay?”

Sitting down at the opposite end of the sofa, she told him about the morning’s drama. By the time she was done, she couldn’t help but laugh. “All I wanted was some damn waffles and it turned into a soap opera.”

Sean chuckled. “So is everyone okay now?”

“For now,” she said. “Hailey’s going to have to deal with this situation her own way. Jack’s not going away—she’s going to have to see him next weekend whether she likes it or not. Ella’s having her own mini-breakdown but at least she's talking about it. Not that long ago she would have kept it bottled up. And Becca? Well…I have a feeling this thing with Max is going to get serious. Fast."

"And is that a good thing?"

Nodding, Angie said, "I think so. He's a really nice guy and from what I can tell, he's just as crazy about her as she is for him. She's never dated anyone like Max before so I'm sure it's a little weird for her."

"Why do women go for guys who aren't good for them?" he asked with a grin. "I never understood that."

She shrugged. "Because we always think we're going to be the ones to change them."

"Is that what you thought when you met me?" he teased. "That you were going to change me?"

She laughed out loud. "Actually, I wasn't thinking that at all. I was thinking we were going to do the traditional maid of honor/best man thing."

He looked at her with confusion.

"You know, we'd sleep together after the wedding and that would be it."

"Wow…that was brutally honest."

"Why lie about it?" she asked and then let out a small nervous laugh. "When we first met, I wasn't thinking about long-term relationships. You lived in New York, I lived here and…you know…that was it."

He nodded as his expression sobered. "And what about now?"

"What about it?"

"Where do you see us now?"

Okay, here it was. Time to throw it all out there and deal with the consequences. "I don't know where I see us," she began honestly. "I was really happy with the way things were…before. And then…"

"I left and screwed up everything," he supplied.

She smiled slightly. "Yeah. That."

Sean stretched out his arms along the back of the sofa. "What does that mean, Angie? I've told you what I want—where I want us to go from here. But if you can't forgive me because of it, then I don't want to waste your time."

"What about your time?" she asked cautiously.

He shrugged. "I'm willing to put in the time—just as long as I know there's a chance. You're worth the wait."

Well damn.

Swallowing hard, Angie slowly rose to her feet. "I can't make any promises to you, Sean. Not right now. I'd like to think there's a chance, but…I can't guarantee it. But I'd like to try."

He stood and took her hands in his and gently squeezed. "Then that's what we'll do," he said softly. "We'll try."

****

Meanwhile, Ella was busy making a romantic dinner for Dylan. Since they'd moved in together two years ago, they rarely spent a night apart. The times when she traveled with Enchanted Bridal for one of their events were the only reason they did—and occasionally Dylan went with her. It was crazy how after all their years together, she still managed to miss him after only one night apart.

Looking around the kitchen, she smiled. Everything was cooking. She'd made all of Dylan's favorites—pot roast, mashed potatoes, carrots, biscuits and gravy. It wasn't glamorous or gourmet, but it was what he loved and Ella enjoyed making it for him.

With nothing left to do – the table was set and the food was doing its thing—she sat down and sighed. Right now, she thought, Angie was out on a real date with Sean. It was—according to Angie—their first date. Ella could only imagine the anxiety her friend must have felt while getting ready and probably during those first few minutes of the date.

In another part of town Hailey was probably still beating herself up over her night with Jack. Personally, Ella thought the two of them were pretty much perfect for each other. Jack seemed like the type of guy who could be a really good balance for Hailey. He would help her to relax once in a while and have some fun and not be so serious and task-oriented all the damn time. Unfortunately, Ella knew that was something Hailey was going to have to figure out for herself. With any luck, Jack wouldn't be content to just sit back and let Hailey get away with walking out on him this morning.

And then there was Becca. Ella chuckled. If their conversation on the last leg of their trip home was anything to go by, she was fairly certain that by now, Becca and Max were together at Max's place picking up where they'd left off this morning. "Good for her," Ella said with a smile. Out of the four of them, Becca seriously had the worst luck with boyfriends. And if there was one thing Ella knew for certain, it happened because Becca tended to choose guys who were all wrong for her. Max was completely different from the rest and she had a good feeling that he was the one for her friend.

"And then there's me," she sighed. It bothered her that so much was…well…bothering her lately. All of the things Ella loved about her relationship with Dylan now seemed to make her feel silly. Inferior. Boring. Having a romantic dinner at home used to be something she would brag about, but now? Not so much.

Looking around the kitchen—the one she'd decorated with her theme of country-chic—she realized it was nice. It was cute.

It was boring.

Standing up, Ella walked with a sense of purpose up the stairs to the bedroom and looked at herself in the full-length mirror and frowned. She looked cute. She looked nice. In a pair of faded blue jeans and a pink tank top she still managed to look…boring.

Feeling defeated, she slowly dropped to the floor and sat down.

That's where Dylan found her.

"Hey, beautiful," he said with a smile as he walked into the room. "What's going on up here?" He sat down beside her on the floor and kissed her soundly before letting her answer. "The scent of dinner hit me as soon as I opened the door. It smells great."

For a minute, all of her worries vanished. Ella felt pride in Dylan's compliment and then nothing but pure happiness.

And then she remembered.

"Hey," he said softly, tucking a finger under her chin. "What's wrong?"

For the next ten minutes Ella rambled on about everything that was going on with the girls.

"O-kay," Dylan said slowly. "So you're upset because your friends are…?"

How could she even explain it? It barely made any sense to her! "Do you think we're boring?" she finally blurted out.

Dylan's eyes went wide. "What? No. Why?"

Ella shrugged. "Everyone is out doing something right now. Something exciting and we're just here—sitting at home and having dinner. We're young, Dylan, and we live like we're old! We don't really do anything anymore."

"We've been busy planning a wedding, El," he reminded her. "We agreed to cut back on going out and doing stuff so we could put the money toward that." He paused and studied her. "What is going on with you?" He rose to his feet. "Honestly, it seems like lately you're just not happy."

Ella got up and faced him, but couldn't make herself speak.

"Ella, we've been together for too long for you to keep stuff from me. How can I help you if you won't talk to me?" he asked sadly.

The next thing she knew she was wrapped up in Dylan's arms because she had burst into tears. She had no idea how long she cried, but Dylan never let her go. He would kiss the top of her head, whisper how he was there for her and how everything was going to be all right. When she finally felt like she could compose herself, Ella raised her head and looked at him.

"I'm sorry."

For the first time ever, Dylan looked worried.

"I don't know why all of a sudden these things are bothering me. I look at everyone around us and see the things they're doing or hear about how they're feeling and…and it all seems foreign to me. It's like I'm some sort of weirdo."

"Ella…"

"And then I look around here and we have a cute

house. It has nice furniture. I wear cute clothes…and it's all so damn boring that I want to scream!" She jumped up and began to pace. "When did we become these people, Dylan? When did we just morph into this couple who's steady and staid and… boring?"

Without a word, Dylan walked into their master bathroom and washed his hands and face. Then he changed his clothes out of the ones he'd worn to work all day. When he was finally done, he leaned against his dresser and faced Ella. "You know what? I don't see us that way and I find it offensive that you do." His voice was completely calm but his expression bordered on fierce.

"Dylan…"

He held up a hand. "You had your say; now I'm having mine," he said firmly. "You want to know how I see us? I see us as people who work hard and are planning for our future. While everyone else is running around—or sleeping around—we're committed to each other. We're not pissing away our money at bars and clubs. We're making sure we're putting money into savings for retirement and college funds for our kids. We don't live beyond our means and we decorated within our budget because we know this is our starter home and someday we'll upgrade."

"I know, but…"

"You're looking around and thinking 'look at all we're missing' and acting like it's a bad thing. I'm looking at all the same people and thinking about it all with relief! You know what, El? I bet if you asked any of them, they'd all rather be us! We've got our shit together! And you know what? They're right! There's security in that that people want!"

"Dylan..."

"If you asked a majority of the people we know what they'd rather have—the crazy bullshit of running around trying to find someone to spend their lives with or having their soul mate—they'd choose soul mate! If you asked those same people if they'd rather be out trolling bars and clubs on the weekend or being totally themselves at home with someone they love, they'd choose staying home!"

Shame washed over her.

He was right.

But before she could utter a word, Dylan spoke up. "I don't know what it is you're looking for," he said, his voice back to being calm and level. "If you're looking to go out clubbing or being immersed in drama, I can't give that to you. It's not who I am. I used to feel confident in what I was giving you and in what we had. Clearly I was wrong."

He walked over and sat on the bed and put his shoes back on and Ella wasn't sure what to do or say to him. When he stood, he looked at her sadly.

"So go," he said quietly. "Go and figure out what it is you want, Ella. I won't stand in your way. All I've ever wanted is for you to be happy. If I'm not able to do that—or be that—for you, then I'm willing to step aside."

Her tears came back in earnest but she couldn't

form a single word. Dylan was moving around the room and putting clothes in a duffel bag.

"I'll be at my folks' place if you need me," he said solemnly.

"Dylan," she finally forced out. "Don't! Please!" Reaching out, she grabbed his arm to stop him from leaving the room. "That's not what I want!"

He smiled sadly at her and reached up with his free hand and caressed her cheek. "The thing is, El…I don't think you really know what you want right now. And I don't want to stay here feeling like I'm the reason you're not happy."

"It's not like that!" she cried frantically. "That wasn't what I was saying!"

Leaning in, Dylan placed a gentle kiss on the tip of her nose. "You may not think that's what you're saying, but it is."

And for the first time in all their years together Dylan walked out and Ella had no idea if he was ever going to come back.

When she heard the front door close, she ran down the stairs after him. But she was too late. By the time she was out on the front porch, Dylan's truck was already pulling out of the driveway.

Ella didn't know what to do. He was her rock, her center of gravity, her…everything! What had she done? Turning quickly, she went back into the house and turned off the oven and began a frantic search for her own shoes and car keys. Her vision was completely hampered by the tears she couldn't seem to stop.

She made it out to her car and even had herself buckled in when she finally stopped. There was no way she could drive like this. No way to get herself even out of the driveway without crashing. And that just made her cry even harder.

If it were any other time or any other situation, Ella knew she could pick up the phone and call one of the girls or even her mother, but this time she was on her own. Why? Because how could she explain to them how she'd essentially ruined the greatest relationship of her life over…what?

Nothing.

Everyone had jitters before their wedding. Everyone had doubts. Why couldn't she look at her life and realize that she was the lucky one and not everyone else?

And how was she going to convince Dylan that she was so sorry?

Eight

“I don’t understand. Why wouldn’t she call us?” Hailey asked, grabbing the bag of takeout from her car.

Becca shrugged. “This is bad, right? Like…really bad.”

Angie nodded. “I’ve been calling her all afternoon and she’s not answering her phone.”

“Maybe she just wants to be alone,” Becca said sadly. “Maybe we shouldn’t be here.”

The three of them stood in Ella’s driveway, each holding their own contribution to the evening—Hailey had the Chinese takeout, Becca had brownies and Angie had the wine. It was a tradition they had started as soon as they were of drinking age—when one of them was in crisis mode, the other three would rally around them with the necessities.

Food.

Chocolate.

Wine.

It was the first time they had to do it for Ella.

“I have to admit,” Hailey said as they walked toward the front door, “I’m not sure how to handle this.”

“What do you mean?”

She stopped. "Ella's ever the optimist. She's everyone's cheerleader. In all our lives, have you ever known her to have a crisis?" Hailey asked.

"There was the whole thing with her mom a few weeks ago," Angie stated.

"Yeah but…she kept it bottled up and then when it came to a head it wasn't anything big. She sort of said her piece and moved on. Ella's quiet and normally nothing keeps her down." Hailey looked at Becca. "You were the one who saw Dylan. How did he look?"

"I almost wanted to cry for him," she said quietly. "He looked so sad, so broken…I'm telling you it was heartbreaking."

"You roomed with her Friday night," Hailey said, turning to Angie. "Did she say anything to you?"

Angie quickly filled them in on her conversation with Ella and then shrugged. "It's the same stuff she's been saying for a while now. I didn't get the vibe that she was going to pull the plug on her and Dylan though."

"I'm stumped," Hailey said with a sigh.

"Yeah well, maybe we need to actually go inside and talk to her so we won't be stumped," Becca said with a hint of irritation. Then she reached into her pocket and pulled out her keys. "If she won't answer the phone, chances are she's not going to answer the door. Unless either of you have a problem with it, if she doesn't let us in after five minutes, I'm using my emergency key."

Angie chuckled and walked up to the front door and knocked. Hard. "Um…yeah. Because suddenly we're all about having manners. Give me a break."

It soon became obvious that Ella wasn't going to open the door so Becca moved forward with her key and opened the door. The house was dark and if it wasn't for the fact that Ella's car was in the driveway, they would have questioned if she was even home. Hailey quickly put the food down in the kitchen and opened some windows. There were pots and pans on the stove and the entire place smelled of rotting food.

Wordlessly, they each moved about the downstairs opening more windows and turning on lights. Then, together, they walked up the stairs. The master bedroom door was open and one small bedside lamp was on. There was a collective sigh of relief when they saw Ella's small form curled up under the blankets.

"I hate to wake her," Becca whispered.

"Maybe we should clean up downstairs first and then wake her up," Hailey suggested quietly.

"Screw that," Angie said, full-volume. "The pity party ends now! Clearly something's wrong and letting her wallow any longer isn't really helping anyone." With that, she walked over to the bed and shook Ella's shoulder. Hard.

"Wh…what?" Ella said groggily.

"Get up," Angie snapped. "Now."

Rubbing her eyes, Ella rolled onto her back before slowly sitting up. Her short hair was sticking out in every direction and her eyes were red. "What are you guys doing here? How did you get in?" Then her eyes went wide. "Dylan? Did Dylan let you in? Is he back?" She went to climb from the bed but Angie's hand on her shoulder stopped her.

"Dylan's not here, El. Becca used her key to get us in. We've been calling you all day," Angie said, her voice softening.

And then Ella's eyes filled with tears. "Oh."

"Ella, sweetie," Hailey said, immediately coming to sit beside her on the bed. "Why didn't you call us and tell us what was going on?"

With a shrug, Ella hung her head as the tears began to fall. "I'm so ashamed," she said, her voice so low they barely heard her.

"Why?" Hailey asked softly, wrapping an arm around Ella and hugging her close.

"I handled everything so poorly. I hurt him," she said, looking up at the three of them. "That wasn't my intention. Ever. Dylan's the most kind-hearted person in the world and I hurt him." She paused and just let the tears come. "I'm so busy looking at what everyone else is doing and what they have that I completely missed how great everything I have is."

"You were freaking out," Angie said carefully, sitting on the edge of the bed. "You're allowed to freak out once in a while. That still doesn't explain why you wouldn't call us."

"I…I didn't want you to know. I didn't want anyone to know."

Becca crouched next to the bed. "Ella, in all the years we've known each other, have we ever judged one another?"

Ella shook her head.

"You've had to sit back and watch the three of us make bad decisions, huge mistakes and just be flat-out stupid. Did you ever judge us for them?" Becca asked.

Again Ella shook her head.

"Then why would you think it would be any different here and now?" Hailey asked. "Ella, honey…we're always going to be here for you no matter what. We may not understand exactly what you're going through, but we can still be here to listen and support you. You do that for us all the damn time. It's about time we get to do it for you."

"Really?" Ella asked weakly. "You're…you're not mad at me?"

They all laughed. "Why on earth would we be mad at you?" Becca asked.

"Because…I'm the reason Dylan left."

"Yeah well," Angie began, "that one certainly gets filed under 'not your smartest move,' but like

Hailey just said, we're here for you."

A small smile played at Ella's lips. "You guys are the best."

"And we brought food too," Becca said. "Are you hungry?"

Her smile faded. "I don't deserve to eat."

Angie rolled her eyes as she jumped up and tugged Ella from the bed. "Enough!" She spun Ella and pushed her in the direction of the bathroom. "You do deserve to eat. You need to eat. And you're going to eat."

"But…"

"But you need to shower first. So go and we'll take care of everything. Be downstairs in fifteen minutes or I'm coming to get you!" Angie said forcefully.

Ella stood in the doorway and gave them all another weak smile. "What would I do without you guys?"

"Good thing you'll never have to find out," Hailey said, coming to her feet. "Now go and shower and we'll meet you downstairs."

They all waited until they heard the shower turn on and then walked down the stairs.

And groaned.

"I don't know about you, but I'm kind of afraid to take the lids off of any of those pots," Becca said.

"Maybe we can just buy her some new pots," Angie suggested.

"Look, it's not going to be pretty," Hailey said firmly, "but if we all sit here and remember how many times Ella's been the one to hold our heads after we drank too much or made us homemade chicken soup when we were sick…"

"She did my laundry when I had the flu last year," Becca said.

"She watched Trampus for me and took him to the vet when he got sick and I was out of town," Angie added.

Then they all sighed.

"So basically we're not getting out of it," Angie stated. Taking a deep breath, she walked into the kitchen and said, "Let's do this."

****

Twenty minutes later Ella came down the stairs. She literally hadn't been down there since she came in from her car four days ago.

Since Dylan left.

Taking a steadying breath, she walked into the kitchen where she heard the girls talking. Hailey was reheating the takeout and putting it all out on the table, Becca was drying dishes and putting them away and Angie was uncorking the wine. The sight of her friends was enough to bring on a fresh wave of tears.

"I was getting ready to come up and get you,"

Angie said, pouring the wine.

Quickly wiping her eyes, Ella moved further into the room. "Yeah, I…uh…I needed a few extra minutes."

"Hungry?" Hailey asked, smiling. The entire table was set and the kitchen looked—and smelled—clean.

With a nod, Ella sat where Hailey motioned her to and then waited for the girls to all sit down. For a few minutes, it was all about serving the food and eating. When they started talking, much to Ella's surprise, it wasn't about her.

"So Sean's coming to the barbecue this weekend," Angie said casually.

"He's coming back to town again?" Hailey asked, brows furrowed. "Good thing he's his own boss."

"Actually…" Angie began, "he never left."

"What?" they all cried in unison.

She nodded. "Yeah…um…we went to dinner Saturday night and had a great dinner and stayed up all night talking. And…"

"Right," Becca teased. "Talking. Good one."

"It's true!" Angie cried and then laughed. "I'm not gonna lie to you; I was a little disappointed at first. I mean…I had totally prepared for him to spend the night."

"Clean sheets?" Hailey asked and Angie nodded.

"Shaved your legs?" Becca asked and Angie nodded.

"Sexy underwear?" Ella asked and Angie nodded.

"I even put out some of those scented candles that I figured I'd run in and light when we got back, but after dinner we walked around downtown, listened to a jazz trio that was playing and just…talked." She took a sip of her wine. "Then we got back to my place and I thought 'Okay, this is it' and Sean came in and sat on the couch and made no attempt to touch me."

"Wow," Hailey said and held up her wine glass. "Impressive."

"I know!" Angie agreed. "Honestly, I didn't know what to do with myself at first. He just kept talking and asking me questions about my job and my family and…you guys…and once I stopped obsessing over the fact that we weren't ripping each other's clothes off, I found that I kind of really liked talking with him."

"Good for you!" Becca said enthusiastically. "Seriously, that's awesome!"

"It is," Angie said.

"So how did he end up staying for so long?" Ella asked, thankful for all of the food in front of her. She hadn't realized how hungry she was until she came and sat down.

"When the sun came up Sunday morning, we were both exhausted. I was almost delirious as I climbed into bed." She paused and took a bite of her dumpling. "I asked Sean to join me and he told me no. He decided to sleep on the couch because he was too tired to go back to his hotel."

"Wait, wait, wait," Hailey interrupted. "He had a hotel room? Even though he knew you guys were going out?"

Angie nodded. "I know, how adorable is that?"

"I was going to say crazy but…whatever," Hailey murmured.

"Anyway, he slept on the couch and I went to bed and we got up around two in the afternoon and I made us lunch and afterwards, Sean went back to his hotel."

"Seriously?" Becca asked. "He was still holding out?"

Angie nodded again. "I know! We made plans to do dinner and a movie and he asked if I would meet him at the theater."

Ella held up her hand. "Wait…why? Why wouldn't he just come and pick you up? It was a date, right?"

"The theater was close to his hotel so I just thought…you know…we'd do the dinner and after the movie we'd go back to his room."

"And did you?" Hailey asked, pushing her plate aside.

"Nope. He walked me to my car and kissed me goodnight. On the cheek."

"Shut up!" Becca cried.

"No way!" Ella said at the same time.

"Yup. The sneaky bastard was making me crazy! I drove home talking to myself the entire time about what the hell was going on! I mean Sean and I had sex like bunnies from the get-go so I couldn't figure out why all of a sudden he was pulling back—especially when he'd been doing nothing but telling me how much he wanted a real relationship with me." Angie took another sip of her wine. "It didn't hit me until the next day that he was doing all of this to show me he's interested in more than just sex with me. It's kind of sweet if you think about it."

"Or incredibly frustrating," Becca said, taking another spoonful of shrimp with lobster sauce.

"A-ny-way…" Angie went on, "I decided to play along and see how things went. I mean…once I figured out what he was doing, I was able to relax a bit."

"And?" Hailey prompted.

"The next night we met up after work—he took me to dinner, we talked about my day and he told me about this project he and his brother are submitting a proposal on…yada, yada, yada…and he walked me out to my car and kissed me goodnight."

"On the cheek again?" Ella asked.

Angie nodded. “But then I turned my head and kissed the hell out of him.” She burst out laughing. “I’m talking I kissed him until he was weak in the knees!”

“Then what? Did you go back to his hotel?” Becca asked, a wide grin on her face.

Angie shook her head. “Nope. Once he was steady on his feet, I wished him a good night and drove home.”

“No!” they all yelled.

She nodded. “True story. And the whole way home I sang at the top of my lungs to every song on the radio—even that new Adele song that’s so depressing—and just felt so damn giddy!”

“Even during the sad song?” Ella asked, miffed. “How is that even possible?”

“It just was,” Angie said as she scooped up the last egg roll. “So I got home and texted him—like I always do so he knows I got home safely—and was feeling all kinds of proud of myself for being the one to leave him speechless. It was a good feeling.” She took a bite of her egg roll and noticed everyone was just staring at her. “What?”

“That’s it?” Hailey asked. “That’s the whole story?”

Angie grinned – the kind of grin only seen maybe on the Grinch. It was slow and just slightly evil.

“Actually…no. That’s not the whole story.”

Ella felt herself holding her breath. When Angie simply continued to munch on her food, Ella finally snapped. "Oh for the love of it! You cannot just end the story there! Out with it!"

Laughing, Angie reached over and hugged Ella. "There's my girl!" She straightened in her seat and looked at them. "So I was walking around the house getting ready for bed when there was a knock at the front door."

"Ooh…I bet I know what happens next!" Becca said giddily.

Angie nodded in agreement. "I knew it then too. But I drew it out just a little bit. Made him knock again before I went to open the door. And once I did, he tossed his suitcase through the door and then picked me up, kicked the door shut and carried me to bed." She sighed happily. "I didn't even go to work today."

"Nice," Hailey said approvingly. "Well played."

"I have my moments," Angie said with a shrug.

"And how do you feel about all of this? You okay with Sean pretty much moving in?" Hailey asked.

"I kind of am," she admitted. "I mean…I'm scared and nervous and I have no idea what's going to happen from here—and you know how I hate surprises—but I'm willing to give it a go."

"Wow," Hailey said with an approving smile. "I'm proud of you."

“I realized how I tend to sabotage my relationships because of the unknown,” Angie said. “Or I stay in relationships I know are bad for me just because they’re predictable. I figured I’d try something new and see if it sticks.”

“But…” Ella began cautiously, “what is it about Sean that made you want to take the risk?”

“Honestly? He’s the first guy who’s ever pushed me for more. Sean made me really look at our relationship and made me stop and take it seriously. We’re far from being settled or perfect and I have no idea if we’ll get married and live happily ever after and all that crap, but for the first time in my life I feel like it’s a possibility.”

“I feel that way with Max,” Becca said. “He’s so different from any guy I’ve ever dated and he just really has his life together. So much so that it makes me nervous.”

“Why would that make you nervous?” Hailey asked. “Security is a good thing. Everyone wants to have that.”

For a minute, Ella simply zoned out as Dylan’s words flashed through her mind. *I bet if you asked any of them, they’d all rather be us! We’ve got our shit together! And you know what? They’re right! There’s security in that that people want!*

“Yeah well…” Becca began, “I mean he’s *really*

got his shit together. And I’m still floundering in so many ways that I’m afraid he’s going to wake up and look at me and think I'm too much of a mess to be with."

"Becs, you're not a mess. You're a pretty stable chick too. You have a steady job, a home…why would you even think that about yourself?" Angie asked.

"I guess I'm still feeling the effects of past relationships. If I was so together, why couldn't I find a guy who wanted to stay with me? Why did my last boyfriend cheat on me?"

"Okay first," Hailey said firmly, "you can't even count Danny as a boyfriend. He was a mistake. A big one. And if you think about it realistically, every guy you date—who anyone dates—before you get married, isn't supposed to be the one. You're not supposed to want to stay with the wrong person. You're simply out…shopping…until you find the right one!"

"But the shopping is so exhausting!" Becca cried.

"And not nearly as satisfying as shopping for shoes," Angie said with a chuckle.

"Truth," they all agreed.

"Look, all I'm saying is that you shouldn't think about the ones who didn't stay," Hailey went on. "They weren't supposed to."

"Maybe Max won't either," Becca sighed.

"Maybe he will," Hailey countered. "You don't know that but if you keep looking back, you're never going to be able to enjoy what you have right now. And what you have is a great guy who is crazy about you."

Becca blushed. "He is pretty great."

"Promise us that you're not going to keep looking back—especially not at a loser like Danny—and comparing him to Max," Angie said. "Because honestly? That's just wrong. Max would never do to you what Danny did. Ever."

"I know…I know…old insecurities die hard though, right?" Becca asked and they all nodded.

By silent agreement they all got up and started clearing away the dinner dishes and made sure the kitchen was back in perfect order before taking their wine into the living room along with the brownies. Once seated, Ella felt like she needed to speak up.

"I don't know how to ask Dylan to come home." Three sets of eyes looked at her with sadness. "I haven't called him but…he hasn't called me either. I have no idea what I can possibly say that would make up for the way I behaved."

"Ella, I find it hard to believe you did anything crazy that Dylan can't get over. You really need to talk to him," Hailey said softly.

They were quiet for a minute before Ella told them how everything had happened days ago. Then she shook her head. "I don't even know how it escalated so quickly. I thought we were just talking and then he just calmly got up, changed his clothes and the next thing I know he's packing." She looked up at them. "It was like I was paralyzed. I couldn't comprehend what was going on but I couldn't stop it either."

Hailey looked at her other two friends before returning her focus to Ella.
"Ella…sweetheart…haven't the two of you ever had a fight before?"

Ella's heart was hammering in her chest as a blush crept up her cheeks. Rather than speak, she simply shook her head.

"How is that even possible?" Angie asked loudly. When everyone turned and looked at her with disbelief, she shrugged. "What? I'm serious here. How can two people be together for like fifteen years and never have a fight? It's not natural!"

"Okay, okay…" Becca interrupted. "No need to add to her stress right now."

"No, it's true," Ella said weakly. "I don't know how it's possible. We just always agreed on everything. It's been like that since the beginning. We were just always in sync with each other. Sure we'd disagree on some stuff—movies or food or silly stuff—but we never really fought. It was scary and I just about died when he walked out the door."

"Sweetie, you know fighting is a normal part of every relationship, right?" Hailey asked, her voice a little cautious.

"I don't," Ella said honestly, her voice getting stronger. "And why does it have to be? For all these years, Dylan and I have been fine without any arguing. I don't understand how this happened and why I should be okay with it!"

"All right, no one's saying you need to be okay with it," Hailey corrected, "but at the same time I'm saying that you don't have to be sitting here beating yourself up over it. Dylan chose to leave rather than staying to talk things through and that's not healthy either. After fifteen years, he should have wanted to stay and fight."

"But we're not fighters!" Ella cried, jumping to her feet. "I just said that! Why would he stay and fight?"

"Because you're worth fighting for!" Becca cried. "Geez, El, don't you understand? You were upset about something and then he got upset about something, but neither of you fought about it together to work it out! He ran and you hid! That's not what you do! Especially after all this time and certainly not with a wedding coming up!"

"So what am I supposed to do?" Ella snapped. "Just pick up the phone and yell at him?"

"No," Hailey said, coming to her feet. "You're supposed to go over to his parents' house—or wherever it is he's staying—and demand he talk to you!"

"Now?" Ella asked. "You mean like right now?"

The girls all looked at one another. "You can," Hailey said carefully. "But maybe you should stop and think about what you're going to say when you see him. Since this is all new to you, maybe it would be better if…"

"No," Ella said defiantly and walked across the room and grabbed her shoes, "I want to do it now."

"Ella…" Becca said hesitantly. "I don't think…"

But Ella wasn't listening. She was walking around the room and grabbing her keys and then looking around wildly for whatever else she might need. Then without another word, she walked out the door, letting it slam behind her.

For a minute, Hailey, Becca and Angie were too stunned to speak.

"We can't possibly let her go there on her own, can we?" Becca asked.

Hailey shrugged. "We shouldn't, but I don't know if it's a good thing for us to go with her either. This is kind of private and I don't think Dylan's going to appreciate an audience."

Angie stood and walked over to the coat rack and grabbed her purse. "Well that's too damn bad because he's getting one. Ella needs some backup right now. She's finally taking a stand on something and showing a little backbone." She paused and huffed with frustration when neither Hailey nor Becca got up. "Come on, you guys! When have you ever seen Ella this worked up over anything?"

Becca finally stood up. "Never."

Hailey stood and nodded in agreement and then went to retrieve her own purse. "She may not want us to go with her."

"And again, too bad," Angie said as they all walked out the door and then stopped. Ella was leaning against Hailey's car. "What the…?"

"Finally!" Ella said as she moved away from the car. "I can't believe you guys were going to let me go all by myself. Now come on, let's go! I need my man to come home with me!"

As Ella climbed into the car, her friends laughed.

"I think we may have created a monster here," Hailey murmured.

"About damn time," Angie said with a grin.

****

Ella was trembling from head to toe.

It was one thing to say she was going to go after Dylan and make things right, but it was quite another to actually do it. It was like an out-of-body experience. She didn't know how to fight with Dylan—or fight *for* Dylan! If anyone would have told her that she'd ever be in this kind of situation, she would have told them they were crazy. She and Dylan were solid. Forever.

Clearly they weren't as solid as she'd hoped.

Hailey pulled up in front of Dylan's parents'

house and parked. She and Becca and Angie all turned and looked at her.

"I can do this," Ella said, but her voice certainly didn't convey any confidence.

"We'll wait here," Hailey said. "Unless you want us to go in with you."

Ella shook her head. "I hope he's here."

"His truck is parked up by the garage," Angie said, "so…"

"Okay," Ella sighed. "I can do this." She paused. "I'm totally ready to do this."

"Do you maybe want one of us to walk you up to the door?" Becca asked.

"No," she replied a little more firmly. "I need to do this on my own." Then she gave them all a lopsided grin. "Well…you know what I mean." Reaching for the door handle, she took a steadying breath and murmured, "I can do this," one last time before climbing out.

Actually, she chanted it the entire way up the driveway and to the front door. If it were any other time, she would have just walked into her future in-laws' home but this time she rang the bell and waited.

It felt all kinds of wrong.

Looking over her shoulder, she gave the girls a quick wave and felt guilty they were going to sit out there in Hailey's car. Ella had no idea how long she'd be here or if they should leave or…

"Ella? What are you doing here?"

Quickly turning around, she faced Dylan and her heart actually ached. For a minute, all Ella could do was stare at him.

Four days.

They had never gone for more than a day without seeing each other since the seventh grade and Ella couldn't believe how good it was to simply look at him.

"Ella?"

She swallowed hard and fully faced him. "Hey," she began softly. "Can we talk?"

If she thought Dylan was going to make it easy for her, she was wrong. "Um…" He looked over his shoulder into the house. "It's kind of late…"

Her eyes went wide and she was pretty certain her mouth dropped open. Was he serious?

Dylan looked beyond her and noticed Hailey's car. "Why are the girls here?"

"They came over tonight to check on me and they were worried about me driving so…"

He frowned. "Why were they worried? Or did they force you to come here and talk to me? Because it's been four days without a word from you, Ella."

"I haven't exactly heard from you either," she accused.

Dylan stepped outside, pulling the door closed behind him. "When I left I told you to get things worked out. I was giving you space." His tone wasn't his usual sweet and even one. This one had a little bit of a snap to it.

And it was that tone that made Ella brave. "Oh yeah? Well I didn't want space, Dylan! For fourteen years we've been together and for most of it, we've been on the same page. And when I suddenly don't fall in line with everything you want or what you're thinking, you pack up and leave? What the hell kind of bullshit is that?"

Now it was Dylan's eyes that went wide. "Ella…seriously?" he whispered. "My parents are right inside."

"You know what? I don't care!" she said loudly. "If I have to yell to get you to listen to me, then I'm going to do it!"

"Okay, you're not being reasonable. Maybe we should talk another time." Dylan turned to go back into the house and Ella grabbed his arm and forced him to turn around. He looked at her hand on him and then up at her face with confusion.

"This is exactly what I'm talking about," he hissed. "I don't know what's gotten into you. It's like I don't even know you anymore!"

"Why? Because I'm sticking up for myself? Because I have an opinion? Because I'm not sitting back and meekly doing what everyone says?"

That made him stop. He stared at her as if seeing her for the first time.

Ella mistook his silence for something else. "I thought I knew you, Dylan, really knew you. I thought we were partners but that's obviously not what you want. You want me to be like some sort of…lap dog or something…someone who cooks for you, cleans for you, has your babies but God forbid I have any thoughts of my own or feelings of my own!" She stopped and caught her breath. "Well…that's not who I am. And if you can't handle that…if you can't love me because of that then…then it's your loss!"

Spinning on her heels, Ella stomped down the porch steps and started to stalk across the front yard to Hailey's car. She could see the girls all staring at her with disbelief but she didn't care. Her mind was too busy reeling with the fact that after all these years, Dylan wasn't the man she thought he was. Her heart broke a little more with every step she took away from him.

Halfway across the yard, Dylan caught up to her and was the one to spin her around this time. "Dammit, Ella!" he snapped. "Wait!"

"For what?" she demanded. "For you to tell me I'm being crazy and need to keep it down? For you to tell me I'm wrong for being upset? For you to tell me how I'm not the woman you thought I was and you don't love me anymore?" Tears welled in her eyes and it was all she could do to will them not to fall. She pulled out of his grasp and crossed her arms across her chest. "Go ahead and say it!"

Dylan raked a hand through his hair. "Say what? What the hell is it you think I'm gonna say?"

"Pretty much everything I just said!" she cried. "Dammit, are you even listening to me at all?"

He took a deep breath and let it out slowly. "Things are getting a little out of hand here and I'm not really enjoying being the entertainment for the neighbors. Can we…can we please just not do this right now?"

She had begged.

She had cried.

She had screamed to be heard.

Feeling defeated, her shoulders sagged and Ella took a single step away from him. "No."

"No?"

She shook her head. "I think it's my turn to leave. And you can take your time thinking all this through and figuring out when is the perfect time for us to have a conversation, but it won't matter."

"Ella…"

She held up a hand to stop him. "I came here tonight to fight for you. For us. And all you can think about is how it looks to others."

Dylan held out his arms helplessly. "What am I supposed to do?"

"You were supposed to fight for me too," she

said sadly and turned and walked away.

****

"That doesn't look good," Angie said quietly, watching Ella and Dylan in the middle of the yard.

"No, it doesn't," Becca agreed.

"Is it me or does this seem completely bizarre?" Hailey asked.

"It's bizarre," Angie said. "Those two have been like Ken and Barbie since day one. I don't think I've ever seen Dylan without a smile on his face."

"He's certainly not smiling now," Hailey said.

"Nope. Definitely not," Becca said. "What are we going to do when she comes back to the car? I hate that we're sitting here witnessing this."

"Me too," Hailey said sadly. "Maybe we should have left. It would have forced them to at least be in the car together so Dylan could drive her home."

"We could leave now," Angie suggested.

"For crying out loud, Ange, she's walking this way!" Becca hissed. "What's wrong with you?"

"What? It would be even better timing to force them to drive together!"

"Just…just stop," Hailey said. "We need to be strong for Ella and just let her vent or cry or whatever it is she needs to do."

"What if she wants us to bring her home and

leave? Do we do that?" Becca asked.

"I'm not leaving her until I know she's okay," Hailey said.

"Me too," Angie said.

"Me too," Becca agreed.

Nine

Judith James was running around her backyard overseeing the proper setup and placement of the extra tables and chairs she had rented for this party. She knew everyone was doing their jobs and had everything under control, but it just wasn't in her nature to sit back and do nothing. As she moved around her mind wandered to the food they were going to be serving, the music they were going to play and if the weather was going to continue to cooperate.

After her fifth trek around the yard, she stopped and smiled.

It was all coming along beautifully.

That's when she allowed herself to simply stop and sit. Across the yard, Hailey was setting up centerpieces for the tables. Becca was working with Max to set up a photo booth. Angie and Sean were stringing twinkly lights around the deck. And Ella had gone and stocked the pool house with extra towels for anyone who felt like going for a swim. Everything was in its place but something still felt…off.

Looking over her shoulder she caught sight of Ella coming out of the pool house. The normally cheery one of the group looked incredibly sad. Judith had heard all about the big break up from Hailey but she had secretly hoped her daughter was wrong—or at the very least, exaggerating.

The thought made her chuckle because her daughter prided herself on never being wrong.

Deciding she needed a little info for herself, Judith stood as Ella approached. "How's the pool house look? Ready for guests?"

Ella gave her a small smile. "Yup. And I put out all of the extra baskets of goodies you had in the boxes. It's a great idea to have those extra bottles of sunscreen, sunglasses and goggles. You managed to think of everything."

"Well, I know we don't often do big parties here at the house, but I like to think I know how to cover all bases," Judith chuckled.

"Everyone's so excited you're doing this," Ella said. "And the timing is perfect. The weather is supposed to be beautiful today."

"As if Mother Nature could stop me."

Ella laughed but it felt a little forced. Looking around the yard, she said, "I guess I'll go and see who needs some help. Maybe Hailey could use a hand with the centerpieces."

"Actually," Judith began, "if you wouldn't mind, I could use your help inside."

"Oh…okay. Sure."

They walked back into the main house and Judith led Ella past the kitchen and dining room where the catering staff was working and back to her home office. Once they were inside, she shut the door and motioned for Ella to have a seat.

Ella looked at Judith with confusion. "I…I don't understand. What do we need to do in here?"

Judith took a seat behind her desk and looked at Ella with a sad smile. "How are you doing, Ella? Truthfully."

Her shoulders sagged as she sighed. "I'd like to say I'm okay, but I'd be lying."

"You don't have to lie to anyone, Ella. We all know how tough relationships can be and there's nothing wrong with letting people know you're hurting."

Ella studied her hands that were folded in her lap and nodded.

"I was surprised you came to the show last night. I appreciated it, of course, but I would have completely understood if you weren't up for it."

"Believe it or not, it was good for me. I've been cooped up in the house pretty much wallowing in my own misery. So going out last night and being around everyone really helped."

"I'm glad," Judith replied. "I know it couldn't have been easy for you."

Ella shrugged. "It's something I'm going to have to get used to." She paused. "Which reminds me, we'll need to cancel my dress order. I…I know I'll lose my deposit and all that and I'm fine with it, but I don't think I could handle having it come and knowing I won't…you know…"

Reaching across the desk, Judith held her hand out for one of Ella's and when Ella did the same, they simply sat in companionable silence for a minute. "I'll do whatever you need me to do, Ella. But…are you sure about this? Are you really sure things aren't going to work themselves out?"

"I don't think so," Ella said quietly, gently pulling her hand back. She looked up at Judith. "You know, in these last couple of months I learned a lot. I learned that I was letting people walk all over me and that I let people tell me it was okay for that to happen. Dylan was one of them. He never liked to make waves and basically, I'm the same way."

"Ella, there's a difference between not wanting to make waves and people taking advantage of you or…walking all over you like you said. You're allowed to tell people how you feel and if they can't handle it, it's their problem, not yours."

"I see that now. I really do. I look at Hailey and Becca and Angie and see how they all do that and I've also seen how sometimes it works and sometimes it doesn't." Her eyes began to well with tears and she immediately swiped them away. "It just stinks that for me, it didn't."

"Yeah, some people just don't take kindly to hearing other people's opinions and feelings," Judith sighed and then stopped to think of how that applied in her own life. She looked at Ella and then cleared her throat. "Maybe Dylan just needs a little time to get used to the new you."

Ella shook her head. "We've been together for so long, Mrs. J, that if he can't grow with me or evolve with me, then I can't do it. I can't be expected to be the same girl I was at fourteen as I am today. It's not fair. And for him to think it—or want it—is just wrong."

"Is there anything I can do for you, Ella? Anything to help you during this time? It breaks my heart to see you hurting like this."

A sad smile played at Ella's lips. "Thanks but…I'm going to get through this. I really am. It may just take a while."

Judith stood and came around the desk and pulled Ella to her feet and hugged her. "You're like one of my own, Ella. You know that. And if you ever need someone to talk to," she pulled back and smiled, "someone who isn't one of the girls, you can always come to me."

"Thanks, Mrs. J. You have no idea how much I appreciate that."

With one arm wrapped around Ella's shoulders, Judith led her out of the office and back toward the yard. "Now come on, we've got a party to go to!"

****

The party was in full swing when Hailey found a quiet corner to sit down with a glass of white wine and simply breathe. Since she had arrived at her parents' house that morning, she had been on the move helping to get everything set up and ready.

"Mind if I join you?"

She had to wonder how a man that size could sneak up on a person and yet it seemed a specialty of Jack's. Without a word she motioned to the chair next to her.

"Your mom certainly knows how to throw a party," he said conversationally before taking a drink from the beer bottle he had in his hand.

"Years of practice," Hailey said, letting her head fall back and refusing to let his proximity bother her. It wasn't the first time she was seeing him since their sexcapade the previous weekend—he had been in the show last night—but Hailey had kept her distance and made sure she was constantly busy.

Until now.

"It shows," he agreed and made himself comfortable. "I heard about Ella and Dylan. Is she doing okay?"

Her heart skipped at beat at his thoughtfulness. Still without looking at him she replied, "I think she's putting up a good front, but I know she's struggling."

"How could she not? It just seems odd seeing her at a function without Dylan. He's a nice guy. Maybe they'll work it out."

Hailey's smile was a little wistful. "I think they will. It's their first real fight."

Jack choked on his drink. "Excuse me?"

Nodding, Hailey opened her eyes and looked over at him and chuckled. "It's true. The two of them have never had a fight. It was almost sickening at times, but now it's just…sad."

He nodded in agreement. "Absolutely. Fighting is a necessity in any relationship."

She looked at him quizzically. "What do you mean?"

"You know…it serves several purposes. No two people can agree on everything. It's just not possible. You need to disagree and maybe fight about things to get to know each other. How else would you know that someone doesn't like…say…the thermostat being set below seventy degrees?"

Twisting in her seat, she faced him. "Well first of all, you could ask. And second of all…who would fight over a thermostat setting? That's ridiculous."

"And yet here we are arguing about it," he teased and winked.

"We're not…" Hailey let out a small groan of frustration. "Personally, I don't think arguing is necessary but it is natural."

"Disagree."

She glared at him. "Of course you do."

"Aren't you going to ask me why?"

In a million years she would never confess that

she was enjoying this crazy conversation, but she was. With a dramatic sigh she said, "Okay. Why?"

Jack leaned in a little closer to her. Close enough that she could smell his cologne and feel the heat coming off of his body. "It's necessary for great make-up sex."

Hailey swallowed hard. Her mouth opened to say something, but she couldn't make any words come out. Images of the two of them from the previous weekend flashed through her mind.

Jack peeling off her panties.

Jack tugging on her hair so he'd have better access to her throat.

Jack's hands and mouth…everywhere.

She swallowed hard again and saw the knowing smirk on his face. Doing her best to compose herself, she shifted to put a little more space between them. "I don't think make-up sex is a good enough reason to fight."

"Then obviously you haven't had great make-up sex," he countered.

Feeling a blush creeping up her cheeks, she came up with a way to put him in his place and get her back on even ground. She shrugged carelessly. "If a man is really a good lover, he shouldn't need the excuse of make-up sex to make things good. He should be able to prove it at any time."

Jack's eyes went wide right before he laughed

out loud. "Is that right?"

Hailey nodded. "Absolutely. It shouldn't take getting angry and yelling and screaming at each other to make for great sex. Maybe some people need that, but it should never be a necessity for it."

Jack looked like he was about to say something and then thought better of it. He stood up and finished his beer. "I'm going to grab a burger," he said. "You want one?"

Actually, Hailey was starving but wasn't sure if she was ready to sit and share a meal with Jack—just the two of them. Then she laughed at the absurdity of it. They were at a barbecue with fifty other people. It was hardly an intimate dinner for two. And besides, she was curious to see if there was maybe something more to Jack that she hadn't allowed herself to see.

Smiling, she stood. "I do," she said. "Why don't you grab us a couple of burgers and I'll get us a couple of sides and salads and we can meet back here."

Jack smiled so brightly, so sincerely, that Hailey almost tripped over herself.

"Sounds like a plan," he said, his voice rich and deep against her cheek as he leaned in and placed a soft kiss there before walking away.

Hailey watched him go for a minute before making her way over to one of the many food stations her mother had set up.

"So..." Angie said as she sidled up to her,

"someone was looking all cozy over there. Are you going to give that sexy bastard another chance?"

"Would you be quiet?!" Hailey hissed.

Angie looked around. "What? No one's even paying attention to us," she said as she began putting salads on a plate. "What's the big deal?"

"The big deal is…no one knows about last weekend so I'm trying to…"

"Pretend it didn't happen? Um…yeah. No."

Hailey looked up at her sharply. "And why not?"

"Because it *did* happen and Jack's a nice guy and if you'd get that stick out of your ass for a few minutes you might actually see that."

Unsure of what to say, Hailey moved along and made progress on her own plates of food. When she reached the end of the table, she turned back to Angie. "For your information, we're eating together. So there."

"Wow…you really showed me," Angie murmured, stepping around her to get to the next table of food.

"Now what?" Hailey sighed.

"Don't make it like you're throwing the poor guy a bone. Why can't you just admit you like him and you want to spend time with him?"

Good question. Taking a minute to herself, Hailey took a couple of scoops of potato salad and then some of the tortellini with pesto before answering. "Because I'm still not sure if I should," she said quietly.

When they got to the end of the table, Angie turned and faced her. "Sean and I are going to join you two."

"What?" Hailey asked, feeling confused.

"We'll all eat together and then later on you and I will talk about how I see things between the two of you."

On the surface it sounded like a good plan but Angie had a way of embarrassing the crap out of people when she wanted to and Hailey just wasn't up for it right now. "I don't know, Ange…"

"I promise not to mention that I know about last weekend and I promise I won't say anything about you being a snob." Her expression was sincere and she was smiling broadly—probably because she knew exactly what was going on in Hailey's mind. "Come on. It will be fun. Plus, I think Becca and Max sneaked off to do it in the pool house and Ella's moping around and I'd really like Sean to hang out with at least one of my friends today."

Deciding to throw caution to the wind, Hailey nodded. "Okay. But I'm telling you now, one snarky comment about last weekend or anything close to it and I will totally start blabbing all of your secrets to Sean."

Angie laughed out loud. "You could try but trust

me, the man doesn't scare easily."

"Great," Hailey mumbled.

"And I have a feeling Jack doesn't either."

****

"If Judith ever sells this house, I'm offering to buy this pool house," Max said breathlessly against Becca's throat. She chuckled. "I'm serious. This place is beginning to hold some of my hottest memories."

They were in the changing room—with the door locked—with Becca's legs still locked around his bare waist. "I can't believe we actually got away with this," she said quietly. "I was afraid someone was going to come in and knock on the door or something."

Max smiled as he gently eased her down until her feet were on the floor. "Why do you think I waited until the food started to be served?"

Becca swatted at him playfully. They quietly fixed their clothes and she was about to move away from the wall when Max cupped her face and kissed her again. She purred at the contact. When he lifted his head, she smiled. "You think she'd get suspicious if we just asked to rent it out once in a while?"

He laughed and took one of her hands in his as he opened the door. Checking to make sure the coast was clear, they left the room and went to the small kitchenette to grab a couple of bottles of water. "Are you hungry? Want to go and grab something to eat?"

"Absolutely." They made their way out of the pool house and across the yard and quickly blended in with the group of people milling about piling their plates with food. When they were done, Becca looked around the yard until she spotted where Hailey and Angie were sitting. Nodding in their direction, she and Max made their way over. "Hey! Is there room for two more?" she asked as she approached the table.

"The more the merrier," Hailey said, scooting her chair over—as everyone was—to make room for them.

"Look who finally made it out of the pool house," Angie teased and Becca stared at her with wide-eyed shock. "Don't even try to deny it."

Out of the corner of her eye, Becca saw Hailey smirk but decided just to let it go. She was feeling too good to let herself get upset over some harmless teasing. "Wasn't planning on it," she said casually.

Angie grinned and went back to her burger.

Ella walked over. "I'm just gonna squeeze in here too. Don't mind me." She pulled a chair over as everyone did another round of scooting to make room for her. By the time she sat down, there was very little elbow room. "Sorry."

"No worries," Hailey said. "We were wondering where you were."

"I was sort of lending a hand wherever it was needed," she replied softly and then shrugged. It seemed like a good thing to do."

"El, you didn't need to do any work. Why didn't you just come and hang out?" Becca asked.

Without looking up, Ella said, "I really didn't think you and Max wanted a threesome in the pool house."

Angie and Hailey both barked out loud with laughter and Becca immediately began to choke on her drink. Jack and Sean exchanged smirks and Max slouched down in his seat as he rubbed Becca's back.

"I am really liking this new Ella," Angie said a few minutes later.

Ella looked up. "What? What did I say?"

Angie's eyes went wide. "You just dished out the ultimate snarky comment and you didn't even blink an eye!" She wrapped her arms around Ella and hugged her close. "I'm so proud of you!"

Ella chuckled. "Yeah, well…I guess after all these years of hanging out with you, some of your sense of sarcasm has finally rubbed off on me."

Angie made it like she was wiping her eyes. "It's one of the proudest moments of my life. You always dream that your kids will turn out like you, but this is so much better!"

Becca was still a bit red in the face but kept her gaze averted as she ate her burger.

"All right, all right," Hailey finally said, "I think that's enough. You've managed to make Becca turn a shade of red that probably isn't healthy. So…change of subject."

Angie quickly raised her hand. "Ooh…I know! How about…"

"Whatever it is," Hailey interrupted quickly, "no!"

"What? But…?"

"I'm thinking of a spa weekend next weekend," Hailey began, effectively ignoring Angie's protests. "We've got the show Friday night but I'm thinking we can meet up Saturday morning and do the luxury overnight spa thing. What do you think?"

"Aren't they normally west of here?" Becca asked. "Like in the mountains?"

Hailey shook her head. "There's actually one only about thirty minutes from here. I met the manager last night at the show. Her daughter's getting married and she was interested in being a vendor at one of Mom's shows so she offered a heavily discounted rate for us to come and check it out."

"I'm pretty sure she meant for that offer to go to your mom," Ella said with a frown. "That's only fair."

Hailey shook her head again. "Mom was standing right there and said she was too wound up for something like that but mentioned that we—as in the four of us—would probably enjoy it and would give honest feedback."

"And she went for it?" Angie asked.

"Yes! Isn't that great!" Hailey said with a smile, looking at each of her friends. "So? What do you say? Are you in?"

"I'm in," Angie said instantly and then turned to look at Sean. "You're going to be back up north all next week, right?"

He nodded. "That shouldn't matter," he said with a smile. "I would never stop you from doing something with your girls. I know better than that."

There were some soft chuckles around the table.

Becca looked over at Max and then back at the group. "We sort of had plans…"

Max reached out and stopped her. "That we can reschedule. How often do you get a weekend away to get pampered?"

She blushed and was about to remind him of all the ways he'd pampered her last night but thought better of it. "Only if you're sure," she said to him softly. "I really wanted to go to the art exhibit with you."

He cupped her cheek and leaned in and kissed her softly. "We'll go Sunday night then. I'll take Saturday night to work on some of my own art and maybe someday we'll be going to an exhibit of mine."

Her shoulders sagged with relief as she briefly kissed him back. "You're amazing, you know that, right?"

Before they could say anything else, Angie called out, "Ella! What about you? Are you in?"

Looking up at all of the hopeful expressions, she simply shrugged. "Sure. It's not like I've got anything else to do or anyone to ask about it."

Hailey reached over to comfort Ella but Angie slapped her hand away. "That's the spirit!" she cried out. "Glad you have a good attitude about it. It's going to be great! Lots of fun. Very therapeutic!"

"I guess," Ella mumbled and then went back to eating her salad.

Conversation flowed around the table with questions about the art exhibit Max and Becca were going to, then moved on to the spa the girls were going to and finally to the next Friday night show. Everyone had finished eating and the sun was setting.

"This was a good day," Hailey said, relaxing back in her seat.

"Agreed," Angie said. "The food was great." She looked over her shoulder. "Do you think they're going to bring out dessert soon?"

Sean stood beside her. "I'll go check." He leaned down and kissed the top of her head before walking away.

"Dessert does sound good," Becca said. "Something chocolate…"

Taking the hint, Max stood. "I'm on it." He

followed Sean.

That left just the girls—and Jack.

Clearing his throat, he slowly pushed his chair back and stood up. "So…I guess I'm going to check and see if there's any dessert out," he chuckled and then looked down at Hailey. "Any requests?"

"I'm with Becca. Anything chocolate," she replied with a smile.

He nodded and then reached over and picked up her empty wine glass. "You want another?"

Hailey nodded. "Please."

With a smile, Jack carefully made his way around the table and then walked off to join the guys in their quest for dessert.

Hailey sighed and smiled and then noticed her three friends staring at her with knowing smiles on their faces. "What? What did I do?"

"Girl," Angie began with a very satisfied smile, "you are so into him. There's no denying it."

Hailey's eyes went wide. "Why? Because he offered to get me some dessert? Please," she snorted with disgust. "That's crazy."

"No, not because he's getting you dessert, dummy," Angie said, leaning forward.

"More like because you looked at him like you wanted to eat *him* for dessert," Ella said and then giggled.

"Twice in one night!" Angie cried and pulled Ella in for another hug. "I love it!"

****

It was late.

The yard was almost empty.

And Hailey was still sitting with Jack.

Becca and Max had left an hour ago with Angie and Sean not long after them. Ella was helping Judith straighten up and if Hailey heard things correctly, her mother had thanked Ella and told her she should head on home.

Which still left Hailey alone with Jack.

Over the course of the day she had learned about his job, his hobbies and his family. If she were honest with herself, this was the most perfect date she'd ever had. Jack was charming and funny and they seemed to have a lot of common interests, none of which she could recall because suddenly Jack wasn't talking and he was studying her. She squirmed a little under his intense gaze until she couldn't take it anymore. Straightening in her seat she huffed, "What? What are you staring at?"

He chuckled. "You know, Princess, I had a really good time today."

Hailey relaxed slightly in her seat. "Oh," she said, smiling shyly. "Me too."

Leaning his arm on her chair, he was close. Hailey could practically see herself in his eyes. Her mind raced as she secretly hoped he'd simply close the distance and kiss her. There. She admitted it. Sort of. Scanning his face, she hoped he understood she wouldn't mind if he kissed her—there was no way she was making the first move.

Again.

Swallowing hard, she whispered his name.

Smiling, Jack reached out and cupped Hailey's cheek. "I'm going to see a friend of mine's band play Wednesday night. They're playing at a club in downtown. Would you like to go with me?"

He was asking her out.

Not kissing her.

Damn.

Although she had to admit, it was nice that he wasn't being overly aggressive and this could work for them too. "I'd like that," she finally said and couldn't help but smile at the pleased look on his face.

He pulled back and relaxed in his chair. "Good," he said with a hint of satisfaction. "That's good."

Hailey waited for him to ask her to dinner first but he didn't say anything. She was just about to question it when her mother walked over.

"Oh! There you two are! I was hoping I didn't miss saying goodnight to you with all this running around," Judith said, her hand fluttering over her heart.

"Mom, you hired a crew to handle all of the cleaning up. Why aren't you relaxing?"

Judith waved her off. "Please, when have you ever seen me sit back and let anyone else do all of the work?"

Hailey chuckled. "Okay, good point. So other than the running around, did you have a good time today?"

"Oh, yes," she replied, pulling up a chair and sitting down. "I am thrilled with the way everything went. It was a total success." Sighing, Judith let her head fall back for a moment before it snapped back and she was looking at Hailey. "I am worried about Ella though."

"Join the club."

"No…it's…I can't quite put my finger on it. She's not emotional, Hailey. She's just not herself. She asked me to cancel her gown today."

Hailey frowned. "Well…I guess it's the next logical step…"

Judith shook her head. "No. Absolutely not," she said firmly. "That girl needs to fight for her man! For their relationship!"

"Mom…she tried. We were there to see it for ourselves; it was awful. Maybe she's realizing it's not the relationship she wants. Maybe now that she's finally standing up for herself she sees that Dylan isn't the one for her."

Leaning forward, Judith slapped Hailey on the arm.

"Ow! What was that for?"

"Do you hear yourself? You and Ella have been friends for just about your entire lives! Can you honestly sit there and believe she and Dylan aren't right for each other? Well? Can you?"

Hailey was still rubbing her arm. "Look, I don't like it either but it's not our call to make! Maybe she needs this time to figure out what she wants. And why should she go into debt with wedding plans and preparations for a ceremony that might not happen?" She paused. "And as for emotional, she spent a week holed up in her house crying! She's drained. She's tired. Right now she doesn't have much left in her to give. What are you expecting?"

Now it was Judith's turn to frown. "I just expected…"

"We all did, Mom. Trust me."

"And I can't believe Dylan isn't doing anything either. I would have thought for sure he'd have come to his senses by now and tried to make things right too."

"I think he's just as confused as she is."

"If I could interject something here," Jack said hesitantly.

"Oh!" Judith said, slightly flustered. "I almost forgot you were sitting there, Jackson. I'm sorry. We didn't mean to exclude you."

He smiled and shook his head before taking one of Judith's hands in his and kissing it. "If you'd like the male perspective…"

"Absolutely," Judith gushed and Hailey rolled her eyes at her mother's exuberance.

"Dylan probably doesn't know which end is up right now. From what I've heard—which isn't much—Ella's come to this revelation about her life and what she wants and doesn't want. I'm sure Dylan's equally confused because he has no idea if *he's* still what she wants."

Hailey and Judith looked at Jack and then at each other before turning back to him. "I'd say that's fairly accurate," Judith said. "I imagine the poor boy is probably afraid to make the wrong move. If he comes after her, he could be pushing her further away."

"Exactly," Jack agreed.

"But," Hailey began, "if he simply sits back and does nothing—which has sort of been his M.O.—they'll never work anything out."

"I don't think it's that Dylan does nothing, Hailey," Judith countered. "He's more like the type of man who is laid back and waits to see how it's all going to play out."

"There's a time and a place for that," Hailey argued, "and by him sitting around and waiting, all he's accomplishing is making Ella feel like she doesn't matter enough for him to fight for. She left her comfort zone and maybe it's time he did too."

They grew silent and stayed that way for several moments before Judith stood and kissed Hailey on the cheek and then Jack. "Unfortunately, this isn't our fight. Ella and Dylan will have to work it out." She looked around the yard. "I'm going to make sure the staff is cleaning up." Turning back to them, she smiled. "Jackson, it's always a pleasure to see you. Thank you for coming. And Hailey, are you still coming for dinner tomorrow?"

Hailey couldn't help but smile at her mother. As much as they could, they stuck to their tradition of Sunday dinner together. "I wouldn't miss it."

"Good. Have a good night, you two!" And with a wave, Judith was gone.

It was getting late and as much as she was hating that the night was coming to an end, Hailey knew she at least had her mid-week date with Jack to look forward to. It seemed like he wasn't going to expand upon it—just going to see a band play—but she figured that was all right. She'd take it and see where it took them.

She stood and stretched. Jack did the same. Picking up her purse, she moved around the table. Jack followed. Silently they made their way across the yard out to the driveway where Hailey was parked. They stopped beside her car.

"So…Wednesday, right?"

He nodded.

Looking around, Hailey noted how there weren't many cars left. "Where are you parked?"

Jack moved in closer until their bodies were practically touching and Hailey was forced to look up at him. He reached up and caressed her cheek. Everything inside of her was screaming *Yes! Yes!! Yes!!!* His name came out as a breathy sigh right before he lowered his head and captured her lips with his.

It wasn't wild and untamed like their first kiss the previous weekend. No. It was deep and sweet and all-consuming on a whole new level. Hailey's purse and keys dropped to the ground as she wrapped her arms around his shoulders and pressed up against him. It didn't matter that they were in her parents' driveway. It didn't matter that the catering crew was still walking around. She'd been waiting for this kiss and wasn't going to let something like people moving around stop it from happening.

Slowly Jack raised his head. His eyes scanned her face before he rested his forehead against hers. "I'll text you the info for Wednesday night," he said softly, placing one last kiss on the tip of her nose before pulling back.

What the…?

"Wait," Hailey said, trying to clear her head. "You're…you're leaving?"

He nodded.

"But…"

Jack chuckled softly. "Believe me, Princess, I'm tempted. Very tempted."

She looked at him expectantly, waiting for him to finish the thought. "But…?"

"But," he finally said, "I don't think it's smart for us to act on anything tonight."

He was seriously killing her. "I don't understand."

Taking a step back toward her and closing the distance between them once again, Jack rested his hands on her waist. "Last weekend was…fantastic. It was unexpected and you completely took me by surprise."

Hailey couldn't help but smile and she placed one hand on his chest, meeting his gaze. "All the more reason we should act on this tonight."

Slowly Jack shook his head.

Now she pulled back. "I still don't understand then."

"Hailey, you and I have been…I don't know…dancing around each other for the better part of a year. In all that time, I was really into you and you treated me like something you wanted to scrape off your shoe."

Shame washed over her. "That's not…completely true."

He cupped her cheek. “It’s okay,” he said sincerely. “I’m not going to lie to you. There were times you came off like a complete bitch and I didn’t like it. But eventually I came to see that part of your reaction to me was because of how you were feeling about Logan.”

At the mention of that topic, she felt herself blush.

“And then last weekend happened,” Jack went on. “I had no idea what I was thinking when I took you to my room. It wasn’t planned; it wasn’t something I had thought about…sort of,” he chuckled, “but once I had you there, I wasn’t sure what the hell was going to happen. But the first time we kissed, I knew immediately I wanted more.”

“Jack…”

“And the thing is, I thought you felt the same way too. That entire night was something beyond anything I’d ever experienced before.” He paused. “And then you sneaked out without a word. Nothing. Not a note, a text, a call…nothing.”

“I…I didn’t…”

He held up a hand to stop her. “I was mad as hell when I woke up and you weren’t there. I searched the whole damn hotel looking for you. When I found out you and the girls had cut out early, I figured it out.”

“What?” she asked quietly.

“That you were running scared.”

Nailed it in one. She wasn't even going to try and deny it. "I was."

A slow smile spread across his face. "Glad you can admit it, Princess," he said softly. "And that's why we're going to say goodnight here and see each other on Wednesday."

Her brows furrowed in confusion.

"Slow, Hailey. From here on out, I think we need to take the time to get to know each other. I'm not willing to just be a way for you to scratch an itch and then hightail it out of there while I'm still asleep again. It's not gonna happen that way ever again."

She swallowed hard and then nodded. "I understand," she said and then tried to look away.

"Hey," he said, gently forcing her to look at him. "Believe me, there is a part of me that is fighting to go home with you and spend the night. I'm trying to be decent here. If I were only looking to get laid, then that's where we'd be heading right now. But like I said, I want more." His eyes scanned her face again. "What is it you want, Princess? Just a night or something more?"

Right now her body was saying the night would be fine, but she knew in her heart that it wouldn't be enough. She was beginning to see an entirely different side of Jack and he intrigued her. She was beyond attracted to him and genuinely wanted to see where this all could go. With a steady gaze, she met his. "I want something more too." Her breath was husky as she said it and she knew Jack was affected by it.

Hauling her close, he kissed her again, kissed her so thoroughly that Hailey thought she would combust right on the spot. And then he released her and moved away. "Give me your phone," he gently commanded and Hailey obeyed. Jack quickly scrolled around and entered his contact information. "Call me when you get home," he said and handed her phone back to her before turning and walking away.

In that instant Hailey was thankful her car was behind her.

It was the only thing holding her up.

****

Ella sat in her car and stared at her house and sighed. It was dark. It was late. The thought of going in there alone was almost too much to bear. Going to the party had been a great distraction but there was no way it could possibly go on forever and Ella knew this was how her day was going to end.

Alone.

It didn't matter how long she sat out there; eventually she was going to have to go inside and deal with the reality—Dylan wasn't there and she was going to sleep alone. Again.

Honestly, it didn't matter how many times she reminded herself of that fact. It still hurt to know he wasn't there. They had never gone this long without at least talking to each other. It felt like a part of her was missing.

With a small groan, Ella climbed from the car and walked listlessly into the house. Locking the door behind her, she didn't bother turning on any lights and opted to just go straight up the stairs to the bedroom. When she turned on the light in there, she was disappointed. In the back of her mind she still kept hoping Dylan would surprise her and just be there.

Or that she'd wake up and realize it had all been a really bad dream.

On autopilot, she moved around the room and got undressed and then slipped on one of Dylan's t-shirts to sleep in. It was silly but it gave her comfort. Ella crawled into the bed and positioned herself in the middle.

It felt weird.

Her mind was still racing a bit with all the thoughts of what could have been and what her reality was, and she knew she wasn't going to fall asleep any time soon. A small sound made her sit up. Realizing it was her phone and that she had an incoming text, she kicked the blankets off and walked across the room to get it.

She fished the phone out and swiped the screen and smiled. Angie had texted to make sure she had gotten home okay. A tear made its way down her cheek. Ella knew she was lucky to have such amazing friends. Her family was not taking her breakup with Dylan well and hadn't bothered to show her much sympathy. But her friends? They were her rocks. They were what kept her sane and smiling when all she really wanted to do was curl back up under the covers and cry.

Replying that she was home safe and sound and that they'd talk tomorrow, Ella put her phone down on her nightstand, crawled back into the bed and turned out the light.

And allowed herself one more night of crying.

****

Hailey paced her bedroom from one end to the other. She had gotten home just a few minutes ago and was in serious overthinking mode.

Text Jack.

It seemed simple enough. Type the message, hit send, end of story. But was it that simple? No. Why? Because she wasn't sure what kind of tone she wanted the text to have. Collapsing on her bed, she sighed. "I have issues."

On one hand, she could simply send an "I'm home" message with a little smiley face. It was short and to the point. But after the kiss they'd shared and the way her body was still tingling from it, she was extremely tempted to send a bit of a flirty text. Something like "I'm home—wish you were here with me" followed by a heart or something.

Growling, she sat up and looked at her phone and

took a steadying breath. "Just do…something!" she admonished herself.

Her fingers moved along typing furiously and she hit send before she could second-guess herself.

Two minutes later, her phone dinged with an incoming text.

Wish I were there with you too. I pretty much kicked my own ass the whole way home.

Hailey smiled.

Good. She was glad to know that she wasn't suffering alone.

Ten

"This is almost too decadent for words."

"Truth."

"Can we make plans to do this every day?"

"I think I've died and gone to heaven."

It was spa day and they had opted to have a group-style massage—like a couples massage times two. And as much as the point of the whole thing was to relax, conversation never seemed to stop.

"Did Sean head back to New York?" Ella asked, her voice slightly muffled due to her position on the massage table.

"Not until this morning," Angie said and then moaned as the masseuse kneaded a knot out of her shoulder.

"I thought he was leaving earlier in the week?" Hailey asked.

"I did too but…oh God does that feel good…he managed to handle all of his stuff via phone calls and FaceTime or whatever app he's using."

"And you're good with it?" Ella asked. "Him staying for so long?"

"Mmm…" was Angie's only reply.

"Why didn't you say anything last night at the show?" Hailey asked and then did her own moaning as her masseuse worked on her lower back.

"I think we were all a little…distracted…last night," Angie replied.

And it was the truth. It was the first time ever that they all seemed that way. Becca and Max had shown up together—as was becoming the norm—and rather than going their separate ways once they got there to do their own thing, they had worked together to get Max's photography equipment set up before Becca had to start getting ready. By the time she had gone backstage, everyone was running around doing the same.

Angie had been late. Sean had surprised her with an early dinner waiting for her when she had gotten home from work. Normally she went right from her job to the show but since Sean was in town, she had opted to leave work early and meet him at her house so they could go to the show together. Once she had walked in the door and seen what he had done for her, she had wanted to thank him properly—which turned into so much more. Before she knew it, dinner was cold and she was late. She left Sean half-asleep with a promise she'd be back as soon as possible.

Hailey, for the first time this season, had not been paired up with Logan for the show. Last night was the first time she and Jack had been paired up. Normally something like that done at the last minute would have thrown her for a loop, but in a move that seemed to surprise everyone, Hailey had simply shrugged and linked arms with Jack as they lined up.

And then there was Ella. It was obvious to

everyone that doing the show was causing her equal levels of pain and pleasure, but no one knew how to handle it. She came and did everything she always did and smiled while doing it, but she didn't want to talk to anyone and she certainly didn't linger before or after the show.

"So when is he coming back?" Ella finally asked.

"I think Wednesday," Angie said. "I'm not sure. I'll talk to him about it tomorrow." She sighed loudly. "What about you, Hails?"

"What about me?"

"You haven't said much about your date with Jack. How did that go?"

"It was…good," she replied and then asked her masseuse to move a little to the left.

"That's it? Just good?"

"We met up at the club where his friend was playing. We listened to the band play, had a couple of drinks and…that's it."

Angie raised her head—much to her masseuse's displeasure—and looked over at Hailey. "What do you mean 'that's it'? So you're done? You're not going out with him again?"

"Oh…no…sorry," Hailey said, her own voice slightly muffled. "I mean that was it for the night. He walked me out to my car, kissed me until I was practically a puddle at his feet and said goodnight."

"I'm noticing a pattern there," Becca chimed in.

"Exactly," Hailey mumbled. "It's becoming his signature move. I both love and hate it."

"So what are you going to do about it?" Ella asked.

"I'm still working on it. We've talked to each other every night on the phone and texted during the day, but…"

"Have you flat out asked him to nail you?" Angie asked.

There was a bark of laughter throughout the room.

"Um…no," Hailey said.

"Maybe you should," Becca said. "It seems to me that's what you really want. Why deny it? And besides, you already know the sex is going to be good. I say go for the sex. Always go for the sex."

Now it was Hailey's turn to raise her head. "When did you become such a sex fiend?"

Becca chuckled and then did her own share of moaning as her back was massaged. "Since I finally discovered how freaking awesome it can be. I'm telling you guys, Max is…"

"LA-LA-LA-LA-LA!" Angie cried out. "Just no! Stop! Do *not* finish that sentence!"

Becca turned her head and looked at her. "Are you kidding me? You're always looking for a good sex story and now you're telling me to stop? For real?"

Shifting on her table, Angie got comfortable again. "Normally I do, but you and Max are like this cute and sweet little hipster couple and that's the image I'd rather have of the two of you. Not one where you're…" She stopped and shook her head. "Never mind. Dammit! Now I almost put the gross image there myself!"

That just made Becca laugh. "Ha! Serves you right!" Then she settled down and sighed happily. "But back to you, Hails. What's your plan?"

"There is no plan. We've gone out once. We talked about it and know we want to get to know each other and he's still…he's still a little freaked out that I walked out. You know…that morning."

"How could we ever forget?" Angie asked sarcastically.

"Yeah, I get it. Not my finest hour. We've been over it. I just didn't think about how Jack would feel about it."

"So he was mad?" Ella questioned.

"Not mad, although he said he was that morning. But by the time we talked about it he seemed like he wanted to be a little more…cautious. I got the feeling he thinks I'm using him."

"And are you?" Becca asked. "You know, because the sex is so good?"

"Ugh," Angie groaned.

"It was one night!"

"One night of great sex," Becca mumbled and they all laughed.

"When are you seeing him again?" Ella asked, trying to get them all to calm down.

"I'm not sure, actually. I told him I'd call him when I got home tomorrow."

"You mean you went out Wednesday and saw him again last night and he didn't mention when he wanted to see you again?" Becca asked, puzzled.

"Um…"

"Wow," Angie sighed. "That…that's okay. I guess."

"You guys," Hailey protested. "It's not like that. We just haven't…"

"Hell, even I know that it's not a good sign when a guy doesn't ask to see you again," Ella said. "What did you say to him Wednesday night to make him not want to go out again?"

"What?!" Hailey cried, pushing her masseuse away. She sat up, clutching the blanket to cover herself. "I didn't do anything!"

"Maybe that's the problem," Becca mumbled.

"Enough with the sex innuendos!" Hailey snapped. "Jack and I agreed to take things slowly. So that's what we're doing! If he didn't want to see me again or go out again, we wouldn't be talking and texting every day." She cursed under her breath.

"Um, ladies," Hailey's masseuse finally said, her voice firm and cool. "This is why we don't normally recommend a group massage. You're all supposed to be relaxing and you're not. I'm going to suggest you curb the rest of this discussion until we're done. Agreed?"

There was a mumbled round of agreement as everyone got back to their spots.

Within minutes, the only sound in the room was the relaxing music being piped in.

****

Two weeks later, Hailey was no closer to any…anything.

She and Jack had gone out multiple times, had seen each other at the bridal shows and yet things were still exactly the same. They met at places—sometimes for dinner or a movie or to see the same band play—and then he'd kiss her goodnight and that would be it.

She was losing her mind.

Slowly. Steadily.

Over the last two weeks, something actually had changed. Everyone was going out more, including Ella. Several times they had all met up—including Max, Sean and Jack—to get a bite to eat. Ella had been with them and didn't seem phased by being the only single girl in the group. Now that Hailey thought about it, she noticed how Ella was actually starting to socialize a little more with everyone—including single men!

So here they were at a club in downtown Raleigh waiting for Jack's friend's band to go on. The place was large, dimly lit and getting crowded. Everyone was there and Hailey was standing next to Jack—listening to him talk to Sean about construction. That was Sean's line of work but to hear Jack talk about it, it could have been his too. His hand was resting low on her back and Hailey found she liked it there. And if she had anything to say about it, she was going to feel that hand in other places tonight too.

"So what kind of music are we hearing tonight?"

Becca asked as she pulled up a stool and placed it next to Hailey. "Rock? Jazz? What?"

"They're like a cover band. They do music from the eighties along with current songs. Some you can dance to, some you can just…I don't know…rock out to," Hailey said with a shrug. "They're really good."

Max walked over and handed Becca a drink before kissing her on the cheek. Hailey couldn't help but smile at the transformation in her friend. Several months ago, Becca had been a little insecure and quiet. Max had changed all of that. Now when she looked at her friend she saw a woman who was happy, confident. She loved that for her.

"It's been ages since we've gone dancing!" Becca exclaimed and then reached for Hailey's hand. "Promise me if they play something danceable, we'll go out and dance! You, me, Ange and Ella! Please!!"

Hailey laughed. "Of course! But you may want to let them in on our plan. I'm not sure we'll get Ella out there just yet. She's making progress but I don't know if it's that much."

Jack turned to them and smiled before reaching out and shaking Max's hand. "What's your plan?" he asked.

"Dancing!" Becca said. "If something good comes on to dance to, we're going to get out there and dance!"

Jack chuckled and then looked down at Hailey. "Dancing, huh?"

She nodded. "It's been years since we've done that. Now we just have to make sure Angie and Ella are on board. I was saying I wasn't sure Ella was up for it."

Nodding, Jack took a pull from his beer. "I think she may surprise you." He pointed toward the other end of the bar to where Ella was standing and talking to one of the guys in the band. "And before you get worried, don't. That's Charlie. He's a good guy."

Hailey looked at Ella with wide eyes before turning her gaze back to Jack. "How good of a guy? Is he hitting on her? Should I go over there?" She made to move away, but Jack simply tightened his grip on her.

"She's fine. You've all been worried about her

and now she's finally starting to socialize again. I think she's all right."

Hailey turned and looked at Becca, still unsure. "What do you think? Should we go over there?"

Becca shook her head. "I agree with Jack. This is good for her. She's never dated anyone but Dylan. Maybe she needs to do this."

"Do what?" Angie said, joining them. Becca explained what was going on with Ella and then pointed her out to Angie. "Oh! Oh! Look at that! And she's actually smiling!"

Hailey and Becca both nodded.

Conversation was going on all around them, but Hailey couldn't focus on even one of them. Her mind was swirling. Ella dating someone other than Dylan seemed wrong. Jack's hand—which was on the verge of cupping her ass—seemed right. Looking over her shoulder, she saw Ella laughing at something Charlie said right before he walked up onto the stage.

Jack noticed the direction of her gaze and leaned down to whisper in her ear. "Stop worrying about her. It's all going to be all right."

With a sigh, Hailey leaned in to him. "I wish I were as confident as you."

He placed a gentle kiss on her temple and straightened as the music started.

****

"I think we may need to do something," Becca

yelled in Angie's ear, trying to be heard over the music. They were currently dancing to a rocking version of "I Will Survive" and Ella was practically dancing on a table.

"Nah," Angie shouted back. "This is very therapeutic for her! Let her have her fun!"

Becca wasn't so sure. She was all for having some fun but knowing Ella the way she did—the way they all did—it was all a little unnerving. Ella wasn't a dancing-on-the-table kind of girl. She was more of a can-I-make-you-a-cup-of-tea kind. Shaking her head, she did her best to enjoy the music and the fact that she and the girls were having a great time. Hailey was right; the band was awesome and even though the bar scene wasn't her thing, she was glad she'd agreed to come.

Looking over at the bar, she smiled and waved at Max. He raised his bottle of beer at her and winked. God, how had she gotten so lucky? How was it even possible she could have met such an amazing guy at the seemingly lowest moment of her life? Max was everything she always hoped she'd find in a man but didn't think existed.

Physically, he wasn't anything like she ever imagined she'd fall in love with. She always imagined herself with a guy who was big and built—at least, that had always been her type. But it didn't matter. He was kind and considerate. He made her smile and laugh and feel good about herself. They could talk for hours and never run out of things to say.

She loved him.

Stopping in the middle of the dance floor, she gasped.

Angie turned and looked at her and leaned in close. "You okay? You look like you just saw a ghost!"

Becca chuckled and then started laughing almost hysterically. Jumping up, she hugged Angie. "I'm in love with Max!"

"Yeah, yeah, tell me something we don't all already know!"

"I need to go tell him!" And before she could talk herself out of it, Becca moved across the makeshift dance floor and walked excitedly back over to the bar. To Max.

He was still smiling when she walked up to him. "You okay?" he asked in her ear. "You looked like you were having fun out there!"

Becca nodded enthusiastically and then took the bottle of beer from his hands and put it on the bar. Then she reached around and cupped his face with both hands and kissed him—the kind of kiss that promised all kinds of sexy things. When she raised her head and looked at him, she said, "Let's get out of here."

Max looked a little dazed as he pulled her in close, his arms wrapped around her waist. "What's going on? I thought you were having a good time and besides, it's still early yet."

She even loved how he could be completely clueless at times. Like now. Leaning in close again, she playfully nipped his ear before saying, "I am having a good time but I'd much prefer to be alone with you and have a great time." Then she pulled back and gave him a sexy grin as if to say "Get it?"

Understanding slowly dawned on his face. Holding up a finger, he stood and turned to pay the bar tab. Turning back to her, he said, "Just give me a minute. I'm just gonna hit the men's room before we go." He kissed her again and then carefully maneuvered around her and through the crowd.

Becca looked around, practically bouncing on her toes with excitement. The song had changed and now it was some classic Bon Jovi and the crowd was still dancing. The girls were still out there and Sean and Jack had joined them. Ella was standing beside the stage and singing along happily.

It was a good night. It gave her such peace to see all of her friends so happy and smiling and…

"Hey, Becs," a deep male voice said from directly behind her.

She froze. No. Freaking. Way.

Slowly, she turned around and found Danny standing directly behind her. He had a smarmy look on his face—bordering on lecherous—and it made her stomach turn.

"Saw you dancing out there," he said, leaning in to be heard over the music. "Looking good."

Ew. Seriously? Becca looked beyond him to see if Max was coming back. The last thing she wanted was to be seen talking to Danny by Max…or anyone really. Without a word, she went to move around him but he reached out and gently grabbed her upper arm.

"What's the rush, babe? Let's get a beer. It's been a while."

Deciding she'd had enough, Becca pulled out of his grasp. "Thanks but I think I'll pass. Excuse me."

She never got to move. Danny had his hand on her again and blocked her path. The wall-to-wall crowd wasn't helping either.

"Oh come on, Bec, loosen up. One drink," he said smoothly.

"Where's your fiancée?" she asked snidely and liked how his smile slipped a little.

Danny shrugged. "I don't know. Home or something. I don't necessarily keep track."

"Charming," she muttered.

He huffed loudly. "You're not seriously going to make a big deal out it, right? I mean she's not here and you are. Let's get a drink." He reached out and traced a finger across her cheek. "I've missed you."

Becca swatted his hand away. "Don't touch me," she spat. "Don't ever touch me again!" Then she stormed around him and spotted Max walking toward her. Without looking back, she met up with him and took him by the hand and quickly led him out of the bar. They were halfway across the parking lot when she heard Danny call out her name. Max stopped and turned around and Becca had no choice but to stop with him due to the fact that they were holding hands.

Danny stormed up to them. “For Christ’s sake, Becca, what is your problem?”

“*My problem*? Seriously? Why would you think—for even a minute—I’d want to have a drink with you?”

“I don’t see what the big deal is.”

“The big deal is that you’re a complete jackass! You were such a tool to me! And you have a fiancée! Or have you forgotten her again? Because you clearly forgot about her while we were dating!”

“Dating? Is that what you thought we were doing?” Danny looked down at her and then at Max and chuckled. “This guy? Really?”

Pulling her hand from Max’s, she got toe to toe with Danny. “Yeah, this guy. Really,” she said. “You could learn something from him—like how to be a decent human being. Just…go away, Danny. Don’t talk to me anymore. I have nothing to say to you.” She turned to walk away.

“You’ve got a hell of a lot of nerve, you know that?” Danny taunted. “You practically threw yourself at me when we met and I was nice enough to spend some time with you. We had some fun but you were always so damn needy and clingy!” He snorted with disgust and then leaned in close. “And you weren't even that good in bed." With a sneer, he looked over at Max. "You're welcome to her. You look more her speed anyway."

Becca wanted to die of embarrassment. How had everything gone so wrong so damn quickly? This was a good night—a great night!—and five minutes around Danny and it all came crashing down. Unable to look at Max, she turned to walk to his car when she heard a loud thud. Turning around, she saw Danny on the ground holding his face. Max stood over him menacingly.

"If you ever come near her again, I'll do worse," he threatened and then turned, reached for Becca's hand and stalked away toward his car.

They were halfway to Becca's house before she was able to make herself speak. "I'm so sorry, Max."

Silence. His gaze was fixed on the road and his expression was hard.

Reaching across the console, she tried to touch him, but he flinched. Slowly, she pulled her hand back and put it in her lap. "Say something. Please."

Silence.

By the time they pulled into her driveway, Becca was more than a little concerned. This wasn't like Max at all. He never got mad, took everything in stride and was normally very laid back and understanding.

Clearly this was a side of himself he'd been hiding from her.

They climbed out of the car and once she had unlocked the front door, she noticed Max didn't seem inclined to come inside. "Max?"

"I…I think I should go," he said quietly, firmly.

Tossing her purse into the house, she faced him. "No. I think we need to talk about this. I don't understand why you're mad at me."

His expression was one of barely banked fury, but he said nothing.

"Will you come inside so we can talk? Please," she begged.

Max sighed and looked down at the ground for a long moment before looking at Becca again. "You know, as I was standing there in the parking lot listening to you, I realized something."

"What?" she asked earnestly.

"When he asked you what the big deal was, I didn't seem to play into the equation at all."

She looked at him, brows furrowed in confusion. "I…I don't understand."

"When Danny asked you what the big deal was about having a drink with him, you said he was a jackass, a tool, he had a girlfriend he was now engaged to…you mentioned all those things but you never said it was a big deal because you had a boyfriend."

Becca's eyes went a little wide as his words sank in. "Max, I wasn't thinking it all through. You know after he broke up with me, I never had the chance to confront him. So when the opportunity presented itself, I guess I just got caught up in it."

He shook his head. "It's more than that."

She reached for his hand but Max took a step back. Now she was beginning to panic.

"And when he stood there mocking me," He paused and shrugged, "You really didn't seem all that bothered by it. You told him I was decent but…"

"Max," she began, practically begging. "It was a shitty situation and I handled it poorly. The whole thing took me by surprise! Please. I'm so sorry that I hurt you. I'm not good at thinking on my feet like that or being confrontational."

For a minute, she thought she had him. His posture relaxed and he let out a small sigh. When he reached for her hand, Becca thought they were good.

"Let me ask you something," he began softly. "How do you feel right now? How did seeing Danny make you feel?"

"Honestly? Embarrassed."

"Why?"

"Because I can't believe I was ever so stupid," she explained. "I see now how much better my life is." She clutched his hand tightly in both of hers. "What we have is so much better than I ever thought possible, Max. I never believed guys like you were real. And when I think of us, I am so thankful. I'm so incredibly lucky because you are everything to me. Don't you know that?"

He smiled sadly. "I thought I did. But…"

"No. No, no, no…no buts," she said quickly and stepped in close to him. "I'm sorry if I didn't act the way you wanted me to but I can't change that. I've never been the type of person who says the right thing in the heat of the moment—especially in a fight." Taking a steadying breath, Becca decided it was time to lay it all out on the line for him. "I love you. I love you, Max, and I hate that I did something to hurt you."

Max studied her face for a long moment before he closed the distance between them and placed a gentle kiss on her forehead. Then he pulled away. "I'll talk to you tomorrow." And with that he turned and walked to his car and drove away.

Becca stood alone in the doorway wondering what the hell had just happened.

****

"I think the nachos may be to blame."

Becca's night wasn't the only one that went downhill. Angie had gotten sick at the bar and was currently curled up on her bathroom floor. Sean was sitting next to her and holding a cool towel to her head.

"Don't blame the nachos," she said miserably. "I refuse to believe that something so good would do something so horrible to me."

Trampus walked in, meowed, and did a slow inspection of the scene before walking out again.

"I should have gotten a dog. They're way more compassionate," she sighed.

Sean chuckled. "You don't need a dog; you have me."

That made her chuckle and then groan. "As much as I appreciate your willingness to compare yourself to an animal, now is not the time."

"Do you think you'll be okay if we move you to the bed or do you need to stay in here a little bit longer?"

"I can't imagine there's anything left inside of me, but the thought of moving is sort of bringing on a fresh wave of nausea."

He kissed her temple before standing up. "Okay, stay put. I'm going to go and take care of some things."

When he left the room Angie found she was mildly curious about what he was doing. Actually, that was a lie. She wasn't curious at all because she felt her entire body going hot again and she silently cursed her rotten luck. With strength she didn't think she had, she quickly sat up and found out she was wrong. There was something left inside of her.

Sean came back a few minutes later and gently scooped her up into his arms. Slowly he made his way to the bedroom and placed her down on the bed. Her entire body was trembling and he helped her get comfortable and covered her with blankets before kissing the top of her head and turning out the light.

"Where are you going?" she asked, her voice barely audible.

"I'll be out in the living room. Call me if you need anything, okay?"

Angie couldn't make herself answer because her eyes felt heavy and all she wanted to do was sleep. Unwilling to fight it, she closed her eyes and prayed she'd feel better in the morning.

****

"This was fun! Wasn't this fun?" Ella asked as she walked arm-in-arm with Hailey across the parking lot. "We should totally do this more often!"

Hailey made a non-committal sound.

"I can't even remember the last time we all danced like that! God, I used to love to dance! Why haven't we done that more? When did we stop doing it?"

Ella was drunk. Hailey couldn't believe her luck. Just when she was all set to pretty much pounce on Jack, Ella had come dancing over and pretty much rained on that parade. There was no way she could let Ella drive herself home and there was no way she was going to trust any random guy to do it, which meant getting Jack to go home with her would have to wait.

Again.

He was walking with them across the parking lot to Hailey's car. "Yeah, Hailey, why did you guys stop going dancing?" he teased.

"Oh hush," she murmured. "Don't encourage this."

"Oh you should to-tally encourage this," Ella sang. "And you know what else you should encourage, Jack-son?"

"Ella, come on," Hailey quickly interrupted. "Let's get you in the car and get you home."

"No, no, no," Ella quickly replied and turned to face Jack. "You should totally encourage this one here," she stopped to point at Hailey, "to loosen up once in a while. And you should totally follow her home."

Hailey quickly unlocked the passenger door and tried to maneuver Ella into the car.

"She's been waiting for you to take her to bed again!" Ella called out over Hailey's shoulder.

"Oh, dear God," Hailey mumbled before buckling Ella into the seat and shutting the door. She knew Jack was watching her and she also knew she was blushing clear to the roots of her hair. Clearing her throat, she forced herself to turn around. "So…"

Jack was grinning from ear to ear. "So…?"

"Drunk Ella is a completely new experience," she said lightly, moving away from Ella's door.

"I can see that," he said and then pulled her in close. "You sure you're going to be okay to take her home?"

She nodded. "I only had one glass of wine and that was hours ago."

"That's good. But I was thinking more about you getting her into her house and to bed all by yourself. I know she's small but…"

"Yeah, I'm kind of wondering that too."

"Tell you what, I'll follow you to Ella's and help you if you need it. If not, I'll head on home. What do you say?"

Hailey couldn't help but smile. "I'd say thank you very much. That's very kind of you."

He nodded. "Good." Then with a quick kiss he walked toward his car.

Hailey climbed in hers and waited until she saw where he was waiting before pulling out. It wasn't a long drive—ten minutes tops—but Ella was already asleep. By the time she pulled up in front of Ella's house, Hailey was relieved that Jack had followed her. There was no way she was going to be able to get Ella inside without one of them getting hurt.

Jack was already opening her passenger side door when Hailey walked around. "Do you have her keys?" he asked softly.

Hailey nodded and quickly made her way up to the front door to unlock it. They worked together to get Ella up and into bed. Once Jack had put her down, he left the room to go and find a glass of water and some Advil while Hailey got Ella out of her shoes and jeans.

"Mmm…" Ella hummed. "Dylan?"

And right then and there Hailey's heart broke a little bit more for her friend. Drunk and passed out and Dylan was still the first thing on her mind.

Gently combing Ella's hair away from her face she said, "No, sweetie. Dylan's not here."

Ella's face scrunched up like she was about to cry before she rolled onto her side. "I miss him so much," she said quietly. "Why won't he come home?"

Jack had come back into the room and put the water and tablets on Ella's nightstand. "Is she okay?"

Hailey leaned against him. "She's so sad."

Wrapping an arm around her, Jack pulled her close. "I know. I'm sure it's not easy to be as close as you two are and not be able to do anything to help her."

"Tonight…I really thought maybe she had turned a corner. And I feel bad because I wasn't really happy about it."

"What do you mean?"

Hailey shrugged. "I want Ella to be happy—more than anything. But I know now that she'll only truly be happy with Dylan. What they had?" She looked up at Jack. "You don't see that sort of love every day."

His gaze was intense but he didn't say a word. He simply held her close for a few minutes. Finally he asked, "Are you going to stay here tonight with her?"

"I thought about it. But I think she's out for the night. Plus, I'm not sure she'll want an audience when she wakes up with a hangover tomorrow." Stepping away from him, Hailey made sure Ella was covered and then fluttered around the room making sure she had a clear path to the bathroom—and even turned the light on in there for her. With nothing left to do, she faced Jack and silently held out her hand to him.

Leaving Ella's house, Hailey made sure the door was locked before walking with Jack back toward her car. "Thanks for following me here. I don't know if I could have gotten her inside by myself." She chuckled. "I didn't think she'd fall asleep so quickly. In my mind we were going to do the drunk walk into the house."

"You mean like the one the two of you did across the parking lot?" he asked, laughing with her.

She nodded. "Absolutely. Then I imagined the two of us tripping over each other as I tried to get her up the stairs." She laughed again and shook her head. "Believe it or not, this is the first time I've ever had to do this with Ella. Angie, yes. Becca, yes. But not Ella."

"I can believe it. I'm sure if she ever drank before, Dylan was there to take care of her."

Hailey nodded again. "It was always sweet to watch." Then she shrugged. "And Ella's really a lightweight. All of this tonight was only after two beers."

"What? No!" Jack said with disbelief.

"It's true. She's always the designated driver because she doesn't like to drink. That's another reason why I was concerned tonight. Everything about her tonight was completely out of character. And seeing her talking to that guy? Charlie? It was just plain weird."

"Come on, you can't tell me in all the years the two of them dated that they never broke up. Not even for a little while? Or that no guy ever hit on Ella?"

"Nope. They started dating in middle school and pretty much everyone knew Ella was off-limits. Besides, it was so obvious that the two of them only had eyes for each other. I never saw Dylan even look at another girl. And believe me, there were a lot of them who tried to get his attention. He just wasn't interested."

Jack studied her for a minute. "This may seem like a stupid question but…has anyone talked to Dylan? I mean, you? Angie? Becca? Anyone?"

"We've talked about it, but we don't want to upset Ella any more than she already is. I mean…it almost seems like a betrayal to do it."

"But maybe it's exactly what needs to be done," he reasoned. "Dylan needs to know how much Ella's hurting and someone needs to give them both a nudge. For all you know, he's as much of a mess as she is and is waiting for someone to give him the green light to come and talk to her." He paused. "I realize I don't know them the way you do, but…"

"No, no…you're right. Someone does need to do something. Maybe Ella will realize she needs to go and talk to him. I'm hoping tonight's behavior will maybe open the door to some dialogue."

Jack's eyes went wide. "Open the door to…? Hailey, everyone's walking on eggshells with this situation and it hasn't helped. The time for sitting back and waiting is over. If the two of them are too scared to do something, then somebody else should! You need to go at this!"

"Go at this? Why me?"

He rolled his eyes. "Okay, you or Angie or Becca or someone! It doesn't matter who, it just matters that something happen. Soon!"

"I'm going to talk with Ella tomorrow and…"

"Why? Why wait? Are you going to ask her permission? Do you need her to give you the okay before you do something that is ultimately going to help her?" He paused and almost growled with frustration. "What are you afraid of? Why can't you simply do something because you know it's right?"

"I'm not afraid, Jack," she said, trying to sound

reasonable. The truth was his words were starting to make her feel defensive.

"Then prove it! Do something! Break the damn rules you seem to live by, Hailey! Take a freaking chance! Stop worrying about how things are going to look to other people and do what you know is right!"

She didn't like his tone or what he was implying. Her back instantly stiffened. "Don't worry about it," she said primly. "I'll talk to the girls and we'll handle it. Like we always have." She crossed her arms across her chest. "It's late and I'm tired. Thank you again for helping me here tonight. I appreciate it."

Hailey knew she had totally regressed back into bitch-mode. Something she hadn't done with Jack in well over a month. And she also saw the look on his face.

Yeah, he was mentally calling her a bitch too.

And that was fine. She was tired and frustrated—not only with their current situation but with Ella and Dylan's too.

Jack took a step back and gave her a curt nod. "No worries. As usual, you're the one in control." He sighed loudly before turning away. "I'll see you Friday at the show."

Hailey didn't even try to stop him. She had done this—pushed him—and she wasn't about to resort to groveling. Mentally she made a note to call him tomorrow and apologize. But right now all she wanted to do was go home and punch something or kick something or…do something to get out this frustration!

By the time Hailey had backed out of Ella's driveway, Jack's car was nowhere in sight. She slapped the steering wheel while cursing herself and him. Her condo was only five minutes away and she spent every minute of it continuing to mentally yell at Jack.

It was easy for other people to offer an opinion on what should be done when they weren't the ones who had to do it. Talk to Dylan? Sure! Why not? Why not stab one of her best friends in the back—even if it was for the greater good! That wasn't the way they did things. Ever. It was one thing if she happened to run into Dylan, but to actively seek him out seemed wrong.

She slammed her car door shut with a little more force than necessary and then cringed. No need to wake up the entire neighborhood. Inside her home, she threw her purse on the sofa and went into the kitchen to grab herself something to drink. Suddenly she wasn't tired; her mind was too busy racing.

Thinking back to their conversation, Hailey was pretty sure Jack wasn't only talking about this situation with Ella and Dylan.

He was talking about her.

Or…them.

What did he expect from her? Hailey had no intention of changing everything about herself to simply suit him. She wasn't the overly-impulsive type—she enjoyed playing by the rules and within the boundaries. She hated coloring outside the lines. The only impulsive thing she had ever done was…Jack.

Dammit.

It wasn't in her nature to be impulsive. Hailey liked order. She hated chaos or going into situations blind. The very thought of going and talking to Dylan made her nervous. Maybe he didn't want to talk about Ella. Maybe he had already moved on. Then what was she supposed to do? What if he told Hailey breaking up with Ella was the greatest thing to ever happen to him? How could she possibly look at Ella again and tell her that? Or worse, how could she keep something like that from her?

And then there was Jack. Yes, she had acted impulsively and kissed him in his hotel room. And yes, it had led to a night of amazing sex. He was the one who said they should take it slow! He was the one who said he essentially didn't want to feel like she was using him. He was the one who made the rules and now…

Cursing, she slammed the refrigerator door closed and stomped out of the room and scooped up her purse and keys.

"He wants impulsive? He thinks I have to wait for permission? Well, we'll just see about that!" Walking over to the front door she pulled it open and froze.

Jack was standing in the doorway.

She wasn't sure if she was surprised or angry or both. Rather than think about it, she reached out and gripped the collar of his shirt and pulled him inside.

"About damn time," Hailey said as she pulled his head down and kissed him.

Eleven

Judith took one look at Angie and immediately gasped. "Oh my goodness! Are you all right?"

It was Friday night and an hour before show time. Angie still felt like hammered shit but she had never missed a show and she wasn't going to start now. "I'm okay. I didn't want to leave you shorthanded."

Judith immediately began to fuss over her—feeling her head and making sure she wasn't feverish. "Hailey said you had food poisoning. Have you gone to the doctor?"

Angie shook her head. "I didn't think it would be necessary, but I can't seem to get rid of whatever it is that made me sick."

"Then you probably shouldn't be here," Judith said lightly. "We'll be fine and I'd feel better knowing you were home resting. And you know tonight is really more of a mini-show. We could have easily made it work."

At that moment, Sean walked over and joined them. "I told her the same thing, but she insisted she couldn't miss a show."

"I feel fine right now," Angie argued. "I took some over-the-counter anti-nausea stuff. I'm not saying I can handle four dress changes, but I can definitely do a couple." She looked at Judith. "Please? I hate to ruin a perfect attendance record."

Unable to help herself, Judith cupped Angie's face and smiled. "Okay, fine. Two dresses. But no more than that and we'll do one at the beginning and one at the end so you can rest in between. Deal?"

"Deal."

"Okay then." Judith looked over her shoulder and called out to her assistant. "Let me go rework the schedule. You go and do your thing. The girls are already back there."

Sean was right beside her when she turned to go and get ready. Before she could take a step, she faced him. "Look, I am so grateful for you staying and taking care of me all week, but tonight I kind of need to be with the girls." She watched his face for any signs of disappointment. "Are you okay with that?"

He leaned in and kissed her on the forehead. "We talked about this earlier, remember? I knew you guys were going to go out after the show and just relax and really, I'm fine with it. I'm going to go and grab some takeout and do some work. My flight out tomorrow is pretty early and I'm landing and heading right to a meeting with a new client so I want to make sure I have everything in order."

"I just hate feeling like I'm leaving you alone when you're leaving tomorrow."

"Ange, we've spent a lot of time together and we're not joined at the hip, remember? Neither of us wanted to be like that."

She nodded. "I know. I know..."

"Go and get ready and tell the girls I said hi. I'll see you when you get home," he said and kissed her one last time before leaving.

Once he was out of sight, Angie moved to the dressing room area and took her spot with the girls. She sighed and let her head fall back as she sat down.

"So you weren't kidding," Becca said. "You look like hell."

"Becca!" Ella cried. "That was just mean!"

"Nah," Angie said without opening her eyes. "She's telling the truth. It's gonna take a lot of makeup to make me look a little less green around the gills."

"This can't be food poisoning," Hailey said as she applied mascara. "It's got to be a virus or something. And now you're just spreading it around."

That had Angie sitting up straight. "You all told me to come!" she whined.

"Sorry…you know I'm a bit of a germaphobe," Hailey said. "So what's going on?"

"Sean thought it was the nachos Saturday night and to be honest, it made sense. But all week I've just been off. I left work early twice because I got sick after lunch."

"Please tell me it wasn't on more nachos?" Becca asked.

"No, smartass," Angie said. "If anything, I was being super cautious—ginger ale, tea, soup. But we had birthday cake for one of the girls in accounting and I had a slice and then…bleh! It was all over. The next time it was someone reheating their lunch in the microwave—something German, I swear—and I was running for the bathroom."

"Uh…Ange?" Hailey asked cautiously.

"What?"

"Is there a chance you could be pregnant?"

All eyes turned to Angie—including some of the other models. "Geez, Hails, are you sure you don't want a megaphone? Seriously, what the hell?"

Hailey gave some rather pointed looks to the people around them before looking at Angie again. "Sorry. I didn't think I was that loud."

"Well you were."

"And I apologized."

"Well you should."

Hailey gave her a knowing smile. "Nice distraction tactic, but I'm on to you."

Angie sighed loudly. "I can't be pregnant."

"Is it even a possibility?" Ella asked softly.

Shrugging, Angie replied, "I don't think so. I mean, I know nothing is completely foolproof but…"

"Okay, this probably isn't the time or place to get into this," Becca said. "We're all heading over to my place after the show so let's table this discussion until then. All right?"

They all nodded in agreement.

****

Three hours later they were all sitting around Becca's living room eating ice cream.

Except Angie.

"Okay, so this has been a completely shitty week," Becca said. "I mean, a week ago I thought we were all on top of the world and it's like the universe swooped in and took a huge crap on us all." Then she glanced to her left. "Well, except for you, Hails."

Hailey blushed.

"Go ahead and give a quick rundown of how awesome your week has been. Might as well start out on a high note."

"Well, I have to admit, if it weren't for Ella's little foray into being a woo-girl, I'd be just as miserable as the rest of you."

"I am never drinking again," Ella said solemnly. "Honestly, what do people get out of that? I felt awful all day Sunday and just thinking about it makes my head hurt."

"You were entertaining, if nothing else," Angie said, raising her glass of ginger ale at her.

"I aim to please," Ella said with a grin.

"Have you thought about calling Dylan?" Hailey asked. "You know you said…"

"Yeah, I know," Ella quickly interrupted. "But…I can't. I need Dylan to be the one to make the move. He was the one who left and even after I went to see him, he still didn't make any attempt to come after me." She shrugged. "I just thought he would have tried more by now."

They were all silent for a minute. "What about you, Becs? I saw Max at the show tonight but didn't see the two of you together like you usually are. Everything okay?" Angie asked.

Rather than answer right away, Becca took a large spoonful of ice cream and slowly savored it. "He came over last night."

"And?" they all asked.

"And…we talked. He admitted – again – how he was disappointed that I didn't stand up for him more. For us. And he thought it was wrong for me to even want to hash things out with Danny. He said if I was truly happy with him then that was all the closure I should have needed."

"Wow," Angie said seriously, "clearly he's never had someone dump him."

Becca nodded in agreement. "That was my argument."

"So then what happened?" Ella asked curiously, twirling her spoon.

"He thought my telling him I loved him was a little manipulative—given the timing and the circumstances."

"Wait…what?" Hailey cried. "You told him you loved him? In the middle of the fight?"

"Yeah, I know. Not the smartest way to go. But honestly, that was the whole reason why we left the club! I finally realized I'm in love with him and I wanted to tell him. Then Danny showed up and ruined the whole thing."

"Typical Danny," Angie said.

"I think calling it manipulative is a little harsh," Hailey commented. "Did you explain to him how, if it weren't for Danny, you were planning on telling him that anyway?"

"I did. He didn't seem like he really believed me."

"So how did you leave things?" Hailey asked.

"We talked for a long time."

"And…?" Ella asked with a hint of frustration.

"And I think we're okay," Becca said with a smile. "We both agreed it was a fight, it happens and we're ready to move on from it."

"But…what about the 'I love you' part?" Hailey asked.

Becca sighed. "Well, he hasn't said it back so…that sucks. But I feel better because I said it. I was scared to and honestly, if we hadn't fought, I think Max would have said it too. It's okay. I can wait. He's worth it."

"Wow," Ella sighed. "That was quite possibly the healthiest example of a relationship I've ever heard. I'm seriously impressed."

"Yeah well…I think we all know I was due. This is the first healthy relationship I've ever had! And I really do love Max. I can't imagine ever loving anyone else. He's it for me," Becca said, taking a spoonful of ice cream. "I'm not pushing to get married or engaged or anything, although I wouldn't mind us moving in together. But again, I can wait."

"So then what was the deal tonight?" Angie asked. "You guys hardly said two words to each other."

"You just got there late," Becca corrected. "We got there at our usual time and I helped him set up and then he went and grabbed me a latte before he needed to get started." She shrugged. "But he knew we were all hanging out tonight so we promised to talk tomorrow. Which reminds me…are we still doing lunch since we're all here now?"

"Um…it's tradition," Ella reminded. "No matter what, remember? And besides, we're all going out tomorrow night too." She turned to Hailey. "Is this the same club as last week?"

Hailey gave them all the updated info. "It's basically right around the corner and the band goes on at ten. You all in?"

"Max and I are gonna be there."

"And I can promise to be the designated driver," Ella said. "I've learned my lesson."

Hailey chuckled. "I'm going to hold you to that because Jack is actually picking me up and we're having dinner first and then going to the club. I fully intend to go home with him so keep that in mind in case you decide to have a drink."

"Not gonna happen. Trust me," Ella said, holding up her hand. "Scout's honor."

"Yeah, that would be a lot more impressive if you were ever a scout," Angie teased.

"Bite me," Ella said, sticking out her tongue. She burst out laughing. "That felt good!"

"So we went all around the room but never got the rest of Hailey's story," Angie said, smirking.

"Noticed that, did you?"

They all nodded.

"Well, Jack and I had a fight in Ella's driveway Saturday night."

"Oh, no!" Ella cried. "Over what? Was it because I was drunk?"

Hailey shook her head. "We were both a little snippy about…well…a couple of different things," she said evasively. "Anyway, he accused me of being uptight and I didn't take too kindly to it. So he took off."

"You're seriously not going to tell us what you argued about?" Becca asked, brows furrowed.

Hailey shook her head again. "It's not important. Anyway, I got home and was still fuming and the more I thought about things, the madder I got. So I decided I was going to go and confront him."

"Here's where it gets good," Angie sang.

"Yeah, yeah, yeah. I opened the door and there he was," Hailey said, grinning. "Then I pulled him inside and rocked his world until the wee hours!" She let out a maniacal little laugh, clearly proud of herself. "I'm not gonna lie, it was even better than the night at the hotel!"

"Yeah, you!" Angie cheered.

"I know!" Hailey agreed. "God, I had no idea I was missing so much! Sex was always…nice. But with Jack?" She fanned herself. "Nice is never going to be a word I'll use to describe the way that man is in bed!"

"Good sex makes everything better," Becca agreed.

Ella sat curled up in her chair, playing with her ice cream. "I miss all the good sex."

“Seriously, El, you need to go and talk to Dylan again. Maybe he just needed a little time,” Becca suggested. “Or do you maybe want one of us to go and talk to him?”

“Oh, gosh no. I think I would die,” Ella said miserably.

“Why?” Hailey asked.

“Because…what if…what if he’s moved on? What if he just doesn’t care anymore? I don’t think I’d be able to handle hearing about it—even if it came from one of you.”

“So…what then?” Angie asked. “Ignorance is bliss?”

“Hardly,” Ella sighed. “I’m not sure what to do anymore.”

After a brief pause, Angie said, “You’re going to keep doing what you’re doing then until you figure it out. And no matter how long it takes, we’ll be right here to support you.”

Ella smiled sadly. “I love you guys.”

“We love you too.”

****

The club was crowded, but not quite as much as the previous weekend. Hailey was standing with her back pressed against Jack’s chest, unable to stop smiling. When he had shown up at her place earlier to pick her up for dinner, he took one look at her in her electric blue dress with matching stilettos and hauled her over his shoulder, up to bed.

The drive-thru burgers they'd had right before showing up here at the club were totally worth it.

She felt his hot breath against her neck. "I'm all for supporting a friend," he murmured in her ear, "but I don't think he'd be too upset if we didn't stay for the entire set."

Hailey smiled. "You're not going to get an argument from me." Turning, she kissed him. Jack's arms immediately banded around her but she pulled back before things got too out of hand.

"Geez, get a room," Becca teased as she and Max approached. They were both smiling and holding hands as they all greeted each other. "I haven't seen Angie or Ella yet."

"Me either," Hailey replied. "Maybe Sean's flight was delayed."

Becca shrugged. "Maybe. But Ella wasn't coming with them, was she?"

"Actually, I think they decided that after you left this afternoon," Hailey said. "Ella said she felt weird about coming alone. I just wish she'd stop being so stubborn about this whole Dylan thing!"

"Her?" Becca asked incredulously. "I wish Dylan would get his head out of his ass and stop pouting! I have to tell you, I've lost a lot of respect for him after this whole thing. He never should have let her go the way he did. It was cowardly."

“Oh, I agree. But…” She stopped when Jack bent down and whispered in her ear that Angie and Ella were walking in. Hailey looked at Becca. “To be continued.”

Becca nodded.

A few minutes later they were all standing together—minus Sean. “I thought Sean was flying in tonight?” Hailey commented after they settled at the end of the bar.

“Change of plans,” Angie said curtly and then looked away.

Ella looked at Hailey and Becca with a sad smile as she shook her head.

“All righty then,” Becca said brightly. “The band is heading up to the stage.” She hooked her arm through Max’s. “You promised me a dance tonight. Don’t forget that.”

Max chuckled. “Only if it’s slow,” he said. “Don’t expect me to go out there like the four of you did last weekend. I’m not dancing to Madonna or anything.”

“Like I’d ever ask that of you,” she replied, kissing him lightly.

Hailey couldn’t help the smile on her face as she watched them. They were going to be fine. They’d had their first fight, their first bump in the road and they’d survived. Looking over at Ella, Hailey only hoped she could soon say the same thing. Even though the two of them had been together for what seemed like forever, technically this still was Dylan and Ella's first fight, first bump. It was just taking them a little longer to get over it.

Then her gaze wandered over to where Angie was standing. Something was definitely up, but here in the middle of the bar was not the place to get into it. Suddenly the thought of hearing the music and having fun lost some of its appeal. Turning to face Jack, she said, "Excuse me for a minute."

She moved quickly and grabbed Angie's hand as she walk by her and tugged her behind her until they made it to the ladies' room. Once inside, Hailey blanched. It was a little dark and dank but it would have to do. "Okay, spill it. What's going on?"

"What are you talking about?" Angie asked, slightly defensively. "It smells like something died in here."

"Then I suggest you talk quickly," Hailey said, using her best no-nonsense tone.

Angie glared at her silently.

"Look, you were fine this afternoon at lunch and now you're not. It doesn't take a rocket scientist to know something's wrong. So?"

For a minute, she didn't think Angie was going to answer her, but then—much to Hailey's horror—tears filled her friend's eyes. Oh God. This was bad! This was bad! Why hadn't she thought to bring Ella and Becca with her? "Ange? Sweetie? What happened?"

Furiously swiping at her eyes, Angie said flatly, "I'm pregnant."

Hailey's heart stopped for a second. "Okay," she said, nodding. "And I take it you're a little freaked out."

"Ya think?" Angie snapped. "This isn't supposed to happen! This wasn't part of the plan!" Her voice was nearing hysteria.

"Okay, okay, okay," Hailey soothed, wrapping her arms around Angie and simply hugging her until she calmed down. After a few minutes, she pulled back. "What did Sean say?"

Without a word, Angie turned toward the sink and bent over to splash some cold water on her face. Hailey handed her some paper towels and waited for her to respond.

"He wants to get married," she said angrily. "Like…seriously. He wants us to get married!"

Hailey looked at her, uncertain of what it was she was supposed to say here. In her mind, it was the correct response for him to have.

"You don't get it, do you?" Angie snapped and then growled with frustration. "Things were just starting to go well—we were settling into this new routine, relationship, whatever!—and now we're supposed to just jump in and get married? This isn't the fifties! People don't have to do that anymore."

Being the level-headed one of the group, Hailey knew immediately why this was the kind of reaction

Angie was having. Her parents had married young—due to a pregnancy—and never seemed truly happy. That was one thing. The other? Angie took great pride in being fiercely independent and not following in anyone's footsteps. So this whole surprise pregnancy thing? Yeah, it was absolutely bringing up all kinds of negative feelings that were overshadowing all the positives of this situation.

"I know you're upset," Hailey began cautiously, "and this is something we are going to have to talk about when you're not feeling so…freaked out."

Angie simply glared at her.

"You're overwhelmed with all of this right now. You know it, I know it and I'm sure Sean knows it. But it's not something that's just going to go away. You're going to have to deal with it and I think sitting down with all of us—where you can verbally unload without any judgment—will go a long way in helping you." Hailey paused and rubbed Angie's arm comfortingly. "We'll do takeout at my place tomorrow night. What do you say?"

"I'd say we've already spent too much time together this weekend," she grumbled.

"Yeah, well…it's a good thing we all love each other or it would really suck." She was relieved when Angie chuckled with her. "Now let's go back out there, listen to some music and put the world on hold for a little while. Okay?"

"I shouldn't have even come," Angie said as more tears welled up in her eyes. "I thought I'd be able to push it all aside and act like nothing's wrong but my damn hormones are all over the place!"

Hailey hugged her again. "And just so you know, when you're feeling better, we're all going to have a *lot* of fun with that."

Angie swatted her away and chuckled even as tears streamed down her face. She turned to wipe them away and check her reflection in the mirror when Becca stuck her head in the room. "Um…you guys need to come out here. Like now."

They quickly followed and all came to an abrupt halt.

Ella was up on the stage—drink in hand—singing "Living on a Prayer" by Bon Jovi.

The girls all looked at one another in confusion. "How long were we in there?" Angie asked.

"Obviously long enough for Ella to have a drink," Hailey said.

"She did shots," Becca said. "Shots!"

Hailey threw up her arms in frustration as she turned and faced the two of them. "Who was stupid enough to let Ella do shots?"

"Don't look at me!" Angie cried. "I was with

you!"

They both looked at Becca. "Sorry. Wasn'tme." She wouldn't make eye contact with either of them and quickly looked over her shoulder at Ella.

Hailey spun her around. "Who did she do shots with, Bec?"

Frowning, Becca said, "I don't want to say."

"Ladies, you're back," Jack said smoothly as he walked over and put his arm around Hailey.

One look at Becca's face and Hailey had her answer. She quickly turned to Jack. "You did shots with Ella? Why? Why would you do that?"

He laughed and pointed to where Ella was screaming out the chorus. "Because she needed this! Look at her! She's smiling. She's happy. I wanted her to have some fun!"

Hailey looked at him as if he were crazy. "What is wrong with you? After everything that happened the last time she drank, you went and encouraged her to do it again? With shots?" She huffed loudly. "Jack…"

He put a finger over her lips to stop her from saying anything else. Leaning down, he whispered in her ear, "Trust me." Then he took her by the shoulders and turned her back toward the stage.

When the song ended, the entire bar exploded in applause as the lead singer introduced Ella and thanked her for joining them on stage. Ella waved to the crowd enthusiastically and jumped down to high five people as she walked by. The band immediately went into their next song—"Surrender"—as she bounced over to the girls. "Did you see me? Did you see me?" she asked excitedly.

“Ella, honey,” Hailey began, “I thought you weren’t going to drink tonight.”

Ella waved her off. “It was just a couple of shots and,” she stopped and turned to look at the band, “I love this song! Woo!”

Hailey looked over her own shoulder at Jack. “Seriously? This is a good thing to you?”

Not answering, he simply held up his beer and took a pull and focused on the band.

“I totally wanna dance!” Ella said. “Come on, girls! Come dance with me!” She didn’t wait to see if anyone followed, she shimmied her way through the crowd and began dancing with pretty much everyone.

“If I had been drinking, I’d swear I was seeing things,” Angie said in Hailey’s ear. “Should we stop her?”

“I don’t think there’s anything wrong with the dancing, but we definitely can’t let her have any more to drink. That could be dangerous.”

“Agreed.”

Over the next few songs, Ella continued to dance while Angie, Hailey and Jack watched in relative amusement. Becca and Max were currently out on the dance floor in their own little world and for the moment, Hailey felt herself relax. A loud ruckus coming from in front of the stage caught her attention. “What the…?”

“Oh, my God! Is that Dylan?” Angie cried. They all made their way through the crowd and saw that it was—indeed—Dylan.

“Dylan!” Ella cried. “What are you doing here?” The band was still playing—loudly—and it was hard to be heard over them.

“What am I…? What the hell are you doing with this guy?” Dylan demanded. People moved away and Dylan reached out and grabbed Ella’s hand but she pulled back. “I came here to see you and you’re…you’re dancing with some other guy?”

“Why are you so surprised?” she yelled back. “What did you think I was doing here?”

Oh, no. Hailey inwardly groaned.

Jack stepped forward and put a hand on Dylan’s shoulder. “Why don’t we go outside where it’s not so crowded and talk, okay?”

Dylan nodded and stalked away, Ella trailing behind him.

“Should we follow them?” Becca asked.

Before Hailey could answer, Jack did. “Give them a few minutes and then go check on them.” He took Hailey’s hand and led her back over to the bar where he ordered another beer, smiling the entire time.

Hailey studied him and then thought about all of the events of the evening—particularly where Jack was concerned. “You did that,” she said, a smile tugging at her lips.

“Did what?” he asked innocently.

“You got Dylan to come here.”

He shrugged. “Maybe.”

“Oh my God!” she playfully slapped his arm. “You totally went and talked to Dylan! When? What did he say? Did he come here to win her back? Is he going to…?”

Jack cut off her words by kissing her. She instantly melted against him and for a little while, forgot all about the drama that was unfolding.”

****

“Dylan!” Ella cried as she tried to keep up with him. He was stalking across the parking lot and she had no idea if he was going to stop or get in his car and leave. “Dylan, wait!”

He spun around so suddenly that she almost ran right in to him. “What?” he demanded.

Her eyes went wide for a minute. “What is going on? What are you doing here?”

“What am I…? I thought you knew I was coming! Jack said you wanted to see me and to meet you here! And then I walk in and you’re all…dancing all over the place!” He paused, stepping closer and sniffed. “Have you been drinking? Jesus, Ella. Is that why you wanted me here? So you could flaunt your newfound freedom in my face?”

“Newfound freedom? Are you high?” she accused. “I had no idea you were coming here tonight. I've been waiting for you to come home for weeks, Dylan. Weeks! Believe me, this is the last place I expected to see you!"

"Then why did Jack say you wanted to see me?" he asked angrily.

"I didn't ask Jack to talk to you! He did that on his own!"

"Why?" he demanded. "Why would he even do that? I barely know the guy!"

"Because I did want to see you! I mean, I do want to see you! Everyone knew how much I wanted that! It wasn't a big secret! But the more time that went by and you didn't come around, the worse I felt! Dammit, Dylan, how could you just leave me like that?"

"You weren't happy! I thought it was the right thing for me to leave and give you some space!"

"I never wanted you to leave!" She paused and pulled at her hair in frustration. "I never asked you to leave nor did I imply that I wanted that! All I wanted was for us to talk! For you to listen to me and know I was having some struggles! I just needed you to understand what I was feeling and help me through it!"

"It didn't seem that way to me," he said firmly. "Every day it was something else—something else you were missing out on. Do you have any idea how that made me feel?"

"Probably the same way it made me feel when you kept letting our parents march all over me and our wedding plans! I kept telling you how unhappy I was and all you would say was that it would be all right. You never took my side or even tried to see things from my perspective."

"I didn't…I didn't understand how much it was all affecting you. At least not at the time," he admitted. "I couldn't understand what the big deal was because all I knew was that we were finally getting married. I just assumed you were thinking the same way."

"Well I wasn't," she said defiantly. "I mean, yes, I was so happy that we were finally getting married but somewhere along the line it stopped being about you and me and started being about our families and only what they wanted."

He nodded. "Yeah. I know. I see that now."

"And then when I came to talk to you, you still wouldn't listen to me! You still made me feel like everyone else's opinion was more important than mine. Dylan, we were supposed to be partners." She sniffed and wiped away the tears that were starting to fall. "You made me feel like I was all alone." She shook her head. "And that's not what I wanted."

"That was never my intention," he said gruffly. "You have to know that."

"And in the end it's exactly what you did—you left me all alone."

And just like that all of the fight seemed to go out of him. “Dammit, Ella. Do you have any idea how badly I wanted to come home to you?”

She had to fight the urge to fling herself into his arms. “Then why didn’t you? I begged you, Dylan! I begged you to talk to me, to come home and you wouldn’t!”

He hung his head as he shook it. “I really thought I was doing the right thing, Ella. You’d been going on for so damn long about all you thought you were missing and I thought if I just gave you some time, you’d see it wasn’t all that it was cracked up to be and come back.”

She sighed with frustration. “I wasn’t the one who left!”

Dylan looked up at her, his expression bleak. “I thought you’d come back again and get in my face and tell me you were wrong and you wanted me to come home.”

It should have irked her that what he really wanted was for her to admit she was wrong but…she was. So very, very wrong. For so long she thought she was the one missing out on some key life experiences when the reality was that her life had been so much better without them. As much as she loved her friends, she wouldn’t trade her life for any of theirs.

Closing the distance between them, she looped her arms around Dylan’s neck and waited until his eyes met hers. “I was wrong,” she said softly. “Our life together was so much better than anything else in the world. I'm sorry I didn't appreciate it more, that I didn't realize what a gift I'd been given. But if you come home with me tonight, I promise I'll never take it for granted again."

He gave her that slow grin that never failed to make her go a little weak in the knees. "I'm so sorry, Ella," he said, his voice gravelly and thick with emotion. "I know I'm equally to blame for all of this. I didn't stand up for you—for us—with all of the wedding plans and I let you carry that burden all by yourself." He rested his forehead against hers. "It won't happen again. I promise to be more supportive, more vocal, and together—when you're ready—we'll have the wedding we've always dreamed of, not the one our families were orchestrating."

Her eyes lit up. "Do you mean it? You still want to marry me?"

He reached up and cupped her cheek. "Ella Gilmore, since the first time I laid eyes on you I knew you were the girl I was going to marry. Not seeing you these last few weeks nearly killed me. I want to see you every day, lie beside you every night and wake up next to you every morning. You're my everything, Ella."

Unable to hold back any longer, she got up on her toes and pressed her lips to his. Dylan met her halfway and as soon as they touched it felt like coming home. She melted against him and felt an overwhelming sense of peace come over her. When

Dylan lifted his head, he smiled at her. "I missed you."

"I missed you too." She was about to suggest that they go back inside and let everyone know they were okay when Dylan bent and picked her up, hauling her over his shoulder. "Dylan!" she cried. "What are you doing?"

"Taking you home," he growled and playfully swatted her ass. "We have a lot of making up to do."

Ella giggled as happiness filled her to the point of overflowing.

And that's how Angie, Hailey, Becca, Jack and Max found them as they all stepped outside. Without a word, Hailey hooked her arm through Jack's and hugged him.

"Thank you."

****

"So…a lot of drama tonight," Jack said as he and Hailey walked up to her front door.

"Honestly, I've watched soap operas with less."

Jack chuckled. "I think the highlight was Ella

singing Bon Jovi. In a million years I never thought I'd see something like that."

"That makes two of us," Hailey said as she opened the door. She tossed her purse on the sofa and asked Jack if he wanted something to drink. Kicking off her shoes, she went to grab herself a bottle of water.

During the ride home, she had meant to talk to him about what had happened tonight, but they only got around to talking about Angie and Sean's situation—which was really enough to keep them talking for days. Unfortunately, she wasn't going to be able to do more than sit and wait until she got together with Angie and the girls tomorrow. Or, at least she hoped they were going to get together. With the new turn in Dylan and Ella's situation, there was a good chance she was going to be busy in the foreseeable future.

"So I have to ask," she called out, "when did you go and talk to Dylan?"

Jack came into the kitchen and took the bottle of water she was offering. He shrugged. "I went and saw him yesterday. Your mom told me where I could find him."

Her eyes went a little wide at that information. "So what did you say to him?"

"I kind of played it vague. I told him how Ella wasn't doing too well and she really wanted to talk to him, but on neutral ground. Then I told him where we'd all be tonight and told him to come by." He smiled. "And the rest…is history. You can tell me I'm brilliant. I can stand it."

She swatted at him playfully and grabbed her own drink. "Like you need that kind of an ego boost?"

"It can't hurt!" he teased as he walked out of the room.

When she came back to the living room, she found Jack sitting on the sofa and all she could do was smile.

"What?" he asked softly.

"You," she replied with a happy sigh.

"Me? What about me?"

How could she even put it into words? He had come into her life in the most unexpected way and had proved how first impressions could be deceiving. To say that Jack had turned her world upside down would be an understatement.

He showed her how much she was missing out on by having such a rigid outlook and standards. He made her laugh and smile and…oh, did the man know how to make her feel good. In the bedroom and out. And to look at him right now, Hailey felt like she was looking at her future.

"I love you," she simply said.

Jack's smile grew. "Is that right?"

Hailey rolled her eyes. Leave it to Jack to

challenge her even in a situation like this. At one time, it would have ticked her off, but now? Now she was able to laugh at herself—and him. So she nodded. "Yeah. I think so."

Slowly Jack came to his feet. “You think so? A minute ago you sounded like you were pretty sure.”

She shrugged coyly. “What can I say? I’m fickle.”

Reaching out he banded his arms around her waist and pulled her close, smiling the entire time. “Fickle, huh? Well…what if I said I love you too? Would that make you a little less…fickle?”

She purred as she pressed closer. “It can’t hurt,” she teased.

Jack’s hand came up and he caressed her cheek, his expression going serious. “I do, you know. I love you, Hailey. I have for a long time.”

“You have?” she asked, her gaze scanning his face.

“Hell, I fell in love with you when you were blowing me off and treating me like I was beneath you.” There was no condemnation in his words, he was simply stating a fact.

“I’m so sorry. I…”

“Shh…” Jack pressed a finger against her lips. “You don’t owe me an apology, Hailey. We’ve been over this before. That’s all in the past. I want to focus on the here and now.”

She smiled. “I want that too.”

Then his smile turned a little wicked, a little sexy. “How about we go inside and work on that?” His hands traveled up and down her sides and then he shifted around so that his hands gently kneaded her ass.

“Ooh…I like the way you think.” Taking him by the hand, she led him to her bedroom and closed the door behind them.

The here and now sounded just about perfect to her.

****

“You look like you’re going to throw up. Again,” Becca said when Angie came back into the room. “Do you need some crackers? Or more ginger ale? Tea?”

“Stop mentioning food or I will seriously throw up again,” Angie grumbled as she curled up on the couch. They were all supposed to meet at Hailey’s but when she couldn’t seem to be away from her bathroom for more than five minutes at a shot, they changed plans and everyone had come to Angie’s place.

And right now she loved and hated them all equally.

Damn hormones.

“Okay,” Hailey said as she sat down at the other

other end of the sofa. “Tell us where you left things with Sean.”

At just the mention of his name, Angie’s heart seemed to kick in her chest. “I told you. He wants to get married.”

"Yeah," Becca replied, "but you never said if you told him right then and there that you didn't want to or how he responded. Stop procrastinating and just tell us."

Angie groaned as she let her head fall back and closed her eyes. "I told him I didn't want to get married, that I didn't love him." She paused. "Basically I told him I had no interest in any relationship with him, that this wasn't working for me."

"Holy shit," Hailey said. "What in the world?"

"Yeah," Ella chimed in. "I thought things were going great with the two of you. You were practically living together."

"They were and…we were, but…it's all just too much," she replied with agitation. "He was smothering me and I couldn't stand it." Before she could say anything else, she was on her feet and running for the bathroom.

"Geez," Becca murmured. "If that's what pregnancy is like, I'll gladly wait."

"It's not like that for everyone," Ella said. "Some women get away with little to no morning sickness. Poor Ange. I hate this for her. To have to be dealing with all the throwing up while going through a breakup at the same time? That's just too much."

"I think there's more to all this than she's sharing," Hailey said.

“What do you mean?” Becca asked as she reached for one of the muffins Ella had brought with her for them to share.

“She was happy with Sean. Not once did she mention that he was smothering her or that she was looking for an out. I know she’s scared because she doesn’t want to end up like her parents but…” She paused. “I’m telling you, we’re missing some key information here.”

“I don’t know,” Ella said thoughtfully, “Angie doesn’t hide anything from anyone. She says exactly what’s on her mind. Maybe she was just going through the motions and trying to make it work and then decided that it didn’t?”

At that moment Angie walked back into the room and they all grew quiet. She growled slightly as she sat back down. “Oh for crying out loud, I know you were all talking about me. No need to stop because I came back in the room.” She sighed and got comfortable. “If you’ve got something to say, just say it.”

Hailey turned toward her. “Okay, here it is. I think you’re full of shit.”

Angie’s eyes went wide. “Excuse me?”

“You heard me, I think you’re full of shit. I think there’s more to all of this than you’re telling us. I think you’re scared and freaking out, but I think you *do* love Sean. So what gives?”

"Ease up, Hails," Becca said. "Can't you see she's still looking a little green?"

"Yeah, I see how she looks," Hailey said but her tone was far from sympathetic. She turned back to Angie. "So? What's your deal?"

"I don't know," Angie replied tartly. "Why don't you tell me? You seem to think you know freaking everything, so why don't you share with the class?"

Hailey stood and paced the small living room. "You are the most fearless person I know. Out of all of us, you're the only one who has never backed down from anything and it kind of pisses me off that you're choosing to do that now, especially because this is something that really matters."

"You don't think I know that?" Angie snapped, coming to her feet. "Do you think I like feeling like this? A week ago, I was in complete control of my life! Things were going along fine with Sean and we were taking things one day at a time! Did I ever think about getting married? Yes! Did I ever think about getting married to Sean? Yes! But it was going to be on *my* terms! And all this?" she cried, pointing to her belly. "This isn't on my time! And I have no idea what to do about it!"

"The baby?" Hailey asked cautiously.

Angie sighed. "No. I'm having this baby. That was never in question. But Sean?" She shrugged.

Hailey's expression softened. "Okay, so it's not quite the way you had it planned, but that doesn't mean it's not good. Plans change. Things happen. Sometimes you need to just roll with it and open yourself up to the possibility that there's a bigger and better plan."

"What? Like you?" Angie asked snidely. "You chased after a gay guy for a year because you refused to open yourself up to the possibility that he wasn't the one. And all along there was a great guy practically jumping through fiery hoops to get your attention and you shit all over him!"

"Yeah. Exactly like that," Hailey said, crossing her arms across her chest. "I'm not going to deny it, if that's what you were hoping for. I pretty much missed a year of my life, when I could have been with a great guy, because I was too stubborn to see what was right in front of me. But—unlike you—I pulled my head out of my ass and figured it out. And now I'm exactly where I'm supposed to be." Turning to Ella and Becca she smiled. "Jack and I said 'I love you' to each other last night."

"You did?" Ella gushed. "That's awesome!"

"Definitely," Becca agreed. "Must have been something in the air last night."

"Why?" Hailey asked.

"Because when Max and I got back to his place, things got hot and heavy quickly and then…just when it was about to get seriously good—you know, naked good—he told me he loved me." She sighed and looked at them with a completely sappy grin. "Life is good."

"Dylan and I spent the entire night saying it," Ella said giggling. "And I have to say, there is something to be said for make-up sex because it was amazing! Seriously, Dylan was like a wild man! And I loved every minute of it!"

"I'm just so glad the two of you…"

"*HELLO?!* Remember me?" Angie yelled out. "I'm the one with the problem here! We're supposed to be focused on *me*!"

The three of them turned toward her with mumbled apologies as they all sat back down.

"Geez," Angie huffed, "you think you can get your minds off of your perfect lives for a few minutes and help me figure out how I'm supposed to be a single mom?"

"First off," Becca began, "none of our lives are perfect. Far from it. And you know it. In case you've forgotten, I've had the worst luck with guys up until I met Max." She shifted in her seat and took a steadying breath. "And the night we met? Max and I? He had witnessed Danny dumping me in the parking lot."

Nobody said anything – mainly because Max had already told them about it. But they never told Becca that they knew.

She nodded. "It's true. I was so humiliated and he was just…he was so damn sweet. It took me a little while to get over that. He literally saw me at my lowest." Then she looked at Angie. "Have you ever been publicly dumped and then find out you were being cheated on all along?"

"Um…"

"No, you haven't," Becca responded quickly. "So yeah, right now? Things are good. But it's been a long road to get here so don't belittle it."

"I'm with Becca," Hailey said. "You already pointed out how screwed up I am. Things are great with Jack right now but they're not perfect. And you know what? I don't want them to be. I'm kind of looking forward to seeing what he throws my way next."

Ella raised her hand to get everyone's attention. "And I nearly threw away a great relationship with the love of my life all because I was so wrapped up in what I *might* be missing. Well, I found out what I was missing and I didn't want it. I don't know how the three of you can even stand it! Being single is exhausting! I'm thankful I have Dylan and I'll gladly sit home and eat macaroni and cheese or peanut butter and jelly sandwiches while we struggle with finances—just as long as we're together." She smiled broadly. "The struggles bring us together and make us stronger."

They sat there and looked at Angie expectantly.

She hated it—even though she was expecting it. This is what they did and at one time or another, she had been the one staring them down. With a shaky sigh, she looked up at them.

"Sean wants me to move to New York."

There was a collective gasp but no one said a word.

Angie nodded. "Things are really moving along with his company and in a year or two, he knows he can move anywhere he wants. But right now? They have a lot of jobs starting up that are based in New York. It just makes more sense for him to be there."

"And you don't want to move?" Ella asked quietly.

Shaking her head, Angie said, "No. I don't. This is where I was born and raised. My family is here, my job…all of you! How could I possibly go through the biggest event in my life—having a baby—without all of you right there by my side?"

"Did you explain that to him?" Hailey asked cautiously. "Maybe if he understood where you're coming from, he'd be willing to find a compromise."

"There is no compromise," Angie replied sadly. "At least not one that's going to be good for anyone."

"Ange…"

"It's true! If I move up to New York, I'm going to be miserable. If Sean moves here and has to commute back and forth several times a week, he's going to be miserable and eventually, so will I. Either way, I'm going to end up feeling like a single parent anyway, so why do that? I'd rather kill the relationship now than watch it suffer a slow, painful death that will end with us hating each other."

They all grew silent.

"It's hopeless," Angie said miserably.

Twelve

A week later they were all sitting in front of the large mirror at Enchanted doing their makeup.

"At least I'm not going to look like zombie bride this week," Angie murmured as she put on mascara.

"Yeah, you were a little scary last week," Hailey agreed. "How are you feeling?"

"A little better. My OB gave me something to help with the nausea and it seems to be helping." She held up crossed fingers. "Long may it last."

"Well that's a good thing," Becca agreed.

Judith walked in and stood behind them smiling. "Do you have any idea how much I love this?"

The girls looked at her reflection and smiled back.

"I was wondering if you could all stay after the show. I'd like to talk with you."

Hailey spun around. "Mom? Is everything all right?"

Judith squeezed her daughter's shoulder. "Everything is fine; no need to go into a panic. I just have something I wanted to talk to the four of you about and I figured once the show is over and cleared up it would be a good time."

"We'll be here, Mrs. J," Ella said. "I'll tell

Dylan I'll meet him at home."

"Same for Max," Becca said.

"And Jack," Hailey smiled.

"Ugh. Enough…we get it," Angie grumbled.

With a small chuckle, Judith waved and walked away.

"What do you think that's about?" Becca asked. "I don't think she's ever done something like this before."

"I have no idea," Hailey replied. "But she's been a little more distracted lately than I can ever remember. I hope everything's okay with the business."

"Please," Angie snorted, "business is better than ever. Her shows are getting bigger and more and more vendors are wanting to work with her. It's got to be something else."

Hailey groaned.

"What? What's the matter?" Becca asked nervously.

"I hope it's not about her and my dad. She's been kind of complaining about him lately. I didn't take it seriously because they've always just sort of…picked at each other. It used to be cute. Now it's just sad."

"Your mom would not ask the four of us to sit down with her to talk about her marriage trouble," Ella said reasonably. "That would just be weird."

"I don't know," Becca said. "Over the years we've helped each other through numerous relationship problems and minefields and managed to work it all out. Maybe she needs a fresh opinion."

"Nah," Angie disagreed. "Mrs. J would totally talk to Hailey alone before bringing it to all of us. It's got to be something else."

"Maybe…"

"Okay, time to start getting our brides ready!" Judith called out and all around, people started scurrying to get ready.

"I guess we're going to have to wait," Hailey sighed.

****

Judith looked at the four faces in front of her and felt tears begin to sting her eyes. The first time they had sat like this, they were five years old. And now, twenty years later, they were grown women—amazing grown women. She looked at them and felt a sense of pride and thankfulness that she had been able to have the privilege of watching them grow into the women they were now.

"Um…Mom? You're starting to freak us out. What's going on?"

With a sigh, Judith composed herself and carefully folded her arms on her desk as she looked up at them and smiled. "Have I told you girls how proud I am of you?"

The four of them looked at one another before returning their attention to Judith, but rather than speak, they simply smiled.

"I was just sitting here and thinking of how long we've all known one another and I can honestly say that I feel blessed. I look at you and see not just my daughter, but I see four daughters. I love you all so much."

"Mom..." Hailey began, her lips starting to tremble.

"Oh, hush. I'm getting to it," Judith said lightly and then sighed. "Okay, here's the thing—I'm making some changes to Enchanted and I'd like for all of you to be a part of it."

"What?" they all asked.

She nodded. "Things are growing—I didn't think it was possible. I thought for a while there that we were going to slow down. With things like Pinterest and people being able to do so much of their wedding planning themselves on the internet, I really thought we were going to have to downsize. But that hasn't been the case."

"That's great!" Ella said.

"But what does this have to do with us?" Hailey asked.

"I have a proposal for each of you," Judith began.

"The things I want to do for the business are going to be too much for me to take on alone. I'm not getting any younger and I know my limitations. I also know the four of you very well—I know your strengths, weaknesses and…more about you than you probably realize."

They all began to shift in their seats nervously.

"We've purchased property and we're going to begin construction on a larger facility." She looked at Hailey. "Your father and I talked about it and—believe it or not—it was his idea. We're going to be more of a full-service wedding planning center now."

"Mom! That's amazing! I can't believe you haven't mentioned this before."

Judith looked mildly embarrassed. "Well, I really wasn't sure it was something I wanted to do, mainly because I thought it was all going to be on me. But…after careful consideration, your father and I worked up this plan."

"I can't believe Dad would even show an interest in this," Hailey said. "He always seems annoyed when you talk about work."

"That's because I've been trying to be like Superwoman for far too long."

"So how can we help?" Angie asked.

"So here's what I'm thinking. Becca," she said firmly, pulling a sheet of paper out of the folder that was sitting on her desk. "You're not happy being in that office where you're working." It wasn't a question. "You know it and I know it. Your parents pushed you into getting your business degree when, really, it wasn't your thing. I don't think it was necessarily bad for you, but it's not your passion." She paused for a moment. "The new location is going to have a coffee shop in it. It's by no means going to have the kind of traffic you'd get if it were in a mall, but I'm thinking that along with being there for walk-in clients and appointments, it would also provide all of the refreshments for our shows."

Becca's eyes went a little wide with disbelief. "And…you want me to work it?"

"No," Judith said seriously, "I want you to run it. Own it. Make it yours. It's my gift to you." She handed Becca the sheet of paper she had pulled out.

Becca scanned it and gasped. "But…this…this says I'll be a five-percent owner of Enchanted. On top of owning the coffee shop." She looked up at Judith. "I don't understand."

"You will," she replied cryptically and then turned to focus on Ella. "Ella, I want to start off by telling you that your dress came in."

"Wait…what? I…I thought we canceled the order."

Judith blushed slightly. "Well, I know that's what you told me to do, but I didn't think it was going to be necessary. So it's here in my closet and ready for you to try on for fittings."

"But…" Ella looked nervously at her friends

before looking back at Judith. "We canceled all of the wedding stuff—the hall, the caterers—everything. We're not even sure when we're getting married!"

Then Judith gave her a patient smile. "Sweet girl, you should never underestimate the power of love, or of a wedding planner who knows what she's doing." She pulled out another sheet of paper. "Nothing got canceled." She held up a hand when Ella went to argue. "During the entire time you and Dylan were broken up, I was in constant contact with both sets of parents. We were all working together to scale down to the wedding you originally wanted and, if you and Dylan are still interested, everything is set—according to your original plan." She handed Ella the sheet of paper.

"Oh my," she said in awe. "This…this is everything Dylan and I first started with." She looked up as tears rolled down her cheeks. "How…how did you do this? How did you get everyone to agree?"

"It wasn't easy," Judith chuckled. "It took several meetings to get everyone to realize how much stress and pressure they were putting on you and how they played a large part in the two of you breaking up."

Ella's brows furrowed. "But that wasn't the only…"

Judith grinned. "But they didn't realize that, did they?"

"Mrs. J, you are an evil genius!" Angie said and reached out to high five her.

"You know it!" Judith agreed and then pulled out another sheet of paper. "Okay, take that home, talk to Dylan and then I made an appointment for the two of you to meet me here after lunch tomorrow to discuss any questions you have."

"I don't even know what to say," Ella said, wiping away the tears. "I can't believe you were able to do this."

"I want you to be happy, Ella," Judith said. "And that brings me to item number two." She cleared her throat. "We've talked a lot over the years about what it is you want out of life and your answer has always been 'to be Dylan's wife and a mom.' And I love that. However, I think you have something unique to offer Enchanted."

"You do?" Ella asked.

Judith nodded. "I do. You see, you've been fascinating to watch during the last year or so with your own wedding planning. You've experienced a lot and I also know you can relate to what most brides are going through."

"I never thought getting married could be so stressful," Ella said with a small laugh. "All I kept thinking was 'party,' but the reality is so much more."

"Exactly," Judith agreed. "My assistant Sharon really wants to start cutting back her hours at the end of the season. She's been my right hand for years and she had a knack for knowing how to talk to the brides who come in here—helping them stay calm and offering a friendly ear when needed. You have those same traits, Ella."

"You...you want me to be your assistant?"

"Yes," she confirmed. "I want you to work with Sharon in learning a little more of the business so that when she's ready to leave, you can take over. Plus, once you're married and starting your family, your hours will be flexible."

"Oh my goodness," Ella said giddily. "That...that sounds wonderful!"

"But there's one more thing," Judith added.

"Oh?"

"At the new location, I want to incorporate a nursery. A lot of families come in with the bride and sometimes they have no one to watch their children. I would like to offer a service where they can bring their children and know they have someplace where they can play and be loved on. I think you would be the perfect person to head that up. What do you think?"

"It's like an answer to a prayer!" Ella gushed. "I mean...I love working at the daycare center and snuggling babies, but...to have something like this of my own? I...I don't know what to say?"

Judith handed her a sheet of paper. "On there is a contract similar to what I just gave Becca, but yours also lists some courses you are going to have to take in order to have the nursery or child-care space be the best it can be."

Ella scanned the sheet of paper quickly. "And you're offering me five-percent in Enchanted too?"

"Of course," Judith beamed.

Jumping up, Ella ran around the desk and hugged her. "I need to go and call Dylan! Is…is that all right?"

"Take your time," Judith said and watched as Ella hurried from the room. She sighed with satisfaction. "Okay, who's next?" she teased.

Angie and Hailey grinned at each other.

"Angie…"

"Yes?" Angie hissed happily.

"You, my dear girl, were a little bit of a challenge for me."

"Me? Why?"

"Because I wasn't sure if you were going to be staying," Judith said bluntly. At Angie's shocked expression, she continued. "That's why what I'm offering to you is something we can work with and can even be handled remotely if you're interested."

"I'm listening…"

"During the construction phase of the business, I'm going to be consumed with that. And even once it's done, there are going to be tons of things I'm going to need to focus on. You are an organizational wizard with a knack for party planning."

Angie grinned and blushed accordingly. "So true."

"I would like you to take over the shows."

"What? You can't be serious?" Angie cried with disbelief. "That's your thing! You're so good at it!"

"Well thank you," Judith said pleasantly. "But you know what? It's a lot of work and it's exhausting and I think it's time for some new and creative ideas to come in—especially now that we're branching out. With your position you can handle all of the logistics and plans and—if need be—hire an assistant to be there on-site for the shows. You know, just in case you're not living locally."

"Wow…Mrs. J, I don't know what to say to all of that."

Judith pulled yet another sheet of paper from her folder but didn't hand it over just yet. "You'll be in charge of organizing vendors and scouting out locations and coming up with new ways to get potential brides and grooms in for the shows and events. Besides your salary, you'll get a percentage of the business."

"But…that hardly seems fair, especially if I'm not even living here."

The girls all gasped.

"So are you seriously thinking of moving up to New York?" Becca asked excitedly. "Are you going after Sean?"

Slowly, Angie nodded and then looked up at them all. "I miss him. And after really sitting and thinking about it—after I was finally able to stop throwing up—I realized I'm nothing like my parents. They were barely out of high school when they got pregnant with my sister and they never had a chance to figure out what they wanted to do with their lives. I'm old enough now where I've experienced so much and know exactly what I want and don't want. And when I calmed down and saw how this situation is nothing like theirs, I was able to see how much I really love Sean."

They all stood and hugged her. That's how Ella found them when she came back into the room. "Oh my gosh! What did I miss?" She immediately hopped into the hug with them.

"Angie's going after Sean," Becca said.

"That's amazing! Yeah! I'm so proud of you!" Ella said happily.

When they broke apart and took their seats again, Angie was wiping her own tears away. "It's stuff like this that I'm going to miss," she admitted. "I don't know how to get by without you guys by my side. It's going to be the hardest thing I've ever done."

"New York isn't that far away," Hailey said. "Yes, it's going to make our Saturday lunches hard, but the end result is so worth it!"

"I was planning on telling you guys all about it at lunch tomorrow."

Judith sat back in awe. The friendship so fully on display in front of her was enviable. She said a prayer of thanks that her daughter had been blessed with three amazing friends.

Clearing her throat to get their attention, she handed Angie her sheet of paper. "This details the basics for you—with the option of it happening whether you live here or New York. But I don't want you to feel rushed to get started. I want you settled with Sean before you start doing anything for Enchanted."

"Well…that might take some time. You see…"

"I know all about the baby, Angie," Judith said.

"How?" Then she turned and looked at Hailey. "You blabbed?"

"Well…"

"Oh, stop," Judith interrupted. "Hailey tells me everything and what she doesn't I can easily see for myself. Although in this instance she did *not* tell me. I knew when you were so green last weekend. It wasn't hard to figure out. You simply confirmed it."

"Sneaky, Mom. Very sneaky."

Judith bowed her head, taking it as a compliment. "Anyway, we'll talk more about it after you talk to Sean."

"Thank you."

"That just leaves you, my darling daughter."

Hailey sat up a little straighter in her seat and took a steadying breath. "I'm ready. Lay it on me."

"I know we've talked about it a lot over the years, and you've never really seemed too keen on the idea of working with me full-time."

Hailey deflated slightly.

"It's okay. I completely understand why. You looked at the business and saw that everything was good and didn't think there was any room for changes or improvements." She pulled one last sheet of paper out. "As you can tell, you were wrong. There is plenty of room for it. Now, I may have found the property and have the initial plans in place for what I'd like, but from here on in, I want your input on all of it." She paused as she felt tears of her own building back up. "This is my legacy to you, Hailey. But I want it to be something you want and that you feel is yours."

"Mom," Hailey began hesitantly, "I was never against working with you."

"It's okay, sweetheart. I know it wasn't a large factor, but it was there. That's why it's so important to me that you put your stamp on this project and really make it your own. We have a meeting with the architect on Monday that you are going to sit in on and the way I see it, Enchanted is going to almost be a brand-new entity when we open in our new location, full of fresh ideas and an exciting outlook."

Without another word, she handed the paper to Hailey.

"Mom!" she cried. "This says that you're giving me forty-percent of the business! That means…"

"That means you are officially the head of Enchanted," Judith finished for her. "That is, if you want it."

Hailey got up and went around the desk as Judith stood and hugged her. "I can't believe you did all of this!" Together they hugged and cried. "I'm completely overwhelmed!"

"Well, that's to be expected," Judith replied. "But I'm not going anywhere. I'm going to be here to help you out for a while. And then…"

"Then what?"

"Your father and I are going on one of those cruise-around-the world vacations. We're going to be gone for a little over three months and focus on our marriage again. It's been way too long since we did that." She paused and smiled at them. "Never take your marriage for granted, girls. Trust me on this one."

They spent the next hour talking about their plans and ideas for Enchanted and as Judith did her best to field questions and simply sit back and listen, she knew she had made the right decision. These girls were going to take the business that was her dream and turn it into so much more.

When she looked at her watch and saw it was after midnight, she stood. "Rome wasn't built in a day, ladies, and this business isn't going to be either.

It's late and I don't know about you, but I would love to get some sleep." She walked around the desk and hugged and kissed each one of them. "Now go home and we'll talk some more next week."

****

"So what's your plan with Sean?" Hailey asked the next day at lunch. "Are you going to just call him and talk it out?"

Angie shook her head. "I'm flying up on Monday and kind of surprising him. Or ambushing him. We'll see how he responds," she said with a nervous chuckle.

"Wow! Look at you being all spontaneous," Becca said. "He's going to be surprised—and in a good way," she quickly added.

"I hope so."

"Have you talked to him since last week?" Hailey asked.

"No. When I told him I didn't want to see him anymore, I also told him I needed my space and that I'd call him when I was ready to talk." She sighed. "I guess he's respecting my wishes."

"Gotta appreciate a guy who does that," Becca said.

"Hell no you don't," Ella snapped. "I mean, yes, it's all fine and well in certain situations but in big, life-changing ones? I don't agree. I wish Dylan had pushed back at me when we broke up. It made me feel like I didn't matter to him—like I didn't mean enough for him to fight for!"

"Okay, okay, shh…" Angie said soothingly, rubbing Ella's arm. "Calm down."

"Oh stop," Ella said, pulling her arm away. "Don't patronize me. I'm trying to be helpful here."

"And you are and I agree—there's a time and a place. But really, this time it was a good thing. I needed this time without Sean so that he couldn't influence my decision. I know now that this is what I want because I came to that conclusion all on my own while sitting by myself. That was very important to me."

"Then I guess it was a good thing," Ella commented with a smile. "Do you need a ride to the airport on Monday?"

"I do. Anyone up for it?"

"I can take you," Hailey said. "I have off anyway so it's not a big deal."

"Only if you're sure."

Hailey nodded. "What about Trampus? What are you doing with him while you're gone?"

"I'm taking him with me. I figured I wasn't sure how long I'd be gone and if things go well, I'm going to want him to get acclimated to a new place."

"You know I would have watched him for you," Becca said. "It's not a big deal."

"Yeah, but like I said, it seemed wrong to leave him behind when we're going to be making this move together. He deserves to be a part of it."

"You know he's just a cat, right?" Hailey asked. "He doesn't have an opinion."

"Bite your tongue! If it were allowed, Tramp would totally be here at lunch with us—he's that kind of cat. He listens to me bitch and complain and in his own way, he understands."

"Um…sure. Okay," Hailey replied and then made a cuckoo sign at her.

They all started to laugh.

"You guys," Becca said suddenly. "Do you realize this could be our last Saturday lunch together?"

They all looked at each other with wide eyes as that statement started to sink in.

"It's not going to be forever," Angie finally said. "I mean, yes, I might be moving but that doesn't mean we'll never have lunch together again."

"No, I know," Becca replied, "but this will be the last time here as our weekly thing. It's like…an end of an era."

"Wow…way to totally bring us down," Angie murmured.

"It's just…" Becca began and then stopped. "We need to go out with a bang."

"I'm listening," Hailey said with a grin.

"No salads," Becca stated. "Today's lunch is an 'anything goes' lunch. Order the most decadent item that you never let yourself order."

"And then get dessert!" Ella cried.

"Yes!"

When the waitress came to take their order, she looked at them in shock after it was all written down. "So…nobody's dieting this week?" she teased.

"Nope," Angie answered. "If anything, add butter to everyone's order."

"I'll see what I can do," she laughed as she walked away.

Hailey tapped her spoon against her glass. "I would like to propose a toast." They each raised their glass. "To Angie and your new adventure."

"To Angie!" they all said.

After they drank, Angie turned to Ella. "So…did you and Dylan talk about the wedding last night? Are you going to see Mrs. J today?"

"We did and we are," Ella smiled. "We had no idea that nothing had been canceled or that this was even an option so it was a great surprise. We celebrated all night," she said with a wink. "If you know what I mean."

"Ugh…I can't," Angie said, holding up her hand. "I just…I can't. It's like Muppet sex."

"Hey!" Ella snapped but then burst out laughing. "We're not Muppets!"

"Technically," Angie replied, "but you're both too damn cute for me to even want to consider the image of you doing it. So just…stop."

Ella laughed a little maniacally. "Seriously, we're both so thrilled that things are going the way they are. I have to admit that I hate that it took such drastic actions to get us here, but in the end, we're going to have the wedding that we always wanted." She turned to Angie. "And you better be here for it."

"I wouldn't miss it for the world. And hopefully I won't be showing too much since it's not that far away. With any luck, I can still fit into my bridesmaid dress as it is without having to get it taken out."

"Either way you're going to be beautiful," Ella said cheerfully.

"Well, be sure to let us know how it all goes after you're done meeting with my mom. And let us know what you need from us because you know we're here to help."

"You got it," Ella replied.

"So does nobody want to address the bombshell that Mrs. J dropped on us all last night?" Becca said breathlessly. "I've been sitting here waiting for someone to even refer to it! Is no one else as excited and freaked out as I am?"

"Are you kidding me?" Hailey asked. "I didn't

even sleep last night!"

"Jack has nothing to do with this and again…stop," Angie deadpanned.

"Oh shut up," Hailey chuckled. "By Monday night you're going to want to be telling us all about your sexy time with Sean so spare me." Then she gave an evil grin. "But Jack did play into part of the reason I was up all night—and he was willing to stay up and listen to me ramble on about my plans for Enchanted."

"You know what the biggest part—the biggest change—is going to be, don't you?" Becca asked.

They all shook their heads.

"We're not going to be the Friday night brides anymore," she said sadly. "There's going to be a new wave of models coming in to take our places. Doesn't that make you sad?"

There was total silence at the table for a long time.

Swallowing hard, Hailey said, "Actually, I think it's a good thing. We had some of our greatest memories during those shows over the years. Now it's time for another group of friends to make their memories."

"Aww…that's really sweet," Becca said, sniffing a little. "I didn't think of it like that."

"It's true. Even if we weren't friends before the shows and before Enchanted, I'd like to think we would have become friends because of it." She placed her hand in the middle of the table. "Do you remember when we first got promoted from bridesmaids to brides? Do you remember how we celebrated after that first show?"

Angie started to laugh. "Oh my God! I haven't thought about that in a long time!"

Becca and Ella joined in the laughter. "That was a great night!" Becca said.

"We thought we had it all worked out," Ella added.

"Do each of you remember what you said? What your future self was going to do?" Hailey prompted. She wiggled her fingers on the table. "I said that my future self was going to fall madly in love with one of the perfect models. And I did. Jackson is my perfect model and I am definitely madly in love."

Ella placed her hand on top of Hailey's. "And I said my future self was going to get married to Dylan in the wedding of our dreams surrounded by my three best friends and a small selection of family because we wanted small and intimate." She grinned. "And we are."

Becca's hand went on next. "Wow, my future self was going to own a café and I was going to be married to a man who treated me like a princess." Her eyes filled with tears. "We may not be married but Max is the first and only man to ever treat me like a princess." She sniffled. "I can only hope that someday we'll be married."

Angie pouted. "I don't want to play."

"Come on," Hailey whined. "We're all doing it."

"Fine," Angie muttered and slapped her hand on top. "My future self was going to grab the world by the balls and blaze my own path because I don't need a man to define me."

Becca cleared her throat loudly.

Angie paused and then shook her head with a chuckle. "But then I'd get swept off my feet when I least expected it."

Hailey grinned broadly at her friends. "We're some pretty smart bitches, don't you think?"

The roar of laughter that followed was the best response ever.

More Wedding Fun!

Read an excerpt from Samantha Chase's

"The Wedding Season"

"You have got to be kidding me," Tricia grumbled as she sorted through the mail that was just delivered. She considered running down the block after her mailman and throwing it all back at him and shaking him until he promised to be more considerate, but then thought better of it. After all, it wasn't his fault she was a single woman.

A single woman who was currently holding three wedding invitations in her hand.

Cursing under her breath, she made her way back up the driveway and into her house, slamming the door behind her. Tossing the pile on her little entryway table without opening it, she walked through to the kitchen to get a drink. The sound of her phone ringing stopped her.

Her foul mood was instantly forgotten when she saw Sean's name on the screen. "Hey! It's you!"

"Hey, beautiful," Sean said with a small chuckle. "How are you doing?"

Walking into the living room, she collapsed on the couch. "Okay…and you?"

"By the sound of your voice, I'd say you are officially lying to me. So what's going on, Patterson?"

She rolled her eyes, hating how he rarely called her by her first name. "Three more came today."

"You're kidding!"

"Do I sound like I'm kidding?"

Sean chuckled again. "How is this even possible? How could it be that almost everyone we know is getting married this summer? Didn't they all get married last summer?"

"That's what I thought," she mumbled and threw her head back with a sigh. "I'm telling you, Sean, I'm nailing the mailbox shut as soon as we're off the phone!" The two of them had been commiserating over the last week about the upcoming wedding season.

"Tampering with the mail is a federal offense," he joked and Tricia couldn't help but smile.

"I'm not tampering with the mail, per se. It's my mailbox and if I want it nailed shut then…"

"Relax," he said smoothly. "Besides, how many more invites could there possibly be? I don't think we know any more people."

"I don't know. I have a feeling we're still missing some."

"Sure but…what are the odds of those people

getting married this summer too? As it is, we're up to what? Five weddings? Six?"

"Today's mail brought us up to six."

"Yikes."

"Exactly." It really was a little more than Tricia wanted to deal with. She was feeling like the proverbial "always a bridesmaid, never a bride" while Sean had complained about how he was tired of people trying to set him up with their "cute" sisters or cousins. "Seriously, we don't have to go to all of them, do we?"

"I mean I guess we don't have to," Sean began, "but…they are all our friends. Whose would we skip?"

Standing, Tricia quickly went over and grabbed today's invitations and then walked to the kitchen to grab the three that had arrived the previous week before sitting back down on the sofa. "Okay, let's think about this. The first one is Tami and Eric on June third." She paused. "Actually, I'd really like to go to that one. They're a great couple and have always been good friends to me."

"Ditto," Sean said. "Next?"

"Linda and Jerry on the fifth. Wow. It's going to be a very full weekend."

"Yeah, but…if we do one, we kind of have to do the other. It will be all the same people and how would we explain going to one and not the other?"

"Good point," Tricia conceded. "Give me a minute to open these new ones and see if any of the dates overlap."

"Wishful thinking, Patterson. Our luck is never that good."

"You know, I can't help but notice how you keep talking about all these events in the plural sense. Does that mean you're definitely going to be back home for the summer?"

"That's the plan," Sean said, and Tricia could hear the smile in his voice. For the last year, Sean had been working as a contractor over in the Middle East and Asia, helping to rebuild areas that were torn apart by war and a tsunami. It was hard work but she knew Sean loved it.

"And you want to spend your free time when you finally get home going to weddings? Seriously?" she asked with a laugh. "What's wrong with you?"

"Well, although it will cost me a fortune, it's a great opportunity to see everyone at one shot and get caught up."

It made sense. "Okay, next up we have…Donna and Jason on…" She scanned the invitation, "the eleventh. That's almost too much, right? Can we skip that one?"

"You can, but I can't. Jason and I played soccer together since we were five. I have to be there."

"Are you sure you're even invited? How often do you check your mail?" She asked with as serious of a tone as she could manage, but Sean knew immediately she was teasing.

"Ha-ha, very funny. I get my mail on a regular basis and although I haven't gotten today's mail – and probably won't until next week – I'm fairly certain I'm invited to all the same weddings as you."

"Fine, whatever. Don't get all defensive." She shuffled through the mail and opened up the rest of the invites. "It looks like we get a break for a couple of weeks and the next batch doesn't start up again until the second week of July."

"So that means we don't have to make any firm decisions right now then."

"You don't, but I do. The first one up in July is Kristen and Bobby. I told her I couldn't commit to being in the bridal party but that I'd be there."

"Okay, fine. Bobby was also on the soccer team so I should be there too."

"You know high school was over ten years ago, right? It doesn't matter that you played on a team together – it doesn't obligate you to stuff for the rest of your life," she said.

"You wouldn't understand," he replied. "We were all close and once I started traveling, I've missed out on a lot. My friends mean a lot to me – you should know that – and as much as it pains me to have to dress up and do the chicken dance, I want to be there for my friends."

Suddenly, Tricia didn't feel quite as antagonistic toward the invitations. "You're right," she sighed. "I guess there's a part of me that just dreads all that goes with accepting the invites."

"You mean the inevitable attempts to fix you up with someone?"

"That and the pity looks I get. And I get a lot of them. You know…the old 'Poor Tricia. You'll find someone soon. I'm sure of it.' I hate those looks."

"Yeah well, I'd take pity over pimps."

She couldn't help but laugh. "Is that what we're calling it now?"

"Might as well. It's pretty much what they're doing," Sean said and then sighed loudly. "I don't know maybe it's not…" He stopped. "Wait a minute," he began excitedly. "I've got it! I know exactly how to get us out of those situations!"

"I'm listening…" she said hopefully.

"We go together."

All of the hope she was just feeling quickly deflated from her body. "That's it? That's your big plan? How is that going to get us out of anything? Everyone is used to seeing us together. And considering you've been out of the country for so damn long, they'll just figure you didn't have time to find a date and so you asked me. I'll be the pity date!" She cursed. "Damn it! I can't escape it!"

"No, no, no…listen. We go together as like, you

know, a couple."

She shook her head. "No one is going to believe it."

"Sure they will. We'll get all cozy and you'll have to look at me as if you adore me – which shouldn't be hard to do – and hang on my every word."

"You're crazy, you know that? I'm not going to hang on your every word and whatever else. It's ridiculous and it won't work."

"Why not? You're telling me you can't pretend to be in love with me for a couple of hours? I'm crushed."

"Don't be such a drama queen, Sean," she said wearily. "It's not just a couple of hours. We're looking at potentially six weddings at six-to-eight hours each with people who've known us for years. It's going to take a lot more than batting my eyelashes at you while holding your hand."

"What have we got to lose?" he asked. "Unless…unless you had someone else you planned on going with."

Unfortunately, she didn't. It had been months since she'd even been on a date. But there was no need to dwell on it right now. "No, that's not it. I just don't think…"

"C'mon, Tricia. It makes perfect sense. We'll test out the theory at the first wedding and see how it goes. I'm sure no one's going to expect us to be pawing at each other to prove we're in a relationship. What do you say?"

"I still think you're crazy but…"

"Look, it's not that big of a deal and I guarantee you we'll have a lot more fun this way. We'll shock everyone and then field all kinds of questions and then we'll get to enjoy ourselves. No ducking behind potted plants or running into the bathroom to avoid the feeding frenzy of well-meaning people who claim only to be thinking of our happiness."

Tricia took a minute to think about it and as much as she believed they'd never be able to pull it off, it was certainly worth a try. "You're right. Damn it."

"Excellent!"

"So that leads me to our other order of business, where you'll be staying while you're home. I hope it's here." Tricia was actually renting Sean's childhood home. From the first time she had walked through the front door, she had fallen in love with it. When Sean's mom wanted to move away and travel a bit herself, she had offered it to Tricia. Someday she hoped to own it but wanted to wait until the time was right.

"I wouldn't dream of staying anyplace else," he said. "Where else could I go for free and sleep in my old room?" He paused. "You haven't changed anything in there, have you?" he asked with exaggerated anxiety.

"No, precious," she mocked. "Your Van Halen posters are still on the wall so you can relax. I'll just have to unlock the shrine and air it out before you get here. Which reminds me, when exactly will you be getting home?"

"End of May. I'm thinking the twenty-eighth but figure you'll have to give or take a day with that. Nothing ever goes as planned."

"And what about your mom? Are you going to go and see her first and then come here or the other way around?"

"Honestly? I'm not sure. Probably after the first round of weddings I'll track her down. Last I talked to her she was going on a cruise with some friends and was talking about yoga classes." He sighed. "Why can't she just be like other moms?"

That made Tricia laugh. Stephanie Peterson had never been like other moms – that was one of the things she'd always loved about her. "You have no idea how lucky you are. Steph gets out there and is enjoying her life. My mom prefers to live like a hermit."

"That's not true and you know it," Sean said.

"Which part?"

"Your mom and John are very happy and they have plenty of friends. You need to stop picking on them."

"Hey, same goes for you, buddy. Your mom is very happy and has a lot of friends. She just chooses to have them all over the world. There's nothing wrong with that."

"I guess," he grumbled. "It's just hard to pin her down sometimes. It would be nice to have a home base to go and see her. I'm never sure where I'm going to find her."

"It's not like you've been home a whole lot, Sean," she reminded him. "I don't see why it should bother you so much."

"Yeah, well, it doesn't just bother me. Ryan complains about it too. Every time I talk to him he tells me how it's easier to find Waldo than it is to find Steph."

"Yeah, well…Ryan's just grumpy. I swear, he's always got something to complain about." It was only partially true. Ryan was Sean's older brother and while he and Sean had a great relationship, any time Tricia was around him he seemed to be irritated.

Sean chuckled. "I don't know where you get it from. Ry's not like that. He does his own fair share of traveling but even with that, Steph has him beat."

"I think that's great for her!"

"You women. Always sticking together."

"And don't you forget it." There was a moment of companionable silence before Tricia spoke again. "So you really think you'll be coming home this time?"

"I do. I know I said that six months ago but then

the tsunami hit. I was already over here with a team. What was I supposed to do?"

"You don't have to fix the entire world, Sean. You have people back here who love you and want to see you."

"Aww…see? You love me. It's going to be so easy for you to play the part of my girlfriend for these weddings!" he teased.

"You're an idiot," she laughed.

"Yes, yes, yes," he agreed. "But you still love me."

That just made her laugh harder. "Knock it off, doofus."

"Come on. I'm not completely hideous to look at, am I?"

"Now you're just fishing for compliments. And besides, you've been gone for like two years. For all I know you could look like some kind of yeti now."

"I promise to shave," he said with a laugh. "Admit it. This is going to be so much fun. We can watch all of their shocked faces and we can be as outrageous as we want."

"I'm sure I'm going to regret this at some point, but okay. Fine. I guess it could be kind of fun. Plus, we'll get to spend a whole lot of time together getting caught up."

"So…it's a plan?"

She nodded even though she knew he couldn't see her. "Definitely. I'll take care of all the RSVP'ing for us if you don't mind."

"Be my guest, sweetheart," he gushed.

"Ugh…knock it off. Save it for the audience."

"You're no fun. How are we supposed to come off as being believable if we don't practice?"

"Sean?"

"Yeah?"

"Let it go. We'll be fine and I don't think either of us is going to have to pull off an Oscar-worthy performance."

"You never know…"

Tricia didn't even want to think about it. All she knew was her best friend was coming home and they'd have a couple of weeks to hang out together. Weddings or no weddings, it was going to be fun.

****

Several things hit Tricia at once as she pulled into her driveway a month later. First, it was too hot to cook. Second, there was bird poop on her windshield so she was going to have to wash her car. And lastly, there was a strange car in her driveway.

"Sean!" she instantly squealed as she parked and climbed out of the car. He had mentioned he wouldn't be home until the end of May and that was still a few weeks away but…who else would it be?

He probably just wanted to throw her off so he could surprise her.

Grabbing her purse, she closed the car door and practically ran up the front steps of the house. Sean still had a key so no doubt he was inside already. She let herself in, dropped her things in the doorway, and went looking for him.

No sign of him in the living room.

No sign of him in the kitchen.

Tricia was about to turn and walk up the stairs to look in his room when she caught sight of him through the French doors that led out to the deck. For a minute, all she could do was stop and stare. He was here, really and truly here. He looked bigger, taller, like he had filled out from all his time in construction. His brown hair looked kissed by the sun but could definitely use a trim, she thought with a smile.

With a contented sigh, she decided she'd be the one to surprise him by sneaking up on him. He may have heard the car, but it wasn't enough to make him come inside to investigate. Toeing off her shoes, she tiptoed through the kitchen and over to the doors. He looked completely at peace, although that could have something to do with the yard. Steph had been a whiz with the landscaping and gardening and she had really created something special back here.

An oasis.

At least that's what Tricia thought of it. With the Koi pond and lush foliage, it was something out of a magazine. And it was hers now – sort of. Tricia was certain that after all of the horrors Sean had witnessed in the last several years, this space must really seem like a little bit of heaven to him. It almost seemed a shame to disturb him but…she needed to. She needed to hug him, to see his face and make sure he was real.

In her best stealth mode, she quietly walked through the open doors and out onto the deck and didn't stop until she was directly behind him. He was standing on the edge of the deck looking down at the fish. Part of her wanted to be playful and yell "Gotcha!" but the softer side – the side that was just so happy to have him home – won out. Reaching out, Tricia simply wrapped her arms around his middle and rested her head on his back.

"I'm so glad you're finally here," she said softly as she squeezed. He cleared his throat and Tricia stiffened and pulled away before taking a step back.

"Hey, Tricia."

Apparently someone wanted to surprise her, but it wasn't Sean.

It was Ryan.

****

He had heard the car pull up.

He had known he'd have to see her.

But being touched by Tricia? Um, yeah. That wasn't something he'd counted on.

Slowly he turned around and faced her. And smiled. Everything about Tricia Patterson was familiar and yet looking at her right now, different. From the copper-colored hair to her green eyes, she was the girl he remembered. But taking in the rest of her? Well, she wasn't a girl any more. She had most definitely blossomed into a woman.

Ryan tucked his hands into the front pockets of his jeans and took a steadying breath. "How have you been?"

Her smile had only faltered slightly when she realized it wasn't Sean she was hugging and now - even though she was still smiling - he could see the apprehension there. "I'm fine. Fine. Um…how about you?"

He nodded. "I'm good." Ryan looked around the yard and knew this peaceful reprieve was over. "You're probably wondering what I'm doing here."

She blushed and ducked her head a little. "Well…yeah. I think the last time I saw you was…"

"About six years ago," he finished for her. "At Sean's graduation."

"Right," she said softly and then looked toward the house. "I'm sorry, where are my manners? Can I get you something to drink?" But before Ryan could answer, Tricia was walking back into the house.

He followed and found her in the kitchen. "I wasn't expecting anyone so I'm afraid I don't have a lot to offer – water, Coke, orange juice…"

"I'll take a Coke," he said, even though he wasn't particularly thirsty. Standing back, he watched Tricia flutter around the kitchen pouring their drinks. When she handed the glass to him, her eyes barely met his. "I probably shouldn't have just let myself in," he finally said to break the silence.

"What? Oh, no…it's fine. I told your mom when she rented the place to me that it's still your family's home. I'm just borrowing it for a while."

"Still…you had no idea I was coming, but I didn't know when you'd be home."

"You could have called," she said and glanced at him through her lashes.

Ryan nodded and placed his glass down on the counter. "Look, Tricia, this isn't really a social call. Which – ironically – is why I didn't call."

She paled and placed her own drink down next to his. "What's going on?" she asked nervously. "Is it your mom? Sean?"

Shit. He hated doing this, hated being the messenger and delivering bad news. "Why don't we go and sit down?" he asked quietly and went to reach for her arm to guide her out to the living room.

"Just tell me," she said, taking a cautious step back. "Please, Ryan." There was a tremble in her voice and it affected him more than it should have.

He sighed with resignation. "There was another storm," he said lowly, watching her face as his words sank in. "It hit in the middle of the night. No one saw it coming."

Tricia's body slowly began to sag to the floor. Ryan tried to reach out and catch her, but all he managed to do was sit down on the ceramic tile beside her. Tricia's green eyes filled with tears as she looked at him. "Sean?" she whispered.

"It's too soon to tell. Mom got the call and then called me. We've been trying to get someone to talk to us but it's chaos over there."

"I…I don't understand," she said as the tears began to fall. "How…? Why…?"

Ryan wrapped an arm around her shoulders – it seemed like the thing to do. "I was out east when I got the call. I had some business out there and I was going to just head back to Jersey and see what I could do, but mom mentioned she was going to call you and I just thought…" He shrugged. "I thought this was something you should hear in person."

It was clearly the wrong thing to say because her expression crumbled and the next thing Ryan knew, Tricia was sobbing hysterically against his shoulder.

"No…no," he said, trying to tuck a finger under her chin to get her to look at him. "We have to stay positive. Just because we haven't heard anything doesn't mean something's happened to Sean."

He only wished he believed it.

“I just…well…I know how close you and my brother are and I felt like it was better if someone was here with you.”

Read an excerpt from Samantha Chase's

"Christmas in Silver Bell Falls"

There was nothing quite like coming home at the end of a long day: kicking off your shoes…having a little something to eat while watching TV…and most importantly, not having to hear any more Christmas music!

Melanie Harper was certain she wasn't the only one who felt that way. It was early November and the holiday season was just getting under way.

"More like under my skin," she murmured as she walked into her kitchen and poured herself a glass of wine. Taking her glass, she went back to her living room and sat down on the couch.

It had been a long day. A long week. Hell, if she were being honest, it had been a long three months. With deadlines approaching, her editor was getting more and more snarky while Melanie was getting more and more discouraged.

Writer's block.

In her ten years of writing, she'd never once suffered from it, but for some reason the words refused to come.

"Figures," she said with disgust and turned on the TV. Flipping through the channels, it was all the same thing—Christmas specials, Christmas movies and holiday-themed shows. Unable to stand it, she turned it off and sighed.

It was always like this. Christmas. The holidays. Every year, if something bad was going to happen, it happened around Christmas.

Not that it had been that way her entire life, but…she stopped and paused. No, scratch that. It had been like that her entire life. Her earliest memory was of the Christmas when she was five. That was the year her mother left. Her father had been too distraught to celebrate that year so she spent the day watching him drink and cry.

There had been a glimmer of hope for the next year—her dad promised her it would be better. The flu had both of them fighting for the bathroom the entire day. And after that, it was all one big, giant blur of suckiness. Between financial struggles and family issues—and that one year where they had gotten robbed the day before Christmas—Melanie had come to see the months of November and December as nothing but a big nuisance. Eventually they stopped even attempting to celebrate.

And now she'd be able to add "getting cut by her publisher because of writer's block" to the Christmas resume of doom.

The name almost made her chuckle.

It would have been easy to sit there and wax unpoetic about how much she hated this time of the year, but a knock at the door saved her. Placing her wine glass down, she padded to the front door and pulled it open.

"Hey! There's my girl!"

Melanie smiled as her dad wrapped her in his embrace. "Hey, Dad." She hugged him back and then stepped aside so he could come in. "What's going on? I thought we were getting together on Saturday for dinner."

John Harper smiled at his only child as he took off his coat. "Is this a bad time?"

She shook her head. "No, not at all. I just wasn't expecting you. Have you eaten dinner yet?"

He chuckled softly. "It's almost eight, Mel. Of course I have." He studied her for a minute. "Don't tell me you haven't."

She shrugged. "It was a long day and I sort of lost my appetite."

"Uh-oh. What happened?"

Melanie led him to the living room and sat down on the couch again. "My deadline will be here at the end of December and I haven't written a thing."

"Okay," he said slowly. "So…can't they extend your deadline?"

She shook her head. "They've extended it three times already."

"Hmm…so what's the problem with the story? Why are you having such a hard time with it?

That's not like you."

She sighed again. "They're pretty much demanding a Christmas story."

"Oh."

She didn't even need to look at him to know his expression was just as pinched as hers at the topic. "Yeah…oh."

"Did you try explaining…?"

Nodding, she sat up and reached for her glass of wine. "Every time I talk to them. They don't get it and they don't care. Basically their attitude is that I'm a fiction writer and I should be able to use my imagination to concoct this Christmas story without having to draw on personal experience."

"Maybe they don't realize just how much you dislike the holiday."

"Dislike is too mild of a word," she said flatly. Taking a long drink, she put her glass down and looked at him. "I don't even want to talk about it. The meeting with my editor and agent went on and on and on today so my brain is pretty fried. The only thing to come out of it is yet another crappy reinforcement of the holiday."

"Oh, dear…"

Melanie's eyes narrowed. "What? What's wrong?"

"I guess maybe I should have called first because…" He stopped. "You know what? Never mind. We'll talk on Saturday." He stood quickly and walked back toward the foyer.

"Oh, no," she said as she went after him. "You can't come here and say something like that and then leave! Come on. What's going on?"

John sighed and reached for her hand. "Your grandmother died."

Melanie simply stared at him for a minute. "Oh…okay. Wow. Um…when?"

"A month ago."

Her eyes went wide. "And you're just telling me now?"

Slowly, he led her back to the couch. "Mel, seriously? Your grandmother hasn't spoken to me in over twenty-five years. I'm surprised I was notified."

"I guess," she sighed. Then she looked at him. "Are you okay?"

He shrugged. "I'm not sure. I always thought when the time came that it wouldn't mean anything. After all, she kind of died to me all those years ago. But now? Now that I know she's really gone?" His voice choked with emotion. "It all suddenly seems so stupid, so wrong. I mean, how could I have let all those years go by without trying to make things right?"

Squeezing his hand, Melanie reached over and hugged him. "It's not like you never tried, Dad.

Grandma was pretty stubborn. You can't sit here and take all the blame."

When she released him, she saw him wipe away a stray tear. "In my mind, I guess I always thought there would be time. Time to make amends and…"

"I know," she said softly. "And I'm sorry. I really am."

"You probably don't even remember her. You were so little when it all happened."

It was the truth, sort of. Melanie had some memories of her grandmother and none of them were of the warm and fuzzy variety. Unfortunately, now wasn't the time to mention it. "So who contacted you?"

"Her attorney. He actually called last night and met me in person today."

"Well that was nice of him. I guess."

"He had some papers for me. For us."

Melanie looked at him oddly. "What kind of papers?"

"She um…she left some things to us in her will."

Her eyes went wide again. "Seriously? The woman didn't talk to either of us all these years and she actually put us in her will? Is it bad stuff?"

John chuckled. "What do you mean by bad stuff?"

"You know…like she has a really old house and she was a hoarder and we're supposed to clean it out. Or she has some sort of vicious pet we're supposed to take care of. That kind of thing."

John laughed even harder. "Sometimes your imagination really is wild; you know that, right?" he teased.

Melanie couldn't help but laugh with him. "What? It's true! Things like that happen all the time!"

"Mel, it doesn't," he said, wiping the tears of mirth from his eyes. "And for your information, there was no hoarding, no vicious pets…"

"Did she collect dead animals or something?"

He laughed again. "No. Nothing like that."

Relaxing back on the couch, she looked at her father. "Okay. Lay it on me then. What could she possibly have put in her will for the two of us?"

John took a steadying breath. "She left me my father's coin collection."

That actually made Melanie smile. "I know how much you used to talk about it." She nodded with approval. "That's a good gift to get."

He nodded. "She'd kept it all these years. Then there's some family photos, things from my childhood that she had saved, that sort of thing."

"So no money," Melanie said because she already knew the answer.

John shook his head. “And it’s fine with me. I don’t think I would have felt comfortable with it. All those years ago, it would have meant the world to me to have a little help so you and I didn’t have to struggle so much. But we’re good now and I don’t really need or want it.”

“Who’d she leave it to? Her cat? Some snooty museum?”

“Museums aren’t snooty,” he said lightly.

“Anyway,” she prompted. “So who’d she leave her fortune to?”

With a sigh he took one of her hands in his. “She left the bulk of her estate to the local hospice care center.”

“Oh…well…that was nice of her,” Melanie said. “I guess she wasn’t entirely hateful.”

“No, she wasn’t,” John said softly. “And she did leave you something.”

The statement wasn’t a surprise since he’d mentioned it earlier, but Melanie figured he’d tell her when he was ready.

“When the attorney told me about it,” he began, “I was a little surprised. I had no idea she still had it.”

Curiosity piqued, she asked, “Had what?”

“The cabin.”

Okay, *that* was a surprise, she thought. "Grandma had a cabin? Where?"

"Up north. Practically on the border of Canada."

"Seriously? Why on earth would she have a cabin there?"

A small smile played across John's face. "Believe it or not, there was a time when your grandmother wasn't quite so…hard. She loved the winters and loved all of the outdoor activities you could do in the snow. She skied, went sleigh riding and…get this…she loved Christmas."

Pulling her hand from his, Melanie stood with a snort of disgust. "That's ironic. The woman went out of her way to ruin so many of our Christmases and now you're telling me she used to love them? So…so…what? She started hating them after I came along? That would just be the icing on the rotten Christmas cookie."

John came to his feet and walked over to her. Placing his hands on her shoulders, he turned her to look at him. "It wasn't you, sweetheart. It was me. When your mom left, grandma wanted us to move in with her—but there were conditions and rules and I just knew it wasn't the kind of environment I wanted you to grow up in."

"Dad, I know all this. I remember the fights but…what made her hate Christmas?"

He shook his head. "She didn't. As far as I know, she always loved it."

"Then…then why? Why would she ruin ours?"

A sad expression covered his face. "It was punishment. I grew up loving Christmas and we always made such a big celebration out of it. It was her way of punishing me for not falling in line. She took away that joy."

Tears filled Melanie's eyes. "See? She was hateful. And whatever this cabin thing is, I don't want it."

"Mel…"

"No, I'm serious!" she interrupted. "I don't want anything from her. She ruined so many things in our lives because she was being spiteful! Why on earth would I accept anything from her?"

"Because I think you need it," he said, his tone firm, serious.

"Excuse me?"

Leading her back to the sofa, they sat down. "I think this may have come at the perfect time."

She rolled her eyes. "Seriously?"

"Okay, that didn't quite come out the way I had planned," he said with a chuckle. "What I meant is…I think you could really use the time away. With the pressure you're feeling about the book, maybe a change of scenery will really help put things into perspective."

"Dad," Melanie began, "a change of scenery is not going to undo twenty-five years of hating

Christmas. And besides, I really don't want the…the cabin. I don't want anything from her. It would have meant more to me to have her in my life while she was alive."

He sighed. "I know and I wish things could have been different. But…this is really something you need to do."

She looked at him with disbelief. "Now I *need* to do it? Why?"

"Melanie, you are my daughter and I love you."

"That's an ominous start."

"You're too young to be this disillusioned and angry. We can't go back and change anything, but I think you need to do this to make peace with the past and have some hope for the future."

"Dad…"

"Three months, Mel, that's all I'm asking."

She jumped to her feet. "You expect me to go live in some arctic place for three months? Are you crazy?"

He smiled patiently at her. "I'm not crazy and you know I'm right."

"No…I'm still going with crazy."

"There's a stipulation in the will," he began cautiously.

"What kind of stipulation?"

“You need to live in the cabin for three months. After that, you’re free to sell it.”

“That’s a bunch of bull. What if I don’t want to live there at all? Why can’t I just sell it now? Or give it away?”

“If you don’t want it, it will be given away.”

“Well then…good riddance.”

“You’re being spiteful just for the sake of it, Mel. What have you got to lose? You work from home so you don’t have that hanging over your head and your condo is paid for. Think of it as a writing retreat. Your editor will love the idea and it will show how you’re seriously trying to get the book done. It’s a win-win if you think about it.”

“Ugh,” she sighed. “I’m not a big fan of being cold.”

“The cabin has heat.”

“It will mean I’ll be gone for Christmas.”

He chuckled. “Nice try. We don’t celebrate it anymore, remember?”

She let out a small growl of frustration. “I’m still going to have writer’s block. That’s not going to change.”

“Trust me. It will.”

Tilting her head, she gave him a curious look. “What’s that supposed to mean?”

"Okay, there really isn't any way *not* to tell you this…"

"Tell me what?"

"The town is pretty much all about Christmas."

"Forget it. I'm not going." She sat back down and crossed her arms.

"You're too old to pout so knock it off," he said.

She glared at her father. "So I'm supposed to go to this…this…Christmas town and then, thanks to the wonder of it all, suddenly I'm going to be able to write this fabulous holiday story and have it become a bestseller?"

"There's that imagination again! I knew it was still in there!"

"Ha-ha. Very funny." Slouching down she let out another growl. "I really don't want to do this."

"Mel, it's not often that I put my foot down. You're normally more level-headed and you're old enough that I don't need to, but this time, I'm going to have to put my foot down."

"Who gets the cabin if I turn it down?"

John sighed dejectedly. "I have no idea. The lawyer didn't say."

"Maybe she left it to someone who really needs it," Melanie said, trying to sound hopeful.

"She did," John replied. "You."

****

A week later, Melanie was in her car and driving halfway across the country to see if she could get her writing mojo back. It was a fifteen-hour drive so she split it up over two days and since she was alone in the car, she had nothing to do but think.

"She couldn't have left me a condo in Hawaii or maybe someplace tropical like the Bahamas? No. I have to go to the tip of freaking New York for this." It was a running dialogue in her head throughout the drive and it seemed like the closer she got, the angrier she became.

On the second day of the trip, when her GPS told her she was less than an hour away from her destination, she called her father and put him on speakerphone.

"Hey, sweetheart! How's the drive?"

"She hated me," Melanie replied. "She seriously hated me."

"I'm not even going to pretend I don't know who you're referring to," he said. "Are you there already? Is the cabin in bad shape?"

"I'm not there yet but I'm driving on this little two-lane road and there is nothing out here. I mean nothing! The GPS says I should be there soon but I haven't seen a city or a town in quite a while. Where am I supposed to shop and get food? Or am I supposed to hunt for it? Because if I am, that's a deal-breaker and you should have told me."

John laughed. "You seriously need to put all of this in your book. It's hysterical!"

"I'm not trying to be funny here, Dad! I'm serious! There isn't anything around!"

"You haven't gotten there yet. If I remember correctly, there are plenty of places to shop and eat. You won't starve and you certainly won't have to go out and kill your dinner so don't worry."

"But you don't know that for sure…"

"Mel, stop looking for trouble. We talked about this. It's going to be good for you. Your editor is thrilled and promised to give you a little extra time so you're off to a promising start."

"Yeah…I'm lucky," Melanie deadpanned.

"You need a positive attitude, young lady," he admonished. "I'm serious. I want you to make the most of this time you have up there."

She mentally sighed. "I'll try, Dad. But I'm not making any promises."

"That's all I ask."

"Okay, well…let me go because the road seems to be getting pretty winding and hilly and I need to pay attention to it. I'll call you when I get there."

"Be safe, sweetheart!"

Hanging up, Melanie frowned at the road. It was getting narrower and the sky was getting a little bit darker. A chill went down her spine and attributing it to the cooling temperatures, she cranked up the heat.

The GPS began calling out directions to her and Melanie feared she was leaving civilization further and further behind. "I better hit the *New York Times* for this," she murmured. A few minutes later she hit the brakes and stared at the giant sign on the side of the road.

"Silver Bell Falls Welcomes You!"

Melanie frowned and then looked around because she was certain she was hearing things. Turning down her car stereo, she groaned when she heard the song "Silver Bells" coming from the massive sign.

City sidewalks, busy sidewalks, dressed in holiday style…in the air there's a feeling of Christmas…

"You have got to be kidding me." Cranking the radio up to block out the Christmas carol, Melanie slammed her foot on the gas and continued her drive. It was maybe only a mile down the road when she spotted a small grocery store, a gas station and a diner.

And that was it.

"I guess I just drove through town," she sighed. It was tempting to stop and look around but she was anxious to get to the house and check it out first. Being practical, Melanie had already shopped for enough food and essentials to get her by for the first night. And besides, she had no idea what kind of shape the house was going to be in.

"Turn left," the GPS directed and Melanie did just that. "Your destination is at the end of the road."

Squinting, Melanie looked straight ahead but saw…nothing. There were trees, lots and lots of trees. Slowing down, she approached the end of the pavement and saw a dirt road that led through the trees and a small mailbox hidden in the brush.

"Charming." With no other choice, she carefully drove off the pavement and made her way over the bumpy road through the trees. It was like a dense forest and for a minute, she didn't think she was going to get through it.

But then she did.

The field opened up and off to the right was a house—not a cabin. In her mind, Melanie pictured some sort of log cabin, but the structure she was looking at was more stone than log. It was a one-story home with a wraparound porch and a red roof. The yard was completely manicured and the place even looked like it had a fresh coat of paint.

Since neither she nor her father had any contact with her grandmother, there was no way for them to know about the upkeep on the place. She had tried to question the lawyer, but other than giving her the deed to the house and the keys, he had very little information for her.

A little beyond the house was a shed. It looked like it was perched on a trailer and it certainly looked a lot newer than the house. Maybe it had been a new addition. Maybe her grandmother hadn't known she was going to die and was doing some renovations on the property.

Pulling up to the front of the house, Melanie sighed. She was anxious to go and explore the space and silently prayed she wasn't going to open the door to some sort of nightmare. Climbing from the car, the first thing she did was stretch. Looking around the property from where she stood, the only thing that was obvious to her was that she had no neighbors—she couldn't even see another house!

Pulling the key from her pocket, she closed the car door and carefully walked up the two steps to the front porch. Stopping at the front door, she bounced on her feet and noticed that the floor was in pretty good shape—no creaking and a lot of the wood looked fairly new.

Not a bad start, she thought and opened the front door.

Stopping dead in her tracks, she could only stare. It was dark and dusty and there was a smell that made her want to gag. Not that she was surprised, but it did cause her to spring into action. With a hand over her mouth, she quickly made her way around the house opening windows. Next, she went out to her car and grabbed the box of cleaning supplies out of the trunk. Melanie knew a certain amount of cleaning would be involved, but she hadn't expected quite so much.

For the next three hours she scrubbed and dusted and vacuumed and mopped. It didn't matter that it was thirty degrees outside, and currently pushing that temperature inside thanks to the open windows; she was sweating. Once she was satisfied with the way things looked, she walked outside, grabbed the box of linens and went about making the bed. Next came the groceries and finally her own personal belongings.

It was dark outside and every inch of Melanie's body hurt. Slowly she made her way back around the house to close the windows and jacked up the heat. Luckily the fireplace was gas, clearly a recent update. She flipped the switch and sighed with relief when it roared to life and the blower immediately began pushing out heat as well.

Guzzling down a bottle of water, she looked around with a sense of satisfaction. The house was small, maybe only a thousand square feet, but it had potential. Grabbing a banana from her cooler, she peeled and ate it while contemplating her next move.

"Shower," she finally said. "A nice hot shower or maybe a bath." The latter sounded far more appealing. Locking the front door, Melanie walked to the newly-cleaned bathroom and started the bath water. It was a fairly decent-sized tub and for that she was grateful. "Bath salts," she murmured and padded to the master bedroom to search through her toiletry bag.

Within minutes, the bathroom was steamy and fragrant and Melanie could feel the tension starting to leave her body. Her cell phone rang and she cursed when she realized she had forgotten to call her father when she'd arrived.

"Hey, Dad!" she said quickly. "Sorry!"

He chuckled. "Are you all right?"

"I am. The house was a mess and once I got inside and looked around, I couldn't help but start cleaning. I guess I lost track of the time."

"Have you eaten dinner yet?" he asked expectantly.

"A banana."

"Mel…" he whined. "You have to start taking better care of yourself."

"I will. I know. Actually, I'm just getting ready to take a nice hot bath to relax. I promise I'll eat as soon as I'm done."

He sighed wearily. "Okay. Be sure that you do. Call me tomorrow."

"I will, Dad. Thanks."

She hung up and turned the water off. Looking around, Melanie grabbed some fresh towels from one of her boxes and set them on the vanity before stripping down and gingerly climbing into the steamy water. A groan of pure appreciation escaped her lips as soon as she was fully submerged.

"This almost makes up for all the grime," she sighed and rested her head back, closing her eyes. "Heavenly."

For a few minutes, Melanie let her mind be blank and simply relaxed. The hot water and the salts were doing wonders for her tired body and it was glorious. Then, unable to help herself, her mind went back into work mode. A running list of supplies she was going to need was first and she cursed not having a pad and pen handy to start writing things down. Next came the necessities of going into town and maybe meeting her neighbors.

And then there was the book.

The groan that came out this time had nothing to do with relaxation and everything to do with dread. "Damn Christmas story. Why can't I write what I want to write?" It was something she'd been asking her editor for months and the only response she got was how all of the other in-house authors were contributing to building their holiday line, and she would be no exception. "Stupid rule."

And then something came to her.

Melanie sat up straight in the tub and only mildly minded the water that sloshed over the side of the tub. "All I need to do is write a story that takes place around Christmas. It doesn't have to necessarily be about Christmas!" Her heart began to beat frantically. "I've been focusing on the wrong thing!" Relief swamped her and she forced herself to relax again. Sinking back into the water, she closed her eyes and let her mind wander to all of the possibilities that had suddenly opened up.

"A romance at Christmas time," she said quietly. "Major emphasis on romance, minor on Christmas.

Technically, I'm meeting my obligations." She smiled. "Hmm…a heroine alone—maybe stranded—in a winter storm and a sexy hero who storms in and rescues her."

Melanie purred. "Yeah. That could definitely work." Sinking further down into the water, an image of the hero came to mind. Tall. That was a given. Muscular, but not overly so. Maybe lean would be a better way to describe him. And dark hair. She was a sucker for the dark hair. "Sex on a stick," she said quietly, enjoying the image that was playing in her mind.

The bathroom door swung open and Melanie's eyes flew open as she screamed. The man standing in the doorway seemed to have stepped almost completely from her imagination. If she wasn't so freaking scared at the moment, she would appreciate it.

"I wouldn't count on sex on a stick or anyplace else if I were you. You're trespassing and you're under arrest."

****

For a moment, Josiah could only stare.

There was a naked woman in Carol Harper's tub.

Holy. Crap.

When he'd driven up to his place a few minutes ago and saw the strange car parked out in front of the cabin, he immediately became suspicious. Hazards of the job, considering he was the sheriff of Silver Bell

Falls. The front door had been locked and the blinds drawn just as they always were, but the car was definitely a red flag. So he let himself in.

And found the naked woman he was currently staring at.

"Who the hell are you?" she demanded, strategically covering herself so he couldn't see what he already saw.

Like he was going to forget *that* any time soon.

About Samantha Chase

New York Times and USA Today Bestseller/contemporary romance writer Samantha Chase released her debut novel, Jordan's Return, in November 2011. Although she waited until she was in her 40's to publish for the first time, writing has been a lifelong passion. Her motivation to take that step was her students: teaching creative writing to elementary age students all the way up through high school and encouraging those students to follow their writing dreams gave Samantha the confidence to take that step as well.

When she's not working on a new story, she spends her time reading contemporary romances, blogging, playing way too many games of Scrabble on Facebook and spending time with her husband of 25 years and their two sons in North Carolina. For more information visit her website at: www.chasing-romance.com.

Other Books by Samantha Chase

Jordan's Return
The Christmas Cottage
Ever After
Catering to the CEO
In the Eye of the Storm
Wait for Me
Trust in Me
Stay With Me
More of Me
A Touch of Heaven
Mistletoe Between Friends
The Snowflake Inn
Duty Bound
Honor Bound
Forever Bound
Home Bound
Exclusive
The Baby Arrangement
Baby, I'm Yours
Baby, Be Mine
Moonlight in Winter Park
Return To You
Meant For You
The Wedding Season
Made for Us
Christmas in Silver Bell Falls
I'll Be There
Waiting for Midnight (Christmas in the City)
Wildest Dreams
Love Walks In
Always My Girl

Where to Find Me

Website: www.chasing-romance.com

Facebook:
www.facebook.com/SamanthaChaseFanClub

Twitter: https://twitter.com/SamanthaChase3

Pinterest:
http://www.pinterest.com/samanthachase31/

Sign up for my mailing list and get exclusive content and chances to win members-only prizes!
http://bit.ly/1jqdxPR